Malkore

Father Of Asgard

Book One

Malkore let out his big warrior's laugh. Kalla was terrified that Dossa had gone too far and that Iyasiil would be offended. Iyasiil, was laughing too hard to come up with a good sarcastic response.

When Iyasiil caught her breath, she looked at Dossa with a look of admiration. Then looked at Malkore, "You're creating Monsters, My Lord Husband. Do you hear how this woman just talked to me?"

Malkore didn't miss a beat and responded with his over-zealous voice of wisdom, "No, My Witchy Wife, I am helping an amazing woman to create an army of empowered women."

She smiled recognizing her words being used against her again. "Indeed . . . Indeed. And what a beautiful, glowing bunch you have gathered so far." She said smiling at him.

Kalla's face lit up, "Mama, are we training tomorrow, just like the men?"

Dossa leaned forward, excited. "That's it. Isn't it?!"

"Shhhhhh." In a very stern voice, Iyasiil said, "Do *not* let anyone, except Frigg or Lord Malkore, hear you say *anything* about it. Am I clear?" Iyasiil said to them, looking around to see if anyone could have heard.

Kalla had never heard Iyasiil speak to her that way, it startled her. "I am sorry Mama. Of course, I won't tell anyone. I am sorry."

Iyasiil took a breath, she felt how tight and scared she was inside. "No, Kalla. I am sorry. We just can't let anyone else hear anything about it. Frigg already figured it out, too. Frigg had a dream about stealing wooden practice swords today. She is bringing them tomorrow."

Malkore laughed at the magic of how it is all coming together. "That's awesome. The clues keep piling up, My Witchy Wife." He smiled at Iyasiil, but he could see she was still a little distraught.

"Yeah, I know. But, My Lord, you don't know what people are like when sexist attitudes get challenged. People can be brutal." She turned to Kalla, "I am sorry I snapped at you. I am really worried about the wrong people finding out. A lot of people will be mad and scared and feel incredibly threatened by women starting to stand in their power. When people feel threatened, the stupid people try to clamp down on what scares them, and it can be horribly ugly. This is part of a cultural change and Asgard is not ready, yet." Iyasiil looked at Kalla and Dossa, "You two are ready now. Frigg is ready. We will bring in all the right women, when the time has come. But for now, *no one* will know. *No one.*"

Kalla nodded, "Yes, Mama."

Dossa said, "Mama, before long, we will slay or subdue anyone who would dare try to sabotage our training. But for now, we will keep it all secret. No worries."

Iyasiil looked at Dossa and smiled. "That is the voice of the kind of Woman Warrior I want in my Army. Thank you, Dossa." Dossa nodded back at her confidently.

Kalla asked, "Lord Malkore, will you help train us?"

Malkore said, "I will be training the men at high sun. And you don't need me to teach you. I believe your teacher has arranged for one of the finest sword masters in Asgard to train you. I have seen their work and trained with them, myself. They are probably better with a sword than any warrior in Asgard. You will be in good hands."

Iyasiil looked at him, "You think so, My Lord?"

"Yes, I was thinking about that while training with St'laad today." He said. "Your Army will be trained very well." He wanted to say it in a flirty way to her but didn't want to give it away to the girls that their teacher was such an amazing fighter. "This has been such a busy day. So many changes have been happening for us all. Maybe we should take a walk in the moonlight before we go to bed." He responded.

"Yes, My Lord Husband, so much happening, so fast." She turned to Kalla. "Kalla, are you still ready to kill Dossa?" Iyasiil looked at Kalla and saw the smile grow on her face, Kalla was glowing again. "Oh, I see." Iyasiil turned to Dossa and repeated Dossa's words back to her. "Lord Malkore's kisses make women glow." Then she turned to Malkore, and said, "My Lord, I feel my glimmer is starting to fade. I am going to need more of those kisses soon, myself, or else I will fade into darkness."

He couldn't remember a time when he felt his breath taken away before meeting Iyasiil, it seemed to be a regular thing when spending time around her. "My Witchy Wife, that's like the sun saying it might run out of light. I am positive that you are the source of glimmer and glow for all the universe – we are all just reflection pools of the light you shine."

She kissed him and Dossa could have sworn she saw that golden light radiating from them again.

Chapter Seventeen
Slowing Down and Speeding Up

It had been such a busy and change-filled day, Iyasiil was glad to feel like all the work of the day was finished. "Let's go for that walk." Then she looked at the girls, "Would you two like to join us?"

Kalla said, "I would."

Dossa used a high-pitched voice and said, "Me too! Me too!" They all laughed and Malkore grabbed Dossa in a hug as he got up and was stepping around the table.

Walking out of the great hall, they all felt the cool night air and it was a welcomed bit of freshness after such an intense day. Iyasiil was walking on Malkore's right side, holding his hand, leaning against his arm, with her right hand holding his right bicep. Dossa was walking on Malkore's left side, holding his hand. Kalla was trailing behind for a moment, looking at the three of them, feeling so full inside, feeling how much she loved each of them. She noticed the way she loved each of them in such different ways. She smiled as she looked at all of them from behind.

Kalla said, "I love you all so much. Thank you."

Iyasiil pulled away from Malkore and turned to look back at Kalla, smiling. She motioned for Kalla to come join them and get between she and Malkore.

Kalla jumped up between them, reached around Malkore's waist and around her teacher's shoulders, and pulled them both into her really hard, making a squealing sound. "OK. That was all I needed." Then she sprang forward a couple of steps and turned around to her left and got beside Dossa. "I was thinking earlier, this is like a new little family that has been born, and I like it."

Iyasiil said, "Yeah, Kalla. It kind of is."

Malkore always stood tall, confident in his presence, and he couldn't believe the difference he felt in how his life seemed different from just five days ago. His heart had been met in a way that seemed to wash his spirit clean of so much he had been holding and carrying.

Iyasiil had felt the same way, but she hadn't had the added weight of knowing she was responsible for guiding the growth of an entire army, not until the last day or so. Now, she felt the weight of that commitment. "My Lord, it must have been crushing to carry the responsibility of growing an empire all alone for so long. I now have my own mission, and it feels very big, but I don't think I could do it without your support."

Malkore said, "Yes, My Witchy Wife, it has been hard. And now, feeling like I have support, I feel like I can do it. I didn't know how badly I needed this kind of support, but there was none to be had for so long. I looked for it, not necessarily in a relationship, but I couldn't find it anywhere."

Dossa let go of Malkore's left hand and wrapped her arm around Malkore's left arm. "If I may, My Lord. You won't ever have to carry the weight of Asgard alone, again. One of us will always be here – each in our own way. Kalla and I can't do what Mama can do, but we will do a lot."

Iyasiil said, "Well said, Dossa."

Kalla chimed in, "That goes for you, too, Mama. Whatever you face, you'll never do it alone."

Malkore couldn't help but laugh, "Why don't all families do it like this? This is how families should be."

Iyasiil said, "That's part of our mission, too. We can't build Asgard strong, without making strong Asgardian families. And we can't build strong Asgardian families without getting Asgardians in touch with their hearts and healing the hurts that keep them from growing their own hearts. It's all about finding peace inside ourself – when we do that, then we love bigger and better."

"I know that I have never loved like this. I didn't even know it was possible." Kalla said.

They walked over to sit on the corner of a rock wall near Iyasiil's chambers. Malkore and Iyasiil sat on the corner of the wall, Kalla and Dossa sat on either side of them. Iyasiil took a breath and looked up at the stars above them. It was a quiet night; the air was still.

Iyasiil told the girls, "Girls, I want to tell you everything now. There is a place out in the woods that I call my Sanctuary. It's a magical place. Malkore and I went out there yesterday to do ceremony. I had a vision which confirmed a feeling I have had for quite a while, but I never saw it clearly, not until yesterday. The thing is, I have never lived anywhere that it was possible.

Asgard is the first place I have ever lived that has the potential to grow into a society where my vision can happen. Asgard is not there yet, but it could be someday. There are so many places that I have lived, where the people will never grow. Essentially, they are miserable people, and they stay miserable, generation after generation. I had a vision of finding my Sanctuary, and when I found it, I knew Asgard would be home for a very long time."

Kalla asked, "What is your Sanctuary?"

Malkore answered, "When she says magical, she means it. You wouldn't believe anything I told you about it, you have to see it."

Iyasiil went on, "I will take you there, in time. Yesterday, I was shown an army of amazing Women Warriors. I saw what their armor looked like, I saw what their training would be like, and I saw how they would be respected and honored by the men of Asgard. The men and most of the women of Asgard are not ready to handle an army of Women – they haven't learned to honor women, like they could."

Dossa added in, "—and should!"

Malkore responded, "Absolutely."

Iyasiil finished, "Yes. So, a cultural change must take place, Malkore now has a platform to teach the men, and it will take a long time, but it can happen. While Malkore is teaching the men, we will begin preparing. We will have to train *twice* as hard as the men to catch up to their training, and we will have to train *three times* as hard to be able to hold our own against their greatest warriors. And we will have to be better than most of their warriors to have any of their respect."

Malkore interrupted, "Excuse me, My Love. We went out this morning —" Then he turned to Iyasiil, "Are you OK if I tell them?" She nodded at him. "We went out to train together this morning and she told me not to hold back with my sword. Your teacher came at me with a skill that is only rivalled by three or four of my men. If I had held back at all, she would have killed me."

Iyasiil said, "That's not true, you were holding back."

Malkore responded, "Not really. I stayed totally defensive for a while, but only to see what kind of skill level you had, and it was nearly everything I had to defend myself. Girls, she is *that* fucking good."

Dossa interjected, "No way. Really?"

Malkore nodded, "Really. You won't find a better warrior to fight beside, anywhere in all the nine realms. I would take her into battle with me tonight, if I needed her."

Iyasiil looked at him with a mixture of gratitude and feeling honored. "If you are lying, I am going to kick your ass, My Lord Husband."

He laughed. "You know that I am not lying."

She went on, "So girls, The four of us, with Frigg will start training tomorrow. Kalla, today was a test. I wanted to see how you would do on the run up the mountain. I wanted to see if it was realistic to start training you the way I want. You did great and I saw that you are ready."

"Thank you, Mama. I was wondering what was up, that wasn't a normal teacher-student walk." Kalla said.

"No, it wasn't. But the talk we had on top of the mountain was. And we will continue to do both." She said.

"How long will it take?" Dossa asked. "How long until I can kick Malkore's ass in a fight?" She leaned over into him, bumping him with her shoulder.

"At least a week, Dossa. Don't be in such a hurry." Kalla said.

"I trained Odin for over a thousand years, and I can still fight him off with an arrow, so it may take you two weeks, Dossa." He said, putting his arm around her, and pulling her in close.

"Girls, it's going to be hard. There is so much to learn. And when you get proficient with a sword, I am going to teach you groundfighting. The men here don't even know, it. It will be a lot." Iyasiil told her students.

"Groundfighting?" Malkore asked.

"Yes, My Lord Husband. That's where I could twist your arm off, or choke you to death, or break your ankle, before you even knew what was happening. There's a whole mindset with it that is great for women fighting men in a one-on-one setting that says, if you don't lose the fight, you will eventually win. Just don't ever lose. You keep yourself in a safe position and let them wear themselves out, then you attack, or escape without having used up all your energy."

"Oooooooo, sounds awesome. I'd love to learn that someday." Malkore said.

Kalla chimed in, "Dossa and I will teach you, right after we learn to kick your ass with a sword, My Gorgeous Waterfall Husband."

Malkore loved their confidence. "That's a deal. I will hold you two to that. I look forward to learning from you."

Iyasiil said, "When we get to that point, it really will be great for the two of you to practice with Lord Malkore. The techniques are made to be effective if you are fighting someone stronger than you. But don't get ahead of yourselves, it may be five or ten years before you get to where you are ready to actually fight someone with a sword."

Dossa said, "I bet we can do it in three years."

Iyasiil said, "That's a lot to ask. That's a big goal, Dossa."

"Hey, We're the Waterfall bitches! We can do amazing things, just watch and see." She said.

Kalla added, "That's right!"

Malkore laughed, "I love that. Put in the work, I look forward to the day when you all come challenge my men."

Kalla yawned loudly. "Mama, I think you wore my ass out, today. I am going to head home and get some sleep. Apparently, I will need to be rested for tomorrow. Dossa, do you want to come now? Or are you going to stay for a while?"

Dossa said, "I am going to come with you, I'm almost tired, myself."

Kalla stood up and said, "My Lord Malkore, will you please stand up. I want to hug you."

Malkore stood up and Kalla came over to hug him. He leaned down slightly to hug her; she wrapped her arms tightly around his neck. She made a squealing/growling sound, excited to hug him. He could feel her excitement and felt his own excitement rising inside as he felt her heart start to wrap around him. He growled slightly and straightened up, lifting her off the ground. She reacted quickly, picking her knees up, straight out to the sides with her knees bent to mend her dress and she wrapped her legs around him. She said, "Oh, Lord Malkore, I love you so much!" When she loosed her grip with her legs, he slowly lowered her down. She put her hands on the sides of his face and looked at him and said, "Thank you for today, My Waterfall Husband." Then she kissed him on the lips. Still holding his face in her hands, Kalla said, "Three years. I'm coming after you in three years." She started to take a step back then bounced up on her toes and kissed his lips again.

As Kalla turned to hug her teacher goodnight, Iyasiil said, "Me too. Me too." Kalla hugged her and told her how excited she was for everything going on. "Everything, Mama! Everything! Thank you for coming to Asgard! Thank you for being the woman to lead us. I love you and I want you to sleep like a cool, deep river tonight."

Iyasiil responded, "Thank you, beautiful woman. I am so excited to have found you and to have you in my life." When Kalla finished hugging Iyasiil, she turned to see if Dossa was finished hugging Malkore, her eyes went wide.

Dossa had stepped up on the short wall on which they had been sitting, she was taller than Malkore and had started kissing him passionately. "Today has been so fun! Thank you for inviting me to put my roots in water."

Malkore was smiling, "It's an honor to get to love you, Sweet Dossa."

Dossa walked down the top of the wall to Iyasiil and leaned over and hugged her while still standing on the wall. She felt silly, then said, "Lord Malkore, this is horrible! Is this what it is like when you hug me? Why would you ever hug a woman who is as short as I am." She jumped down off the wall and finished hugging her teacher. "Mama, get some rest tonight. We have work to do tomorrow."

Iyasiil said, "Indeed we do, you amazing little fireball. Sleep well."

When the girls left, Malkore and Iyasiil sat back down on the wall again. Both of them took a big breath.

"What a day, huh?" Iyasiil said.

"What a day, indeed." He responded.

Iyasiil got excited, "Oh Malkore, I haven't even heard how training went today, except to hear about Scout and --" She started laughing. "Scout and P— . . . Piii -- . . ." She wrapped her arms around his arm and leaned her head onto his shoulder laughing so hard she couldn't talk.

Malkore asked, "You mean, Lord Pigfucker?" She screamed, with laughter. He went on, with a straight face, "Is that who you are talking about? Lord Pigfucker?"

She laughed like every bit of tension and worry she had been carrying over the last day and a half were being released through her laughter. She almost screamed, "My Good Lord Pigfucker!" She kept laughing.

"Yes, My Love. What would you like to know about our Good Lord Pigfucker." He was managing to almost keep a straight face.

"How did that really happen? I can't imagine."

He told her the story. He told her how it had been Odin who called the man out and Odin who had started calling him by that name.

"So, Odin was good with you, then?" She asked.

"Iyasiil, it was amazing. It was like I got my student back." He took a breath and almost shed a tear, feeling just how much he had missed Odin over the years. "Odin was like a son to me for centuries, and we were *so* close. I never thought he would drift so far away like he has, then today, he was right there with me, step for step with everything that I said. He was finishing my sentences and listening and sharing from the heart with the men. I couldn't believe it. He apologized for having lost his way and showed me that he remembered all the lessons that I had ever taught him, he was teaching those lessons from a thousand years ago to the men, it was astounding. Then, tonight, the girls told me that Frigg had given Pigfucker one of her mushrooms, seeing the change in him, it all made sense."

"Oh, Malky, that sounds so wonderful." She said.

"Did you just call me, Malky?!" He said.

She giggled. "I guess I did. How funny . . . I didn't mean to."

He laughed. "Just don't let anyone else hear you call me that."

"Yes, My Lord Husband . . . King of FeetFuckia, My Man Malky." She said.

"Oh no, it just keeps getting worse." He said laughing and leaning his shoulder into her.

"No, My Lord Husband, it keeps getting better." She said looking at him like she adored him.

"Yes, My Witchy Wife. It does keep getting better. Better and busier. We both have armies to build and an entire cultural ethic to re-train. This is a lot of work that has been handed to us." He said, putting his arm around her and pulling her closer.

She took a deep breath, "Yes, it's quite a lot. And right now, I don't care about any of that. That's tomorrow's work. Today's work is done. I just want to sit here with you and then take you to bed."

He smiled and in a high-pitched squeaky voice he said, "Me too! Me too!" Then he squeezed her a little tighter around the waist, "And I wanted to see if you need to talk about everything from the day, it's a lot to step into."

She felt the weight of what she was looking at doing. "While Kalla and I were going up the mountain today, I was pushing myself and thinking about training the women. I was flooded with images of what to do with them. I'm really excited and it is a daunting task."

"But no one is better for it." He replied.

"Yes, I know, it isn't too much – It's just a lot." She said.

"Would you like to train together again, in the morning?" He asked.

With a very measured tone, she said, "My Lord, do you feel like you need my help, training with a sword, in the morning, before training your men?"

He laughed. She meant it to be a ridiculous question. "That's not what I meant. No, of course not, I wasn't thinking that you needed to practice to get ready. I was thinking of getting to spend time with you in the morning and doing something fun."

She looked at him like she wasn't quite sure that she believed him. When she looked into his eyes, she saw something different. "I only have until sundown tomorrow to be married to you. I *definitely* want to spend the morning with you, and I don't care what we do, as long as we do it together, My Lord."

He was smiling so big, "Good. I am still getting used to this. I keep thinking you might not be as crazy about me as I am about you. I loved spending the morning with you this morning; the training; the talk in the grove; the few moments we got alone after dinner; sitting here now. I feel like I can't get enough of you, right now."

She snuggled into his arm, "I'm not as crazy about you as you are about me. I'm much crazier about you than that. I loved my whole day, and we do important work, but every moment away from you, I kept feeling like it would have been better if you had been there."

"It was the same way at training today. And talking with Dossa. I missed you and wished you had been there." He said.

With an excited squeal, she asked, "Oh, tell me about that. How did that go with Dossa?"

"Do you see what's happening?" He asked.

"What? With Dossa?"

"No, right here. The only thing I want to do is take you home and feel your naked body and I love talking with you so much that we keep sitting here." He said.

"I know, it feels so good. Malkore," She looked up at him, "Malky, there is a really good chance I am going to be in love with you all day tomorrow – right up until sundown."

He let out his big warrior's laugh. "Same here." He smiled looking into her eyes, "OK. I will tell you about talking to Dossa, then no more talking tonight, only nakedness."

"Agreed." She took a big breath and rubbed the side of her head on his shoulder. "So, you were sitting in meditation, and she came in to talk with you, right?"

"No, she didn't know I was there. She was just bringing food, so you would have food when you got home. She didn't see me, until she had been there for a few seconds. When she saw me, it startled her. She immediately went into that apologizing thing and tried to leave, but I had the sense that she didn't really want to. I just kept asking her time and time again, to check in deeper with her feelings and to feel what she really wanted. The task for her was to accept what she really wanted, accept that her feelings were OK, and to share them without hiding it all because she was scared. You know, it's the same stuff we see in people all the time."

Iyasiil said, "Yes, that's her pattern. But I am curious how you got her to drop in so deep and make such a huge change so fast. I wish I could have seen it."

"I wish you could have been there. It was a long process of tiny steps – you saw how we had those same conversations with Kalla, when it was all four of us." He said.

"My Lord, I have had men trying to get close to me for Five Thousand years and I haven't found anything that excites me for millennia. You excite me, like I've never been excited before and it's not just me. Kalla and Dossa are besides themselves with how they feel about you. You have a different effect on people."

"I think I only have a different effect on people who want to grow and open more. I've been here for years, and I haven't had an effect on many people here." He said.

"Then they are idiots, yes." They both laughed. "I get that they haven't been ready until now, but just look at what have you done with Kalla and Dossa. And me!"

He looked at her not really knowing what to say, "I guess it's the same thing you do: I stay open to connect, I feel when someone isn't being more present, I invite them to be more present, I invite them to first get in touch with what they are really feeling. Then it's one of two things: I invite them to step through the shit that's blocking them and be how they really want to be, or we focus on the hurt that is blocking them from being how they really want to be. Either way, eventually, I invite them to step into the parts that are really wanting to come out. But, the biggest thing, is two things: One, I know that I am OK, so I don't often block connection with any fear of what others are going to think of me. And two, I want to be close without fear of *not* being close. If I am *not* going to be close to someone, I am OK with that. If they can't connect, I'll just love my own company and go find other company that feels good, so there is no pressure to connect with that particular person that is right in front of me. I have always trusted that," he gestured to the night sky, "the stars would put enough of the right people in my path eventually, so I would be surrounded with people I love and who love me."

"Mmmmmm. I love that." As she snuggled into his arm again, she asked a leading question, "How's that plan working for you now?"

"Right now?" he asked sarcastically. She nodded. "Right this minute, you mean?"

"Yeah." She said, smiling.

"You're asking me right this minute how my plan is working in this minute right here. Am I understanding you correctly?" He asked.

"Yes, My Lord. That is exactly what I am asking you." She said, ignoring his sarcasm, only adoring him.

"Horrible." He said. "I just keep talking. Talking like I haven't had someone at my own level to talk with for Thirty-Five Hundred years, and I am trying to get all the conversation in; as if there is some kind of deadline; like I want to share everything before sundown tomorrow because I don't want to miss out on anything. And it sucks, because," he got up and took her by the hand, "all I want to do is go home and make love with you." He started leading her back to her chambers.

When they walked in, the room was warm. Before going to their own home, Kalla and Dossa had stopped by their teacher's chambers and stoked up the fire, and made sure there were light snacks, water, and mead waiting for when their teacher and Malkore got home.

"Damn, those girls are good, look how much they love you, My Witchy Wife." He said.

She walked over to him with a smile on her face and wrapped her arms up around his neck, "Damn, those girls are good. Look how much they love their Waterfall Husband."

He chuckled, "Point taken. I like what they have said, they love each of us, and they love us as a couple."

"There we go, again." She said.

"What?" He said with a confused look on his face.

"We keep talking . . . You need to stop being so interesting and take your clothes off." She said.

Without saying a word, he picked her up and walked over to the bed. He put her down so that she was standing right next to the bed. While making eye contact with her, looking deeply into her, he gently brushed her hair back from her face, if was such a gentle, tender, nurturing thing. She could feel his intensity, the intensity of his presence, it made her heart speed up and her breath quicken. He slowly loosened the laces on the front of her dress and untied the wrap around her waist. While keeping eye contact with her, he untied the shoulders on her dress and slowly guided it down past her shoulders. When her dress was down past her elbows, he dropped her dress to the floor.

She was standing naked in front of him. He never broke eye contact with her, except the split second he pulled his shirt over his head. He untied his belt and let his pants fall to the floor, then stepped out of them. He gently put his hands on her shoulders and surprised her by quickly turning her around.

She expected him to bend her over, and she would have loved that. Instead, he surprised her again, by reaching down and pushing his right forearm between her legs and reaching up with his left arm and hooking his elbow over her shoulder at the base of her neck with his left forearm firmly across her chest. He lifted her up quickly. She gasped with a hint of a startled scream. When she got high enough that she could have reached up and touched the ceiling, her feet were over the side of the bed and her head was pointed towards the wall. He turned her around and when her head was over the side of the bed, he started moving her head down towards the bed. He stepped his right foot onto the bed and swung her body down until she was being held, hovering horizontally above the bed, and he gently laid her down on her stomach.

She couldn't believe his strength. He seemed to flip her around like and toy, and yet he was so gentle.

He pulled his arms out and straddled the tops of her thighs, putting his lips and nose into the back of her heart.

She felt like his lips were penetrating deep into her heart. Her sexual desire melded with wanting to be torn open wide, emotionally and spiritually, by this man. She felt herself longing to surrender and be totally consumed by him.

Silently, he said to her, "I love you. Thank you for being the woman that you are."

Then she felt his tongue lie wide and flat on the back of her heart. She could feel him moving his nose and chin in tiny circles; she felt his tongue only reaching deeper into her soul. She felt an animalistic desire from deep inside. *"Take me. I am yours."* She thought.

He pressed his chest and stomach into her lower back and into her ass. He felt like he was pushing his heart into her, it's the only place he wanted his heart to be. He lightly grabbed the skin on the back of her heart with his teeth and held the back of her heart like he was biting her. It didn't hurt, but just as she was about to brace for a little pain, she felt his tongue caressing the skin between his teeth. She melted a little more and he released her from his teeth.

He slid his body upward, towards her head, slightly lifting his hips, and laying his cock in the middle of her ass, then moved his knees up to straddle her hips. He pressed his hips into her and pressed his heart into the back of her heart. He slid his right hand from the side of her ribs, across to the middle of her spine at the base of her neck. He slid his hand with his fingers spread wide, up back of her neck and combed his fingers up into her hair, curled his fingers, and gently but firmly grabbed a handful of hair on the back of her head, then guiding her head to turn to the left. He put his head down to her left ear, and lightly stroked her ear with the side of his nose, then he rested his lips on her ear and softly whispered, "I am totally enthralled with you . . . I want to spend every minute I can making love to you . . . until sundown tomorrow."

Her body shuddered. She reached up with her left hand and cradled his head. He tuned his head down and kissed her shoulder with his lips and his tongue. He pushed his heart into the back of her heart again and felt like he was being wrapped in a warm energy field that tingled every cell in his body and every part of his soul. He rested his forehead on the back of her head and took a breath. Everything inside him felt gratitude in that moment, "My Dear Goddess, thank you." He said to her.

"You said no more talking." She responded, playfully, raising her butt, pressing it into his hips.

He smiled, "Indeed, My Love, forgive me." He moved his weight to his left knee and reached up to the table beside the bed and got the bowl of oil they had been using for massage. He got back to his straddling position and scooted back down to straddle her knees. He took some oil and spread it across both hands, the inside of his own thighs, then began massaging the backs of her thighs. He made long strokes from the back of her knees to her butt with his fingers spread wide. He used lots of oil and within minutes his hands were sliding deeply into her skin across her thighs, butt, and up her back. Then he rubbed up the inside of her left thigh with the fingers of his right hand, finishing with light pressure on the soft skin on the left side of her yoni. Then up the inside of her right thigh with his left hand finishing the same way.

She could feel her body relaxing in the way that only this kind of massage could bring. She felt her body respond like it had never responded to anyone before. She was so turned on and wanted him to make love with her and with every massage stroke, she felt her body relax and get more receptive and even more open to him than before.

As he made massage strokes up from the back of her thighs and across her ass and up her back, he slid his hips up the back of her thighs, sliding his cock up the back of her thighs until it either pressed against the outside of her yoni or slid up the middle of her ass. She wanted him inside her so badly, she began arching her low back to try and guide his cock inside her.

He made one last massage stroke up her back and lowered his chest into her low back and kissed the back of her heart again. When she felt his lips and nose on the back of her heart, she melted even more, she felt so touched, so loved, and she felt herself drop into a deeply vulnerable place inside. She stopped trying to control or have any say in what was happening, she relaxed her whole body and except to use her elbows and squeeze his forearms against her ribs. She felt herself start to cry, she couldn't imagine feeling more happy or more loved or more thankful. As soon as she felt her heart that little bit more, she felt his cock slide inside her, but just a little bit. She gasped with pleasure and felt her whole-body tense with excitement, then relax into surrender so quickly she almost didn't even notice.

She felt him moving his cock a tiny bit, just barely inside her. She wanted more, her body was screaming for more, and she felt lightning shocks shooting through her body as his cock moved inside. She tried arching her low back again but couldn't slide his cock any deeper inside her. She even tried scooting her whole body back into him — it didn't work, all that happened was he pulled his cock out and leaned his head down to her ear and whispered, "Are you finished trying to decide what I do with my cock?"

"*Damn, he got me.*" She thought. "Yes, My Lord." She said, acquiescing.

"Good, now relax your body and trust that you're going to get everything that you need and everything that you want." He said.

"Oh fuck! Yes, My Lord." She said, but she didn't relax her body.

"Now, relax." He said.

She let her whole body go again and felt his whole cock start to slide slowly into her, every time she thought it was all the way in, it slid in deeper until it took her breath away for a second. She had never felt so filled up and then felt him press his lips and tongue into the back of her heart again. She felt like her heart exploded in love; a scream came from her lips. Her palms were flat against the bed, and she grabbed the blankets with her fingers, while squeezing his forearms tighter against her ribs with her elbows.

She felt him rolling his hips, making subtle movements of his cock deep inside her. She was feeling tingles and touches in parts she didn't even know could tingle. "Oh! Oh! Oh!" She screamed higher and higher pitched. He kept making circles with his hips, each circle pulling his cock further and further back at the bottom of its circle before climbing back to its deepest point inside.

She almost couldn't take it, every part of it felt so good, her heart and body both felt like they couldn't take it anymore, her body started shaking. His hips kept making larger and larger circles until he was making full-length strokes inside her with his cock, each time pulling is cock out to where it was just touching the outside of her yoni, then plunging deep inside of her again.

She buried her face in the bed and screamed as her body began to shake harder and harder and she kept screaming and gasping as she felt lightning exploding through her whole body. Then a final scream as her entire body tensed up, she squeezed his cock inside her and he held his cock in the deepest parts as her body convulsed.

She felt his body shudder, and she felt like all the lightning in the biggest storm had just exploded inside her.

He laid his nose on the side of her neck, just below her ear and he kept making subtle little movements with his nose, that kept sending shudders through her body and heart.

Just as her body started to relax, he pulled his right leg back and put his weight on his left knee as she lifted her right hip and laid her on her side. She was still breathing hard and shaking, he wanted to move her quickly before she started thinking about what was going on again. He braced the inside of his left thigh against her low back and put his left hand down on the bed in front of her hips, then with right hand, she pushed her knees forward until she was laying on her side with her knees almost up to her chest. He slid his right knee up to the back of her knees and slid his cock inside her again. She had barely been aware of what was happening and felt shocked by how good his cock felt sliding in "sideways."

He had his left hand on her hip, feeling her more. He couldn't believe how good she felt, not just physically – she felt good to him in his heart and all the way into his soul. He wanted to make love with her forever. He looked at her laying there on her side, looking like she was in pain, sounding like she was in pleasure, with her hair tussled across her face, her beautiful rich skin, such tenderness, such strength, so beautiful in every way.

He wanted to keep diving into her heart; he also wanted speed up and fuck her harder; and he wanted to slow down and savor every single little feel of her. He felt like his head was breaking as his heart and body were both fighting for dominance in his awareness. He couldn't tell what he was feeling at any one moment, because every next sensation was overpowering the last – He only knew that he wanted to keep feeling it.

He felt like such a lucky man, being with such an amazing woman, and he hadn't been with a woman in so long because he hadn't met anyone like her. He slowed down physically and raised his energy up higher. He imagined his whole body was entering her entire body, he could feel the inside of her arms with his arms; he could feel the inside of her chest with his chest; he could feel his face kissing her throat from the inside.

"Ahh Ahhhhhh" She sang a perfect fifth that turned into a cry, that turned into a moan. She felt like she was being sent on a journey through the stars, she couldn't tell what he was doing, but her body and spirit were responding to it.

They made love for quite a while longer, rolling with each other all over the bed. While Iyasiil was on top of him, looking in his eyes, she asked him, "Malkore, tell me what you did when you made me sing before. What was that?"

He had no idea what she was talking about. He shook his head looking at her blinking quickly, trying to figure out what she meant.

She stopped moving her hips but focused her energy and awareness on feeling his cock, he felt it. It felt like his cock was being massaged in every direction and consumed at the same time.

"I – I can't – I can't talk if you keep doing that . . . what was I doing? What in the fires of Muspell were you just doing?!" He said.

While playing coy, she answered him as if it were a petty thing she had just done, "Oh, that? I was just devouring your cock. Only without moving physically . . . That's all."

Malkore's breath had been taken away, "Shit, woman! You're amazing!"

"Well, I haven't made you sing . . . So, tell me, what were *you* doing?"

"When?"

"It was over there." She pointed to a corner of the bed. "I felt like your whole body was inside me, filling up every part of me and I felt like you were singing through my throat from the inside." She said while making circles with her hips, feeling every possible sensation of him inside her that she could.

He understood now. So, in a mocking tone he said, "Oh, that? I was just nurturing your soul, adding wood to the fire of you bringing all of who you are out into the world, through your throat, while selfishly swimming inside you, and selfishly enjoying your body . . . That's all." He smiled. He loved their sarcastic banter that always sounded like it would land as an insult and turn into some type of adoration.

"Malkore." She said, looking deeply into him. "I love you like I never thought I would be able to love anyone." She kept looking into him, making rocking motions with her hips, feeling like his cock was about to pierce her heart, physically, loving how he had already pierced her heart emotionally.

"All day, until sundown tomorrow, My Love." He put his left hand up on her heart, nestled between her breasts and his right hand halfway up her ribs. He pressed his hand into her heart and couldn't tell if he was giving or taking away, it felt like both. Loving her felt like he was being given so much and loving her felt like all the light of the stars is flowing through him and into her.

"Until sundown tomorrow . . ." She lifted her knees, so she was in a squatting position over his cock and started ever so slowly rising up and down on him while keeping her eyes locked with his. "Until sundown tomorrow." She repeated.

He felt like the air was being taken out of his lungs, he had never felt such free-flowing sexual energy being fueled with so much spiritual expansiveness and emotional openness. It was making his whole-body shudder. She had a look on her face like she had been saving this trick, just to destroy him, and prove her dominance in their ongoing sarcastic banter.

He tried to say something, he tried to make some kind of smart-ass comment about how she had won and that he surrendered and would gladly bow down to her for the rest of his life . . . until sundown tomorrow, but all that came out was, "gah ooaahhh" as his body was shaking and his heart was melting, with tears starting to well up in his eyes.

She had tears welling up, too. She put her feet back behind her, so her weight was on her knees, and she collapsed onto his chest and let out a cry that pierced his heart. He wrapped his arms around her and pulled her tightly into his chest and said, "sundown tomorrow."

Book Two

Iyasiil
Birth Of The Valkyrie

Chapter Twenty
Women's Warrior Training

All four of the women had met on the edge of the east meadow just before high noon. They were all so excited, they had all shown up a few minutes early.

Frigg and Iyasiil had met on the way. Frigg carried the four practice swords, and four long strips of cloth wrapped up in a blanket, as she'd been instructed. Kalla and Dossa had gotten there first. They were waiting, sitting close to each other on a large, flat boulder.

Dossa had been so excited about training and had so much confidence going in, she had been motivated to work hard, but she didn't know the first obstacle she would face.

"Wow! Look at those beautiful bitches!" Kalla said as Frigg and Iyasiil approached them.

Dossa said, "I know. I can't wait to learn to kick both their asses, just so I can tend to them afterwards and get me a new beautiful wife."

Kalla started laughing at the way Dossa put phrases and ideas together. She was so funny – she had always been funny, but now she had become bold. "Dossa, do me a favor, will you?"

Dossa said, "Of course, anything for you, My Love. You know that."

Kalla asked her, "If kissing Malkore is your secret to being more funny than usual, don't ever stop kissing him!"

Dossa laughed and quickly responded, "Oh, Love, if you think I am funny now, wait until I get to fuck him and feel that amazing cock of his tearing me open. I'll be the funniest bitch in all the nine realms."

They both laughed and were still laughing as Frigg and Iyasiil got to them.

Iyasiil asked, "What are you two beautiful women laughing about?"

"We are talking about fucking your husband, Mama." Dossa said, matter-of-factly.

Iyasiil laughed, and her face lit up, thinking about him, "You really ought to try it sometime. It's the most amazing experience I have ever had in a bed."

Frigg was shocked at what Dossa had said to Iyasiil and surprised by Iyasiil's response. Frigg said, "I need to spend more time with the three of you. I've spent too much time with women who don't respect themselves and treat sex like a heartless man or women that are so scared and insecure and act like crazy, jealous b tches all the time. I don't know what you three have going or, but I want more of it."

Iyasiil said, "Absolutely, love. It's all a part of the training. Ladies, you can't know your feminine power without knowing your sexual energy's full strength and you can't know that, unless your own heart is full. If a woman is jealous, she doesn't know her own beauty and isn't feeling her own radiant love or she's feeling needy and see's the other person as the source of her security and then she will be afraid of losing the other person. So, teaching you to fight is teaching you how to bring all of you -- your whole heart, your faith in yourself, your confidence of knowing you will create an amazing future. And what may be the most important piece, you learn acceptance and approval of yourself, so you never look to another person to know your worth."

Kalla said, "Oh shit, Mama. Say all that again."

"I will. It will all come up again. Right now, we have other matters to attend. Frigg, did you bring the practice swords and strips of cloth, like I asked?"

"Yes, Mama. What are the strips of cloth for?"

Iyasiil pointed to the woods and started walking. Iyasiil wanted them to get used to wearing their swords, so they feel as comfortable wearing a sword as any other piece of clothing.

When they all got to a secluded area behind the tree line, Iyasiil took the bundle from Frigg. She folded one of the long pieces of cloth and folded it in half to find the middle, then wrapped it twice around one of the practice swords, just below the guard, tied the cloth in a knot around the sword, then tied the rest of the cloth around her waist, like a belt. "Did you all see what I did?" All the girls nodded. "Tell me. What did I do?"

Kalla said, "You wrapped the cloth around the sword, then made a belt of it."

"No." Iyasiil said.

Dossa said, "You wrapped it twice, then made a belt of it."

"No." Iyasiil said again. "Frigg?"

"That's all I saw." Frigg grabbed another piece of cloth, folded it in half, doing exactly what Iyasiil had done.

"That was it. Kalla, what did she just do?" Her teacher asked.

Kalla said, "She got a piece of cloth."

"No." Iyasiil said. "Dossa, what did Frigg do?"

"I don't – Oh. She folded it in half." Dossa said.

"Yes. Now, why am I asking you this?" Iyasiil asked.

Dossa said, "Because I said I wanted to fuck your husband and you're trying to be bossy to establish dominance as the top bitch?" Frigg's mouth hung open; she couldn't believe what Dossa had just said. Kalla was terrified that Dossa was in trouble. Dossa feigned innocence and just looked at her teacher, cocking her head sideways, as if she were waiting to hear if she got the right answer.

Iyasiil dropped her head laughing and took the two steps to get to Dossa and hugged her. Iyasiil's body was still shaking with laughter when she tried to speak, "N- No- Noooo, sweet Dossa. You crack me up, girl. I love you so much."

Then Iyasiil's tone changed to her teacher's tone, "Sword training is about paying attention to the smallest details. I was making a point because I want Kalla and Frigg to learn to pay attention to the details that will keep them alive. I don't care if you make jokes, I like your jokes. And if you don't pay attention, we will have to let you die on the battlefield, and I don't want to lose you – you're too important to me."

"Yes, Mama. I understand." Dossa said.

While Iyasiil was talking, Frigg had secured her practice sword to her hip. Kalla hadn't started getting her wooden sword wrapped and tied, she had been looking at her teacher as she spoke.

"Ladies, I don't care how you tie or wear your swords, as long as it works, I know this has worked for me. What I *do* care about is that," in a lightning-fast motion, Iyasiil had drawn her sword and swung it at Frigg's neck, stopping it just before she touched Frigg. "you learn to focus on the details." She was looking into Frigg's eyes with a seriousness and determination. Frigg felt like Iyasiil could easily kill her right in that moment. "I want you to be *dedicated* to mastering the details."

"Oh fuck, Mama." Frigg said.

As Iyasiil held her practice sword against Frigg's throat, she kept making eye contact with Frigg as she spoke to everyone. "For example, there are times when if you are holding your elbow high like this, you can block any attack, no matter how strong the attacker. Other times, if your elbow is high like that instead of pointed down like this, your opponent will put your ass on the ground and probably take your sword, knock you out, and take you back home as a slave to be raped and abused. The point is, it's a small change, but knowing when to make that change and when to *not* make that change, will save your life and it will save mine. If you aren't dedicated with your *first* focus on mastering the details of all the techniques I will teach you, then you will be sloppy and die, and I won't have any of that. Does that make sense, ladies?"

Dossa said, "Oh shit, Mama. I think I just peed myself, but I get it."

"Yeah, oh shit, Mama." Kalla said.

Frigg said, "You're going to teach us all that, right?"

"Of course, Love. I don't expect you to know anything right now." Iyasiil told her.

"So, teach me something, teacher. How do I get out of this? You have your sword to my throat. If I reach for my sword, you cut my throat. If I try to get away, same thing. What do I do?" Frigg asked.

"Good question. You have three options, all of them are risky, but doable. Well four options, but the fourth comes much later in your training. Let's talk about all that when we get to the top of the hill. OK? Kalla, Dossa, get your swords secured." Iyasiil said.

Kalla said, "Oh shit." She knew what was coming.

Iyasiil made a double loop around the tip of her wooden practice sword, then slid it all the way down to the guard, as if she were putting a sword in a scabbard. When Kalla and Dossa had their swords secured, Iyasiil started walking up the trail towards the top of the mountain. She was walking fast. Kalla knew it would get faster.

"Ladies, just keep up with me." She spent the first five minutes walking quickly up the mountain. Then she stopped and started doing push-ups. "Do ten of them, ladies." All of them did their pushups, then headed up the mountain faster than before. After another few minutes, she stopped and turned around to face the girls and said, "Ten more, facing downhill." They were harder, but all the women did them.

Iyasiil started running up the hill and opened up a gap of about five body lengths within about thirty seconds. Kalla could feel her legs burning but passed Frigg and started closing the gap to her teacher. Frigg let out a frustrated groan and sped up to keep up with Kalla. Dossa saw that she was ten or fifteen strides behind Frigg and yelled, "Me too. Me too." And Dossa started speeding up.

Iyasiil started past a tree with a low hanging branch. She grabbed the end of the branch and held on to it for a couple of strides, pulling it up the hill, then let it go. The branch swung back and smacked Kalla in the face.

Kalla was breathing heavily, but still yelled, "Shit, Mama. That hit me in the face."

Iyasiil yelled back to her, "Don't block an attack with your face. That's lesson number one." Iyasiil kept moving without pausing.

Book Two is Available Now!

Malkore
Father Of Asgard

Marcus Ambrester

Dedication

More thanks than words can express go out to Cheryl, Steve, Duey, Alyson, Leo, Joe, Mike, Sue, Richard, Gordon, Gene, Carrie, Amita, Patrick, Jonathan, John, Jon, Joseph, Jen, Brent, Charlotte, Vanessa, Fire Circle, and all those who have chosen to come sit and talk.
Special thanks to Bug & BoBo.
And to Iyasiil for reaching across the galaxy to say hello and share our tale.

Introduction

Viking legends will tell you that Asgard was made great by conquering other worlds.

The Medicine Women of Asgard have a different story to tell – a story that was lost until today.

Ten Millenia ago, long before Thor and Loki were even born, before Asgard was a glorious kingdom. Asgard was just a small village that raided other villages and hadn't discovered it's Magic, yet. But that was about to change.

When Odin was just a small boy, his father had asked Malkore, the greatest warrior and the wisest man he had ever met, to teach his son. He wanted Odin to grow to be the man who could make Asgard into a great kingdom. Odin consistently failed to learn.

It was only when the great women of Asgard collected their talents and joined Malkore that Odin began to learn, heal, and transform into the amazing man that could lead Asgard into become the greatest kingdom in all the nine realms.

Chapter One
A Good King

All the men were ready to celebrate in the great hall when they got home, all but one. Malkore was angry and disgusted with the young king. The newly crowned King Odin had been arrogant and stupid leading his men into battle the day before. Malkore was ready to throw him into a tree.

Malkore and the king had not spoken all day as the men made their way back home. There were over a hundred men travelling together on foot and Malkore hadn't spoken to anyone all day.

It was just about to get dark as they made their way across the final open field on their journey home. The men were happy. They were all high on a successful raid – they were high on the blood of their enemies. They still wore the blood of their enemies like trophies.

The singing hadn't begun yet. When the men were ready to celebrate after battle, sometimes the singing would start an hour or so before they arrived home in the great hall. They only suffered a few losses in battle this time; they carried blankets and bags full of the spoils of war – cups, platters, plates, jewelry, food, tools, and a couple of slaves . . .

The young king had been moving around the group all day as they walked, talking to each man. He'd been listening to their stories, as good kings do. He'd been glorifying himself in his own stories, as all kings do. Odin was full of himself after a whole day of this and he was hoping that what happened in battle hadn't been real and had just disappeared. After convincing everyone, and almost himself, that he was an awesome and amazing warrior king, he found Malkore near the lead of the pack as they got close to home.

"Old man!" The king exclaimed in his biggest warrior's voice. "Malkore, the oldest and greatest warrior who has ever lived! It was glorious, huh!? . . . This raid, yeah!?"

His boisterous tone was annoying to Malkore. Without missing a beat, Malkore quietly, gruffly said, "Walk with me, My King." Malkore gently pulled Odin's arm as he turned off towards the oak grove and the king walked with him. Malkore gestured for the king to lead the way to show everyone the king was to be respected. But Malkore was not just any man in Asgard, Malkore was the one man who's respect the king had to earn on a daily basis.

Everyone stopped. No one would move toward home without the king.

They all watched the two men walk away. Malkore knew the men would be watching them and the men would be curious about what was going on, so when Malkore and Odin were about 40 paces away from the rest of the men, Malkore said, "Shove me like you just made a joke."

"What?" Odin asked, confused.

Malkore gruffly said, "Let the men see us laughing and joking. Fucking shove me!"

King Odin shoved Malkore's shoulder.

Malkore laughed so loudly that the men heard him. Malkore went over and wrapped his arm around the king's shoulder, to give everyone the impression that everything was going great.

Everyone knew Malkore was the greatest warrior, older than any other man by at least two thousand years, but he wasn't the king. Malkore was always close to the king, and the king would listen to him, as much as he listened to anyone. For centuries leading up to being crowned as King of Asgard, Od n quit listening to anyone. Malkore still tried to teach Odin, but his teachings often fell on deaf ears. Odin was too busy trying to make himself look like an all-knowing, all-powerful king to listen to anyone. Malkore could shut him up quickly if he wanted to, but out of respect, Malkore would never disrespect the king by making him look foolish in front of the people.

As they approached the grove of large oak trees, Odin knew he was about to get a serious reprimand by his old teacher. Odin stopped near the large oaks. Malkore took a few more steps so he was hidden from the men, behind a huge tree. "Point your finger at me and step over here so the men can't see us."

The king had been learning the duality of keeping a show up for the people against how hard it is to be responsible for the well-being of an entire kingdom. Odin pointed his finger at Malkore and gestured like he was talking, as he stepped behind the large oak.

When Odin was hidden from the army's sight, he asked, "What?!"

Malkore grabbed him by his armor and shoved him against a tree so hard it would have broken a lesser man. Malkore spoke in a tone that made the king's blood grow cold.

"My beloved king," he said through gritted teeth. "If you think you can lead your men into battle like that, you're not worth being covered in the blood of the men you killed." Slamming Odin into the tree again, "You don't get measured like other men! You were trying to get half these men killed because you wanted to prove to everyone what a giant dick you have . . . These men look to you for guidance and leadership, and you acted like a fucking fool!"

Still mashing him up against the tree, Malkore asked, "When you first saw their camp, what should you have done? What plan should you have made?"

The king was put on the spot, and he knew that nothing short of a masterful plan would satisfy his old teacher. The king was fumbling for his words. His eyes were darting back and forth as he was looking for a plan that would satisfy his teacher. "I should have made it look like eight or ten men were foolishly charging into their deaths, while forty were hidden to strike from behind and two more forces flanking both sides that come out of nowhere. Show them eight men, while a hundred are waiting to strike."

Malkore shoved him into tree again and said, "Good. That is the plan of a king, not the suicide of a fool. So, when you come up with a plan, then what do you do?"

"Implement the plan." Malkore looked at Odin like he was stupid. "What?!"

"That's what you did yesterday, and you lost four good, young men." Malkore said.

Odin was confused. He didn't understand what Malkore was trying to say. "I don't know . . ." Then Odin realized his mistake, "Oh shit. I should have told the men, so everyone knew the plan."

Malkore shoved him into the tree again, "If you're ever pull that stupid shit again, I'll kill you myself." Still with a fierce and grim look in his eye, Malkore said, "Now, your men have been waiting all day to sing a great victory song. The women are waiting in the great hall. So, it's time for you to sing your men home." Malkore kept looking him in the eye, "Sing!" Odin looked shocked. He didn't know what had just happened. Malkore shoved him into the tree again and yelled, "Sing!"

The king started fumbling through his mind for a song. He thought of an old song from his grandfather's day. It was a teaching song, telling of a boy who was sent out of the house because his family didn't want to bother with him and through his cunning, was able to protect his family from a thief and murderer who was coming to rob and kill his family. "He gave me a sword. He gave me a shield." Malkore joined in. "Grandfather told me to guard the field. I fought for you. I fought for him. I brought you his lamb, I brought you his hand."

As they sang, Malkore transformed into a warrior celebrating the greatest battle. His face lit up. He smiled as he sang, even his eyes were smiling as he sang. It was an act that Malkore would put on for the people, but he was not happy inside. The joy he showed on his face was a teaching for Odin, too.

The king felt the infectious, deep-souled joy that Malkore was projecting. Odin felt his own energy rise; he felt his heart again. He had passed Malkore's test. The king began to feel like a god again – he felt like the god he'd pretended to be with the men all day.

By singing with him, Malkore was telling him to go celebrate in the great hall, Malkore didn't care that he'd been stupid and foolish. Malkore wanted Odin to grow into the great king that Odin was born to be.

They walked back out from behind the tree and were still singing as they walked back towards the men. They sang so loudly the whole village probably heard them from 20 minutes away.

The men began joining in song. Malkore and the king were radiating celebration and greatness from every cell in their bodies – they were almost glowing as they returned to the group.

Everyone began heading towards home again and as they arrived in the great hall, the amazing women of Asgard were waiting with everything the men would need as they came home.

This time, the men were ready to celebrate. Sometimes the men come home and there are no songs, there is no celebration, only women taking the men into private chambers because the men need to be tended to for days or weeks, before the men's hearts are restored.

When the warriors are bloodsick, wounded, and their spirits are broken, they require mending -- that's what the time of Tending is for, to restore the souls of warriors who's spirits and bodies have been broken in battle. The women of Asgard know that the warriors go to fight battles to support, protect, and provide for the kingdom and they do their part by always providing exactly what the men need to be restored when they return home.

The women always begin preparing for the warriors return, sometimes even before the men go off to battle. At this point, most of the women had been in the great hall for days. Nothing was ever said about when the men would return, they just knew. They always knew because they were always in touch with themselves, either one of them would dream it, or they would hear it in the wind, or an animal would come tell them — the women always knew.

These women were learning to be incredible healers. The women were secretly growing a culture where the young girls who had potential to be great healers were recognized early by the grandmothers, the grandmothers would talk to them — take them in, teach them. By the time they were adults, they were healers of broken souls, menders of wounds, listeners of stories, the wisest of counsel, the loving-est of lovers, always carriers of fierce, passionate love. They channeled the love of the universe in how they nurtured wounded souls. The men knew nothing of this growing culture in Asgard.

This time, the women had prepared the great hall for a grand celebration. The food was laid out on the big table in the great hall just before the men walked in, the mead barrels had been rolled in, and the women knew the celebration would last for days and days -- many stories would be told, a lot of love would be made, a lot of playful fun would be had.

One of the women began to prepare a plate with roasted bird, a bowl of stew, bread, and a larger horn of mead - she would not be staying in the great hall. She already had two of the younger girls take extra food and drink to her private chamber for later that evening.

She was new to the people, no one really knew where she came from or what she had done in her life. All they knew was that she was amazing to be around. She made everyone's life better just by being around them. She glowed from within.

In the short time she had been with the people, she had been helping all the women to step into their own radiance like no one had ever done before. She carried a medicine and magic that resonated deeper than anyone in the kingdom. Some of the women were beginning to realize she had come to teach them all.

She had a quiet confidence about her. She had a confidence that wasn't about herself, it was a confidence that the love of the universe would always flow through her. She was a walking blessing everywhere she went. She had lived past *asking* that goodness to flow through her, she had outgrown being scared of doing the wrong thing -- she just let her hands do what needed to be done for the highest good of the people, without question, with gratitude and grace.

One of the other women saw her preparing a plate, they knew she wouldn't be at the celebration, and said, "Hey Mama, you beautiful bitch. We are all with you, always."

Another woman added in, "Yeah, Mama. We'll be breathing your breath and holding your heart. Our love goes with you -- all of us." They honored her sacred mission. They knew she would be tending to one of the warriors, they just didn't know who.

She felt their love and support. Since she had arrived to live with the people, she'd re-invigorated the grandmothers in teaching all the women to enjoy being the love they were born to be. She knew she would be home in Asgard for a long time.

As she was walking out, a few of the younger women began to talk about her, "How did she get to be so awesome?" "How old do you think she really is?" "She's soooo beautiful." "I hope I get to work with her someday. I'd love to have her be my teacher . . ."

Off she glided, she flowed out of the great hall to meet a man she had never met, except in her dream. She would tend to his every need for the next three days to three months, however long it took.

In the last 30 or 40 yards before they reached the great hall, Malkore started drifting back from the front of the group, expecting that he would be the last to reach the great hall. He would grab some food, and quietly leave.

She had gotten out the door with the plate of food before the men got to the door. She walked to the spot outside where she had seen him in her dream.

When she was Five steps away she saw him, she felt her heart fill with love and compassion. She started feeling the kind of love you feel when your child is scared and you hold them, the kind of love you feel when someone is hurting and you want so much for them, the kind of love born from gratitude when someone has worked hard to help you selflessly, the kind of love that gives like a waterfall, the kind of compassion that comes from the source of all things and never needs to be refilled.

As the men got to the great hall, the women inside got animated and as loud as the men. The song had slowly changed into yells and screams as the celebration started its path towards being way out of control. This celebration quickly started to look like it would go for days and days . . .

There he was. He had been peeling off from the group.

There she was. He didn't even know she would be there.

She spoke to him in a soft, respectful tone that carried a deep heart resonance, "I have food for you, My Lord. I didn't know if you would want to stay long in the great hall." She said.

She knew he didn't want to go into the great hall with the men, not even to get food, and she knew he needed food. She just didn't know if he needed to show up in the great hall to support the men as an elder.

He smiled at how it happened. He smiled that she had met him here, right here, at the right time. *"Magic."* he thought.

He shook his head to her and took the plate and the horn of mead from her, "Thank you, My Love." If he didn't know what amazing healers could do, he would have wondered how she knew that he didn't want to go into the hall.

If he hadn't seen amazing healers before, he would have been freaked out that when he felt the impulse to drift off to the side, a woman magically appeared with food and drink, but he knew that magic is what we truly live for. He knew that magic is what we are all made from, and these women are beginning to learn to be truly magical, but he had never felt such a presence as hers.

He was almost too tired to notice how beautiful she was. He noticed that her beauty glowed from within, and that was besides the shape of her face and body and beautiful head of hair. He also knew he was too tired to even pay attention to her like that. He needed food, rest, sleep, and calm.

She motioned with her hand for them to walk towards her cottage, "We have a quiet place ready where we can just sit and eat, My Lord."

As they walked, she put her hands on his tricep and the outside of his bicep - not really taking his arm, but almost. She was holding his arm just to slightly connect in a warm, nurturing way, letting him know she was there, and that he was being cared for.

They walked into her chambers; she had rolled up several hides and blankets so he could lean back while sitting on the bed. "I've prepared a place for you to sit, My Lord."

He set his food down on the small table beside the bed. She began unlacing the straps on his armor as if she had done this for him a hundred times. Her movements were fluid. Everything she did, she did with a flow and grace and a feminine power that made Malkore stop and take a breath, even in his state, he noticed.

He didn't know how long she had lived with the people or where she came from, but he was thankful she was there. She quickly and delicately took off his armor and laid it on the floor near the bed.

"My Lord, would you like a fresh robe to put on, or do you want to sit for a while?" She asked.

"I'll just sit for now. Thank you." The thought of cleaning up or changing clothes was too tiring for him in the moment.

He started eating, almost moaning with joy at how good the food was.

She sat on the bed by his feet, and turned towards him with one foot still on the floor. She was ready to get up if he needed anything, but her focus was on him. She ate a bit of food herself. They sat quietly, enjoying the food.

He finished eating a piece of bread by soaking up the last of the juice from the bird he had been eating.

"Would you like another plate of food, my Lord? We have plenty for you." She asked in a soft, warm voice.

Everything he needed was there before he even realized he needed it. "No, not right now. Thank you. Right now, I'd like to enjoy the quiet."

She took his plate, put a bronze cup of water next to him, and took his horn to refill his mead. When she returned from the other side of the room, the water cup was empty, she left the full horn of mead, and went to fill the water, again.

He thanked her with a curious look on his face.

She sat back on the bed after setting his water by the bed. She had laid her hand on his ankle very naturally when she sat down. Her attentiveness and her touch said two or three things that were greater than anything Malkore had ever seen all in one place: One, if there is anything you need (physically), I am here to provide for you as you recover. Two, I am here, being present with you, so you can be nurtured as you recover. Three, her touch conveyed a love, a deep presence, support, and compassion.

Even being so tired, he could sense that she carried a love so powerful that anything un-loving could not exist in her presence. The love in her touch went as deep as the oldest see-er, was as comforting as a hundred friends, and radiated like the warmth of a thousand suns.

He looked her into her eyes, appreciating the woman that she was, and he appreciated how at ease he felt being with her, that was unusual for him, "You're amazing. Thank you for being here."

"My Lord, if I were the one coming home from leading the raid, you would do no less for me." She said with a tone of gratitude and grace.

"Indeed, I would do no less for you." He said smiling again, raising his horn of mead to the truth of what she'd just said.

The battle was over. He was home in his village. Malkore began to relax.

His laid his head back against the wall and closed his eyes. He felt his body settle into the bed. His feet were pulled up, so his knees were up in the air. She was almost sitting on one of his feet and she wondered to herself if she had scooted closer to him without realizing it. He took in a deep breath that seemed to last forever. Then he let out a half sigh, half "ahhhhh", half growl that lasted for even longer.

"Yeah, that sounded like it felt good." She said. She took in a long breath and let loose her own sighing growl with the full voice of a woman who never holds anything back, Malkore noticed her fully embodied voice. She put a hand on each of his knees and squeezed. "Again!" she said, patting him on the knee.

They both breathed, they both growled, then they both laughed – silly, relieving, playful laughter.

While they were laughing, she leaned against his shin with her breasts on either side of his knee, not meaning to, she was just being free in the laughter, but it happened. It was like a small little lightning bolt that tickled her whole body. She was a little taken aback, often men need nurturing after battle – they need a bit of mothering when they are being tended to. Either that or they just need to fuck something to help them get back into their body. This man wasn't one of those. He didn't need mothering. He wasn't interested in empty sex. She could feel his presence and that energetic lightning bolt went deep into her soul.

She could feel the wisdom that ran so deep in him. She felt a wisdom so deep that she felt certain these people in Asgard weren't ready to absorb it all, yet.

With him not going to the party in the great hall, she knew his heart was hurting. She knew he was tired beyond tired. She didn't expect to feel that little bit of erotic, flirty energy. She smiled. She trusted her body, and she wouldn't have felt it if that part of him weren't ready to feel deep-hearted connection too, just not tonight.

She is a healer whose intuition guides her body and heart. *"He's more ready to live again than I thought."* She said to herself, but still, he held himself at a distance.

He felt that jolt of energy, too. He felt the energy between them, and he felt a little possibility that maybe he didn't need to hold back with her.

They made eye contact; they recognized something in each other. His nerves were still on edge, but his heart just relaxed a bit - his chest felt a little warmer. He suspected that he wouldn't have to hide during this time with her – it had been a long time since he'd met someone who didn't need to be coddled. With the thought that he could be met by someone who didn't need him to hold space for them, he almost shed a tear.

"Thank you for being here." He reiterated.

"Even the greatest warriors must rest when they come home. Even the greatest teachers have to be tended to." She said, not realizing the weight of how her words would land with him.

He had been carrying too heavy of a load for far too long. He was tired. He was tired down to his soul.

He'd been holding it all together for centuries, while carrying a foolish king onto the throne, while carrying the king's army into battle, carrying the king's men through battle, and he felt like this young king is a heavy charge that won't seem to end . . . So much to carry.

He felt the shield that contained and protected his heart. He felt how he wanted to drop that shield from his heart. He was always on guard with people, he was always fighting, or he was teaching, or he was fighting while teaching, and he was always monitoring the king to know what to teach him next, and the lessons never ended. He hadn't given up on teaching the king, even though the king had quit listening centuries ago.

He was tired.

Malkore said to her, "Sometimes, taking care of the childish ones is like getting kicked repeatedly in the balls. I've been watching over that little fucker since before he could hold a sword – since before he was born."

She smiled because he was talking, he had just shared something that was a clue to his vulnerability. She noticed. She didn't know who he was talking about, but she was glad he wasn't going to spend much time being guarded.

She knew that it said a lot about him that he could feel that it was safe to share with her, and she smiled because she had heard of his stories, and she knew she was about to hear one of his stories now.

"Wait, My Lord. Do I need to know which "little fucker" are you talking about? Remember, I'm new around here . . ." She said playfully with a smile.

He laughed. He laughed for real for the first time in a long time.

"When Odin was just a boy, his father, Borr, who even though he was an asshole, he was my best friend, he asked me to teach Odin – to get him ready to be king, to teach him not just to be a warrior, but to be a man worthy of having a great people follow him . . . *that* little fucker." He said.

They both laughed a little. Then she took a breath and spoke with measured, heart-felt words. "My Lord, the people love that little fucker. They trust him, they respect him, and they believe in him. The truth that's written in the stars is that you've served your friend well in getting Odin to this point, My Lord." She meant it.

"He's done well. He's a good king." Malkore said, staring off into space.

"But . . .?" She asked.

"No. He's a good king. He serves his people." He said very diplomatically.

She let her hands slide slowly around the sides of his knees, he could feel the heart-presence in her touch. With a compassionate tone, she said, "My Lord, it's just us here. I've seen the rise and fall of empires. I've learned that the only time a people advance is when the truth is spoken. So let this chamber be a place where we only speak the truth with each other."

Malkore nodded to her in agreement, feeling grateful for the invitation to share openly. "I am sorry. Not many people can handle the truth. I know you can handle it. It's just been a long time since I have been around anyone who doesn't have to be taught." He paused as he looked into her eyes and nodded to show the massive amount of respect that she had earned in just a short time. "The truth is: Odin is a good king, but he is not a great man – He is not a great king, not yet. He wants too much, he wants to be too great, he thinks winning battles and getting attention means greatness . . . He may have a reign of bloodlust before he begins to learn. I wish I could do more. And I don't know if I can."

She nodded, "I see the same. The people will prosper. He will build Asgard into the greatest kingdom the world has ever known, I have seen that. He is good, you have served his father well, and it may be that only experience can teach him from this point on." She held up one finger, "And it just may be that *only* experience will get him to hear the lessons you have been teaching all along. He may have learned all he is capable of learning from you, because of his own ignorance and fear. It may soon be time to move on, but I know this, My Lord, you will always be welcome in his high court. His love for you is so apparent on his face."

"Yeah, well, I almost had to kill him yesterday." Malkore said, half laughing.

She didn't even flinch, she just smiled to hear the story. She kept listening.

"He got hungry for glory, like he was invincible. He almost got half his men killed because he was reckless and stupid."

"I'm sure you'll set him straight, My Lord." She said with an alluring smile.

"Oh, I already did. I made him wait all day until we talked." He took another big sip of mead. "Then, I scared the shit out of him to make sure he was listening. While he was still pissing himself, I made him start celebrating in song to show the men the victory they had earned."

"Ahhhh, that makes sense, now." She said.

"What? What makes sense?" He asked with a curious look on his face.

She got up as she began talking and got a basin of warm water from near the fire and brought it closer. She put the clean robe across the foot of the bed as she spoke, "We knew the energy in the great hall would be wild tonight when you all returned, but I could only feel a somber, desperate sadness inside. Then all of a sudden it shifted, and I felt like I could breathe again. I began to smile, and right then, we started hearing the song across the valley."

"You see much, My Love." He said as he raised his horn of mead to her again. He felt a little different when he called her "My Love" that time – it was like a little wisp of a possibility.

He thought to himself, *"What the fuck?! I must be more tired than I thought, I've already fallen in love with her four times in the first hour of knowing her . . ."*

Lightening the mood, she said playfully, with just a hint of seductive flirtation, "I see a great many things, My Lord. And one of the things I see is a man covered in the blood of many much lesser men." She grabbed his hands, pulled him to his feet, and began unlacing his shirt to undress him. "I see a man ready to lay down for the night. I see a man who has long since passed given his due service to the people and is way past the point of needing to rest and sleep." She un-looped his belt and let his pants fall to the ground.

"Indeed, wise see-er of things. Indeed." He said with a tired smile, resigning to the tiredness that ached in his bones.

When he was standing in front of her naked, she never broke eye contact with him, she took the warm, wet cloth from the basin and began wiping off his face, neck, shoulders, and chest.

He welcomed the bath, but it was the nurturing that struck him. He put his hands on her shoulders, not to stop her, not to try and have sex, just to ask her to feel this moment with him.

He took a big, deep breath, breathing in the comfort of her care. He needed this so much.

He took another deep breath. She took one with him. She felt him and felt his immense heart, she felt his tiredness, she felt his pain, she felt the hard-earned wisdom, and she could feel what a great man he was.

She leaned forward and with her hands on his chest, she put her forehead onto the top of his chest. They stood there for a second, still breathing, still feeling, and they felt that feeling that tells you that *this* moment was one of life's moments. She almost gasped as she felt herself falling into his heart and into his spirit. She breathed that feeling in deeply.

His hands dropped to the back of her shoulders. Her hands wrapped around him – her right hand slid up to the base of his neck, her left hand went under his shoulder to the back of his heart.

His strong arms pulled her into him, and one hand went to the back of her heart, the other reached up and held the back of her head.

For a moment, she didn't feel like a caretaker, she didn't feel like she was there as a nurturer. She felt like a woman. She felt like a woman with an amazing man.

In that moment, she could feel what an amazing man he is. He wasn't a great warrior who needed to come down from the pressure of war, he was a true servant of the people, a greater leader than any king, but this man led by doing it all to serve the people. He fought with a fierce passion. He taught with wisdom. He protected. He watched over the people like they were all his precious children. He didn't ask for glory; he didn't want to be king. All he wanted was for the people to grow and to learn, so they would never face the trials he had been through. He was amazing. He was just like her – she had never met her equal.

He thought, *"There is something special about this woman. She is truly, truly amazing."* He had never felt anyone be able to receive all of the heart and presence that he carried. And he knew he was too tired to see all the way into her, but he could feel that this woman had a wisdom and a peace inside that he had never seen before in anyone else. She was a person whose experience, presence, and awareness of people was like none other. She was just like him – he had never met his match.

He straightened up, looking in her eyes. "Well, this was unexpected . . ." He said.

"Yeah." She responded. "Let's get you cleaned up and get you to bed, it's been a long journey."

He got the possible double meaning, *"It's been a long journey, getting to you."* And also, the immediate, *"You've had a long journey today and need to rest."*

She continued to wash his body. He was covered in blood. He looked like he must have killed 20 men by himself. She washed his front. She washed his back.

He continued to touch her while she was washing the blood and funk from his skin. He wasn't trying to seduce her. He was tired down to his soul. With his touch, he was begging. His hands were the conduit for his soul - he was sucking the nurturing from her as he touched her.

She felt it. That is what she is here for. Without using her voice, she said to him - to his heart, *"Take all you need, My Lord. Take all you need, My Love."*

She reached for the clean robe she had already prepared for him. He took it from her as he looked into her eyes, he tossed the robe aside.

She kept looking into his eyes and unlaced the shoulders and waist of her dress and let her dress fall to the floor. Then with a playful smile, she pushed him back to lay down on the bed. He fell back onto the bed and laid down with a smile on his face. She covered him with the blankets, and she walked around the bed.

She laid down, snuggling him – one leg across his muscular thighs, her stomach and chest snuggled onto his side. She could feel her breasts on his skin; she laid her arm across his chest. She took a deep breath and let her body melt into him.

He felt her skin as she laid into him. He could feel that she was like a storm that cleans the air and makes everything fresh again. He heard her breathe. He took a breath, too. He pulled her close, saying *"Thank you"* to her in his heart.

She felt like they were melting into each other. She was still aware that he was heartsick, if not bloodsick, and needed rest, she felt the energy in her body of being his nurturer, of being a healer, and what surprised her is right here in this moment, she felt like a woman. She felt her ovaries tingle, she felt her face flush, she felt her body wanting to rub up on him for a while. Her body was excited. The nurturer in her knew that he wasn't ready to open up like that, but that energy was still stirring between them, nonetheless.

He took a few more deep breaths, and he felt his cock come alive, and he felt himself relax more. Then with two more breaths, he was sound asleep.

It had indeed been a long journey, and the greatest part had just begun.

Chapter Two
The Fastest Cure

He hadn't slept that hard, that deep, or that long in decades. Every time he began to stir, he felt her body nuzzle into him a little more and he would be asleep again. It was like he'd been transported into another world.

He needed the rest, but normally didn't get it, and as the morning grew to midday, he woke up almost smiling.

He opened his eyes; there was the smell of fresh food in the air. Two of the younger women, who were quickly becoming her students, had brought in food, added wood to the fire, quietly checked in with their teacher to see if anything else needed to be done, then left with Malkore's dirty clothes to clean them.

Part of the culture is that the whole community helps when warriors return from a raid or battle. Everyone knows the warriors fight to protect and provide for the whole kingdom, so everyone helps the warriors recover from battle. It is not on the warriors to bear that burden alone.

She had woken up, washed her face, then sat in meditation while he slept. As he began to wake up, she put a hot cup of tea and a small bowl of stew by the bed, then gently slid back into bed herself.

He groaned and stretched and did a half roll to end up laying on his back, she snuggled half-way onto him resting her head on the front of his shoulder, pressing her body into him, one leg across him, laying her hand directly over his heart, and she let her body relax. "Good morning, My Lord." She said softly.

"Mmmmmmmmm. Yes, but it doesn't look like morning, the sun is too high." He said.

"Yes, it felt like you got a restful sleep." She spoke with a soft, heartful, nurturing tone.

"I haven't slept like that in years . . . Thanks to you." He said gratefully.

"Me? What did I do?" She said with a low-key playfulness.

He put his other hand on top of hers while gently pulling her into him more and said, "You are truly amazing." He was not trying to flatter her; he was acknowledging the masterful presence she has. "You're taking care of me from the inside out - You know what I need before I need it. The women here can't do what you do. A younger man would think you have some kind of magic. But I know the truth."

"What truth is that, My Lord?" She asked, playfully feigning innocence.

"You are magic itself." He said.

"It's what we do, My Lord. We protect and care for our own." She said with a gentle gravitas that touched him so deeply he almost shed a tear.

She recognized that they were on the same level. Her heart always felt full, it's part of who she is, and she knew the same was true of him.

He pulled her in a little more closely, grateful for the care.

"Has Frigg finally chosen Odin, yet?" He asked.

"No, No, No, No, No." She startled him with her quick, terse response. "You will do NO teaching today, My Lord. No watching out for the people today, not the king, not anyone." She lifted her head to look him directly in the eyes.

Her tone was firm and still warm, but Malkore knew she was serious. You don't cross a woman like this; she would probably turn you into a goat or a frog for a day to teach you a lesson.

She continued. "You will not protect anyone today, not even me, My Lord. Today is all about you - only what you want, only what *you* need. You have done too much for this entire kingdom and so much for these people – more than they even know. My Lord, you have done more than they can realize, and you will continue to serve them well - but not today."

She looked at him to make sure he understood. He nodded with a slight grin on his face.

As she looked more deeply into him, he felt her even more. He felt her energy in his heart.

She took a breath and looked into his eyes. Her face softened, "My Lord, you are the greatest kind of warrior. You fight to make the people great in every way and you *don't* do it for your own glory – you do it for the people to know *their* own glory. You fight every minute of every day for the people to learn to live their own greatness. *That* is the *greatest* service to the people. You do so much every day. So, you are taking the entire day to only take care of you. You and I are going to stay right here, we are going to eat some delicious food, and we are going to do nothing except what feeds and fuels your soul. And if you try to get up and go do anything for anyone else, I will *personally* kick the ass of the greatest warrior in the kingdom. Are we clear about this, my Lord?!" She was playfully poking him in the chest with her finger as she "threatened" him.

No one spoke to him this way. No one *could* speak to him this way, because no one saw more than him. No one, until now.

He had an amused look on his face. No one put him in his place, but he felt her power – he felt the power of her words – he felt the power of her presence. She cut through his bullshit and put him directly in touch with all those parts of who he is. This woman who he'd just barely met could see deeply into him. He was surprised. He had forgotten how intoxicating it is to feel like someone could really see who he was. "Yes, My Love. Thank you."

She knew that she would probably have to give him the same speech tomorrow, but she would wait until tomorrow to let him know she wasn't letting him up then, either.

She laid her head back down on his chest. She felt him breathe and she could feel that he was relatively calm. His nerves were not frazzled, especially for a man coming home from battle, but he wasn't quite at peace inside.

He was worn down, tired deep in his soul – some of it was battle, but it was something else. This man had been at war for too long, but not with a sword in his hand. He was in some other kind of war, a war inside, constantly in some kind of turmoil. He needed the kind of rest only she could tend to.

For the men, returning from battle is *not* the time to be on guard. It is time to let go of the hyper-focus of battle, to let their nervous system calm down after battle — to return to being a "normal" person. It takes time, and that's what the time of Tending is for.

"There is some stew and some bread beside you. Are you ready to have a little food, My Lord?" She asked.

He nodded. "Yes, please."

As he was sitting up, she seemed to pull the pile of blankets and hides out of nowhere, to put them behind his back. Without looking, she reached behind her where she had put another bowl of stew for herself.

They sat and ate in silence for a bit except for the occasional moans of joy at the taste of the stew. She was tickled and impressed with how much he let himself enjoy the food.

These amazing women healers know the best way to support the men after battle is a delicate mix of tending to their simple needs, like food and drink, and their deeper needs, the emotional needs, their spiritual needs — to soothe their spirit.

Everyone in the kingdom knew that being bloodsick after battle is a soul problem that can only be healed through nurturing. Nurturing in all the ways that feel like nurturing to the man at the time.

All the good stories need to be told, and all the most horrible stories need to be told, especially the especially horrible stories. The men don't need to carry terrible memories inside. When bad memories stay in the body, they turn poisonous. The women listen without fear and honor the men for being willing and courageous to do the horrible things that war demands.

She had heard the most horrible stories of war in her time. She had heard the most glorious battle tales. She listened patiently. She always listened long enough and been nurturing enough to hear the stories and the fears that truly terrified the toughest of men. She knew it couldn't be rushed – it takes time.

After several minutes he had devoured the stew and drained his tea.

"There is still so much food. Eat as much as you want, if we run out, my girls will bring more." She said.

"Before you came, the younger girls didn't know how to serve in this way." He said.

"My Lord today is about you, *not* about what the women are being taught. Do we have to go over this again?" She said as she put his bowl and cup on the table.

"No, no, no. That's not what I am saying." He said it with such calmness and thoughtfulness that she knew he wasn't just arguing about keeping his attention on his own needs for the day.

They laid back down and she snuggled her body into his.

He felt the deep pain rising up from his chest. "I am saying that before you came to be with the people, the women were good and tending to the men when they returned, but there was a whole other level that they didn't understand." His voice was almost cracking.

"My Lord, it's what we do." She said, reiterating what she had said before.

"Yes, it's what *we* do. It's not what *they* do. There's a level that they don't understand." His voice started shaking a bit, "I have been with these people for a long time . . . and they . . ." His speech was flustered; he couldn't find his words.

She listened more, waiting. She nuzzled her body into his chest a bit more. She squeezed his thigh between her thighs.

"They . . . they . . ." He couldn't find his words.

She pressed her hand into his heart with more force than he would have thought possible. Then, all of a sudden, a scream erupted from him. It was a deep, guttural scream that sounded like it had been building for a hundred lifetimes.

As he screamed, she felt the wall falling down from around his heart. She was hearing the deepest part of him.

She never lifted her head from his chest and shoulder - She melted deeper into him as this ferocious warrior screamed – this was the opening to his heart.

She began crying as she felt the depth of his spirit and the depth of his pain. She pushed the side of her nose and the side of her mouth into his chest and rolled her head, so she felt him with her cheek and then her ear.

"Yes." She whispered. He had just said so much in that scream. She took a breath and said, "Tell me again, My Lord."

Tears were rolling down his face. He pulled her closer still. "I haven't been able to teach them. I haven't been able to. These people are the first people I have known who can grow into a truly great people, and I haven't been able to teach them all they need to know. I have tried. I have tried so hard." His chest was heaving as he let himself feel this pressure that's been building inside for so long.

"Oh, My Lord. *That's* the pain that's been boiling inside. I didn't know what it was." She said to him.

He nodded as the tears continued to flow. "What a manipulative witch you are. I have barely known you for a half a day and already you have made your magic on me to where I share what no one here could hear in over a thousand years."

There was so much to say and especially so much more of that pain inside to let out, but she started feeling something different.

She was smiling as she swung up on top of him. "I bet you have barely been interested in a woman here, because they all seem like children, right?" He nodded while drawing in a deep breath. "And even though you have been teaching and leading and teaching how to lead, it has all felt like you pour yourself out until you are empty – fueled only by the love you have for the people. Am I right?"

He nodded.

She smiled a happy smile and said, "My Lord, I am not the only one here with witchy ways. If there were any woman in this kingdom who caught your attention, you would have her bare her soul in less time than this. Am I right?" He just smiled at this.

While straddling him, she was making subtle, almost imperceptible movements with her body to accentuate her point.

Just feeling her on top of him may have been better that any sex he could ever remember because he could feel her heart in every inch of her skin. And she was so captivating . . .

Being sassy, she said, "Excuse me, My Lord. I didn't hear your answer."

He nodded, smiling, "Yes, My Love."

"Yes, and no matter how much you teach, they don't seem to understand *all* of what they could get out of it?" She asked while still barely moving her hips on his hips.

Then, without missing a beat, she raised her body up and reached down, without any awkwardness of having never touched it before, she pulled his cock up and laid it flat onto his stomach and sat back again.

"And tell me, My Lord, do the people here with potential do their very best to learn, even though they always seem to fall short of learning?"

Again, he nodded.

"And, My Lord, do the well-meaning, good-hearted people among them, who are complete fools, just want to be buddies with you, to try and get your acceptance, because they can't comprehend the incredible gap that exists between their understanding and the vast vision that you see?"

He was starting to laugh by this point, and she was still making more than subtle movements with her hips to accentuate the points she was making.

He was smiling at her, waiting to see where she was going with this. Her tone was getting more playful, almost like she was making light of his pain, but she wasn't. She was calling out his pain more plainly than he had ever heard or even voiced himself, it was reassuring and comforting.

"My Lord, have you ever waivered in your commitment to the people?" She had balled her hands into fists and placed them on his chest. "Have you ever failed to offer the teachings that they need? Have you ever failed to offer it to them, regardless of whether or not the people could take it in?"

"No, My Love. Never." He had a tear welling up again. He felt like he and everything he had been working for was finally being seen and was being honored. Most of the time he felt like all his diligent work was invisible.

Her tone and rate of speech had been building almost like a volcano rumbling.

"Then tell me my, My Lord," she said in a tone that was almost condescending, "have you forgotten the thing I keep telling you?!"

Again, no one talks to Malkore this way – no one *can* talk to him this way, much less have anything to say that is worth him hearing. That was, until this woman showed up.

He was smiling again. "What's that, My Love?"

She gently hit her fists into his chest, and whispered forcefully, "*It's what we do!*"

He nodded again. Besides feeling his heart being touched, his could feel his cock getting excited too. He was also starting to wonder if the excitement she was feeling was just to help him heal and recover during this time of Tending or if she had really shown up to be in his life for a long time.

Maybe she was one of those miracle goddesses who pops in to help someone heal, then disappears without a trace. He had been that miracle healer who showed up in a village before and left things better than he had found them, never to return again. Maybe she would be gone as soon as he was restored and ready to return to the people.

BAM! She pounded her fists into his chest. "I am here. You are not going to be alone again." He felt the power of her. She continued to look deep into his eyes. His cock was growing now.

He thought, *"Fuck! She's inside my head. This woman is good!"*

"You are not going to be alone again. We are going to stay here and rest and play and talk and cuddle and sleep and eat and do whatever the fuck we want for as long as it takes. As long as we are here, I am going to honor the Tending and let myself fall totally in love with you and honor you for the incredible man that you *so clearly* are. Then, when the Tending is done, we will know what to do. But for right now, I am going to be madly in love with you forever. I trust my body. I trust my Heart. What I feel inside is overwhelming and intoxicating. I have never felt this before with another person, so we are just going to go with it. Maybe it will last two days, maybe it will last two months, maybe two millennia, maybe it lasts for more than a thousand lifetimes, and maybe you and I will be finished four minutes from now. Whatever it is, right now, it is just you and I, yes?!"

Bam! She hit him in the chest again with both fists. "I've been alone, too. I have walked a path that taught me more than anyone else ever could. I too, have never met my match, until now. It's thrilling and scary, and stupid to even think such thoughts, but the magic of the Tending should *never* be questioned. My vision of you was clear before you even returned home. I am here. I am yours. You are not alone."

And like a magical witch, she slid down on his cock, sliding it deep inside her, never breaking eye contact, never taking her hands off his chest; only flattening out her hands on him. She gasped. Took a breath. Her eyes began filling with tears.

They looked into each other's eyes; their bodies motionless – feeling the moment.

He kept looking at her. He wanted to move and couldn't figure what to do – nothing could be better than this.

She whispered, "Malkore, My Love." She hadn't said his name before.

He asked, "What's your real name? Not what they call you here, your *real* name?"

Her name hadn't been spoken in centuries, no one had asked. She was delighted to not keep it a secret from him, "I am Iyasiil."

She felt his cock throb inside her when she said her name. "The Iyasiil? I remember hearing stories about you. I thought the stories were just myths. I didn't think you were real."

He put his right hand on her heart, between her breasts. He was touching her so deeply; she felt it all the way into her soul. She took his left hand and put it on her right breast, holding his hand on her breast. Her left hand was on top of his hand covering her heart. "But you feel real enough to me!" He said playfully.

She began moving her hips slowly as if she were on a galloping horse, she was rocking her hips forward and back, but never losing the deepest penetration. Her eyes closed for a moment then she looked back into him.

"You. *You!*" She said, not knowing where that sentence was going.

"Yes, Love." Then with the half growl of a warrior, he said her name, "Iyasiil." The pain he'd been carrying had been lifted for the moment. He only felt elation, love, and the lust of a whale.

"Yes!" she squealed, sighed, then collapsed her body onto his chest, never stopping her rocking hips, using her weight to press his hands further into her heart.

They made love for what seemed like an hour.

He still had waves of exhaustion flow through him. When one of those waves would start to come on, she would stop, grind her hips into him that little bit more, and lay on him being very still. "Breathe with me, My Lord. We have all day. We have all week. Let me have your heart. I'll have more of your cock in a bit. For now, let's just breathe." A few minutes later, when his energy came back, with his cock still inside her, they would make love more.

At one point, the exhaustion hit and hit hard. She felt the energy drain out of him. She stopped moving and laid her body on his. She had her head lying on his chest. She reached up with one hand and held the side of his face and felt him nuzzle his face into her hand. She stayed there until his cock slid out of her.

After a couple of minutes of feeling her weight on him, feeling his hands touching her, lightly and gently stroking her skin.

She raised up and put her forehead on his forehead, lightly grazing the side of his nose with her nose. She whispered, "I am going to get us some of that delicious food the girls brought us, then we will see what we want to do."

She quickly prepared two plates of food. And filled his large horn of mead.

When she returned from the other side of her chamber, she looked at him and smiled. He was sound asleep again.

Chapter Three
Healing the Body

He slept for almost two more hours. She had a short nap with him, then she ate a bit of food again. When the girls had come in to check if she needed anything, she asked the girls to gather several handfuls of the red tinted grass that grew on the edge of the oak grove.

She instructed them on how to make a medicine tea from the grass, and what other herbs to put into it. The grass was to be chopped into fine pieces, then ground into a paste, and boiled with the other herbs.

The girls were curious what it was for, but she only told them to be careful not to drink any of it themselves and to wash the pot and utensils after making the tea.

She knew he would be hungry when he woke up. So, she heated up the lunch that had been brought to them.

As if by magic, she put their food by the bed, just minutes before he woke up. She took off her robe and slid back into bed, gently snuggling up to him.

He wasn't quite awake, but he could feel her laying behind him, with her hand on his hip and her breasts against his shoulder blades.

Before she realized he was awake, she felt him reach for her hand, pull it in front of him, and press it into his heart. She squeezed him and put her nose and mouth into the back of his neck, while wrapping her leg over him, snuggling his top leg.

"You fucking witch." He said smiling to himself.

With a playful tone, she asked, "Yes, My Lord. What can this fucking witch do for you?"

"Even her voice is sexy! This woman is amazing." He thought while chuckling. "Did you fuck me into unconscious oblivion, you witch?"

"It was not my intention, My Lord. But if it happened, you must have needed it." She said.

"Indeed. I hadn't realized how much I needed to sleep." He said.

"Yes, My Lord. It seems much needed and long overdue. When you're ready, we have food for you My Lord."

"Mmmmm, yes, Love. Food is a good thing. It smells good." He said.

She kissed the back of his neck and squeezed him with her entire body before sitting up and reaching for the bolster for him to sit up and lean against.

As he was sitting up, he groaned a little. "I didn't realize how intense that battle was. I am actually sore today. After we eat, it may be good to go for a little walk."

"That sounds good, My Lord. Maybe after we eat, my lord will let me massage him as I intended to do before the nap."

Then with an infectious, flirty, laugh, she said, "I got distracted earlier."

He laughed as he was sitting up and getting settled, but he was still surprised that she had felt excited enough with him to get distracted.   "That was, without a doubt, the greatest *distraction* I have ever known. Thank you."

"Oh no, My Lord. Thank *you!* That was me being selfish with you." With a sarcastic tone, she said, "Such a travesty – a severe transgression - no one should ever put their own needs and desires first while Tending to a warrior during the time of Tending. I hope my lord will forgive me for that."

Matching her sarcasm, "Yes. Very true. And seeing how much I obviously needed time in that unconscious oblivion, I think you get a pass, this time."   Then he looked at her for a moment. With a clumsy, but still gentle, hand he started patting her face as if he wasn't sure what he was feeling. He patted h s hand all over her face, then he poked around in the front of her shoulder while looking at her curiously.

Caught off guard, having no idea what he was doing, she was holding in a laugh and asked, "What is that? What are you doing, My Lord?"

"I just wanted to make sure you're real and that you're really here. It might be easier to believe that I am still dreaming and you're just a dream fantasy. If you aren't real, please don't wake me up. This looks like it could be *too much* fun!" He said.

She laughed and leaned up and kissed him. "Well, if I am just a fantasy, you've created a pretty happy experience for me in your dream – I am loving being here with you, My Lord."

She grabbed his plate and handed it to him, then got her own plate. She settled herself at the foot of the bed, so they were facing each other. They ate and talked; he devoured his plate full of food. She asked if he wanted more.

"Yes, please. That's delicious and I'm still really hungry, Love." She got up to refill his plate.

He was caught off guard and how beautiful she was walking across the room naked. He ate an entire second plate of food and finished a cup of tea after each large horn of mead that he drank.

"I'm glad to see your appetite is so strong, My Lord." She said while taking their plates away.

"Why is that, Love?" He asked.

"Well, on one hand, it shows that your energy is strong. On the other hand, you may need lots of strength if things keep up like this between us." She said with a flirty smile.

He grinned and let out a little laugh; her playful smile was adorable.

She sat back at the foot of the bed. Getting back under the blankets and pulling them up around her stomach.

He looked at her and felt what it was like to feel so free, like he could share anything with her, like she could see so deeply into him. He felt what it was like to have this woman be here with him who could handle herself and bring such a strong, capable presence.

The light in his eyes disappeared. He suddenly looked sad and took a big breath.

She cocked her head, "What is it, My Lord?"

He took another big breath. She breathed with him. He tightened his lips and shook his head slightly.

"Malkore, tell me." She said.

He let out a little laugh, exasperated by how he felt inside. "Do you have any idea what it's been like to feel so full and still feel so alone for so long, because no one can understand?"

"Indeed, I do, My Lord." She said.

"But, --"

"My Lord, if I may?" He nodded to her. "My Lord . . ." Her voice dropped to a more personal, soft tone. "Malkore, I said last night that if it were me who had just returned home, you would be doing no less for me." She paused.

"Yes, indeed." He responded.

"Even though none of the men here know what it is to tend to anyone, like we do, *you* would tend to me masterfully. Right?"

"I would hope. You deserve nothing less than masterful care and to be loved masterfully . . ." He said.

"Yes, and if I were the one sitting there being tended to, I would be freaking out and wondering if I were going crazy to be falling in love with a man I'd only met less than a day before. And on top of that, I would be sobbing and crying, inconsolably, all day. I would be feeling the longing I had felt to feel something like this for longer than most of the people here have even been alive. *And*, if I were not being fed so much by the energy of the Tending, I would be freaking out now. It *is* hard! It is *so fucking hard*! It's hard to carry the weight of being responsible for evolving and growing a people. It's not a smal thing! And to do it alone, while it has its own gifts, it is incredibly hard to not have support from other people."

That touched a deep place inside, his heart felt jumbled and warmly comforted at the same time. "Yes. Thank you. Being here with you is delicious, and I have felt so happy with my life; so full. Caring for the people and teaching the king is a great charge to have, no doubt, but I have had this fantasy and desire that went beyond anything I have ever known and beyond anything the people could ever grasp. You're the only one I have ever met that seems like they are capable of meeting me in that place that I created in my fantasy. Does that make sense?"

"Yes, of course." She said.

He nodded at her seeing that she understood. He went on, "There is a piece I don't understand. Things that just feel jumbled up inside. I felt like I was constantly failing to teach the people what was possible for them and the desire to teach them felt so huge. That desire felt like it was important *for* the people, not like a selfish desire."

"It *is* important for them, My Lord." She interjected.

"Yeah, and I always know how to teach every lesson that I teach. Even when it takes time, it just takes time, no problem. But this has been a mystery to me. There is a deeper understanding that these people don't have, and they *need* it to go where they need to go as a people. They don't understand and they don't even know there is more that they don't understand. I used to trust that it would become clear when it was time, but it is becoming time. And it's not working." He had been looking down with his eyes looking left and right, searching through all these jumbled feelings. Then he looked up and made eye contact with her.

She was smiling with tears rolling down her face. "I have had the grace to spend so much of the last centuries by myself, in communion with the forest. But I've been seeing all the same things for these people. It must be maddening to be among them and be given the mandate to teach something that can't be taught, yet."

He nodded. "That is what has weighed on me so much. And I suspect *that* is what needs to be tended to in me more than anything."

She smiled, "My Lord, I have felt the same frustration. I felt it before I even got here, for decades. It has been a constant letting go of what I cannot change."

"So, what the fuck are we doing here?!" He asked.

She smiled and felt her energy shift away from what he was talking about. She knew they would not find any answers in this moment. "I suspect that right now, I am here to massage you. Is there anything you need before we begin?"

"No, My Love. Thank you." He grabbed a blanket and folded it up like a small wedge and put it under his chest as he laid on his stomach diagonally on the bed.

She straddled his left foot and took a liberal amount of oil into her hands and began rubbing it into his calf muscle. She could feel the strength in the mass of his muscles, and she could feel the tension he was holding. She was aware that the first goal of massage is to nurture the soul, and second to release tension in the body. She started working deeper into his muscles than she normally would on anyone else, but the sheer muscle mass on this man needed some pressure, just to provide a deep flush to the muscles. She leaned her weight into him with her hands making wide, nourishing strokes up his calf.

After several minutes, she used the flat of her forearm, then both forearms at angles to flush his calf.

As she got up into his hamstring, she was straddling his calf, feeling herself moving slightly on his oiled calf. She wasn't paying attention to it, but she could feel it. As she was working into his hamstring, she felt how physically focused he was in receiving. If she could feel his erotic energy getting stirred up, it would guide how the massage would go. For now, she would focus on relaxing his physical body, and nurturing his spirit.

Twenty minutes later she had moved up to working deep into his muscular ass. As she rubbed deep with her forearm, she could feel him relax more and he was groaning and moaning with how good it felt.

"I've never had a massage that goes this deep. Usually during a tending, I get oiled up and barely touched. It feels good, but most of the time it does nothing for the muscles." He said with a low, relaxed, gravelly voice.

"I can't wait to teach my girls to do this." She said.

"If you ever need someone to demonstrate on while you are teaching the girls, I will be there to support you." He said, only half-joking.

"Of course, My Lord. I would need someone who can tell the difference when their spirit is being loved on or just their body being touched – someone who could possibly give them feedback on their presence." She said.

"Mmm. Yes, is that how you were taught?" He asked.

"No, most everything I know I was taught by the forest and by the land itself. And in dreamtime, of course. Same as you, I suppose." She said.

"Yeah, it seems we are the tip of the spear on this journey." He took a deep breath and turned his attention to relaxing his whole body. He imagined melting into the bed, then he started thinking, "*After this Tending is over, I am going to do a full Tending for her. She does so much for the people, she needs to be supported, too.*" That thought made him feel really happy inside. He imagined making the space for her to not have to take care of anyone. He kept imagining massaging her, giving back for all she was doing for him.

She gently said, "Let yourself receive, My Lord. You will never owe me anything for this. You have already paid with your service to the people."

In a fake bravado, as if he were making a proclamation, he said, "The fucking witch will now get out of my head!" They both laughed.

She was 45 minutes into the massage and moved back down to his left foot, then moved to his right foot and began slowly working her way up the back of his right leg.

After finishing his right leg and his ass, she asked him if he would like to sit up and have some tea.

"Mmmmmm, that would be great." Sitting up, he reached for his tea. "Thank you, that was wonderful." He figured an hour and a half was all the massage he would get.

"Oh, My Lord. We are *not* finished. I've barely done a quarter of your body. We have time and nothing else to do." She said.

"*Wow!*" He thought. "You give so much, so well." He said.

"Thank you, My Lord. But would My Lord do anything less for anyone else?" She asked.

He smiled as he looked at her. "Of course not. This tea is great. Is it one of your recipes?"

"It is. I made a large batch based on what all the men needed after this raid, but I doubt much of it is being consumed in the great hall today." She said with a smile. "The girls said the celebration is still going strong and wild. It's pretty raucous over there."

He wondered if he needed to make an appearance in the great hall tonight.

"My Lord today is your day for *you*. Your men can make fools of themselves without you." She said.

"Witch! Get out of my head!" He laughed and jokingly said with a smile.

She had a big, flirty grin on her face, "But My Lord, I like being in your head."

He kept smiling with her. He hadn't smiled this much with anyone else in forever. He took a deep breath, looking deeply into her, "I like you being in my head. I like feeling so close."

"It's been a long time, for me. But never this close and deeply connected for me." She was a little caught off guard that she shared that, she hoped she wasn't putting any pressure on him that would hinder how safe and free he felt, this was *his* time.

"Have you been to the hot springs up on the mountain, yet?" He asked.

"Nooooo, but that sounds fun!" She said with a girlish wiggle.

"They don't carry medicine like some springs do, but it's a wonderful trip to take. I like making a two-day trip of it where I pack food and spend the night by the springs."

"Oh, Please! That sounds fantastic!" She said.

The girls gently knocked on the door and came in with a pitcher of mead and a smaller pitcher of tea. One of them asked, "May I refill your drinks?"

"Please." He said. He had put on his warrior's celebration voice.

"Would you like tea or mead, or both, My Lord?" The girl asked.

"Both!" He said with a boisterous growl.

She came over with both pitchers, not making any notice that they were both sitting on the bed completely naked. "Is she taking good care of you, My Lord?"

"Young lady, she is taking better care than anyone has ever taken care of anyone in the history of time." He said.

Not really catching the gravity of what he said, she responded, "Good." Her lack of presence was markedly different to the energy in the room while it was just the two of them.

She filled both of his drinks, filled her teacher's tea, and the other girl knelt on the other side of her teacher, placing a horn of mead on the table by the bed.

Iyasiil motioned for the first girl to lean down to her and whispered something into her ear. The girl looked surprised for a second. Iyasiil nodded to her.

The girl turned to Malkore and squatted down next to her teacher. "I'm sorry, My Lord. Tell me again. Is she taking good care of you?"

Malkore smiled. "Good job, young lady. Now take a breath and let your heart get big inside." Iyasiil put her hand on the back of the girl's heart. The girl took a breath and put her hand on Iyasiil's thigh. "This woman has a wisdom and power, the likes of which I have never seen." The girl looked at her teacher and smiled. "I have been a warrior since before your great-grandfathers were born and I have never been taken care of better. No one has ever been Tended to like this woman does. Tending, like all good magic, comes from an expansive heart. Now, imagine a wisdom, power, and a capacity to love that goes far beyond what you have ever imagined."

The girl said, "Yes, My Lord."

"No. Do it right now, close your eyes. Take a deep breath, let your body relax, then let it relax a little more." He looked to the other girl, "You too." He wanted to make sure they both got the lesson. The other girl closed her eyes and began breathing.

"Imagine the greatest love, the warmest love in the universe flowing into you. Breathe it in. Breathe it into every part of you." He instructed.

The girl sitting on the bed next to Iyasiil, Dossa was her name, her mouth opened. She felt like she had just had a love bomb go off in her heart, both girls did. Iyasiil put her hand on Dossa's knee as Malkore looked at her. She felt like she had just been given a gift, but she didn't even know what it was. She opened her eyes with a look of wonder on her face, "Yes, My

Lord." She put one hand on her heart and bowed her head slightly to say thank you. She looked to her teacher, then back to him, then back to her teacher. "What just happened?" She asked, lightly patting her heart.

"*That* is your first real lesson from your teacher." He said while pointing at Iyasiil.

"Girls, that is the heart space from which true Tending is done, and it gets even bigger." Iyasiil said.

The taller one, Kalla, squatting next to the bed, said, "Wow. Ok. I don't know if I could handle more."

"You have the best teacher to help you learn." Malkore said.

"Yes, My Lord." She said. Still feeling as if she had been transported into another world, she caught herself and looked to the other girl and nodded. "Is there anything else we can do before we go? We'll bring dinner in two or three hours and the medicine tea you asked for is on the table, cooling."

Iyasiil looked at Malkore and asked, "My Lord, is there anything else we need, right now?"

He shook his head, already wanting the girls to leave so he could have Iyasiil all to himself again.

"Thank you, girls." She said to them. The girls got up and started to leave.

- - - - - - - - - - - - - - - - - - - -

As the girls left their teacher's chamber, they began walking back towards the kitchen behind the great hall. Kalla asked,

"What just happened?! I felt like my heart was going to explode!"

"That's not all! I thought I was going to leave a puddle on the bed, I felt like my whole body and my heart was about to have an orgasm." Dossa said. "You could feel it in the room when we walked in. It's like another world in there. That is amazing. What do you think she is doing in there?"

"I don't know, I've never felt that before. But I didn't want to leave, I just wanted to stay in there with them." Kalla said.

"We can't do that, Kalla."

"Oh, I know. I wouldn't have. I just wanted to." She said.

"Yeah, me too. We have some time; we could make a lap around the great hall and refill everyone's mead."

"Or we could just go lay down and rest for an hour or so. I'd rather do that." Kalla said.

"Yeah, let's do that." Dossa said.

- - - - - - - - - - - - - - - -

After the girls left her chamber, Malkore and Iyasiil felt the energy both settle and come back up in intensity. They just sat there on the bed and looked at each other.

"Thank you for playing along with the girls. That seemed like a good chance to catch them off guard and give them a glimpse of what we do. And I love how you caught their attention then spoke to their hearts. It was like you were tricking them into feeling more than they had ever felt before." She said to him.

"Oh, of course. Thanks for trusting me to play along." He started to get up, "I am going to get another bite of food, wou d you like anything?"

"The girls would have been happy to get you another plate, My Lord." She said.

"No, it's not that. I need to get up and move a little bit. Besides, I wanted them to go soon -- I was the one feeling selfish and wanted you all to myself for a while longer." He said.

"You can have all of me you want, My Lord." She said as he was sitting back on the bed with a bit of food.

"I think I may want a lot of you, witch!" He said, playfully.

He had a couple of small bits of meat and a medium size piece of thick bread. He tore the bread open, put the meat inside, and took a bite. "Mmmmmm. You women are amazing. This food is so good." The meat was so tender it almost melted in his mouth.

That wasn't the kind of compliment anyone needed to make. He didn't need to say how amazing the women are just because the food is good.

It's true the food was amazing, and the women had worked hard to provide for the men returning home, but she *felt* his appreciation. He *really* appreciated it, and he was so generous with his energy! So much love flowed from this man – he loved so freely. She felt her heart spinning in her chest.

She sat and admired him and felt warm inside seeing his simple gratitude and joy for the food. She sipped her mead and couldn't imagine anything being better right in that moment. She was eager to continue his massage. Selfishly, she wanted to get lost in his energy again, while nurturing him to relax and open even more. She didn't know how the rest of the massage would go; she couldn't feel if it would stay physical or if his erotic energy would begin to rise.

He finished his food and stood up, stretching tall. Then he squatted down and twisted his body back and forth. "Wow, My Love. Nice work. My hips feel great." Then he stood up again and took his plate to the table.

As he laid back down on the bed, he asked, "So, this time is all about what I need, right?" He had a tone to his voice, she couldn't quite tell what it was, but he sounded happy and energetic.

"Yes, My Lord." She said.

"Well, as I look deep into my own heart and soul, and take stock of everything inside, would you like to know what I need?" His tone was a tiny bit boisterous and a bit sarcastic.

She was smiling, enjoying his playfulness, "Yes, My Lord. I would *indeed* like to know what you need." Matching his sarcasm with over-earnestness.

"After looking deep into my very own soul, I have come to see that it is very likely that I need a really big hug, right now." A big smile on his face. He wanted to hug her. He wanted to feel her energy close.

She laughed and with an equally sarcastic tone, she climbed on him with her hips pressed into his hips and her body hovering above him, she said, "I am here to provide whatever My Lord needs and desires, today."

She leaned down, smiling, and kissed him, repeatedly. *"I'm always smiling with this man; this isn't just a Tending."* She thought.

"Now, My Lord, when I am finished kissing you, I am getting back to the very serious business of massaging you. Would you like me to start on your back or start on your chest?"

"As long as you take your time kissing me, I will leave it up to you, My Love." He responded.

The kissing took on a passionate, and still playful, almost celebratory, tone and it seemed like it would lead into more sex, but she stopped and grabbed the oil. "Turn over big guy. Let us see what a warrior's back feels like a couple of days after battle." She sat straddling his upper hamstrings and began rubbing into his lower back and sides.

He moaned with pleasure, and she dug deep into his muscles. When there was a spot that he wanted her to focus on, she let his moans guide her to keep focusing on that spot. His back and neck were soaking in the nurturing love and while his muscles were not softening much, his nerves were.

He kept playing the battle through in his mind while she was massaging his back. He had such clear pictures in his head of how badly things could have gone for his men, for Odin's men, if he had not intervened. She could feel his body flinch a little as he pictured the battle in his mind, but he was not getting more tense about it, that was rare. She suspected he hadn't been bloodsick at all after this battle, he just needed to decompress from the stresses of teaching such dire lessons.

"My Lord, will you tell me what you are watching in your mind?" She asked.

"What?"

"Are you watching the battle again?" She asked with a soft, nurturing tone.

"Yes, you fucking witch." He said laughing. It caught him off guard that she knew what was going through his mind. *"That shouldn't surprise me . . . But it will take some getting used to."* He thought.

"I'd love to hear about it. If you care to share." She said while rubbing her elbows deep between his shoulder blades.

"A group of the men didn't know what to do at one point, they had never seen a battle unfold like this, they weren't prepared – they hadn't been taught. It could have been very bad." He said.

"What did you do, My Lord?"

"Aaaaahhh, they just needed me to step in and take care of a few things, you know." He said, deflecting attention away from what he had really done.

"My Lord, I would love to hear the truth. You should tell me what *really* happened." She said, still with a soft tone.

He lifted his head and turned it halfway towards her, then shook his head, as if he were shaming her. "And she's a bossy witch, too." He wasn't complaining, he said it adoring her.

She leaned down and whispered in his ear, "It's what we do, My Lord."

"This has to stay here." He told her.

She nodded. "Of course, My Lord. I won't tell anyone."

"There was a group of eight or ten men who got cut off from the rest of the group in the battle and they were almost surrounded because Odin made a rash decision to attack before he thought out how to move forward or even informed his men of what he was doing. He was stupid and completely fucking reckless. I had planned on sitting back and staying out of the battle to see how the Odin would handle things. Then, right as I was about to ask King FuckBrains to tell me his plan, he yells and starts running into battle without even telling his men what he was thinking."

"How did the men respond?" Iyasiil asked.

"They weren't even ready. So, they just took off with him. That little stupid little fucker . . ." Malkore said, letting out a long sigh. "Anyway, I saw what was about to happen away from the main force and so I took off to keep from losing too many men. There were six or eight of us against 30 or so men. We only lost one from that group and there was nothing I could have done about that one." He said matter-of-factly.

"How are you doing with that, My Lord." She asked.

"It's OK. He was a good kid, but he never should have been put in that position." He said with compassion. "I did actually *enjoy* killing the four men who had ganged up on him." He chuckled.

"We will send up love and prayers for him." She interjected.

"- and for the men who killed him." He said, finishing her sentence.

"Yes, My Lord." She was glad to hear that he didn't have any judgment about the souls of his enemy. *"Yeah, this warrior is not bloodsick. He just couldn't talk about what was really weighing on him and it was growing toxic inside him."* She thought.

He continued to tell the story where Odin and the largest part of the men wound up all on one side and this small group of younger warriors got isolated, and how it likely would have led to Odin's forces being divided and suffering bigger losses. He talked as if he had watched his own failure and how that if he hadn't stepped in to fix it, it would have been a catastrophe. He took it on himself that he had failed to teach his student better.

"I basically had to cut a swath through their forces to create a space for our men to begin isolating them." He said.

"So, My Lord, what you're saying is that you went in and killed about 20 plus men by yourself to turn a stalemate into a grand victory?" She asked.

"I shouldn't have had to." He said.

She laid her body on his back and melted into him, kissed him on the back of his neck, then said, "I understand that, My Lord. The part that impresses me is your mastery of men and measure to be able to see, analyze, assess, respond instantly with a masterful plan, and then to skillfully fight your way through so many men without even being wounded yourself, and then turning the tide of the battle all on your own. I have seen a lot in my days, and I have *never* seen the likes of you." She exhaled deeply with her mouth and nose burrowing into the back of his neck.

"Well, my chest is sore. That's kind of like being wounded, isn't it?" He said, being silly and downplaying what he had done.

"Well then, My Lord, perhaps it's time for you to turn over and let me tend to your wounds." She said playfully. She had been working deep into his back for over an hour. As he was rolling over, "It's probably a good idea for us both to have a cup of tea before we go further."

He sat up. She handed him his cup of tea. They sat in silence and enjoyed their tea.

When Malkore finished his tea, he set his cup on the table beside the bed, closed his eyes, and took a long, slow breath. Seeing this she smiled and thought, *What an awesome man.* "My Lord, before we get started again, I am going to take a break for a minute or two."

"Of course, Love. Do whatever you need to do." He thought she was probably just tired from working on his body so deeply and needed a break. He was wrong. That was not the kind of break she wanted.

"Thank you, My Lord." She climbed up on him, straddling him, wrapping her arms around him without hesitation or reservation. "I am going to be *really* selfish with you again." She kissed him like she wanted to devour his mouth as well as his heart and soul.

"Yes. Please and thank you." He said, pulling her close. He took a breath – breathing her in. His body shuttered as he felt how she felt touching him. He wasn't just feeling how amazing her body felt – he was feeling what it was like to feel her heart be so present with him. He could feel her heart and spirit and her wisdom and her love.

He kept one hand on the back of her heart and put the other hand on her sacrum, pulling her hips and her heart closer. He could feel that she was already getting excited. He could feel how wet she was on the top of his cock. He just sat there, holding her, amazed at how good his heart felt with her there.

"My Lord, I am going to finish your massage now."

"OK. You go do that." But he wasn't letting her go. Still holding her firmly into him, he said, "Go do your thing, witch.

I'm not stopping you." His strong arms had her firmly planted against his chest.

She only nuzzled his neck with her nose and mouth, feeling her heart melting into his chest.

"My Lord." She didn't finish that sentence; she just took more heavy breaths.

"Yes, My Love? Is there something the fucking witch would like to say?" He asked smiling.

"The fucking witch doesn't ever want you to stop holding her like this." She said. She couldn't believe she said that. "The fucking witch wants to finish your massage, because she knows you will like it very much. The fucking witch knows how much you need the massage. *AND*, the witch is getting bewitched and doesn't want to stop feeling this long enough to move, My Lord." She kissed him again.

"Yes, witch." He said.

"My Lord. The fucking witch is going to start massaging you in a minute and she may stop to take breaks to come right back here, like this, at any point. OK?" She said, softly.

"Yes, witch." He said, pulling her even closer, pushing her hips onto him even more, pulling her heart into his heart even more. He moved his hand from the back of her heart to the back of her head and held her head against his face and neck.

Without moving, she asked, "Are you ready, My Lord?"

He slowly slid his fingers up into her hair and grabbed a handful of hair gently and still firmly. He turned her head to bring her lips to his and he kissed her. Her whole body shuddered.

"I am yours." She thought.

"Now. Now I am ready. I just wanted to kiss you first." He said. He felt like his heart was flowing like a waterfall. Part of him wanted to throw her down on the bed and make love with her the rest of the day. He hadn't felt that kind of erotic excitement in his body in millennia, but it was here now.

She sat up, still straddling him. She put her hands on his chest, looking him in the eyes and she forgot about her sexual excitement, she forgot about massaging him. She just got lost in feeling what this man felt like to her. "Thank You." She said.

Then she slid off of him, had him lay down, and began massaging his chest.

- - - - - - - - - - - -

Kalla and Dossa had left the chamber and went ahead and gone to check in with the women in the kitchen, they got a small bit of food for themselves, and went back to their cabin to lay down for a while.

As they laid down on their beds, Dossa said, "Well, that was stupid. We should have come straight here. I lost that feeling by going into the kitchen."

"Yeah, I'm going to breathe and see if I can find it again. Come lay here with me, D."

As Dossa laid next to Kalla, Kalla rolled onto her side, so the entire length of her body was touching Dossa's body. She laid her hand on Dossa's heart and began breathing and relaxing her body, just as Malkore had instructed them to do in their teacher's chamber.

"Breathe with me." Kalla said. Dossa began breathing deep, slow breaths. Mimicking Malkore's words, Kalla said, "Let your body relax as you breathe. Feel the love of the universe flowing into your heart and filling you up." Kalla felt it in her hand and her own heart as she laid there with her hand on Dossa's heart.

Dossa gasped, "Oh . . . I can feel it. Your hand feels warm. It's making my whole chest feel warm."

"Yeah, good. Keep breathing. Keep feeling it." Kalla said. She knew she was mimicking Malkore and her teacher and she wasn't sure what to do next.

"Oh wow!" Dossa said softly, "You feel so good." She laid her hand on Kalla's hand, and they just kept breathing. After another minute, Dossa moved Kalla's hand over to her breast and mashed Kalla's hand into her breast.

Kalla froze for a second. She felt excited but wasn't sure. "I don't think that's the point, Dossa."

"Shut up and feel me. Breathe with me, you sexy little bitch." The both giggled. Kalla relaxed her hand and started moving her hand, caressing Dossa's breast.

They started kissing and fondling each other. They stayed in bed, making love for over an hour, loving on each other and feeling each other.

As they were getting up and getting dressed, Kalla kept giggling at how much fun they had. Dossa came over and straightened Kalla's dress and said, "This is wild. I have never felt so much love, ever! Not even when I am in a relationship. What just happened?"

Kalla said, "Dossa, I don't know. But I don't think we should tell anyone about this right away. They won't understand."

"Oh Stop. They have never cared before. No one cares." Dossa told her.

"Well, if this were just sex, that would be fine. No one cares about that."

Looking at her with her head cocked and her eyebrows scrunched up, Dossa asked, "What do you mean?"

"This is something different, it's not just sex. It's something more. It's . . . It's . . . like it's . . . I don't know what the fuck it is!"

Dossa was laughing. She felt the same way. She didn't know what it was, but she liked it.

- - - - - - - - - - - - - - -

Malkore was laying on his back, Iyasiil had been kneeling on the bed beside him, massaging his chest. She was making strokes with the heels of her hands, the length of his chest muscles, going from the center of his chest all the way out to the top of his arm. Each stroke getting progressively firmer, from medium firm strokes to deep, slow strokes that were just on the edge of painful, but it was amazing how high his pain tolerance was.

He noticed how much she was working as much his heart and spirit as she was working on his muscles. He felt like she was equally building up the amount of love in his heart as she was breaking down the tension in his muscles.

He had spent so long feeling like he was dragging boulders along everywhere he went. Feeling worn down and overworked was an everyday thing. He was so used to keeping his energy to himself. Showing up only as *The Teacher* or *The Warrior*, never having time to stop and relax, never having peers with whom he could share his real thoughts. It had been wearing him down.

She could feel the strength in his muscles, he was so solid. He was like an immovable force of nature. He didn't just feel strong physically, he was relaxed, and his heart was expansive. She kept feeling herself drop into admiration and a delicious sense of "awe" while she was massaging him. Those feelings felt like her own personal, selfish feelings – not what one often feels like being in a place of service.

Often being there, supporting someone during the Tending feels like putting part of yourself aside to take care of someone else, which has its own rewards, but it's different. This felt much more integrated, she knew that both of those sets of feelings were compatible, they both supported Malkore during this time of Tending. She felt like she was getting her personal needs met, too. Connecting with this man was thrilling!

He was soaking it in. *"This woman is amazing. I think she is inside my body, feeling what I need without me telling her."* Every time, she rubbed a spot that was sore, and he wanted more work in that spot, she focused on it more.

She changed sides and knelt on the other side of him and worked on the other side of his chest.   Overall, she had been working on his upper body for over hour, then she straddled his massive chest. Her knees didn't even touch the bed on either side of him, so she wiggled her feet under his shoulders and was basically squatting on his chest. She was relaxed but didn't feel heavy on him.

She was reaching down and massaging his neck. She was pressing her fingers into the back of his neck, then slightly arching her back to make deep, pulling strokes around the sides of his neck. Then she put her thumbs at the top of his shoulders and pressed them behind his collarbones to his sternum and then up the sides of his neck to the base of his skull, behind his ears.

At first if felt strange, no one had ever touched him like that, and after four or five times through that motion, he felt the tension in his neck start to dissolve.

She massaged his face, working deep into the muscles of his jaw, the bottom of his jaw, and the bottoms of his cheekbones. She massaged his forehead and all around his eyes. He hadn't even been aware he had been holding tension there.

As she finished up on his upper body, she scooted back to straddle his hips. She laid her body onto his and relaxed. She had her head laying sideways on his shoulder and let out a big breath.

There was a little more to come and she knew they both needed to get up and move a bit before anything else was done. After all the massage, he needed to move a lot of blood through his body, and she needed a break from holding such intense space for him in the Tending.

Chapter Four
Clues

He was feeling refreshed like he had never felt before. He was excited to see what the rest of the day would hold for them.

It was hard to grasp that less than a day ago, the sun had been going down as he and the raiding party had been walking back into Asgard. He had been so angry and so tired. It seemed like three or four days had happened since then – since he had met this woman.

They decided to go for that walk he had mentioned earlier.

The girls had washed his clothes. He put them on. He started to put on his bear skin robe but stopped. She had just wrapped a blanket around her shoulders before walking out. He took the blanket off of her and wrapped her in his bear skin. She was surprised, it was a really sweet gesture. The robe was so warm, but didn't feel heavy, at all.

When they went out the door, if they turned right, they would pass by the great hall. If they turned left, they could wander out towards the edge of the village and stroll down past the gardens and into the woods. They chose to stay away from lots of people, towards the woods they went.

As they walked, she noticed that he comfortably strolled along looking all around. He moved like an exotic animal, so soft and relaxed, yet capable of the most destruction. It was a beautiful balance.

"You move with grace, My Lord." She said to him.

"What do you mean?" He asked.

"You are the greatest warrior, capable of killing so many with ease, and yet, there is no 'brute-ish-ness' to you at all. You walk like a man at peace with the world." She said.

"Says the witch who's feet have yet to touch the ground, only gliding above the path."

She laughed. "My Lord, just because you can't see my feet beneath this robe of yours, doesn't mean they aren't touching the ground."

He stopped, grinning at her. She stepped closer to him and held his hands. He said, "Iyasiil, My Love, Asgard itself should pray to be worthy of feeling the touch of your feet. You are made of grace itself and you glide as you move."

She just smiled.

They continued their walk and kept holding hands. Their hearts both tingled a little bit, it was like their hearts were having a conversation through their hands that they couldn't hear, but they felt it.

He pointed out a few things about the village as he looked around, sharing memories and little bits of the history of the kingdom.

The few people they saw yelled out a greeting to one of them.

"Malkore, you're amazing!" One man yelled. Malkore would just wave.

"Mama, we missed you in the great hall last night." A young woman said. Iyasiil just smiled and blew her a kiss.

One young man, who talked and carried himself like a little boy, came up to them and said that he had heard about the raid and wished he could have been there. "My Lord, Malkore, it sounded like you defeated the entire army yourself, you are indeed the greatest warrior! Is there anything I can do for you?"

Malkore smiled and grabbed the boy in a great bear hug, with his boisterous warrior's voice said, "I'm glad you weren't there! If you had been there, there would have been no one left for me to kill! You would have taken them all down yourself!"

"My Lord, I know that I need to practice with the sword. I believe I am ready to start going on the raids. I want to learn from you. Will you teach me?" The boy said with a bit of admiration and a bit of a desperate tone.

"Ahhh, young man. In a week or so, you should come find this woman and ask her." Malkore said shifting from the warrior's celebration voice to his 'wise, old teacher' voice.

The young man looked confused. He looked at her and nodded out of respect, then looked back at Malkore. "I don't understand, My Lord."

"When this woman tells me that you have learned to sit in silence. Then you will be ready to learn with me." Malkore said.

The young man looked to Iyasiil, then back to Malkore, still confused, "I still don't understand."

Iyasiil said to him, using *her* wise, old teacher voice, "You will, My Lord. Don't take Lord Malkore's offer lightly. If you want to be a great warrior, like you say, come find me at the end of next week. OK?"

"Next week?" He asked, he had been so excited hearing all the stories from the raid, he wanted to get started right away.

Malkore said, "Son, the waiting is part of the teaching. Why else would I tell you to do it?! Until then, make the time to go for long walks in the woods by yourself. If you don't follow these instructions, I'll know that you weren't serious about learning, and you weren't worthy to be a real student with me."

The young man got a little glimmer in his eye and cracked a half-smile. "Yes, My Lord."

Putting on his boisterous warrior's voice again, he said, "Now go join the men in the great hall. Enjoy the celebration."

The two of them walked off towards the gardens, immediately wrapping her arms around his arm and snuggling into him as they walked. "My Lord, you show great trust in me, sending me your students already."

"Yeah! I heard that come out of my mouth. I hadn't planned on saying that; hadn't even thought it. I hope you are OK with that." He said with an amused tone.

"Well, you asked what we were both doing here in Asgard. That could be a clue." She said.

"Hmm. Yeah. I don't even know what you do, I just know that I want some of it for myself. But as far as the people go, I trust you to teach them well." He said.

"It's what we do, My Lord." She said smiling as she leaned her head on his shoulder, and he pulled her arms tighter into his ribs with his elbow.

They walked on, around the gardens. They talked brief y with a couple harvesting some of the Fall vegetables. Malkore thanked them for all they were doing for the people.

"We are just farmers. We grow vegetables, that's all." The man said.

"Ahhh. But that's where you're wrong!" Malkore said with only half of his boisterous warrior's voice put on for effect. He pulled a Teeda Root out of the basket and held it up, "It all starts here. Do you love what you do?" They both nodded. "Do you care for these plants like they are your own children? Do you nurture them so they will grow strong?" They both smiled. He gestured with the Teeda Root in his hand, "Asgard starts here! Our lives start here! Without you, I would still be suffering after returning home last night, *you two* have been a vital part of that. Without the love and care you give to the people; we would all starve."

"My Lord, thank you." The young man wanted to get down on one knee in front of Malkore, he was so touched and honored by Malkore's words.

"No, son. Thank *you*." He turned and nodded to the young woman. "Thank you both."

The young woman wiped a tear from her face and said, "Blessing to you both, My Lord."

Iyasiil smiled and held eye contact with her and said, "Come say hello sometime." The woman bowed her head slightly in acknowledgment. "Now, if you two will excuse us, I am taking this gorgeous man for a walk tonight." Wrapping around his arm again, she snuggled into him as they walked. "Their harvest will be Thirty percent bigger next season from what you just did, My Lord."

Not really grasping what she said, "Well, they need to know. I'm sure no one has ever taught them how important the work they do is to the people. Wait. Thirty percent?"

"Yes, Thirty percent. And no doubt that no one has ever taught them until now. Possibly another clue, My Lord." She said, elbowing him in his side.

Shaking his head, amazed at this woman, "It's what we do, My Love." They both laughed a little.

They turned to walk down by the oak grove and looped back up into the far side of the village. At some point soon, they would have to decide whether or not to avoid walking by the great hall. They hadn't planned it, but as they walked, they found themselves there.

"Would you like to go by the blacksmith's shop and go back to my cottage, My Lord? Or would you like to walk by the great hall?" She asked, still being mindful of guarding his energy against people being a drain on him.

"If we keep it short, it would be good to stop in for a minute or two. If you're OK with that." He said.

"If it's what My Lord wishes, it will be done. And I don't want you to be drained a single bit, even though I know you are feeling good. So, when you're ready, let me know. I'll make sure we get out quickly." She said.

As they approached the great hall, they could hear the drums and horns being played; they could hear the yelling and laughing. It sounded like a raucous party, just as they both suspected.

They had only gotten a step into the door before Odin yelled, "Malkore!" then Twenty more men and women yelled his name, then twenty more after that.

Odin grabbed a full horn of mead and came over to Malkore, screaming his name and gave him the horn of mead. Odin was happy to see him and kept his warrior's "celebration" persona on. "Malkore, feast with us! There is enough food for ten armies!"

Odin and Malkore talked for a moment, then several men came up and hugged Malkore or punched him on the shoulder, yelling his name.

Iyasiil stayed close, but let the men have their moments with him. He kept talking to a few of the men. Odin turned his attention to Iyasiil and hugged her as if she were just any woman. He hugged her with a hunger to enjoy her beauty. She could feel his hunger, but it didn't feel good to her. He felt like a drunk, teenage boy who didn't know how to handle himself. She was used to it, every woman is.

Odin looked at her, his eyes half-glazed with mead, and said, "Maybe you should stay and celebrate with us, my young beauty!" The intention was clear, he wanted to have sex with her in the celebration.

"My Lord, I have been Tending to warriors returning home since before your father ever carried a blade, and Tending to *this* great warrior is what I will be doing tonight." She said to Odin.

Odin was caught off guard, he hadn't realized that Malkore hadn't really been part of what was happening in the great hall. He looked at Malkore, then back to her, then back to Malkore, then back to her. He just then realized that something was going on, he couldn't tell what it was, but he felt something.

Odin asked, "How is he doing?"

Her face looked warm, and her smile said it all, "He's doing great, My Lord. He is truly an amazing man."

"Yes, he is." Odin's whole demeanor changed. He began to feel his respect and admiration for his teacher. "I wouldn't be who I am today without him."

"He has more to teach than anyone I have ever known, My Lord. So much of what he has to teach, most of the people here aren't even ready to begin learning it. He has already seen what Asgard can become, and he is the man to teach it."

He looked at her, not knowing what to say.

She smiled at the king and continued, "My Lord, you won't believe the heights to which you will lead Asgard."

He looked at Malkore, then back to her. But at the same time, Malkore had turned to her and gave her a look and nodded his head. Malkore was saying he was finished and was ready to leave.

Odin still wasn't sure about what she was saying. He chose to blow it off and go back to celebrating. "To Asgard!" He yelled, raising his horn of ale.

Everyone in the great hall yelled it back, "To Asgard!"

When Odin turned back, Malkore and Iyasiil were gone – to him, it looked like they just disappeared.

They walked out without anyone noticing. Odin looked around quickly, he wasn't sure what had just happened. The woman tending to Malkore had just said something about Malkore seeing how great he would be, then she was gone. *"Where the fuck did they go?"* He wondered.

Walking out of the great hall, Malkore said, "That was nice. I am glad we didn't stay long. I didn't expect to get away so easily."

"My Lord, I may have helped a little with that." She said as she wrapped her arms around his arm again and snuggled into him.

He dropped his head and started laughing, "You *fucking* witch!" He imagined things like that, but never had he made himself disappear.

Feigning innocence, she said, "My lord, it was much better to do it this way than if I had taken your sword and shown you how it's meant to be used, killing every warrior who wanted your attention."

She spoke with such confidence. He believed her for a moment; he believed she really could have done it.

"Yes, I see your point. That would have put a damper on the evening, wouldn't it?"

"It's almost time for dinner, My Lord. I thought maybe we can find a nice place to eat outside, in a secluded spot, away from people."

He said, "That sounds great. It's such a nice night. I can't remember such a beautiful night with such enjoyable company in all history."

There was a bench in the back of where all the hides were processed, and a table had been put outside. There was no one in this part of the village this time of day and the girls would be walking by this spot soon to check in, so they sat and looked out across the meadow and just breathed in how beautiful this place is. Every now and then they could hear the wild screams and laughter from the great hall.

"You know, they may still be going at it, just as strong tomorrow night." He said.

"As well they should. The men were coming back feeling strong and their hearts were full. That's always worthy of a celebration." She said to him.

He put on a (sarcastic) sad voice, "Yeah, but I just keep feeling sorry for them, though."

"My Lord, why?" she asked.

Squeezing her hand, "Not one of them is getting to enjoy *this*."

She leaned her head over onto his shoulder and snuggled her face into his shoulder, "I know. Those pour souls."

He looked out to the horizon, leaned back against the wall, and took a deep breath. He hadn't taken in the beauty of this place in quite a while. He looked at the mountains across the meadow. It was only a day's hike, and it looked so much further.

"After dinner, we will finish your massage." She said.

"What? There's more? Nooo, you have already done so much. There's no need, Love." He said.

"Hey!" She said, lifting her head to look at him. "My Lord, for such a great warrior and such a wise man, you sure are full of shit sometimes, you know that?"

"What?" He asked. He was caught off guard, shocked even. He wasn't offended, but it caught him off guard and he started laughing.

"My Lord, you would do no less for me, so don't even tell me I have done enough. And, I will decide when you have had enough – have you forgotten who you're dealing with?" She looked at him warmly and still firmly, "During the Tending, it is safe to assume that I am," she turned on her sarcastic tone, "*far, far* wiser than you. So, the only thing you need to say," poking him in the ribs, "is," then looking him in the eye with a flirty look, "Yes, My Love.""

He kept looking at her, smiling, recognizing defeat, taking a deep breath. "Yes, My Love, the mountains themselves are not as wise." He took another breath, breathing her in. "You are truly amazing. I am so thankful for this time with you."

She wrapped her arms around him again. They sat, not talking much, both just enjoying the evening as the sun was starting its evening escape from the day.

They could see the girls walking towards them from a little way away. Dossa was carrying a pitcher of mead in her left hand, a pitcher of tea clenched between her elbow and her side, and two horn mugs in the other hand. Kalla had a platter of food with two clean plates and two fresh cups balanced on top of the platter.

When the girls saw their teacher, they both smiled. They were excited to tell their teacher all about what they had experienced when they had gone to lay down, they had so many questions. They also knew that their questions would have to wait. The girls knew enough to know to *not* disturb the Tending. They would stay focused on being in service and not their own needs for the time being.

Kalla said, "Hey mama. Hello, My Lord. We have brought dinner." Then she saw the table that was behind the tannery. She looked confused, "Has this table always been here?"

"I've never seen it before." Dossa said.

Iyasiil smiled, "We were thinking of eating outside this evening and then we saw this table by the bench. We just need to bring the table around here to where we are sitting." Malkore started to get up to move the table. Before he even leaned forward to stand, Iyasiil pulled him down. "The girls will get it, My Lord. Let them serve you."

"*Fuck! She read my mind again.*" In a low, soft grumble, he growled the word, "Witch." He could *not* contain the smile inside.

She was smiling too. She reached up and grabbed his head with one hand and pulled it towards her and kissed him on the cheek and let her cheek and the side of her nose linger, and she felt his skin with her face.

The girls gracefully lifted the heavy table and walked it over to where their teacher was sitting and began arranging the cups, plates, and putting the platter where they could both reach the food.

Dossa said, "I was wondering why I made sure to bring two new plates and four new cups even though you had everything you needed in your chamber. I didn't understand. It didn't make sense; I just felt like I needed to do it."

Malkore was the one who responded. "Good job paying attention. It seems like magic doesn't it? We wanted to eat outside, a table appears, and you magically have the thought to bring everything for a meal."

Dossa looked at him confused, "My Lord?"

Iyasiil finished the teaching, "Don't you think the universe is smarter than we are? Don't you think that the pulse of this planet and the heart of Asgard itself is wiser and more knowledgeable than any of us can be?"

Kalla was creeping forward, she felt her heart get warm, and she wanted to make sure she heard what her teacher was saying.

Dossa wasn't sure what the right answer was. She looked at her teacher, then at Malkore, then back to her teacher. "I don't know, I would guess so." Her voice was shaky. She was scared to offend her teacher if she said that anything was smarter or wiser than she and Malkore. Even if it was true, is the Tending the time to tell a warrior that he isn't the wisest?!

Kalla interjected, just blurting out, "Of course they are. But how --"

Malkore said, "How were the two of you feeling when you went into the kitchen to prepare this feast for us?"

Kalla looked at Dossa. Dossa looked at Kalla. They both giggled, wondering if they should really say.

Iyasiil smiled and laughed a little and said, "It's OK. This is important. Tell us."

The girls giggled again. Kalla said, "We . . . uh . . ."

Dossa interjected, "We were both so happy and feeling great."

"Yes, it's when you're having the most fun that you will feel the impulses to do what is needed and you won't even know why." Malkore said.

"Yeah, it just felt like the right thing to do, even though it didn't make sense." Kalla said.

Iyasiil was grinning, she knew the answer, but she asked anyway, "What had you two so lit up?"

The girls giggled again. Kalla looked at her and was smiling. "Ummm . . . well." She looked a little embarrassed and also like she was about to burst with laughter.

"Kalla, it's OK. Do you think you're going to tell us anything that we don't already know? Tell us what had you two so lit up?" Iyasiil said.

Kalla said, "When we left your chamber a couple of hours ago, we were so lit up after you," nodding to Malkore, "had us do that breathing and feeling thing . . . We went back home to lay down for a while, and –"

Dossa interjected, "but first we went to the kitchen to see if anyone needed any help, and it felt like shit."

Kalla continued, "Yeah, we shouldn't have done that. It just killed all the good feelings. So, when we got back home, we laid down, I put my hand on her heart and we started breathing, just like you had us do before and the feeling came back."

"Yeah, it did! It really came back, big!" Dossa said.

"Then we kind of got carried away with it." Kalla said, still not sure if she had done something wrong or not.

Malkore started laughing quietly to himself.

"But it wasn't just sex. It was something more, it was bigger than any sex either of us have ever had. Does that make sense?"

Iyasiil answered, "Of course, Kalla. That's the most powerful energy in the universe and you can only feel it when your heart is open, and your spirit is clear."

"Consider that your second lesson from your teacher." Malkore said draining his cup of mead.

"But it wasn't like any sex either of us have ever experienced before, with a man or a woman." Kalla said, almost pleading to understand and to be understood.

"Yes, we get it. It's powerful energy to tap into. It's healing and nurturing, it calls us to grow, and it is the next level of living and the next level of loving. We will get into the deeper mysteries of Sacred Sex Magic as we work together. You are just beginning to experience what's possible." She said to the girls.

Malkore finished her thought, "And you're right, it's not just the sex, it's about living every day in the magical place of emotional openness and spiritual expansiveness so that you can access those states of being. It doesn't matter if you use that presence for sex or any other creative thing you do, even if it is," motioning to the food, "just to infect a delicious meal with big-hearted love that nourishes people's souls."

Kalla looked at the food that she had laid out, then back to Malkore, then to Dossa. "Oh Shit!" She looked shocked, "We did that. I didn't realize it, but that's what we did. I was feeling so much love for you," nodding to Iyasiil, "and feeling so happy to get to serve the two of you. I was feeling all that while we prepared this food; I almost started crying. All day, I have been so overwhelmed by loving you so much."

"That's it!" Malkore said. "Now imagine if you felt it every day, not just during the Tending. What would your life be like?"

"Everyday?" Dossa asked.

"How much love can you handle flowing through you, Dossa?" Iyasiil asked her student.

Dossa took a deep breath, trying not to show any emotion. "I feel like I am about to explode. I feel like I can't take it and I don't want it to stop. I'm excited. But, I am scared." She started to tear up.

Iyasiil motioned for her to come around the table to sit next to her. "Come here sweet girl."

Dossa sat next to her teacher on the bench and leaned over to put her head on Iyasiil's shoulder. Iyasiil wrapped her in a hug, wrapping Malkore's huge bear skin robe around her, and started whispering something to her. She had never really shared any big feelings with her teacher before, this was a bit of a breakthrough with her student.

Kalla suddenly realized that all the attention had been on her and Dossa while this is supposed to be Malkore's Tending. She looked shocked and a little panicked for just a moment. Then she turned to Malkore and silently mouthed the words, *"Are you OK?"*

He smiled a peaceful smile and nodded.

Kalla felt the impulse to come around the table to Malkore. With her teacher occupied, she wanted to make sure Malkore was being Tended to. Then she got scared and didn't do it. She looked at Iyasiil holding Dossa, and her heart opened again feeling how much she loved Dossa. With her heart open, the impulse came back. Kalla came around to Malkore's end of the table and leaned down to him, put her hands in the front and back of his shoulder, and whispered into his ear, "Is there anything I can do for you, My Lord? Or anything else I can get you?"

He reached up to pat her on the back and whispered back, "No, Love. I am doing great. Thank you."

She felt his touch on the back of her ribs. It was like getting a lightning bolt of that same amazing energy all through her body.

He felt it, too. He could feel how present she was and how open her heart was by how she felt when he touched her. He could feel that as he was touching her, she was touching him back through the skin on her ribs; receptive to the connection on a deeper level, at least that's what it felt like to him – like she was touching him in response.

His touching her was completely innocent and his touch felt welcomed; his touch felt received and returned.

What he had noticed over the years is that he could feel if someone was really emotionally present through the touch. When someone is not present, it doesn't feel good. Not even sex felt good with someone was not emotionally present and in a spiritually expansive place.

He was about to turn his attention back to his plate of food. Kalla, again had felt an impulse, then got scared to act on it, then felt the impulse again and acted on it the second time – all that happened in a split second. She slid her hands down to the front and back of his heart, stood up a little straighter, and took a long, deep breath.

She was wondering if she could do what her teacher had done to her and what her teacher was doing now with Dossa. She just imagined the love of the universe coming up through her feet, through her heart, out of her hands, and into his heart. She imagined feeling the flow of love that a great warrior deserved. She pictured a flow of love as big as her hands flowing through her and into him.

If she couldn't do it right, she would feel stupid for trying to act like she was awesome like her teacher, but she tried it anyway.

He felt it. It felt for those moments like this was no longer a young woman who was just learning who she was. Right then, she felt like a wise old woman with nurturing and presence to spare. Her touch felt warm, comforting, expansive, and relaxing.

He put his hand on top of hers and gently, but firmly, pressed her hand into his heart and he took a long breath and then another. Then, he patted her hand, gently, to thank her and to acknowledge that he was receiving what she was sending. He looked up at her and nodded, then mouthed the words, "Thank you."

She smiled. She was feeling quite accomplished but didn't know if she was doing something wrong because it felt really intimate, *really* intimate. She cut off those feelings and went back into "service mode," or at least the kind of service she was used to. She went back to the other side of the table and refilled his cup of mead and topped off his tea.

In just a couple of minutes, Dossa's nervousness had settled, and she was wiping away her tears and sniffing hard. She had sat up straight, then looked at her teacher and leaned forward touching foreheads with her teacher for just a few more seconds. Quietly, but still loud enough for Malkore to hear, she said to her teacher, "Thank you, mama. And I am sorry I interrupted."

Iyasiil said, "This isn't an interruption. I wouldn't have asked if it wasn't a good thing to do."

Dossa nodded and started shaking off all she had just been feeling and looked at the table to see if anything needed to be done, then looked at Kalla.

Kalla said, "Everything is good."

Dossa looked at Malkore and asked, "Is there anything we can do for you before we go, My Lord?"

Malkore knew she was feeling flustered and said to her, "Young lady, you have blessed this meal with your open heart. Sharing your raw, heartfelt presence is the biggest gift you could have given me tonight."

"Thank you, My Lord." Dossa bowed her head to him.

"No, My Love. Thank *you*." Malkore responded.

Kalla and Dossa looked at each other to acknowledge that it was time to go and Kalla said, "If there is nothing else, we will come check in before it is time to sleep." The girls started to walk off, "Oh. And your special medicine tea is in your chamber, should I put it by the fire so it can be warming up for you?"

Iyasiil said, "Oh, yes. That would be wonderful, just make sure you don't drink any of it yourself. Thank you, girls."

The girls walked off holding hands, then Dossa wrapped her arms around Kalla's arm and put her head on Kalla's shoulder as they headed to their teacher's chamber to clean up and prepare the chamber for their teachers return.

Malkore looked at Iyasiil and nodded, "You're doing wonderful work with them, My Love."

"The transformation you see has only happened in them in the past day." She responded.

"What do you mean?" Malkore asked.

"Until they saw us together and felt us together, they could only hear me tell them things to do. They've always had massive potential, but it has been like talking to a couple of rocks. Being with us this afternoon, tapped into their hearts in a way I couldn't do on my own. I can feel them now – they are feeling now." She said.

"Just today?"

"Mmm hmm. My Lord has that effect on people." She said laying her head on his shoulder.

"No. No, he doesn't." He protested. "I have been around those girls, and they never even noticed I was there. It isn't me." He said, beginning to eat.

"No, My Lord. I think it is *us*. They were ready and hungry to learn, but nothing would seem to get in, no matter what I did. Then suddenly, they got cracked open when they were with us today." She said.

"Why? What is going on with that?" He asked.

"Clues, My Lord." She said with a flirty wink.

He looked at her, taking in all she had been saying about the "clues" on their walk tonight. He just kept looking at her, taking some deep breaths. "Does that mean we really are going to keep working together?"

"I'd love it!" She said with whole-bodied excitement. Then she took a very measured breath, "Of course, this may just be what we both need for the Tending, but this feels like day one of something wonderful. I *am* taking care of you a little bit, but not much. I don't feel like I am outside looking in, like I normally would in a Tending. I feel like the universe ordered me to do the most selfish thing that has ever been. I feel like all I am doing is getting to know you in the best way possible. Loving on you and spending the day with you has felt mostly like I'm just being me with someone who can actually receive me and fully *meet* me. I am getting to be *me* with someone who can take in everything I bring. Like I said earlier, I'm just going with it. We will see what unfolds as time goes on. For now, you still need several days of hard rest. This is a big, energetic reset, but nothing like a normal, bloodsick Tending. This is more like a reset and starting a new phase."

"Wow. Yes, on all counts. Yes. So, we'll just eat this delicious dinner and see what happens next." He said.

"Oh, I know what is going to happen next." She said with an excited tone.

"Ahhh. That's right. Maybe we can eat then walk down to the oak grove and watch the sun go down before we go back to your chambers. I'd like that." He said.

"Ohhh, fuck yeah! That's a wonderful idea! Yes, let's do that." She said excitedly.

They kept eating and talking a little, but mostly they just enjoyed the cool night air, the amazing food, the view, and the company.

When they finished eating, they strolled down to the oak grove. Malkore sat against the base of a large tree. Iyasiil sat in front of him, turning his big bear robe around to use as a blanket as she leaned back into him. They sat in silence and watched the sun slide down the valley and slip behind the distant hills. After the sun was gone, they stayed. They kept enjoying the time together; they kept enjoying the land.

"We should do this again. This has been a fabulous day. Maybe we should build a bench down here to watch the sunset on the clear nights." Malkore said.

"That would be so much fun! Maybe make a fire pit and make it a regular spot. What do you think, My Lord?" She asked, feeling really excited about the idea.

"As long as we don't tell anyone about it." He said laughing.

She laughed too, "No. No. We won't tell anyone about it. It will just be our spot." She said leaning back into him even more and wiggling a little to get even closer. He pulled her closer and felt how good she felt all over again.

As darkness was setting in, they made their way back to her chamber. As they passed the bench where they had eaten, all the plates were gone, and the table had been put back where they had found it.

"Your girls are pretty good." He said.

"I bet they built the fire up inside and have everything ready for us, My Lord."

"You are teaching them well, My Love."

Just as she predicted, her chamber was warm when they walked in. The warmth felt good after the chilly night air. All the plates in her chamber were gone from earlier in the day and a few light snacks had been left for them. Two large horns of mead and two cups of tea were topped off, sitting by the bed.

"Good job girls." He remarked, even though the girls were not there. "They are honoring their teacher well." He said to her.

He picked up a small bowl of vegetables and a piece of bread and walked over to sit on the bed. She had hung up his robe, then slipped on her lightest weight dress that was little more than nothing. She joined him on the bed and began sipping her mead.

"What a beautiful day so far." She said. "Is there anything I can do for you, My Lord."

"Yes. I would have the fucking witch look deep into my heart and see how happy of a day this has been for me. Thank you . . . you fucking witch." He said with his whole face lit up with a smile.

"Ohhh, what a happy smile that is. Thank you for this." She responded.

He was finishing up his snack and took a moment to look at her hair dancing in the light of the fire, framing her face. He just started shaking his head. "Wow."

"Yeah, wow." She said, smiling back at him. "Now, if My Lord will stand up and let me prepare him for the night's massage."

"Yes, My Love." He felt softer now. He was ready for whatever she had in store for him.

He stood up and she got the bowl of warm water the girls had put by the fire. She put a piece of cloth in the bowl and set it on the table by the bed. She had planned on undressing him as she had done the previous night. But as she stood before him and was about to reach up and untie the shoulders on his shirt, then she looked at him silhouetted by the light of the fire and her arms dropped. She stepped forward and wrapped her arms around his lower back and buried her face in his chest and neck. "Yeah, wow." She repeated.

He chuckled. "Yeah, wow. I feel like the most fortunate man in Asgard."

They stood there and hugged for a full minute, each of them taking a breath that refocused their awareness of how they felt right in that moment and then again in the next moment.

"This is not fortune, My Lord. This is our due for all the work we have done and all the preparations we have made that got us here." She said.

"Yes, of course. And I still feel lucky." He said playfully.

She giggled, "Me too."

She took in another deep, full breath and straightened up, laying her hands flat on his chest and looked him in the eyes. "It's time to begin." She began undressing him. She took the piece of cloth from the bowl of warm water and began wiping him down. She started on his face. She washed his shoulders, under his arms, his chest, his back. She washed his stomach, his cock, and the inside of his thighs.

The warm water felt good, but it had never felt this good. It didn't feel erotic, it felt nurturing.

When she was finished, she dried him off with another piece of cloth and asked him to lay on his back in the center of the bed. "When we are finished tonight, I have a cup of medicine tea for you. It will help you sleep and get a full night's rest."

She began by massaging his right shin with lots of oil. She started off lightly with lots of nurturing. She was rubbing the inside of his shin, into the muscle, right behind the bone. She rubbed the outside of his shin, and the muscles burned and relaxed as she worked on him. Her long strokes got progressively deeper into his muscles. He relaxed more and more. As he relaxed more, she pushed more and more love into him.

She was stopping right above his knee. After 15 or 20 minutes, she switched to the other shin and worked it just as well. Then, she straddled his knee and worked the strong muscles in his thighs pretty hard. The outside of his thighs were tender, and she slowly worked into them. The front of his thighs and inside of his thighs were not as tender, so she worked them deeper and harder. This work into his thighs didn't feel so nurturing, it was some deep physical work. She was still very mindful of flowing lots of love as she was working, it just didn't feel like it with the pain he was feeling at the moment. She switched legs and worked his other thigh just as hard. She had actually broken a sweat working so deep into his thighs.

Then, there was a marked difference in the energy in the massage. The physical work ended, and the erotic part of his spiritual energy came to the front. She knelt and sat on her feet between his knees. She got a little more oil on his thighs and was making long nurturing strokes on both thighs at the same time. She began focusing on his heart while rubbing on his thighs. She would take a breath and empty her mind and listen to how she felt right at that moment, *"You are such an amazing man. Thank you for all you do."* She said silently to his heart. He felt it. He didn't hear words, but suddenly took in a deep breath.

Another long, slow stroke up his thighs, *"You have been working so hard to prepare the people for the journey ahead of them. You have been masterful."* Another long stroke where her thumbs were on the inside of his thighs from the top of his knees all the way up to the crease between his thighs and his body, *"My Lord, you honor us with your presence and your service and your love. Allow us to love you now."*

His breathing got more intense, and a tear rolled down from his eye.

Over the next 30 minutes, she worked deeper into his legs and into his heart and was finishing her massage strokes up into his genitals. Using more oil, she gently massaged his balls and focused on the area under his balls for a while, she lovingly massaged deeply into all the connective tissue all around his genitals and his lower abdomen.

He felt like she was pushing erotic energy into his cock and his balls. He was getting aroused, and it felt great. She wasn't trying to give him an orgasm, she was nurturing his heart and sexual energy! She was building him up.

He couldn't believe how erotic this was – he had done the same kind of massage for women to help them re-connect with their own heart and their own presence, but never had anyone given him the same in return. She was being so patient. She was letting his energy rise naturally without expecting any kind of response. She was loving on him, but not to build their relationship and not so she could get something herself; she was loving on him so he could feel his own energy. She wasn't getting distracted by her own desire, which would cut the process off before his energy was built up as big as it could get.

"My Goddess! This woman is amazing! How intoxicating it is to be in the presence and in the hands of a true Goddess." He thought.

His cock was more engorged that he could ever remember, she had been building his energy up past the point of excitement. His whole body was flickering with lightning bolts and shockwaves. His breathing was still intensifying. He couldn't wait for her to massage his cock. He hoped she would, and he also loved the anticipation. He didn't want it to end.

"You fucking witch." He said with labored breath and his voice cracking as his body twitched.

"Breathe, My King. Feel your own energy and just let us love you." She said in a soft tone that still carried authority.

He kept breathing, not knowing how much more he could take and welcoming more. He couldn't remember his energy ever being built up this high with another person – No one had ever stayed so present after the energy got built up so high.

He was barely able to utter the word, "Witch" again. He called her "Witch" as a playful, joking, and honoring way of saying "thank you." It was hard for him to accept so much love and attention and so much care. He had spent so long taking care of everyone else, he only took care of himself in the deepest ways. No one ever took care of him in the deepest ways.

She smiled as she kept loving on him and building his energy. She felt like her heart had created a large channel that was flowing right into his groin and up to his heart. Although it felt good to her too and she loved how excited he was, she was only doing this so he could move forward in his own life. Her sole focus was supporting him and his enlightenment.

She pushed from his knees, up the inside of his thighs, and made a circle around his balls and cock with her thumbs and fingers, then pushed on up through his stomach into his heart. As her hands pushed up to his heart, her body was stretched out above his body. She laid her forehead on the base of his cock and took a breath and said a prayer thanks. Her prayer of thanks was not her personal gratitude; it was gratitude that this man existed, it was honoring this man and all he had gone through, all he had suffered; it was gratitude for all the work he had done to become the man he is.

Then her hands slid back down his body, her hands almost wrapping around his hard cock, but returning to his knees. She began another stroke up his thighs, her thumbs deeply pushing energy up to his groin. Her hands split as her left hand went up to his heart again and her right hand wrapped around the outside of his left hip. She slid her left knee over his right leg to where she was straddling his right shin, and she leaned down and rubbed her breasts up his thigh and rested her breasts around his cock while still holding his hip with one hand and pressing into his heart with the other hand.

His hips moved up into her. Her body shuddered, too. Her left hand stayed on his heart, her right hand went down to his knee again and began a stroke up to his groin. She wrapped her hand around his cock and pressed it into her heart and began rhythmically making small wave-like movements through her body which had her breasts move up and back on the sides of his groin. She was moaning too. She felt like she was going to have an orgasm in her heart.

His energy kept building with every touch. He had already reached the point of pleasure where he normally would have orgasmed and this time he didn't. The energy and excitement and pleasure kept building. She slid her dripping wet yoni down his shin and then slid her breasts up his thigh again, pressing them around his groin. She repeated this motion, sliding her left hand from his stomach up to his heart as her breasts were sliding up his thigh. Her breasts settled at an angle on the base of his stomach, across his cock. She pulled her left knee up to his hip and squeezed his right thigh with her knees and shins, this was another way to snuggle him, another way to hold him, and just another way to push love into him.

Personally, of course, she wanted to make love with him right then, but this was about nurturing him and helping to fill up his spirit, so she just took a breath and let her body go limp. She kept breathing and let her body move however it was going to move. She started arching then rounding her back, making her breasts move up and down on his lower stomach and groin. She kept that motion going as she began moving her breasts further and further up his stomach to his chest. Straddling the top of his thigh, she was massaging the top of his thigh with her yoni.

He reached another level of pleasure where normally he would have orgasmed. He had rarely gotten to this level before and never beyond it. His whole body was shuddering with pleasure. He was groaning and growling with pleasure.

When her breasts were on his heart, he reached up, put his hands on the back of her heart and pressed her into his heart. He was trying to speak, and only tiny sounds came out. She was already moving to swing her right leg over him, and his right hand pressed on the outside of her hip to guide her hips on top of him, then his hand pressed her hips down into his body, the force of his hands had her pinned to his body.

She slid her hands under his shoulders and squeezed his ribs with the inside of her forearms. Feeling his chest on the side of her face was better than any sex she had ever had, and she didn't ever want to stop. She couldn't move under this man's strength, and she didn't want to. She pressed her heart into his heart even more as she began moving her hips, grinding her yoni on top of his cock. She felt like her entire body had become the love of her heart – she felt his heart reaching out in every inch of his skin.

He almost sounded like he was in pain. He let out a half scream as he pushed her body down onto his cock. She took the full depth of it inside her and soaked him as her body released in orgasm. Now, she let go of any awareness of nurturing and taking care of him – no more Tending for now. Now, she was a woman, making love to a man who's touch and presence was thrilling to all her senses.

She slid her hands onto the fronts of his shoulders and pressed herself upright. He arched his hips and slid into the deepest part of her. She felt her body resist for a second and she let go, relaxing even more down onto him, letting him into her more and more in every way, on every level. She felt like her heart had expanded beyond her physical body and she was aware that they were wrapped in a glow of golden light.

His pleasure again had gone up to yet another level, and it kept building without a physical orgasm. His whole body was electrified like every part of him was orgasming. She kept moving, rocking her hips, him rocking his hips. She felt like her heart was being wrung out and refreshed again, filled up with the purest light of all that is.

His pleasure reached another level and another, still without a physical orgasm – he felt like he couldn't breathe. His face and neck tingled with pleasure; his hands felt like they barely worked any more. He felt his spirit lifting off and floating, as if they were making love in the sky. He could hardly move. His pleasure went up another level again, he was gasping for breath. He was just along for the ride now.

She felt his cock throbbing inside her. His cock was growing even more, the pain of it didn't hurt, she relaxed into the sensation and felt her soul expand even more. She couldn't tell when one orgasm ended and cascaded into the next one.

He was trying to grab something above his head and knocked over the table beside the bed as his whole body was climaxing. He was almost screaming. She leaned down just enough to grab his wrists. Her first two fingers pressing into his palms and her thumbs and other two fingers held his wrists as she pumped her hips on his cock.

Then, as he hit the final plateau, his cock grew even more and throbbed and pulsed inside her. He let out a scream that rumbled from the depths of forever and roiled up through every part of him before exploding into the world. To him, her yoni was a magnetic force that started pulsing the cum from deep in his soul. His brain quit working.

She could feel him cumming inside her. She felt like she was making love to magic itself. As his cock continued to throb and pulse inside her, she kept feeling like she was getting hit by wave after wave of sacred, cosmic lightening, blasting through her body. Tears were rolling down her face and she collapsed onto him, still making tiny, residual, rocking motions with her hips.

He looked like he was in pain, sounded like he was half-laughing/half-crying, and he felt like love itself had taken human form just to change his life.

He couldn't speak. She slid her hands under his ribs and let her body be heavy on his body. They laid there together for quite a while. She didn't move. She loved feeling him still so deep inside her. He tried to reach up and hold her and there was nothing in his arms, his arms fell back to the bed. He tried to say something but didn't know what he would say and only a squeak came out.

"Breathe, Love." She said softly.

He just made another deep squeak in response, acknowledging that he couldn't talk. It seemed like an hour that they stayed like that, it was actually about 30 minutes. The cock and yoni have their own timing, they both knew this. They didn't move until their bodies were finished. Then finally when they had both taken a deep breath at the same time, it was done, but neither of them moved.

They hadn't even realized, but at some point, the girls had brought in more food. They had come in the back door of their teacher's chambers and barely entered the room, left food on the far table, then quietly left.

Iyasiil kissed him, then hovered her face over his face, and looked deep into his eyes. He was glassy-eyed, but not on mead, on the nectar of the universe. He still couldn't really talk.

She started to get up to get them both drinks and just collapsed on the bed next to him. He just half-rolled to snuggle her. It was another 20 minutes of them feeling their hearts intertwine before she could get up.

He felt wasted and energized all at the same time. She got him another big horn of mead and poured him a cup of the special tea she had the girls make that afternoon.

"A full week has passed since last night at sundown. It's hard to believe we only met yesterday." He said.

She made a face that said, *"Can that be right?"* "Yes, you're right, My Lord. It doesn't seem possible, does it?"

He was sitting up in bed now, and was breathing normally, but still had a look of wonder on his face, like he still wasn't all there, he was still halfway into the spirit world. Then he saw the table laying on the floor beside the bed. "Did I do that?"

She laughed, "I had my little part in it, too."

He got up and set the table upright then sat back on the bed.

She handed him the horn and held up the cup of tea to show him, "I have some tea for you. This will help you to sleep tonight and you'll probably continue your journey in dreamtime, but don't drink it until after you have finished eating." She said.

He looked at her with a curious look on his face. Then shook his head, shaking off the thought, then with a smile, he said, "OK. I trust you, witch."

She smiled and got him a small plate of food. He had a sip from the horn and let out a big sigh. He ate and finished his horn of mead.

She took the cup of medicine tea and had a tiny sip, just enough to get the flavor. Her face lit up, "Oh, nice. It actually tastes good, this time. Sometimes it is really bitter, but not today."

"What is it?" He asked as he took a big sip.

"It's only got four or five roots and flowers in it, but the part that will help you sleep tonight is actually a grass that grows here. It's not good to drink it very often. But tonight, it will serve you well, My Lord."

He drank the tea and put the cup on the table. "Now what, you witchy woman?"

"Now I am going to kiss you." She climbed on him and straddled him, letting her body melt into his, pulling the side of his face into her cheek.

"My Goddess, you are delicious. You are the most beautiful of things. I don't think I could ever repay you for what you've done for me today."

"Malkore, you paid by bringing our men home. You've paid by preparing the king to lead. You've paid by walking the path you have walked, and you have paid by what you will do for these people over the next five hundred lifetimes. So, hush!"

"Yes, My Love." He pulled her close and kissed her with gratitude and praise. He kissed her with selfish joy.

About ten minutes later, she felt his energy drop. *"The tea is working quickly tonight."* She thought. "Let's lay down, My Lord."

Another ten minutes later, he was asleep with her wrapped around his body.

Chapter Five
Better, but Still Tending

Malkore slept late again, which was strange for him. The tea she had given him last night had done its job. The last 36 hours had been so packed with emotional and spiritual intensity between them it was good that he was sleeping so much.

Iyasiil had woken up a little earlier and had only gotten up to get some tea. She laid back in bed and did her morning meditation lying next to this amazing man.

She noticed her mind was full of questions. She wasn't sure what today would hold. Normally, the time of Tending was predictable to her in a lot of ways. After millennia of Tending to warriors retuning home, she had seen and heard and healed every kind of emotional and physical wound there was.

The time of Tending is so important to the people. If the warriors don't heal their emotional wounds, the men get lost – their hearts get lost, they stop growing, and they stop being a good presence to the people.

Some places she had lived there was no Tending and no special attention given to the Warriors after they returned home. It tore the communities apart. The warriors stayed angry, and the men and their families grew apart. Asgard had done a good job of Tending to their warriors, their kingdom had stayed strong. They just hadn't grown emotionally and spiritually into the people they would become.

Iyasiil tried to quiet her mind to all the questions she had about how the day would go. There was a piece that was missing, a piece of information she didn't understand. Why had she been given such a clear vision to Tend to Malkore, when he wasn't bloodsick? Why did she meet him as the men were returning home from a raid, instead of meeting another time? Well, she knew the answer to that. He needed to connect with someone who was on his own level, and having time set aside to block out his normal everyday life, set the time up for healing and transformation. In her heart, it was so clear that he needed this time, but for what?

This felt to her like it was going to be a powerful time of transformation. But she still wasn't sure exactly what it was that was transforming. She had her own fanciful desire, and she knew the difference between her own desires and that deep, peaceful, resonating place where she could feel what was for another's highest good.

Malkore wasn't recovering from being bloodsick, after battle, but something powerful was going on. He still needed to be wrapped in a sacred space; be protected from and unconcerned with everyday life. He needed to be given the space to discover something new without old influences, old patterns triggering old ways of thinking, old ways of being around people. He needed to feel *free*. He needed to feel free to bring all of who he really is to the people of Asgard.

She knew and trusted that feeling like she was falling in love with him, was a part of that *free*-ing process, but she wanted to know what the end goal was so she could help shape their time together.

All these questions were draining, the worry was draining. This wasn't the emotional place to be in, not for herself, not for Malkore.

She refocused her attention on only relaxing her body without any thought of all those questions. She imagined her body was floating on warm water at the hot springs Malkore had mentioned. She imagined being at the hot springs with him and how much fun it would be. Then she let that thought go, too. She relaxed a little more.

Just then, she felt a hand on her heart. She was a little startled, but she only took a deeper breath. She opened her eyes slowly.

It was Dossa smiling at her. Dossa quietly whispered, "Good morning, Mama."

Iyasiil put her hand on top of Dossa's hand and took another long, slow deep breath. Then slowly and carefully started to get up, mindful of not waking up Malkore. She motioned to the other side of the room, slipped her robe on, hugged Dossa, and walked over to the other side of the room with her arm around Dossa's shoulders. Both girls looked radiant this morning, Iyasiil would need some of that radiance. She hugged Kalla and took in a deep breath.

Iyasiil began whispering softly, "Girls, thank you so much for being here. I need your help this morning."

"Anything, Mama." Kalla whispered back.

"Yes, anything." Dossa added.

She started to say something about what she needed, then shook it off and asked, "How are you two doing? How was your night?"

Kalla said, "We are both doing great. I slept so hard and was so excited to see you and Malkore this morning I woke up early and prepared your breakfast. I even had to force myself to wait before coming in this morning."

"Dossa, how about you? How are you feeling this morning?"

"Pretty much the same. Something happened to me last night when I cried at your dinner table. I'm sorry if that messed up your work, but I feel more alive than I ever have."

Iyasiil looked at them both and took a big breath. "No. The timing was perfect, Dossa. It was great for me to feel you un-guarded, and it was a blessing for Malkore. In fact, he even said that to you last night. He meant it." She turned to Kalla, "Say more about being excited to see us this morning. Tell me what that feels like to you. I think that's what I need to hear."

Kalla looked at her a little confused. "Ummm. I don't know."

"Close your eyes, take a deep breath, and remember preparing breakfast." Kalla's face lit up with a glowing smile. Iyasiil saw Kalla's face light up and said, "Yes, *that* feeling, what does that feel like?"

Kalla opened her eyes, "I feel so happy -- like my heart is filled with love and I am so excited for you. But,"

"But what?" Iyasiil asked.

"But I feel selfish. Not jealous, but selfish. I want to be with you two so I can keep soaking up what it's like to be with you." Kalla was still glowing, and a tear was welling up in her eye. "I want to get in bed between you two and feel all that all around me." Dossa let out a small laugh, trying to be quiet. Kalla got embarrassed, she couldn't believe she said that. "Shut up, Dossa."

"No. I get it. You're not wanting to interfere or add yourself to it, you just want to feel it more, right?" Iyasiil asked.

"Yes. Absolutely." Kalla said.

"Dossa, do you feel the same? What does it feel like to you?" Iyasiil asked.

"I don't know. Yeah. Except when I started crying yesterday -- that hurt so bad, but then I felt so free. Except for that moment when I cried, I got so turned on when I was here, but it wasn't just for sex. It was amazing. I felt like my heart was turned on. Is that what you mean?"

"Yeah, OK. Thank you, girls. That answers all my questions." Their teacher said.

"Why Mama? What's going on?" Dossa asked.

Iyasiil took a breath and wondered if she should share her own vulnerable doubts with her students. Since she was teaching these girls to pay attention to their own feelings on a deeper level, she quickly decided to share. "I woke up a little worried that by feeling so enthralled with him that it would make me miss something important – that I was missing something I need to be doing to support him. I am just as excited as what you guys are feeling. It's not like a normal Tending. He's not bloodsick, like most men returning from battle - this is something else. It's some kind of powerful, powerful growth and transformation time for him. He needs the same attention and the same space as if he were healing from battle, but this is different. Does that make sense?"

They both nodded. Dossa asked, "What can we do?"

She smiled and said, "Keep feeling that excitement for as long as it lasts. Keep loving what you are feeling."

Both girls smiled. Kalla said (half sarcastically), "Keep wanting to be in bed with you two. Got it." All three of them laughed.

"Now, I want both of you to sit right here on the floor with me, right now." They all sat on the floor. "Scoot close and hold hands with me. Let's breathe together for a moment. Let's all imagine being washed clean under a waterfall. Feel the water coming down and washing away everything that you don't want anymore. Imagine the water is washing away any hurt and is filling you up with the love of the stars. Now, imagine being in the forest and feeling the pulse of the forest. Imagine getting quiet enough inside to hear the voices of the trees communicate under our feet. Imagine you can hear the grass telling you which way to go to find anyplace you want to find. Imagine hearing the trees sing loving songs of gratitude to all of us as we walk and imagine singing those songs back to the trees. Get quiet enough inside to listen to the planet and every living thing on it."

They sat in silence breathing, then a few moments later all three of them let out a big breath at the same time. It hadn't been planned, but that's how they knew their moment of quiet was finished.

Kalla said, "I just kept picturing the two of us hugging you from each side."

Dossa said, "Oh wow. I just pictured both of you hugging me. I guess I need a little more love right now. I am sorry."

"No, don't be." Kalla said.

"Dossa, when it's the three of us, always tell the truth. Please. If you need a little more love, right now, it's OK to need it. It's OK to feel it. It's OK to ask for it. And it's OK to share it. I love you. You are such a sweet treasure, and I am so happy you are here right now." Turning to Kalla, "Maybe before you two bring lunch, you should make the time to lay down and hold her for a bit. This will be good practice for you and part of the next phase of teachings. Just let yourself feel the love flowing through you and you feel your love for her. OK?"

"Yes, Mama." Kalla replied.

"Malkore is going to be awake soon." Smiling, she said, "That medicine tea I had you make really did its job last night. Even though he was only awake half the day yesterday, he slept like an old rock last night."

"We will see you at lunch time. I had the feeling we should bring four meals today, does that sound OK?" Kalla asked.

"Perfect. That sounds great. Thank you, My Dear Sweet Loves. I will see you two later." Iyasiil said.

The girls left and dropped things off at the kitchen, then went back to their cottage. Iyasiil took a moment to breathe and get centered before she got back in bed. She slipped her robe off and laid down, snuggling into him pretty hard while trying to be gentle enough to not wake him up.

As she lay there snuggled into him, she felt her body relax, she felt her breasts loving the way they felt against him. She loved the way her thighs felt wrapped around his thigh. She let her body relax even more and she was surprised that she felt her body drifting off to sleep again.

Almost immediately, she dreamed she had Odin off in the woods by himself, talking with him, teaching him. Whenever

Odin got to one of his personal roadblocks, and began arguing with her, Malkore appeared out of nowhere and he would elbow Odin in the back hard enough to jar him into listening more and looking inside of himself more. Even in her dream, she laughed at how warriors have their own code.

She woke up as Malkore was starting to stir. She reached over him and put her hand on his heart and lightly pressed her nose and lips into the back of his neck.

In a half growl, while moving his hand to press her hand into his heart, he said, "Is she still real?"

"That depends on which "she" you're asking about, My Lord, Malkore."

"The fucking witch who cast a happy spell on me and then drugged me last night." Then he started laughing. What he said was really funny to him. He kept laughing.

She started laughing too. "My Lord, Malkore. I hope you slept well."

"Indeed."

"Any dreams that you remember?"

He thought for a moment as he took in a big breath, "Yes. A couple of dreams. Lots, actually."

As he started to stretch, she rolled away from him a little and gave him some room. He sat up at the head of the bed and yawned a big, growling warrior's yawn.

"I'll get us some tea, My Love." She got up and grabbed two cups and the small pitcher of tea. She took it to his side of the bed and poured them each a cup, handed him his cup, put the pitcher on the small table beside the bed. "Try not to knock this over, just yet." She said playfully with a flirty smile, referring to how he had knocked over the small table last night while they were making love.

He let out a big laugh and said, "With you around, I'm not going to make that promise."

She pointed between his legs, "May I sit right there?" He scooted up a little and spread his legs enough to make room for her.

Handing her cup of tea to him, she sat down and leaned back onto him. She laid her head back into the top of his chest.

He handed her the cup of tea and asked, "What shall we do today? Is my Tending finished? Or are you going to keep me captive here for another day?"

"You're still my captive and there is nothing you can do about it, My Lord." She said with a half flirty/half happy tone.

He laid his arm across her arm and rested his hand on her heart and said, "Oh no! The greatest warrior captured by a witch, helpless to resist. What a tragedy."

She put her hand on top of his and took a breath, breathing him into her heart. "I believe we have an opportunity to help you to *not* ever live with the frustrations that had built up to what you were feeling two days ago. I don't know what you were like with the people before, so tell me if I am wrong. I want to make this time available to you so you can find the bridge to being the teacher the people need you to be in the centuries to come. They need you."

"That's pretty generous of you, My Love. But you know that I could find my own way to what I am here to do." He said dismissively.

"Yes, and I have one of those 'you fucking witch' feelings that tells me you'll be able to do in a couple of hundred years what it would take a two millennia to do on your own." She said.

"But Love, you're not here to serve me for the next hundred years. You have your own vision to follow." Malkore said.

"Of course, My Lord, Malkore. And I *will* follow my vision before anything else, whether you and I are connected or not. And one current part of my vision started two days before all you men left on this raid. What was that? Five or six days ago? I saw you in my dream. I saw meeting you by the top of the stairs near the great hall. And I saw spending time with you until the work with you was finished." Then she added in a sarcastic tone, "So if you recall, when it comes to the Tending --"

"You are far wiser than me. Yes, My Love. I remember. Clues, huh?" He said.

She pressed his hand into her heart a little more and said, "Clues."

"Well, that's what I was hoping, but didn't want to seem stupid if you had a different idea." They both laughed. Then using his big, boisterous warrior's celebration voice he said, "Because how dumb would people have to be to think they were falling in love after one day?! Especially if that day was in a sacred ceremony like the Tending."

In her most sarcastic voice, she said, "Indeed. Only the stupidest people would think that." She took a big breath, rubbing the side of her head on the front of his shoulder. "My Lord, will you tell me about your dreams."

"I had one silly one at the end, but most of my dreams were about Odin and teaching him and fighting lots of battles to show him the way. But the biggest battle he has to fight- the only battle that makes any difference is to learn to feel the feelings inside that truly scare him. If he makes a life out of constantly trying to prove something, then the whole kingdom stays stuck because they can't grow larger than his small-minded fears. When he can feel those fears and not get scared, then he can learn to lead these people to great heights."

"Some powerful teachings, My Lord. Your vision is clear. I had one about you teaching him, too. I'll tell you later." Then with a playful tone, "What was the silly dream? I'd love to hear that one too."

"Oh, I don't really remember that one."

"My Lord," she said with a reprimanding tone, "do please remember who you are talking to. You, I, Odin, & Asgard itself can only grow when the truth is spoken. This space, when it is the two of us, is a place where only the truth is welcome."

"Ahh, fuck. Sorry, I forgot what it was like to be in the presence of such an amazing woman. Forgive me, Love." He said.

"Thank you, Lord Malkore." She said with a mothering tone.

"I dreamed I was standing under a waterfall surrounded by three wives."

"Not silly at all. That actually happened, My Lord. Just before you woke up, the girls were here. We did a visualization where we were standing under a waterfall, holding hands. It was part of the meditation to get us all into the place to support you today."

He let out a boisterous laugh. "No shit?!"

"Yes, and during this time of the Tending, the energetic dynamic is that the three of us are energetically committed to you, so that dream totally makes sense." She said.

"Wow!" He said. *"What a gift to be in the presence of a strong, secure, amazing woman."* He thought. She turned her head enough to wink at him. "Did you hear that, too?"

"Hear what? That you'd love to have three wives?" She said, teasing him.

Another boisterous laugh, "No. Just that it's amazing to be around a woman so secure within herself."

She smiled at him, "Yeah, the feeling is mutual."

With her head still on his shoulder, her hand on his hand over her heart, feeling his legs cradling her hips, and her body snuggled into his, she asked, "Any thoughts on what you would like to do today, My Lord?"

"I don't care as long as I get to keep feeling you like this." He said.

"Mmmmmm. Yes, that sounds good." She said.

"Do you have any thoughts, My Love?" He asked.

"Nothing specific, yet. But right now, this is where I want to be. I'd love to hear about your life and how you got here." She said.

"I don't know if I could tell one single story of it, but it would probably happen through a thousand little stories."

She squealed. "Oooooo! I love hearing stories. Tell me one."

"What would you like to hear about, My Love?" He asked.

"All of it. Tell me how you came to be here in Asgard." She said.

After a while, she got up and got them plates of food. She handed him a plate that was full of food, refilled his tea, and sat at the foot of the bed, facing him. They ate and talked. They talked for hours, trading stories, each listening to the other with rapt attention.

The first time she got lit up, excited by one of his stories that reminded her of something she wanted to share, he noticed it and said, "Remember that. I want to hear it." Then he finished his story. When he finished, he made it a point to ask her what his story had excited in her and what memory it brought up. Then she shared her story.

Then she saw his face light up when she was talking. She said, "Remember that. I want to hear it." When she finished, she asked him to share.

They both wound up sharing about their time traveling from different places, living with different peoples, and the lessons they learned.

He pointed out that he had realized it was most important to notice the lessons he *didn't* learn. He said those are the ones that hurt the most, because he could always feel that space he wanted to grow into, and he missed it when he didn't grow into it. "I guess, the lessons I didn't learn have taught me the most, because they created the desire to learn them. Everyone, everywhere seemed content with their losses, content with their pain, content with all the conflict inside, and I always wanted more."

She totally understood. She had always wanted more, too. She felt like her heart was being held and loved, talking with him. She had never heard someone describe what she had been feeling. "For a long time, it was confusing to me that people were so unhappy, and they never came to the understandings that I had. Finally, I came to accept that some people just take longer. Some people will take thousands of lifetimes longer than others to reach the same understanding."

They kept talking. They were both so excited to hear more and they were both so excited to talk and share more. They both felt like there were so many things that no one else could really relate to. They were both loving having someone listen who could really understand the depth of what they were sharing and what it all meant to them.

They talked until the girls came in with their lunch. Dossa fed the fire, as she always did right when she walked in.

Malkore and Iyasiil had been so enthralled with their conversation that they hadn't even moved their plates since they stopped eating.

Kalla came over to the bed and got their plates, "Would you like some more, My lord?"

"Yes, please." He couldn't believe he was still hungry. He turned to Iyasiil, "You amazing ladies have taken such good care of me the last two days. Thank you, My Love."

"My Beautiful Mama, would you like more, too?" Iyasiil shook her head.

Kalla refilled Malkore's plate while Dossa refilled both of their cups of tea. Then Kalla brought them both a horn of mead. Kalla squatted down next to her teacher, put her hand on her teacher's leg, and asked, "How are you two doing?"

Malkore and Iyasiil looked at each other and smiled. He noticed she was glowing. His smile was coming from a deep, relaxed happiness inside.

She said, "We were just having the most wonderful, rambling conversation ever, talking about everything."

Kalla looked more closely at her teacher and saw her glow. In a half-teasing/half-celebratory tone, Kalla remarked, "Mama, you're glowing. Do you know that?"

"Well, look at the company I'm keeping. Any woman would be glowing." She said.

"Ohhhh, I'm so, so happy for you two." Kalla said.

Dossa came over and knelt on the bed next to her teacher. "I've taken care of everything here, is there anything else we can do to help."

"If Lord Malkore won't mind, in the afternoon, I think I'm going to get you two to help me in here for several hours."

Kalla turned to Malkore and asked with a slightly flirty tone, "Lord Malkore? Would you mind that?"

He smiled at her. "First, I want to thank you all. I have felt so loved and cared for these days here and I am grateful."

Dossa said, "Of course, My Lord. It's an honor. I didn't know what this was going to be like, but I felt like it was going to be something really big. I didn't know it was going to touch me so deep and be so personal for me, or for Kalla."

Iyasiil looked at him with a devilish grin and said, "Lord Malkore, tell them about your dream."

"Ahhh, yeah. I had a dream this morning right before I woke up, where I was standing under a waterfall with 3 women surrounding me holding hands with each other."

Dossa's mouth fell open. She looked at her teacher, then she turned to Kalla, then back to Malkore. "What? But we –"

Malkore was smiling. "I heard that you two were here just before I woke up, right at the time I was having that dream, visualizing standing under the waterfall, getting to an emotional place clean enough to support your teacher greatly."

Dossa interjected, "And to support you, My Lord." Then she felt embarrassed, afraid her attraction to Malkore had just been found out, but she wanted to say it.

"Yes. And I feel your support -- I even felt it in my dream." Looking deeply into Dossa's eyes, "Thank you. You two are learning from the best."

Kalla sensed it was time to go. She asked, "What can we do for you two before we go?"

"After we eat, I think we may go for a long walk. When we get back here, that's when I will need your help, but I may not need your help at all. It all depends on how the day goes. So, thank you girls for everything you are doing. Love you both." Iyasiil said.

Kalla said, "Love you both, too." Then she realized what she said and got really embarrassed. Dossa laughed. Kalla's face was red. She turned to Malkore and said, "Oh shit. I'm embarrassed. I don't -- I mean. I'm – I mean --. I am. I am. I am feeling so much love for both of you."

Iyasiil was laughing at how awkward Kalla felt and laughing because she knew there was nothing to feel embarrassed about.

"Kalla, come here." Malkore said.

She walked over to him, not sure what was about to happen. Kalla's face kept turning more and more red with every breath, "Yes, My Lord."

"Kalla, I feel your love. And your love is wonderful, it's CK. One of the most powerful parts of what she is teaching you is to feel more and more love flow through you." He didn't know if Iyasiil had ever talked to either one of them about this, but he knew it was true.

Kalla started to tear up, and she started nodding her head. "Oh, I'm sorry." Then Kalla started crying harder. It came out of nowhere. One second she was feeling so much love, the next she felt like such a fuck-up.

Iyasiil asked, "For what? What are you sorry for, Love."

"I'm sorry for crying. I don't even know why I'm crying. I'm sorry." Then she laughed because she realized that she had just apologized for apologizing.

Iyasiil motioned for Dossa to hand her a blanket off the shelf by the bed. Iyasiil put the blanket behind her back and told Kalla to sit in front of her and lean back on her. Kalla did. Kalla was so tall, she had to scoot down a little to get comfortable, then she realized her feet were about to touch Malkore at the other end of the bed and she pulled her feet back a little. It didn't look comfortable.

Malkore said, "It's OK to put your feet here if you want." She moved her feet towards him, and he picked up her feet up and put them on his thigh and just held her feet. "Is that OK? Are you OK with that?"

Kalla nodded. She was still sobbing a little. "Fuck! What the fuck is wrong with me. I feel like I just screwed this up."

Iyasiil said, "I want you right here with me," squeezing her around the shoulders, "You didn't fuck anything up. This is perfect for what Lord Malkore and I have been talking about all morning."

Malkore looked at Dossa. "Take a bunch of big, long, slow breaths. As Kalla breathes and lets herself feel your teacher's love, she is going to feel my love flowing in through her feet, you just keep breathing and notice what you are feeling inside." Dossa nodded.

Iyasiil spoke in such soft, nurturing tones in moments like this, her voice was like a gently, soothing hug that you feel in your bones. "Kalla, why don't you tell Lord Malkore what you said you wanted this morning."

Kalla didn't remember. "What did I say?"

"You were talking about your excitement to come see us this morning and how you were feeling selfish . . ."

Right then, Kalla and Dossa both realized that Kalla had said that she wanted to be in bed between Mama and Malkore and that it was happening right now.

Dossa's jaw dropped, again. She felt like these two are just magic and magic keeps happening with them.

Kalla looked up at her teacher and with a whiny voice, asked, "Oh shit! Do I have to?" Her face was turning red again.

"No, it is just important to share." Her teacher said.

Malkore lightly squeezed her feet and asked, "What did you say you wanted? I'd love to hear."

Kalla acted really shy and almost whispered, "I said I woke up feeling selfish that I wanted . . . I was just wanting to feel more and more of what this feels like to be around the two of you."

Iyasiil said, "How did you say it this morning?"

"I said I wanted to be in bed between you two. But not to get in the way or to be part of it."

"Just to soak it up – to soak in more of the love, right." Iyasiil said.

"Yes." Kalla was almost covering her face.

Malkore began to speak. He spoke with such a gentle tambor. "Well, Kalla, you are getting exactly what you wanted. I know this isn't how you pictured it, but I think I know something about you."

Kalla looked at him, "What?"

"I bet you have lived your whole life feeling like you love most everyone more than anyone else seems to know. And you don't know why more people are not loving just as big. Am I right?" He asked.

"Oh shit! I mean, My Lord. I mean . . . Oh shit, My Lord. How did you know that?" Kalla felt her energy lift. She felt like a weight was lifted from her heart.

He looked at her and motioned between himself and Iyasiil and said, "Because we recognize our own. Your teacher and I are the same way. That's why she chose to work with both of you and become your teacher. You didn't just ask her to teach you, she *chose* you both. She had already identified both of you before you asked her."

Kalla looked at Iyasiil and said, "Is that true? You already knew?" Iyasiil nodded while smiling at Kalla.

"Wow." Dossa interjected.

Kalla realized a little more how amazing her teacher was.

Malkore said, "Yeah. Wow! Your teacher is *that* amazing. And girls, I have lived over 5000 years, and I have never met anyone as amazing as this woman. She has more to teach than you could even realize, she has been hiding most of it from you until you are both ready. So, work hard. But work hard in here," he said pointing at his heart. "Right this moment, take a breath and feel what it feels like to be wrapped up in your teachers love and feel what it feels like to have me loving you through your feet." He took a big breath. "Are you letting yourself feel it?"

"I can't feel it in my feet as much." Kalla said.

Malkore leaned forward a little bit and put her feet right over his heart and pressed them into his bare chest. She let out a half-gasp/half-scream and her right leg shook for a second. Her eyes got big. "What is that? What just happened?"

"What did it feel like?" Iyasiil asked.

"It felt like lightning went up my leg, through my whole body, and it felt like . . . like. Well, it felt like my knee just had an orgasm." She expected Dossa to laugh at her for saying that, but Dossa was just looking at her with so much love. It made Kalla start welling up with tears again. "Dossa, I love you! I love you so much."

Dossa leaned over and laid her head on Kalla's thigh and curled up in a ball.

Iyasiil said, "This all started when you said that you loved me and Lord Malkore, too. Are you ready to try something?" Kalla nodded. "Kalla, I want you to say, "Mama, I love you so much and for the rest of this Tending, I am going to let myself be crazy in love with you in whatever way I happen to feel it.""

Dossa started nodding her head in agreement with her head still on Kalla's thigh.

Kalla said, "Mama, my love, I love you, I love you, I love you and I am not going to stop. While we are here, I am not going to stop. And thank you."

Iyasiil said, "Good. How did that feel?" Kalla nodded. "Now Kalla, there's something you need to know. Every man you have ever shown any affection to has immediately tried to fuck you, right?"

"Uuuuhhh, I guess so. I hadn't thought about it like that. But, yes, Mama." Kalla said. Dossa nodded in agreement again.

"What you need to know is that Lord Malkore, while probably being the greatest lover in the world, is not that way. You can tell him that you are feeling love for him, and he won't take to mean anything other than what *you* mean. He will take it the way you meant it – he will feel it how you meant it. Does that make sense?"

"Yeah." Looking at Malkore, "How do you do that?"

Malkore smiled, "I grew up. That's how. I'm not an adolescent boy in a man's body who can't think past his own dick."

All three of the women laughed. The girls had never met a man like him, so they were not really sure what all that meant, but they seemed to take it in OK.

Of course, Iyasiil hadn't met a man like him before, either, except in her dreams, but she really *did* know what it meant. Being around him, something in her heart relaxed into a peacefulness and something in her body woke up and got excited.

Iyasiil said, "In other words, girls, your heart and your body is safe, with him. So Kalla, I want you to try this: Say, "Lord Malkore, for the entire time we are here in this Tending, I am going to love and support you the best I can, and I am not going to hold back from loving you."

Kalla sighed. Something inside her just relaxed. She turned her head towards her teacher and asked, "Even if I love really big?"

Iyasiil smiled, "*Especially* because you love really big."

Kalla looked at Malkore and said, "My Lord," a tear came up in her eye, "While you are here in the Tending, I am going to support the two of you the best I can and part of that is to love you both so much. I know I am not anywhere near what my teacher is, but I am just going to love you how I can love you."

Malkore was smiling at her, "Beautiful. Take a breath. Now say it again and feel it even more this time. Say it like you aren't scared to tell me."

She sat up and leaned toward him a little. He really felt her presence now. She felt it, too. She let out a small scream, "Ahhhh! This is scary." She leaned back into her teacher for a second.

Her teacher said, "It's OK. That fear is the excitement of feeling how big your love is, you just aren't used to it."

Kalla leaned forward again, "Lord Malkore, for this entire Tending I am going to love you so big, every day." She held eye contact with him for a couple of seconds.

Without even picking up her head, Dossa said, "Me too."

Kalla looked down at Dossa and looked back up to make eye contact with Malkore as she put her hand on Dossa's head and said, "Dossa too." Then she smiled even bigger at Malkore. "I want to hug you right now, but I'm scared, so maybe tomorrow." Then Kalla took a deep breath and collapsed on Dossa, where her head was resting on the side of Dossa's hip, acting exhausted. "Oh shit. What is going on? What just happened? Is this how I get to where you two are?"

In unison, Malkore and Iyasiil said, "Yes." Then they both laughed. Iyasiil was smiling at him and mouthed the word, "Clues."

"I'm exhausted now. What did you people just do to me?!" Kalla asked, as if she were complaining.

Malkore laughed. "I know it is so hard being so loved, isn't it?" He wasn't sure if she would get his sarcasm.

Kalla sat up, "Oh the tough guy thinks he's funny, now. Is that it?!" Then she got scared that he would be offended.

Malkore let out the biggest, most boisterous, warrior's laugh of all time. "Iyasiil, My Love, you are creating monsters. The men of Asgard are not ready for women like this." He was still celebrating and laughing.

"Then you *get* them ready, My Lord." She said with a firm, challenging tone.

"Indeed." He said, raising his horn of mead.

It was time to start teaching in a different way, but he didn't know what that way was. It had eluded him for centuries, but now he felt hopeful.

He mumbled to himself, "Clues . . . clues."

Chapter 6
The First Challenge

Iyasiil and Malkore went for a walk. They found another place where they wanted to build a bench. They had walked out of the village and up the mountain on the same trail that goes up to the hot springs. They both felt strong, relaxed, and refreshed. These two days had been exciting for them both. The walk on this mountain with her was beautiful. She stopped every few minutes and talked to a tree or a plant. Sometimes she would see an animal and it would look at her and cock it's head. She would talk to it, and it would come over to her and act like a pet.

Whenever he had been up this hill before, he had walked like a man on a mission. He had walked quickly or run up the steep trail. He was always keeping his body strong, making sure his legs and back were strong enough to never tire in battle. A couple of times he had even pulled himself up the entire mountain with his arms as if his legs didn't work anymore. Few students trained like that with him, none for very long. Since Odin was at the end of his adolescence, Odin always came up with an excuse not to work as hard as he could have, he was too scared of failing – he was always too scared he wasn't good enough, (as if training would prove that he wasn't good enough,) so Odin didn't try to do much, except build his ego.

Malkore felt like he had been locked in a room with his frustrations for centuries. He did everything he could to teach

Odin and anyone else who showed promise, and something about it wasn't working. He had spent a century trying to figure out what was wrong, why the teachings were not landing. He looked only to himself.

Now Odin was looking to marry Frigg, and she was repulsed by him. She had been the most promising woman in Asgard, but Malkore didn't fault her at all – He wouldn't marry Odin either!

No one saw the benefits of what he had to teach, they didn't want to hear about their own heart, they didn't want to hear about spiritual expansiveness. They only wanted to get by without feeling horrible – that was enough for them. They didn't know what feeling really good was. They didn't know what was possible for them and they didn't care. They were a small-minded people in some ways, better than a lot of places he had lived, but not nearly the people they could be.

Malkore and Iyasiil had been sitting on the hillside, enjoying the sun and the view from a part of trail up the mountain when Iyasiil spoke, "It is wonderful to spend time with you like this, My Lord, Malkore, and I can feel the heaviness on your heart."

He nodded. "Yes, it is our boy king. He weighs heavy on me."

"My Lord, may I share something I have noticed about Odin?" She asked.

"Please, Love."

"I don't know what the council meetings are like, but I get the sense that no one challenges him. It is so important that people learn to not just show respect, but to actually *have* respect. We don't respect what cannot withstand a great test. I have not been with the people long, so forgive me if I am far from the truth." She said.

"I don't want to disrespect him in front of the men." He said.

Patiently, Iyasiil said, "I understand, My Lord. I want to kick his ass every other time that I see him. I am sure My Lord feels the same."

"Indeed, I do." Malkore said.

She turned her head towards him and said, "When the men see him rise to a *real* challenge from you, they will respect him more than ever."

He knew she was right, and he knew just how to do it.

After another fifteen minutes of sitting, they made their way back down the trail and decided to stop in the great hall to have a little food with a few other people. The walk down the mountain was relaxing, they took their time. Malkore had always been able to connect with the plants and trees and animals, but he only did it when he needed something, never for the daily joy of it. He watched her blessing and being blessed by the leaves that hung low over the trail. He realized that living this way each day was probably more important than anything else in life.

As they walked back into the village, several people came up to them to say hello. The young boy who had asked Malkore to help him learn with a sword came up to them and asked if there was anything he could do for them. There wasn't anything, but they said they were going to get some food in the great hall and invited him to join them. The boy's face lit up!

"Really?! You would let me come with you, My Lord? They told me to leave, last night." Like all good Asgardian warriors (and wannabe warriors), the boy wore his sword everywhere he went. He struggled so hard with feeling worthless and wanted to "earn his place" among the men, hoping he would finally feel worthy.

Malkore said, "Of course, but only if you can answer one question."

So excited to be getting attention from Malkore, the boy said, "Anything, My Lord."

"Do you remember the specific instruction you were given yesterday?" Malkore asked.

"Yes, My Lord, Malkore. Next week, I am to find your wife and ask her to help me learn, so I can get ready to come learn from you." The boy said excitedly.

Malkore and Iyasiil looked at each other at the boy saying they are husband and wife, she thought, *"Yeah, we have been married for a long time, almost 37 hours now."* She snickered to herself.

Malkore said, "That's right son. Do you remember why?"

The boy said, "It is about being quiet, or something like that. Is that right?"

Malkore laughed his loud warrior's laugh and grabbed the boy in a big hug and said, "Close enough, son. You are about to embark on the greatest adventure of your life. And don't worry about walking into the great hall, when you are with me, no one will send you away."

The boy had no idea what Malkore meant about the adventure, and he had no idea what he was getting himself into, but he loved the attention.

As they were walking towards the great hall, Iyasiil and Malkore had started holding hands and chatted as they walked. Kalla and Dossa had seen them and come up and joined them. Kalla, Dossa, and the boy trailed just behind.

They were about 50 yards from the great hall when an arrow passed about five feet in front of their faces, sticking in the wall to their right. Dossa gasped, the boy froze in fear, Malkore just dropped his head, already knowing what was about to happen. This was Odin.

Odin and several men had been around a corner and stepped out or to the street. Odin yelled from only ten meters, making sure that everyone could hear him, "Malkore, you should have come on the hunt with us this morning instead of hiding in a woman's bed."

Immediately, Iyasiil acted like she was surprised and delighted to see Odin. She walked over to him, exclaiming, "Odin! My Lord, Odin! I'm so excited to see you!" Her tone was overly excited.

Odin assumed she wanted to get close to him, she was acting like she was fawning for the King. Just before she got to him, he loudly said, "You should come visit me tonight, My Beauty." The men let out a light chuckle at his brazen invitation.

As she got close to Odin, at the last second, her face changed. Only Odin could see the look on her face. She acted like she was going to hug him and kiss his cheek. He put his arm around her, as he would any woman fawning over him. She whispered in his ear with a firm and measured tone, "My Lord, Odin. All the people need to have respect for the time of Tending, especially you, if you want Asgard warriors and Asgardian families to be strong. The people look to you for guidance." She pulled back her face to look him in the eye and patted him on the chest with her other hand still on his waist. "Now."

Her certainty gave Odin a chill. *"Who the hell is this woman to talk to me like that?! But she's right."* He thought.

She walked back over to Malkore and took his arm.

Odin felt like he now needed to make himself look wise in front of all his men and sound "king-ly." Speaking in a loud voice, as if he were making a proclamation to everyone. "Yes. Yes. We all should honor and respect the time of the Tending. Otherwise, how will our warriors grow strong to defeat our enemies!" Odin saved face by turning Iyasiil's teaching into a battle cry.

The men yelled.

Odin went on, "Malkore, the men didn't see you fighting in the raid. I told them you had probably been sitting under a tree because you had gotten too old to fight." Even though he had just been corrected about how important the Tending is, Odin ignored it. Odin wanted to challenge Malkore, to prove that as king, he was a great warrior. During the last two days of drinking and telling lies about his glorious leadership, he had started to believe his own lies.

"No, My Lord. The only people that saw me in the fight, never saw anything again." Malkore said, looking Odin in the eye.

The men laughed their warrior's laugh.

"I told everyone one that surely you still have at least a little fight in you – that I would at least have to break a sweat to put you down today." Odon said while pulling out his sword, dropping a clear challenge.

Malkore smiled and started to pull his sword. Iyasiil's hand covered his hand before he could begin pulling his sword from its scabbard. Malkore thought she was trying to prevent him from fighting Odin because he was still in the Tending. She wasn't – she had a better plan.

"It's OK, My Love. This will be fun." Malkore said with a confident smile.

She looked Malkore in the eye with an intensity that filled his heart with love and his body with fire. "No, My Lord. It's time you show him who he really is. It's time you show him who you really are." She took two steps to the wall with the arrow sticking out. She pulled the arrow out of the wall and handed it to Malkore, "Use this."

Malkore saw the wry grin on her face. It was a clear challenge from her. It was a challenge for him to step up and show Odin that Odin was nowhere near the warrior she knew Malkore to be.

He grinned back at her, nodding in agreement. She pulled his sword from its sheath, so he only had the arrow to fight with, he couldn't pull his sword as a back-up. They both knew that if he really did what he was capable of, he wouldn't need a back-up.

Iyasiil knew it wouldn't be a problem for Malkore, and she knew Odin would be embarrassed. She hoped Odin would respond well. Iyasiil took a couple of steps back and put the tip of Malkore's sword on the ground and gently rested her hands on the butt of the sword.

Odin got scared of being horribly embarrassed in front of his men, but he was too arrogant to acknowledge it. Instead, Odin loudly yelled, "Ahhh, she's tired of him already. She wants him to get killed so she can come be in my bed tonight!" The men laughed.

The girls were confused. Why was the king acting so strange? Why was he challenging Malkore? They had never seen the king act so belligerent; it was a turn-off.

The boy had no clue what was going on. He was scared and didn't understand why Iyasiil had taken Malkore's sword from him.

Malkore walked towards Odin slowly with his hands to his sides, not defensive, not feeling as if he needed to protect himself. He swung the arrow in a circle as if he were loosening up his wrist with a sword.

"You are very full of yourself today, My King. I can't believe you would want me to embarrass you in front of your men, like this. You can walk away now."

Odin got mad. He was embarrassed already. This was the first time Malkore had ever been disrespectful in front of other people. He knew he needed to put Malkore down for real to show his men that he really was a great warrior. He also knew that he had no chance against Malkore.

Odin yelled and charged towards Malkore, swinging his sword from above his right shoulder down towards Malkore's neck. Iyasiil grinned at what she was about to see.

Kalla gasped. She saw that Odin was swinging to kill. Dossa covered her eyes, afraid to see Lord Malkore killed. The boy was paralyzed with fear.

Without even lifting his arms, Malkore had spun to the left, letting Odin's momentum carry him forward. As Odin went by, off balance, Malkore poked Odin in the side with the tip of the arrow as Odin stumbled forward.

To make his point, Malkore added, "Hey! Where are you going? I'm over here, My King."

Odin knew he should stop. Malkore hadn't toyed with him like this since he was an adolescent. But Odin felt like he needed to prove himself!

He ran towards Malkore again with a forward thrust of his sword. Again, Malkore waited until Odin had committed his body weight in one direction, then side-stepped the thrust of the sword doing a spin move, again. He smacked Odin on the ass with his arrow before walking away from him towards Odin's men.

A couple of the men looked shocked, a couple of them just had their jaw hanging open. Malkore looked at the toughest of them, a man Malkore had offered to train himself and said, "Aren't any of you going to defend your king?!"

Only one of the men started to reach for their sword, Odin's lead warrior, St'laad, the toughest one, stopped him. This was between Odin and Malkore, and he was sure he wouldn't want to challenge Malkore, either.

Odin tried again and again, each time easily being brushed aside by Malkore and his arrow. Malkore even gave him a small puncture wound on his cheek with the tip of the arrow for good measure. Finally, coming at Malkore with his sword in both hands raised above his head. Malkore moved as fast as lightning towards Odin and caught Odin's hands before he could even swing his sword downward.

Holding Odin's hands above his head, preventing him from using his sword, Malkore started pushing Odin backwards towards the wall. Odin was strong, but he was no match for Malkore, especially no match for Malkore when he ignored the basic body mechanics that Malkore had tried to teach Odin in his youth.

Odin was off balance from the moment he had tried to strike. His weight was moving backwards. That was all the opening that Malkore needed. He never let Odin really get his feet under him. Malkore kept him moving backwards until he had Odin against the wall, Odin quietly said, "What are you doing? Everyone can see us."

Malkore said, "Maybe you should have been listening to me all along, My Lord. You have never trained hard enough to best me in a fight. You've lost your way and gotten sloppy in your technique and sloppy in the head – you are going to make Asgard sloppy and the whole fucking kingdom will suffer for it, unless you decide right now how great you want Asgard to be."

Odin was a mix of feelings. *"How could Asgard be great if their king was openly humiliated? But how great could Asgard be if their king couldn't even beat an old man in battle?"*

"Malkore, stop." Odin said to him, hoping Malkore would relent.

"You've got some decisions to make, My King. Do you want to be a King worthy of these men's respect? How great do you want Asgard to grow? Because Asgard will follow you – You can go far, or you can go nowhere." Malkore said looking Odin in the eye, with his teeth gritted for effect. Malkore wasn't even breathing hard.

"I don't know what has gotten into you, but I don't like it." Odin said to him.

"It's not about me, My Lord Odin. It's about you having a great vision for Asgard. Now, cover your ass in front of your men. Smile and laugh." Malkore said. "Do it!"

Odin was confused. Malkore started smiling and laughing so quietly that no one could hear it. Odin started catching on and started smiling. He put on his big warrior's voice again and said, "Well. It looks like you were all wrong. The old man does indeed have some fight left in him." Malkore let Odin's arms down and Odin put his sword back in its sheath. "Is there anyone else who wants to bring their sword against this old man who fights with a stick?" No one answered. "Come men, we have a feast to finish!"

Odin walked to his men, and they moved off towards the back entrance of the great hall, where Odin's chambers were. St'laad made sure to make eye contact with Malkore and nod his head in respect, before walking off with Odin.

Malkore nodded back to St'laad, then looked to Iyasiil, she was laughing and trying to hold it in. As he got over to her, she wrapped her arms around his arm and leaned in, "Do you think he got the message?"

"An arrow? Seriously?" He asked her quietly.

"It worked, didn't it?" She was still laughing, squeezing his arm.

Kalla stepped forward and put her hand on the back of his other arm and said, "What the -- Excuse me, My Lord. What the fuck was that?! It looked like you were just playing with him!"

Malkore, wanting to protect his king's image said, "No. No. No. Odin is a great warrior. He was going easy on me." He kept looking at Kalla, then winked at her as if to say, "*We are just going to pretend that's the way it is.*"

Kalla smiled and then let out an exasperated sigh and said, "Yes, My Lord." Her head was spinning. Ever since she had come into her teacher's chamber early the day before, she had felt nothing but the most intoxicating, gentle love coming from him. Now, he felt like a masterful force of destruction. He wasn't like the other warriors. She had respect for what they do, but she didn't like a lot of them, personally. She had heard stories that Malkore was the greatest warrior in Asgard, but after she met him, she assumed those stories weren't really true – He was too kind and compassionate. Now, she didn't know what to think.

The boy was still shocked.

Dossa was just catching on to what had happened, her brain couldn't make sense of it, but her body knew immediately what was going on. She was so turned on that she almost felt embarrassed, again. She couldn't stop looking at Malkore and her teacher, she just kept picturing them making love and she kept getting more turned on. She grabbed Kalla's arm and held onto her as they followed towards the great hall.

The boy asked, "Why was Odin so mad at you, Lord Malkore? And why did you fight him with just an arrow?" He looked at Iyasiil, wondering why she had put him in danger by making him fight against a sword with an arrow.

Malkore looked at him and just said, "Patience, son. You'll see. You will see, very soon."

The five of them walked into the great hall. Iyasiil and Malkore sat to have some food and were surprised at how many people were there. They imagined that so many people had been celebrating so hard the last two nights that most of them had just woken up, mid-afternoon, and gotten to the great hall to have some food before the next night of partying began.

When they walked in, Kalla and Dossa had prepared two plates and delivered them to their teacher and Malkore.

Malkore and Iyasiil were sitting at the main table with another couple who had come in just minutes before they did. The other couple, who had gotten their own plates of food, looked a little surprised when the girls had delivered plates of food to Malkore and Iyasiil.

Dossa asked the other man if he wanted his cup of mead refilled. The man looked surprised again, "Thank you, My Love. That would be wonderful." Since the couple was sitting with their teacher, they got a few of the honoring courtesies as well.

Kalla asked the woman, "Beautiful lady, is there anything I can get for you, right now?"

The woman looked at Iyasiil quickly, surprised at how gracious her students were, then turned to Kalla, "You are the beautiful one, My Dear. Just teach me how to get that radiant glow." Kalla picked up the woman's hand and kissed it, then turned to walk to the food table to get her own meal.

Kalla motioned for the boy to come with her. The boy was surprised and delighted to be noticed. But he also wondered if he had done something wrong, he had sat by himself against the outside wall. He got up and walked to catch up to Kalla. He caught her just as she got to where all the food was laid out, Kalla handed the boy and plate and told him that he could eat with her and Dossa, "We will sit back where you were, that's a good spot. We can keep an eye on Lord Malkore from there."

Malkore and Iyasiil were eating and chatting with the other couple. After they finished eating, their conversation went on for another fifteen minutes. Then Odin walked in from the back of the hall, his men had been waiting outside of Odin's chamber for about twenty minutes.

Malkore wasn't sure how Odin would behave around him after having just been humiliated. There was a 50% chance he would get belligerent and start criticizing Malkore publicly, making a case for everyone to shame him. Odin made eye contact with Malkore and nodded respectfully.

Odin walked to the head of the table where he usually sat. He picked up a horn of mead and stood on the bench to make an announcement. Raising the horn into the air, he yelled "Asgard!"

Everyone raised their horns of mead and yelled to toast their Kingdom, "Asgard!

"Asgard. Listen to your king! Everyone needs to hear this and spread the word, so no one will miss out. Two days from now, at high sun, warriors will gather by the oak grove."

One of the men yelled, "What's going on, Odin? Is it time for another raid?"

Odin waived his hand to dismiss the question and continued, "We are embarking on an adventure *far* greater than a simple raid." There were murmurs in the group, they couldn't imagine what it could be. "I have been given a vision of how great Asgard can be!" People cheered. "And I have seen how hard we must work to make that vision come true. I can't do it alone! Will you join me in making Asgard greater than your greatest dreams?!" There were more cheers from the whole hall. "How many of you would like to celebrate in a great hall made of pure gold and have riches so grand that you couldn't count it all in a day?!"

Malkore thought, *"Well Odin, at least you know how to sell something. Now, where are you going with this?"*

Malkore looked at Iyasiil and made an expression that said, *"We will see . . ."* She looked back at him, feeling curious of the same thing.

Odin caught his expression out of the corner of his eye and wanted to bring even more energy to make sure everyone knew he was serious.

Odin stepped from the bench up onto the table and yelled, "Warriors of Asgard! In two days, we will begin the hardest training of our lives! It is only when we do what no one else is willing to do that we become greater than anyone else has ever been!" The people cheered.

Right then, Malkore felt pressure and a warmth in his heart. It didn't feel like something pushing down on his heart, it felt like his heart growing bigger than his chest.

Iyasiil reached over and held Malkore's hand. *"It worked."* She thought.

Odin went on, "Brothers of Asgard, as great as we are, we have not grown as great as we need to be. No one has ever trained hard enough and had the discipline to rule all the nine realms. The first step is warrior training. No matter how great you think you are, each of us will begin" he pointed at Malkore, "Malkore's Warrior Training!" The room erupted in cheers. A couple of warriors slammed a fist onto his shoulders to celebrate him.

The man sitting with Malkore was one of the wiser men of Asgard. He turned to Malkore smiling and said, "I knew it."

In his biggest warrior's voice, Odin went on, "Lord Malkore has more lessons to teach than you could imagine. You will listen to him! You will follow him! Or you will face my sword yourself. If you ever want to go on a raid for Asgard again, you will train with Malkore, until the day comes when we are *all* swimming in gold!" More cheers from everyone. "Brothers, I won't lie to you, it will be hard! Ladies, your men will return to you each night hurting and tired, I promise you that. Warriors, you will be pushed harder than you think you can take, I promise that to you, too! I also promise that I will never ask you to do anything that I won't do myself -- just keep up with me. Learn with me. Malkore has been waiting for us to be ready. Now is the time! We have two days to celebrate, then the work begins." This brought a big cheer from the crowd. "Carry on."

Iyasiil turned to Malkore again, "I guess you got your answer."

Malkore responded, "Thanks to you."

"Ahhh, Lord Malkore. You need not forget . . ." she looked deep in his eyes with a hint of flirt in her eyes, then leaned forward and put her lips softly against his ear and whispered, "Clues."

He let out a big laugh and leaned forward, wrapped his hand around the back of her head, pulled her into him, and kissed her on the cheek. She wrapped her arms around him, then slid forward and spun around to sit sideways on his lap and kissed him repeatedly.

A couple of people yelled when they saw Malkore and Iyasiil kissing, as they would when they saw anyone kissing in the great hall. Then people started to realize, no one had ever seen Malkore kiss a woman in their life. Iyasiil had not been with the people very long, and no one had ever seen her kiss anyone either.

Normally, when people aren't married and don't have relationships with anyone, it's because they have no desire to – they just don't seem wired that way. It was obvious with these two that there was plenty of desire, but there was something different. It almost looked like they were glowing and there was a golden light coming from between them.

A couple of people turned and asked those around them. No one seemed to know what was happening between Malkore and Iyasiil, but they were curious.

- - - - - - - - - - - - - - - - - - -

After returning from their walk, which turned into Malkore's challenge from Odin, their meal in the great hall, and Odin's announcement, Malkore and Iyasiil had returned to her chamber.

They stood there in the center of Iyasiil's chamber together. They were holding hands and just looking at each other.

"What a welcome surprise to return home from a raid and find you here." Malkore said.

"No bigger of a surprise than it has been for me, My Lord Malkore." She responded.

"How about we lay down and do nothing for a while?" He suggested.

"That sounds perfect." She said.

They laid down and snuggled for a while, at times they didn't talk much. Other times, they wouldn't shut up – they laughed, told stories, kissed, and talked some more.

After an hour, the girls had come in, with another bowl of massage oil, because their teacher had used so much of it yesterday. They also brought a light snack, even though everyone had already eaten a big meal. The girls had wanted to talk with them, but quickly felt the energy in the room was quiet and very calm. It didn't feel like a time for teaching and questions. Even though this was supposed to be a Tending, Iyasiil and Malkore had both been doing so much teaching to them both.

Dossa built up the fire and came over to ask her teacher if she needed anything. Her teacher just shook her head, so Dossa leaned over and kissed her teacher on the forehead and then backed away.

Kalla had walked over to Malkore's side of the bed and knelt next to him. Iyasiil was laying with her hand on Malkore's heart. Kalla put her hand halfway on her teacher's hand and halfway on Malkore's chest directly. She felt that same deep, warm feeling as she had before. "Is there anything I can do for you, right now, My Lord."

He looked up at her, and put his hand on top of her hand, but without the same intensity or depth of connection as before and said, "No. Thank you, My Love."

"Very good, My Lord. You two have a great time. We will bring dinner late this evening." Kalla said.

Without even lifting her head, Iyasiil said, "Bring four plates, four horns, and a large pitcher of mead." Then she raised her head to look at Malkore and asked, "Only if that is alright with you, My Lord?"

Kalla looked at Malkore and put her other hand on Malkore's shoulder and asked him with a slightly flirty tone, "Lord Malkore, are you OK with that?"

"What? Having dinner with three beautiful, sexy women?" They all laughed. "Yeah, I think I'll be OK with that." He reached up and patted her hand which was still on his chest.

As she was getting up to leave the room, she said, "Very good. Have a good evening. We will see you two beautiful, sexy people later tonight." She got embarrassed again. She was glad she was already turning to walk towards the door. Only Dossa could see her face. Then she remembered, what she had practiced saying earler that day. She stopped, turned back around. Malkore was looking at her smiling with his finger pointed at her. She laughed and blushed more. With a smile, she looked him in the eye and said, "Lord Malkore, you and Mama are beautiful and sexy! I love you both, all day."

From across the room, Dossa added, "Me too."

Kalla added, "Dossa too." Repeating what she had done this morning.

"There it is. Good afternoon, ladies." Malkore said.

The girls left and Iyasiil rubbed her hand on Malkore's heart, "Thank you for loving them and helping teach them, My Lord."

"It's what we do." He said with a slight laugh. "Seriously, it's nice to be with you and it seems they are part of the deal for these days that we are together." He said.

"My Lord, I can't tell you how proud and happy I am for you with what happened with Lord Odin today." She said.

"Well, we will see how things go when the work begins. t's easy to make grand speeches. The real challenge is if he will not only push himself, but inspire the men when training begins to hurt. I don't know if many of them will be willing to train like I do, they just don't know what it's like to do it every day."

"If Odin backs you up, the men will learn. You may only have to embarrass him three or four more times to get him in line." She said playfully.

"Ha! Yeah, just three or four hundred more times." He responded with a laugh.

The two of them kept winding down their energy. Although not much had happened physically, and the walk had been easy and refreshing, a lot had been changing inside him. He had been re-orienting, changing how he was with the people. Like all changes, they happen first inside, and this was a big one. As fit as he was, it always surprised him how exhausting it is when emotional and spiritual changes are made, living a physical life, he would forget that the majority of who people are is energetic, their spiritual self.

"A lot must be changing inside. I can feel my body drifting towards sleep again. I can't believe I have slept so much since I've been back."

"You have needed the time to rest. I do believe a lot is changing. What happened in the great hall is proof of that." She responded.

"Oh, I wanted to ask you. What was it like for you when Odin was yelling that stuff, trying to get you to come to his bed tonight?"

"Oh, My Lord, I think he was really just trying to get you mad, to get a rise out of you." She responded, but he recognized the shift in her tone.

With a measured tone, sounding very serious, Malkore said to her, "My Love, it's been my experience that people can only move forward and grow when the truth is spoken." She recognized her own words and started smiling, "When it is just the two of us here, let only the truth be spoken." He was smiling, glad that she caught his sarcasm and accepted him using her words to call her out on hiding her real feelings.

"Oh, shit. Yes, My Lord." She said, shaking her head. "Yes, let this be the place where only the truth is spoken. When I was younger, I would have been disgusted by it and felt pressured. But now, I know who I am. When he says something like that, it's not a mandate to me. It is solely my decision who I get into bed with. I sleep with every man who excites me, it is only the most amazing man that can spark my interest. I just haven't met anyone that has sparked my interest in quite a while. I have felt like I am the most amazing lover who never has sex. So, when a little boy like Odin calls out as if getting in his bed is a privilege, just that fact that he cannot feel that I am disgusted by him, and only feels his own low-level desire, is proof that he doesn't have the emotional depth to be present during sex. So, it doesn't interest me at all."

"Wow! Yes! Well said. I think that's exactly why I haven't had sex in forever! My Dear Goddess, you are amazing."

"No, My Lord, Malkore." She started climbing up on him, straddling him. "You are amazing. I'm just the woman who is woman enough to get you in her bed." She said, lifting his cock up so it was laying on his stomach and planting her hips on top of it, then laying her whole body onto him and laying her head on the front of his shoulder.

He wrapped his arms around her, one hand going to the back of her heart, the other on the back of her hips. He pressed on the back of her heart, pushing her heart into his. He took a big breath and focused his attention on his skin. He wanted to feel every bit of how she felt.

She could easily take a nap, too and she didn't want to pass up the chance to snuggle him like this for a few minutes. "Just ignore me, My Lord. I am going to stay here for about three minutes, then we are going to nap."

He started laughing, "Yes, My Love. I was ignoring you already. I didn't even know you were here." He said as he pulled her a little more into him, pressing her heart into his heart and pressing her sacrum down onto his hips.

She felt her heart's and her spirit's happiness flutter through her body as this connection grew. "So silly."

"What is so silly, Love?"

"That boy. It was so silly of him to refer to me as your wife." She said sarcastically.

"Yes. What a foolish child. We have not even known each other two days now. What would give anyone that impression?! A couple that's married, should feel like they have both met someone who is truly their equal and recognizes the greatest parts of them, while supporting them in being their true self and inspiring them, even challenge them in an inspiring way, to grow into the greatest possible version of themselves."

Her body melted a little more. She felt the same way. It wasn't the idea of being married that excited her, it was the kind of connection he was describing. As she relaxed, she felt even more excitement at the same time, her erotic energy started stirring. If this lasted after the Tending, she didn't know how he would support and even challenge her, but the idea of it was exciting. "My Lord, you need to be quiet now and we will take a nap. If you keep talking like that, I will not let you sleep." She added a little grind of her hips on his cock to emphasize her point.

"Yes, Love. I will be quiet now. And I will say more another time, so you can keep me from sleeping." Their playful sarcasm was fun. He had never had that with anyone. He loved playfulness.

After another minute, she slid off of him and laid snuggling into him. They both took deep breaths, and both felt their bodies drifting off into slumber. She had her head on the front of his shoulder and barely tuned her head to press the side of her mouth into the top of his chest while pressing her hand into his chest, she wanted to bite him right then. She felt like a perfect mix of sleep and sex. Every time her body relaxed and got closer to sleep, she felt a delicious desire stirring inside. Every time she thought about how good he felt and how much she wanted to make love with him, she felt how much she wanted to stay in this relaxed feeling and take a nap with him.

They both drifted off to sleep. They slept for nearly two hours.

Chapter Seven
Teachings

She woke up lying on her left side facing away from him, feeling his strong body cradling hers, from her feet to the back of her head. She tried to scoot back into him even more.

He started getting up before her. "Is there something I can get for you, My Lord?"

"I am getting some snacks for us, Love. Stay there." He responded.

She rolled over to face his side of the bed and propped her head up on her hand to look at him across the room. He was quite a sight to take in. It was surprising how quickly her erotic energy had gotten stirred up with him. She always felt it within herself, but she hadn't felt her body wanting to pull anyone else close to her for centuries, and that's all she wanted to do with him – She wanted to pull every part of him into her. Her heart was being touched so deeply and she wanted to keep feeling him in all the deepest parts of her.

He piled up a blanket at the head of the bed and leaned back against it with a big bowl of fruit and cheese the girls had brought in earlier. "I think this is the best food I have ever eaten."

She kept laying there with her head propped up, looking at him. He seemed giddy at how good the food was. He was Five Thousand years old and still had a boyish charm that was adorable.

"My heart is so full, Lord Malkore." She said, then she worried that she was putting too many of her own feelings onto him and wasn't giving him the space that he needed to feel as free as possible during his Tending.

He looked down at her, "Don't do that. If you hold back, it will ruin my tending, ruin the teaching of your girls, and Asgard with crumble." Then he started smiling.

"*Oh shit! He heard me!*" She thought. She started laughing and dropped her head onto the top of her bicep. "This is crazy, right?!"

"Probably." He said smiling at her. Then with a sarcastic tone, he said, "I want you to look me in the eye and say, "Malkore, My Love, I am going to love you like no one has ever loved for as long as we are here." His whole face was lit up, repeating the lesson Iyasiil had taught to Kalla earlier.

Without hesitation, she rolled towards him more, tilting her head and bit him on the shoulder, growling at him.

"Come on, you fucking witch, say it." He was laughing as he popped small pieces of fruit into his mouth. "Say it!"

She was laughing so hard and her heart felt so full she was almost crying, She looked him in the eyes and said, "Malkore —" Then her face changed. She looked pained. Her eyes started filling with tears. "Shit! My Lord! Oh Shit! I love you so much! It's a little overwhelming at times. I just got scared that I wasn't supporting your Tending because I was feeling too much of my own love for you."

He knew she had just said the most intimately vulnerable and raw thing she could have said. But, he didn't acknowledge that to her. Instead, he kept smiling at her and with a little more sarcasm, he said, "OK, that was a good try. We are going to try this again and do better this time." He looked at her and felt his heart about to burst. Giving her the words to say, he said, "Malkore, My Love, I am going to love you like no one has ever loved for as long as we are here."

They were both laughing, she got up on her knees, took his bowl and put it to the side. As she was climbing up onto him, to straddle him. She laid her hands on his chest with the tips of her fingernails barely poking into his skin, as if she were holding on to him a little. She started repeating what he said.

He reached over to pick up his bowl of fruit and popped a piece of fruit into her mouth and said, "Good."

He was laughing and smiling so hard that his face almost hurt. She couldn't believe how silly she felt; silly and loved so much.

"My Dear, Lord Malkore. In all of the millennia that I have been alive, I have never met the likes of you. What a thrill! And so intoxicating!" She just looked at him, feeling totally exposed. "Shit! I'm doing it again."

He popped another piece of fruit in her mouth and said, "Me too, My Love. I have never felt so relaxed and so excited. And you are right, it is crazy." Then he popped another piece of fruit into his own mouth. "You are sooo delicious, in every way."

They just sat there looking at each other. Neither one of them knowing what else to say. They just kept smiling at each other.

He set the bowl of fruit on the side table. "Now get off of me. I'm hungry." He said, pushing her down on the bed, beside him. He had spun her down, so she was laying with her head on the pillow. He moved down to put his face between her legs. His legs were still out to her right side, and she reached over to touch his leg. Without stopping kissing the front of her hip, he grabbed her hand and moved it over to lay it on her own heart.

"My day. My rules. Just breathe, My Love." Then laid down with his head at the foot of the bed and picked her up by the hips, turning her over. She was startled by his raw strength; she was basically hanging in the air from her hips. He gently lowered her hips down, so she was straddling his face.

"Oh fuck, yes." She said wrapping her hand around his cock to put it in her mouth.

Again, he reached for her hand and took it away from his cock, then said, "My day. My rules. The only thing you are allowed to do is lay your head down and breathe."

"You're going to fucking kill me, aren't you?!" She said, not sure if she could take the excitement.

"I am certain that you will be safe, My Love. Now, if you will be quiet, there is something I need to do." He wrapped his lips around her clitoris with his tongue pressed firmly against it, both sucking blood into her clitoris and massaging it with his tongue.

She let out a half-yell, half-moan that sounded like her breath had been taken away. She grabbed the blanket with both hands as she pressed the side of her face into the front of his hip, just inches away from his cock. She felt like she was going to explode.

He had one hand holding her ass firmly, then reached down and held one of her breasts with the other hand. He pulsed his hands in the same rhythm that he was pulsing the suction on her clitoris.

After just a few minutes of this, she buried her face into the front of his hip and was almost screaming. *"Dear God! What is that?! Where did he learn that?!"* she had been with women and had them feeling like they were going to explode before, but never like what she was experiencing now. She couldn't tell what was happening from one moment to the next, her whole body felt like it was being pummeled with lightning bolts, never in the same place twice in a row. Her brain was overloading with pleasure.

She couldn't count the times she had climaxed, and she felt her body building up even more. Her cervix was pulsing with his tongue, reaching for him. Then he plunged his tongue deep inside her, tilted his head slightly, and started rubbing the front wall of her yoni with the side of his tongue. That was it! She pulled the blanket up into her mouth and screamed with her whole-body convulsing. She was gasping and moaning, her body gyrating to its own rhythm.

He knew that too much stimulation after that point could be painful, so he just held his lips against her yoni without moving for a while and kept feeling his own desire and excitement flowing in through her yoni, straight to her heart.

He rolled her onto her side and swung around to snuggle up into her. He knew that after moments like that, she would probably need to be held. He laid down next to her and gently rolled her over to half lay on him. He reached under her head with his left arm and around her back with his right arm. He hooked his heel behind her left leg and pulled her left thigh right up onto his left thigh, while laying his left calf on her right knee and shin. He squeezed her left thigh and knee with his right thigh and shin. There was no way he could have made more skin-to-skin contact without disturbing her too much. She was moaning, it sounded almost painful, and her body kept shaking. Her moaning turned to sobbing. She nuzzled her face into his chest and wrapped her left arm around him, holding him tight.

He couldn't remember a time when he had felt so thankful. He had a few tears rolling down his face, too.

She kept sobbing and he kept holding her. He kept breathing and feeling how good she felt to him.

Several more minutes went by and as her breathing had almost returned to normal, she said to him, "You fucking witch!" They both started laughing. His whole body was shaking with laughter, it made her start laughing harder.

"By all the stars in the sky, I love you!" He said, squeezing her a bit more.

"Yeah, what the fuck was that?!" She asked, she had never felt so much pleasure exploding in her body at one time.

"I told you I hadn't had made love with anyone in a long time, I have a lot of time to make up for, My Love." He said, playfully. Then with sarcasm, he added, "but if you didn't like it, I won't ever do it again." He was trying to keep a straight face and not give away his sarcasm.

"If you don't ever do it again, I'll fucking kill you, My Lord. I think I may need that every day for the rest of my life!" She told him, letting her head fall more into his arm. She felt like she had been exploded by love, itself.

"Hey, you didn't even knock over a table." He joked with her.

"No, but I almost bit a hole in your leg. I'll need to be careful of that. We can't have the greatest warrior in Asgard showing up to a fight with a severe limp."

"No, that wouldn't be good. But, if you told everyone what happened, I am sure they would forgive you." He said.

She laughed. They were both laughing. She rolled up onto him, straddling his hips, and laying her body on his. "Two more minutes like this, then I may be back to where my brain is working and I will be good to Tend to you, again."

"I don't need any Tending, right now, My Love. You stay there as long as you want." He said.

Making fun of herself for not being in a space to take care of him, she said with a breathless tone, "Lord Malkore, you are in Tending. As long as you are in Tending, I am smarter and wiser than you. Do you understand that?"

He started laughing at her adoringly and pulled her even tighter against his chest, "Yes, you wise fucking witch. I will do whatever you tell me to."

"I think I need a drink." She laughed at herself. He was happy to get it for her. He got up and got the large pitcher of mead and brought it over to the bed where he filled her horn and filled up his large horn. They sat up at the head of the bed and drank their mead.

Iyasiil turned her head to look and see if it was dark outside, yet. It was. "The girls should be along shortly. Are you ready for dinner, or would you prefer to wait a while?"

"I think I can wait a while, that fruit was good for me."

"I am going to share a question that I had. It isn't something I would normally share with someone while Tending to them, but this is different. I am sharing it because I am not getting a clear answer, and I would love to hear if you have any thoughts or feelings about it. Does that make sense?" She asked.

"Yes, of course. What is it?" He was curious.

"Normally a Tending is too fragile of a time to bring students in and teach them, the men are too fragile and too scattered for it to work --"

He finished her sentence, "But, again, this is different."

"Yes. I had the thought, and do not let the girls' teaching influence your answer, OK?" He nodded. "I was thinking about massaging you again tonight, maybe with the full sacred sexual energy build up like last night. I don't know what kind of space the girls will be in when they come in, but if they are in a good space, would you mind letting them learn while massaging you?"

"If they are in a good place and aren't detracting, that will be great."

"Yes, of course. I wouldn't hesitate to ask if this were weeks after your Tending, but so much is shifting so quickly, and I still want you to have the safe space to grow into what is changing in you. If they don't feel good to either one of us, I'll just ask them to leave, no question."

"I know Kalla will be eager to try it, if she isn't too scared, but I am not sure Dossa is ready for the kind of work that you do. She may explode or crumble."

"I know. And she is also full of surprises. There have been times she has shocked the shit out of me with the wisdom and presence she brings." Iyasiil said.

"Oh, really. OK. I haven't seen that part of her, yet. The only thing I have seen – I see and feel her potential -- but I have only seen that she is courageous in the face of being terrified, and everything seems to terrify her." He said.

Iyasiil laughed and said, "I know.   She isn't normally so timid; I think she just woke up to who you really are, and she can't handle how much she wants to fuck your brains out."

"What?! What do you mean?" He asked.

"You can't see it?   It has really caught her off guard, she is scared of being so attracted to you that she gets out of control." Iyasiil was snickering to herself, surprised that he couldn't see how much Dossa was turned on by him.

"What?! Seriously? I can't believe that." He responded.

"Lord Malkore, you are going to have to accept, once and for all, that during the time of Tending –"

He cut her off, holding up his hand, "You are so wise and all-knowing, I get it. But that only applies when you are not full of shit, My Love."

She smiled at him, "You really don't see it do you?"

He was at a loss for words, "No. No, I don't. I have seen Kalla wanting to mimic you in her healing style, so she has been dancing on the edge of being flirty with me, but still very reserved. She is trying her best to accept her own heart – Nice work with her this morning, by the way – but I can't see it in Dossa."

"OK. Well, that's a whole different issue and as time goes by, I will remind you and make fun of you that I told you about it on the second day that we knew each other." She said laughing.

He started laughing, too. He still couldn't imagine but acknowledged that he could be completely blind to something, "OK, My Love. You do that." He was smiling so big and shaking his head. *"How amazing it is to be with her!"* He thought.

About then, the girls walked in with a large platter of food, four plates, and two extra horns for mead. Dossa immediately tended to the fire, Kalla gathered their horns to refill and picked up the empty fruit bowl.

Iyasiil said, "Girls, pour mead for us all and come sit on the bed with us. We will eat later." Malkore and Iyasiil stayed sitting at the head of the bed.

Kalla delivered full horns to her teacher and Lord Malkore, then returned to the table to fill her own and Dossa's horns. "Dossa, I have your mead. Come join us in bed."

"I'll be right there. Let me get two more pieces of wood from outside." She went out the door and came right back in with more wood that went onto the fire.

Dossa dusted herself off and rinsed her hands in the bathing bowl by the fire. She walked towards the bed, "Is there anything else before I sit down?" She asked.

Iyasiil responded, "Thank you for taking care of the fire so well this whole time, Dossa. Join us, it's time for mead."

Dossa seemed relaxed and smiled at her teacher and sat next to Kalla. Kalla handed Dossa a horn of mead and told her, "Drink, You sexy bitch!"

Kalla was at the foot of the bed across from Malkore. He was sitting with his legs bent and his knees up. Kalla put her legs out and put her feet on top of his feet. "See, I am not hesitating, now." She giggled.

"Good." Iyasiil said.

Kalla wiggled her feet on Malkore's feet to exercise the fact that she wasn't holding back. He wiggled his toes into hers but couldn't feel her presence through her feet. "Kalla, I want you to really feel me through your feet. Take a breath and take your awareness to the bottoms of your feet."

Kalla responded, "I can feel you."

Iyasiil told her, "That's not what he means. You can feel h s feet, physically. But, he can't feel you, through your feet. He can't feel your heart touching him, through your feet."

"How do I do that?" Kalla asked.

"You did it last night at the table outside, when you put you r hand on my heart." Malkore said.

Kalla said, "Yes, but that —" then she blushed. "Yes, My Lord." She started laughing.

Iyasiil asked, "But that -- what?" She wanted to hear Kalla's objection, it was important to know more about how to teach her.

Kalla blushed again, "But it felt so intimate, last night. I got really turned on." After saying it, she wasn't blushing, she was glowing. "I don't want to screw it up, by getting turned on, again."

Malkore gave Iyasiil a look that said, *"I will take this one."* "Love always excites us -- sometimes it feels erotic, sometimes it feels nurturing, sometimes it feels compassionate, sometimes it feels sisterly or brotherly. How ever it feels in the moment when you feel it, it is OK. Those feelings will either tell you One, what the other person needs, if you are emotionally clear, Two, it might tell you what you need, and if you are not clear, you might try to put your needs onto them, or Three, it may show you a beautiful part of who you are right in that moment. In all cases, enjoy it."

Iyasiil responded, "Well said, Lord Malkore. Does that make sense, Kalla."

"So, I could feel feelings that aren't really mine, I could just be feeling what someone else needs?" Dossa asked.

"Yes, and you always get to choose for yourself whether you give it, based on how you feel with that person." Iyasiil told her.

"No, I get it." Kalla said, "If someone needs a hug, I might have the feeling of really wanting to hug them, because it's what they need."

"Yes," Malkore added, "and the more clear you get in your own feelings, the more you can tell the difference between what they need and what your feelings are."

"OK. I get that, too. So, what about last night? What was I doing last night?" Kalla asked.

"When you put your hand on my heart?" Malkore asked. Kalla nodded. "Go back to that moment, how did you feel?"

"I was feeling two things. First, I was feeling so happy for the two of you and so happy to get to be a part of it and support you, Mama. Second, I felt the impulse to come around the table to you while they were busy. I wanted you to know that you were being cared for. Then, when you touched me, I felt it through my whole body; It felt warm."

"He touched you? I missed that." Dossa said smiling, wanting to mess with Kalla.

Ignoring Dossa, Kalla went on, "The thing was: I was about to walk back around to the other side of the table, and I felt an impulse again to put my hand on your heart. I was nervous, but I just did what I thought Mama would do. I just felt so much love for you. Did I do it wrong?"

"No, it felt awesome to me. It felt great. How was it for you to feel that much love flowing through you." Malkore asked.

"I was just loving you so much." Kalla said.

"Yes, that's what it feels like." Iyasiil said, "And can you tell what kind of way you were loving him, right then?"

Kalla's eyebrows went up, "I don't know. How should I have felt?"

"There is no correct way to feel. It's just a matter of feeling however you felt it at that moment." Malkore said.

Kalla nodded, looking back in her mind to the scene last night, "I don't know. It was big! I felt like how I feel with you two – I felt like I was loving really big."

Iyasiil said, "It sounds like you really were loving big. That's awesome. Did you feel like you wanted to Marry him? Did you feel like you wanted to tear his clothes off? Did you feel like you wanted him to feel good in his own life? Did you feel like he was important to Asgard, and you wanted to honor that? Did –"

"The last two. I wanted you to feel really good and I wanted to show respect." Kalla said.

"And it was really intense." Iyasiil asked.

"Yes. Really intense." Kalla answered.

"Was there more with it?" Her teacher asked.

"Like what?" Kalla asked.

Malkore took this one, "To me, I felt the respect and the support, from you. That was great. Did I also sense a little flirty energy, too?"

Kalla scrunched up her face. Acting like she was scared to share bad news, she said, "Yes. Is that bad?"

They all laughed at how cute she was. Iyasiil said, "Of course not, My Love. If it is how you felt, then it is just how you felt. Did you feel like Lord Malkore was wanting flirtiness from you?"

"No." Kalla said.

"Did you feel like you were wanting or needing to get something from him by feeling flirty?"

Again, Kalla said, "No."

"Was your heart full and were you feeling respect, honoring, and flirty?"

Kalla looked a little embarrassed and said, "Yes." She looked like she was shrinking a bit. Then she remembered that she wasn't supposed to hide her feelings of love and affection for the whole Tending. She looked Malkore in the eyes and said, "But it is OK until the Tending is over to love you. A lot! Right?"

Iyasiil said, "Yes. And girls, the point of all this is not to get you to show love for Lord Malkore. The point is for you to be aware of your real, authentic feelings and to accept those feelings and honor them. Whether you choose to share them or not is up to you, just don't hide who you really are from yourself or anyone close to you. Does that make sense?"

Dossa nodded. Kalla said, "Yes, Mama."

Iyasiil went on, "Kalla, this whole discussion started because you put your feet on Lord Malkore's feet, and he couldn't feel your presence through your touch. So, Kalla, right now, try to feel those same feelings of respect and honoring and imagine those loving feelings flowing into Malkore through your feet as you touch him."

Malkore said, "Better."

Iyasiil said, "Now do you still feel any flirtiness while you are doing that?" Kalla nodded, then looked sheepishly up at Malkore. "Then sweet girl, feel it! Then look Lord Malkore in the eyes and say, "My Lord, may I flirt with you through your feet?"

Dossa was really paying attention. Talking like this was a whole new world for her and she was loving it. She was starting to think that someday she may understand herself; she really needed this kind of thing.

Kalla looked at Malkore and started to get nervous, then took a breath and tried to say it, but the words didn't come out. She tried again, and still she was fighting inside. Finally, she said, "This would be easier I could just say, "I want to fuck the shit out of your feet with my feet. Is that OK?""

Malkore laughed his big laugh and Iyasiil was trying not to laugh too hard. Dossa, started laughing and leaned over on Kalla's shoulder and wrapped her arms around Kalla's arm and said, "I love you so much, Sis."

With a big, loud comedic style, Kalla said, "Yeah, I am just going to start going around to every woman who looks amazingly happy being with her husband," gesturing to her teacher, "and tell her that I want to fuck her husband. That's going to go well."

Everyone was laughing. Then, with a serious look on her face, she looked at her teacher. Her teacher was smiling at her, Iyasiil could tell how hard she was working inside. "You are doing great. Stay with it."

"Why is this so hard?" She asked.

Iyasiil said, "Take a big breath and relax your body."

Kalla looked at Malkore and she let her body relax, "My Dear Lord Malkore, there is something about you that is so amazing. I don't know whether to love you like a dad, love you like a King, love you like a teacher, sit on your lap and kiss you, or love you like, like, like I don't know what! But, right now, I feel all those things, and I don't want to stop." She kept looking at him.

"There it is. That is your *real* voice." Her teacher said.

"Now. Now, I can feel you. Now, I feel like I can love you. You just opened the door to your heart to love and be loved back. Thank you, sweet Kalla." Malkore said with a calm, soothing, compassionate tone.

"By all that is Sacred, this is work. You two are serious? Is this what it takes to be as awesome as you?!" Kalla asked.

Malkore laughed. He remembered feeling that same feeling long ago.

Iyasiil laughed a little, too. "Yes, you beautiful little bitch! This is what it takes. I can feel how much I love you right now. Before two days ago, it was just a theory. Now, it's real."

"And it's worth it?" Kalla asked.

Malkore pointed at her feet on his feet and said, "Ask your feet if it is worth it. Ask your heart if what you feel coming through your feet is worth it."

She refocused her attention on flowing love and feeling how she felt for him, it felt even bigger, now. "But, I -- So, you are really OK if I fall in love with you?" he was about to nod at her, when she added, "for the rest of this Tending." She meant it to be funny, and it was.

"Yes, My Love. I am OK if you fall in love with me for the rest of this tending." Malkore said.

Kalla kept looking at Malkore and without looking at Dossa, pointed her finger at Dossa. On cue, Dossa said, "Me too."

Kalla said, "Dossa too."

Dossa was smiling at Malkore, then suddenly realized that he was still in the Tending and all the focus had been on her and Kalla. Dossa took a big breath and looked at Malkore, "My Lord, how are you doing? This is your time of Tending."

"Yes, My Lord, is there anything we can do for you. Can I get you anything?" Kalla asked.

Malkore finished his horn of mead and handed it to Kalla. She got up to refill it, then sat back at the foot of the bed. She put her legs under the covers and put her feet on Malkore's feet directly.

Dossa asked, "Mama, can I get you anything?" Iyasiil shook her head.

Malkore felt a difference in Dossa, "You seem so much more relaxed, Dossa."

"Yeah, Kalla had to kick my ass while you were sleeping." Turning to their teacher, "You would have been proud of her, Mama."

Iyasiil asked, "What happened this afternoon? Why did she have to kick your ass?"

Kalla said, "I just told her to quit being so scared and to try to let how she was really feeling come out. Just like you have been trying to get me to do. I told her that," turning to Malkore, "you remember when you said that I love bigger than everyone and that it is really scary?"

"And frustrating." Dossa added.

"Well, we talked. Dossa told me some stuff that I didn't even know about how she has felt her whole life like she has been shunned and insulted for loving as big as she loves. I get it, she has good reason to be scared."

Iyasiil spoke to Dossa, "The reason I have asked you two to be such a big part of this Tending is for you two to have the experience of what it is like to be in the presence of a man who is safe, who can see the best in you and who doesn't want to take anything from you."

Dossa piped up, "I get that, and I was scared that everyone would think I was weird if you knew how I was really feeling. am not so scared now, especially after hearing all that w th Kalla." Then with a comical tone, "But Kalla isn't very nice sometimes."

Malkore was amused. "Kalla, what did you do to her?"

Kalla looked at Dossa, with a slight giggle. Then she turned toward her teacher with a look that asked if it was OK. Her teacher nodded. Then Kalla looked at Malkore, "I just told her that if she kept hiding, I would make her pay for it."

Malkore said, "OK. That tells me exactly nothing. What did you tell her?"

Kalla tightened her lips, then exploded in laughter. Dossa started laughing. Kalla looked up at her teacher, while laughing so hard. She tried to breathe, then Dossa spoke up again, "Go ahead. Tell them what you said" goading Kalla on.

Iyasiil was laughing at their infectious laughter. Malkore was smiling, his curiosity was peaked.

Kalla finally stopped laughing enough to speak, "After we left this morning, I kept kidding Dossa about only saying "Me too" when you were getting me to not hold back about loving you two. All day long, I just keep saying "Me too. Me too." She finally got sick of it and snapped back at me. Please understand that this was just me getting her to stop being scared." Kalla looked at Malkore and started blushing. "Shit. This was just me messing with her, agreed?" Malkore nodded. "But it could be kind of flirty, so maybe I should just say it for real. Anyway, I told her that if she kept being scared, and kept hiding her feelings, I was going to do everything she wanted to do to the two of you. I told her I was going to fuck both of your brains out and she would just have to sit there and watch."

Dossa and Iyasiil laughed out loud. Iyasiil was clapping, she was laughing so hard and squealing with laughter, she said, "Oh, that's awesome! Good Job, Kalla! It worked, didn't it?!"

Malkore didn't know what to think. *"Shit! She was right. Dossa really was feeling a little attraction to me."*

Iyasiil reached over to Malkore and squeezed his leg, then poked him in the thigh as if to say, *"I told you so!"*

Dossa looked at Malkore and said, "Lord Malkore, I hope you aren't offended by that. I hope you don't think I am stupid or something. But after this talk, I am trying to be OK with it. I made a deal with Kalla that I wouldn't hold back for the first five minutes we were here tonight, and then I would decide if I wanted to shut down and hide again. It's been more than five minutes, and I am still OK."

"Who's idea was that deal?" Their teacher asked. Looking at Kalla, "Did you think of it, like that?"

"Yes, Mama. Is that wrong? I didn't know what to do." Kalla said.

Iyasiil said, "No, I think it's brilliant. Often, healing is about tricking people into being their real self, sounds like you did great."

Dossa kept looking at Malkore and asked, "You didn't answer, My Lord. Is it OK? I mean, for me too?"

Malkore sat there smiling at her, "How does it feel to you?"

"Like I am going to shit myself and throw up." They all laughed at her frankness, "Seriously. It's scary, but I don't know why. Nothing about being with you two feels scary, at all. It is just . . . I don't know. What if – What if I am wrong? What if you think you made a huge mistake being my teacher? What if I really am a degenerate for loving sex so much? What if I screw up your work in this Tending because I get turned on?" She looked up at her teacher, "it's scary."

"Oh, sweet girl, don't you know how wonderful every part of you is? Don't you know how much I love you and how much I love *all* of you, that includes your sexual energy? Come here." She motioned for Dossa to come sit in her lap. Dossa crawled over and sat sideways on her teacher's lap facing Malkore.

Then Dossa looked at her feet next to Malkore, she felt her body stiffen up. "See. Like, right now, I just wanted to put my feet in your lap. Then I got scared you would think I was stupid for wanting to do that. It's that kind of stuff. It's stupid, I know."

Iyasiil said, "It's not stupid to want to be accepted, My Love." Petting her on the head, "I bet Lord Malkore would love to hold your feet if you want him to."

Dossa looked up at Malkore and took a big breath, "May I?"

"Please." He said to her. She put her feet on his lap. "Now, let me really have them. Let your feet be held."

Iyasiil continued, "Everyone in this bed has the most powerful sexual energy, it's part of why I chose the two of you to be here right now. The two of you need to learn the spiritual aspect of it. Sex without heart expansion, while it can be fun for a little while, leaves you empty. I have been bringing you into the conversations with Lord Malkore, so that you can learn to let your heart expand and grow as big as your spirit."

"Dossa," Malkore added, "I can feel you here so much more. I couldn't feel you before. I couldn't feel your presence. I knew you had massive potential, but that's it. Thanks for coming to the party."

Dossa smiled at him, "Oh. You never answered my question. How are you? This is your Tending, and all the energy has been on us."

"I'm in bed with three awesome, beautiful women. What could be better?!" They all laughed.

Kalla spoke up, "Seriously, how is your Tending going? We know it's not the usual kind of Tending, but how are you?"

Malkore was impressed that she didn't let him get by with waving the question off with a joke. "Kalla, I never dreamed that these days, returning home would be so amazing. I have been hurting deep inside, for a long time. I don't feel like I am hurting anymore."

Dossa asked, "Can you tell us what happened with King Odin today?"

"Yeah, what was that all about? Everyone has been talking about it, all day." Kalla added.

"A long time ago, when Odin was just a boy, Odin's father, Borr, asked me to teach Odin. He knew that Odin could become the greatest king in all the nine realms. And sometimes we need our teachers to give us a kick in our complacency, that's what you saw today. I just needed to rattle his cage a little, today."

"Well, you did a lot more than that." Kalla said. "The whole kingdom has been talking and telling stories about how great you have been in battle. They started talking about how you went in and killed Forty men by yourself in the last raid."

"It was more like Twenty-Five or Thirty, but yeah. It was about to be really, really bad for the people. I'm glad it went well." He said.

Iyasiil spoke up, "Girls, anything that a warrior shares during the Tending stays here in this sacred space. You do not share it with anyone outside of the four of us. When you are with other people, outside of here, you bury everything you hear, and act like you never heard it. OK?"

"Yes, Mama." Dossa said.

"Absolutely. Does that mean you can share all the dirty details about Odin and all the High Council while we are here?" Kalla asked with a playful excitement.

"I am afraid that you would be bored if I talked about all that stuff. The high council just gets together to make itself feel important most of the time." He responded.

Iyasiil said, "*That* is the kind of thing that doesn't leave this room."

"Yeah," he said laughing, "No one needs to hear that Malkore said the high council just gets together to make itself feel important." The women laughed.

Kalla said, "Of course not, My Lord."

Malkore took a deep breath, then another. "Ladies, I have a question."

"Anything, My Lord." Dossa said.

"I want to hear the truth. And in this space, it is good to tell the truth, and it won't help me if you don't tell the truth. OK?" The girls nodded. "I would love to hear your truthful thoughts on Odin. What kind of a man does he seem like to you? What kind of a person is he? What has Frigg said about him? What is it like for you when you are around him? That kind of stuff."

The girls were quiet, not sure what to say. Iyasiil spoke up, "How has he treated each of you as a woman?"

Both girls let out a groan. Dossa said, "Years ago, he kept telling me I should come to his chambers, he just kept bugging me about it. Finally, I went. Then, he acted like he didn't know me and has only ignored me since. The shit part about it was that he was horrible in bed; so fast and I think I could have just put a bowl of thick boar fat under him, and it would have all been the same to him."

Malkore said, "Dossa, I am so sorry for that. I am sorry you went through that. That's exactly what I have been afraid of. And, I am sorry he was such a shitty lover. I am sorry he is such a shitty man."

Kalla said, "I just try to stay away from him. I will fill his drink, if I am there, but only after he gets drunk. After he gets drunk, he won't remember who he just invited into his bed, so I can get away. I don't like being around him."

"Do either of you talk to Frigg?" Malkore asked.

"Yeah, we talk a lot. She mostly complains about Odin." Dossa said.

Kalla continued, "About three weeks ago she was complaining that she knew she was supposed to marry him, she saw it in a vision, but she can't stand him. She doesn't know how he is ever going to change. That is what she says."

Malkore asked, "She said that? That she had a vision and was supposed to marry him?"

"Yes, My Lord. She kept saying, "He's not supposed to be this way. He's not supposed to be this way." But then, this afternoon, she said that she has a plan." Dossa said.

Iyasiil got curious, "Did she say what her plan is?"

"No. She just said that she was waiting for the Mother and Father of Asgard to show up. She said they are coming soon."

Iyasiil and Malkore looked at each other bewildered. *"Who are the Mother and Father of Asgard?!"*

Iyasiil turned to the girls, "Will the two of you go –" Turning to Lord Malkore, "My Lord, how are you feeling? How is your energy, right now?"

"I'm doing great! Why?" He asked.

"I want the girls to go and see if they can bring Frigg back here to talk with us, tonight. But only if you are up to it, My Lord." She said.

"No. That's a great idea!" He said.

"OK, girls. Go to the great hall, wrap yourselves up in good energy, because it will probably be shocking to you after being here to walk into the raucous energy of the celebration. See if you can get Frigg to come see us, right now." The girls started getting up. "Remember to wrap yourselves up."

As the girls were leaving, there was a new energy in the room. It was a faster pace – the kind of energy where things get done quickly. They both felt it.

Malkore put some clothes on. Iyasiil put on her dress.

- - - - - - - - - - - - - - - - - -

As the girls walked into the great hall from the kitchen entrance, they saw Frigg. She was talking with a few of Odin's top men. As soon as she saw Dossa and Kalla, she waved to them and motioned for them to come over to her.

Dossa asked, "Kalla, did she know we were coming to get her?"

Kalla responded, "It looked like it."

As they got to Frigg, she turned to them and said, "I just need two minutes, then I will be ready."

"OK, thank you, My Love." Kalla said. Then turning to Dossa, "I guess she did know we were coming to get her."

Frigg finished up her conversation quickly. Then Frigg excused herself from the group of men and grabbed Dossa's hand and started walking towards the kitchen.

When they got away from people, Frigg asked, "What's going on? I sensed that I was about to get pulled away, what is it?"

Dossa told her, "It's Mama and Lord Malkore, they want to talk with you, it seemed important."

"It seems it is. I felt like I got a lightning bolt up my spine about five minutes ago." Frigg said.

They walked through the kitchen and Frigg said, "You better get another pitcher of mead. We are probably going to need it."

Chapter Eight
Planning

After getting dressed, Malkore and Iyasiil were standing by the fire, holding hands, and kissing.

When the girls and Frigg walked into Iyasiil's chamber, Frigg came in first. When she saw Malkore, she instantly felt her heart warm up and get really big. She had never felt excited to see him before and she felt her face light up as if she had been waiting to see him for a long time. "Lord Malkore! I am —"

Iyasiil stepped around Malkore and stood next to him.

When Frigg saw Iyasiil standing by Malkore, she let out a half-gasp/half-yell and fell to one knee, bowing to them. "By the eyes of Ve, I did not see it. The Mother and Father of Asgard, my eyes are opened." She stood up tall and looked Malkore in the eye, "Malkore, forgive me because I did not see who you are, I meant no offense." She looked to Iyasiil, "Sahnshii, Mama, I am sorry for not seeing you until now."

Iyasiil spoke to her in a warm tone, "Frigg, it is time the people know my real name. I am Iyasiil."

Frigg fell to one knee again, "Iyasiil, of course. No one else could be the Mother of Asgard. Thank you, Mama. We need your help so badly, now."

Kalla was standing behind Frigg off to the side with her mouth hanging open. "Wait. Iyasiil? The one from the stories? Those are *real*? That's *you*?!"

Dossa started laughing, "No shit, Mama! You really are the baddest bitch in all the nine realms!"

Kalla backhanded Dossa on the arm, "Shut up!"

"No girls, nothing changes. It's me, just like I was to you five minutes ago."

Dossa hit Kalla on the arm, "See, it's just Mama." They all laughed, including Frigg.

Frigg asked, "Where can we sit and talk. There is so much to catch you up on."

Malkore and Iyasiil were excited and intrigued to hear. Malkore gestured to the bed and said, "Welcome to our council chamber."

Frigg laughed and with a big smile said, "Well, if that's how this party is going to go, I think I need a drink."

Kalla immediately moved to get an extra cup of mead. As everyone was getting onto the bed, she handed her large horn to Frigg, then made sure everyone else's horn was full. She kept one of the smaller metal cups, that had probably been stolen on a raid, to drink out of for herself.

Frigg saw the metal cup in Kalla's hand and said, "Well, that just won't do, will it?" She reached under her robe and pulled out a large horn and handed it to Kalla.

Dossa asked jokingly, "Do you always carry a horn around in your robe?" Iyasiil looked at Frigg and realized her magic had grown much bigger than she realized.

Frigg responded, "No, I just reached into the kitchen to get it." Iyasiil smiled.

Dossa was confused, *"Did she mean that she got it in the kitchen as we were leaving?"* She told herself to ask later.

Malkore laughed as he was getting into his usual spot, "I've never been in this bed with clothes on before."

Frigg said, "Well, if we all keep drinking enough, clothes will start flying off before too long." Everyone laughed.

Frigg didn't hesitate to put her legs under the covers at the foot of the bed and get really comfortable. Malkore and Iyasiil had put their legs under the covers, too and Frigg immediately snuggled her legs and wiggled her feet into Malkore and Iyasiil's legs.

Seeing this, Kalla saw how quickly and easily Frigg let herself enjoy snuggling into them with her legs and thought, *"Fuck! It really is that easy, just enjoy the people you are with."*

Kalla had sat halfway up the bed and immediately laid her ribs down across Malkore's lap, propping herself up on one elbow between he and Iyasiil. Dossa sat at the edge of the bed in front of Iyasiil. Iyasiil smiled when she saw Kalla getting more comfortable with Malkore and brushed Kalla's hair with her hand.

Iyasiil said, "OK. Tell us. All we know is that you had a vision that you were to marry Odin, and that you have been disgusted by him, rightly so, and the girls told us that you have a plan of some sort."

"And I have been waiting on you two." Frigg said.

"How have you been waiting on us?" Malkore asked.

Frigg spoke quickly and in a direct, steadfast way. She had been waiting for the chance to share all she had been carrying. "OK. Years ago, I started having dreams. When I was awake and when I was asleep, I dreamt of a place, just a spot on the ground. I was so drawn to it. I couldn't get it out of my head, I was being called to it. I had never felt anything like that before, but I am sure the two of you have callings like that all the time and are used to it."

Malkore and Iyasiil turned to look at each other and both said, "Yeah."

"Well, I wish I had come and asked, because it was fucking with me. Then one day, I went out to find the spot. I went out every day for a week before I found it."

Kalla was excited, "What was it?"

"Nothing. There was nothing there. But then I had a dream about it again that night. I dreamt I was crawling down into a hole there. So, the next day I went with tools to dig. I didn't have to dig far. I found one of these." She reached into the leather pouch she wore around her neck and pulled out a small ball of something. She squeezed it to show how soft it was. "This is what will change the course of Asgard. But I can't do all of it alone."

"Is it an herb or a mushroom of some kind?" Malkore asked.

"Yes. After I found the first one, I had a dream about another spot, and another. So, for years, I have been gathering these. I have a lot of them, now."

"What does it do?" Dossa asked.

"It puts us in touch with our true self, the part of us that walked out of the fires of Muspell, but that's not as important. Let me tell you what has happened. I was laying in Odin's bed weeks ago, listening to him whine about how much he loves me and whining about how I never let him fuck me." Turning to Dossa, "He is so disgusting."

"*Yeah*, he is." Dossa replied.

Frigg put her hand on Dossa's back and motioned for Dossa to come closer and lay across her lap. Frigg laid her hand on Dossa's back and kept stroking her back and hip as she went on.

"I fell asleep and had a dream that Odin was a woman and when I rolled over to kiss her, I started treating her like he treats women, then I called in a bunch of men to fuck her, over and over again."

"That's brutal." Malkore said.

Frigg looked up at him and matter-of-factly said, "The way Odin doesn't respect women is brutal. It's a brutal assault on women, emotionally. It's a brutal assault on who we really are and who we are supposed to be."

All the women knew exactly what that was like, they had seen it their entire lives. The girls let out a groan. Malkore understood, too.

Frigg went on, "I knew that we were going to have to change Odin into a woman for a while, but I didn't know how." Iyasiil smiled. Malkore laughed and nodded. Frigg asked him, "You see?" They all understood what change that would make. "As I thought about it, I kept feeling these," patting her medicine pouch, "would be a big part of it. One of these is enough to make drastic change in a person, seven will put him into a place where his physical body will be in a state of flux where he will only be feeling the part of himself that is eternal, he won't even know he has a body for a short while. That is when everything about him will be open to change. But I still didn't know how to make it happen, so I just kept picturing the change I wanted to see happen and waited. Then I started hearing a voice in my head, it was *my* voice, answering me, saying, "The Mother and Father of Asgard will make it happen.""

"I know the place." Iyasiil said.

"You do?! Oh thank, you Mama!" Frigg dropped her head and slumped her shoulders with relief. She acted like this was such a huge relief.

Malkore looked at Iyasiil with wonder, "*By the wonder of All, this woman is full of surprises!*" Iyasiil turned to Malkore, "If this keeps up," she motioned back and forth between them, "I will take you there."

Malkore smiled at her, "You did it again, witch." Then Malkore turned to Frigg, "I know how to help Odin make the transition into a woman. I don't think it will be hard at all. I know exactly what he will need."

Frigg looked at him. He spoke so confidently, but not arrogantly, it was such a quiet confidence that added weight to his words. Frigg thought, "Oh *shit, My Lord. How did I not notice you?*" She had a feeling growing inside that her heart wanted to wrap him up and be wrapped up by him. "*This man is really something special.*" Then she looked at Iyasiil.

Iyasiil nodded, "I know, right?!" They just smiled at each other.

Then Frigg looked back at Malkore, "I feel so stupid. How did I never see who you really are?"

Malkore responded, "No need to ask that question, My Love – You're not stupid, you just had to get to right here, right now."

They all continued to talk. Iyasiil suggested that when they transform Odin, they bring her back to the village and introduce her as a new woman in town. Iyasiil said she knew how to wipe his memory if needed, so he would feel like he had always been a woman who just didn't remember anything from before her time waking up with her and Malkore. Frigg added that it would probably be good if they kept Odin a woman for at least eight or ten days, so he really got a taste of what it was like being a woman among the men of Asgard.

They were all excited. The girls were still in a bit of shock that they were listening in to a conversation about true magic that would change the path of the entire world.

Iyasiil asked, "When should we do this?"

Malkore said, "If Odin is serious about having the men train with me, he will need to be there leading the men for at least three weeks before he disappears for ten days."

Frigg interjected, "Oh, Lord Malkore, he is serious about the training. He has been talking about nothing else all afternoon. He has been telling one story after another about when you were teaching him when he was young."

Malkore just smiled, "Good. I hope he keeps it up. So, if he needs to be at training every day, we will need to help him make his transition no sooner than in a month or so."

Iyasiil looked at the girls, "And no one outside of this circle can know anything about this. We all have to bury the knowledge of what we are doing anytime we are among other people." The girls nodded.

Iyasiil was excited. Then, she realized this probably meant that Malkore's Tending would be over soon. She felt a little tinge of sadness that what they had been feeling was going to end soon. She immediately realized how bad that thought felt. She didn't want to feel bad right now, so she just took a breath and let herself feel the love she was feeling for him in the moment and the sadness and fear went away.

Malkore felt it too. He looked at her, "You aren't getting rid of me that easily."

Iyasiil laughed, *"Fuck, he read my mind, again."*

Frigg looked at him with an alluring grin and asked, "Lord Malkore, do you always read people's minds?"

Iyasiil answered, "Only when he wants to fuck with someone." They all laughed. The girls were both amazed and wondered if he had been reading their minds the whole time.

Frigg was so tuned in at the moment, she could see Malkore clearly, "Lord Malkore, your Tending is not over, just because we are beginning to do a lot of work. We can get together again in the coming weeks to make sure everything is in order. I don't think there is anything more we need to talk about, right now. How does that sound to everyone?"

Everyone nodded in agreement. Iyasiil said, "Yes, that sounds great."

Frigg turned to Malkore, "My Lord, there is nothing left to discuss tonight, so let us support you, for the rest of the night."

"I agree." Iyasiil added.

"What can we do?" Dossa asked.

Frigg responded, "First, we are all going to drink and bring the energy down to a soft, nurturing, warm tingle. Then, --" Frigg paused.

"Then, we are going to get you naked, Lord Malkore." Iyasiil added. She and Frigg were on the same vibration. She had thought earlier about having the girls help with Malkore's massage tonight. With Frigg here, she felt confident that the girls would be able to stay in a good place to help.

Malkore looked surprised. He hadn't had much attention from women in millennia, and never like this. It caught him off guard. He was never at a loss for words and only said, "Well, I . . uhhh . . . I . . . uhhh." Malkore was never speechless.

Iyasiil looked at him with a smile and said, "My Lord, you are still my captive. You don't have any choice." He grinned at her.

Then Frigg asked, "Besides, Lord Malkore. If given the free choice to have four amazing, beautiful, sexy women loving on you and nurturing you, without them wanting or needing anything for themselves, only loving you for your highest good, would you say 'Yes'?"

Iyasiil giggled. That was exactly what she would have said. Malkore laughed and said, "Indeed, I would."

Frigg added, "Besides, would you do any less for one of us that worked so hard to serve the people?"

Malkore looked at Iyasiil and pointed to Frigg, "Oh, she's good."

Iyasiil said, "I told you she was good." Then turning to Frigg, "I always knew you could carry such big medicine, but I didn't realize you had grown into it so much. You are doing great."

Frigg dropped her head, "Mama, I am just now getting my feet wet with it. I didn't want to let you in until I felt confident within myself. I felt like I needed to stand in it, give myself permission to stand in my vision, before I shared it with anyone, but from the moment you got here, I have never been far away from asking for your help." Then Frigg's mouth hung open, "I just realized we have all been calling you "Mama", all along, and you are the Mother of Asgard in my vision."

"Wow!" Dossa said.

Kalla looked at Iyasiil, "Did you sexy bitches have this planned out ahead of time?" It all seemed too perfect, like it was unfolding too well.

Iyasiil answered, "No. This is just how it goes when you flow from the source. The Universe and all the nine realms have already been putting it all together. We have just needed to all be ready to step into it."

Frigg was in such a good place inside that she was able to read Malkore's energy and direct the conversation a bit. "Lord Malkore. It seems like so much has changed for you in the last two days. Changes like that can be really hard, but you seem like you are growing stronger with every breath. Has Sanshi –" She caught herself using the name Iyasiil went by when she arrived. "Has Iyasiil been taking good care of you?"

Malkore smiled a big, relaxed, patient smile and said, "The best care. No one else in all the Nine realms could have done what she has done."

Frigg's face lit up, she looked and Malkore and Iyasiil, "The two of you being together feels so good to me. You are both *so far* beyond this world, you make a good fit to be together for this time of Tending. I have tried to stress to Odin how the time of Tending can be such a powerful time of growth for the people – Not just for the warrior, but for the whole kingdom. He doesn't fight it, but still sees the time of Tending as an incicator of weakness. He thinks no one should ever need to be cared for. He is so closed off and so scared and he doesn't even know it."

Malkore felt a pang of sadness. "I know. I worked hard to keep him from getting stuck in that mindset. Obviously, I failed."

Frigg almost snapped at Malkore, "No, My Lord. Banish that thought!" Frigg took a big breath, holding fierce eye contact with Malkore and said, "Odin was so beaten down by his father, Borr is the one who failed. You are the only thing that kept him from completely dying inside. He won't admit it, but he still thinks of you as his *real* dad – you are the one who helped make him the man he is today. He is scared that talking about any of that stuff makes him look weak, but it comes out privately when he is frustrated about something. He really is grateful for you."

Dossa added, "We all are." Then she got embarrassed, she had been feeling so much admiration for Malkore while they all had been talking and just wanted to express it, then got scared it was inappropriate.

Frigg looked at Dossa with an expression that said, "*I didn't realize how much that needed to be said.*" Frigg said, "Well said, Sis!" She turned back to Malkore, "Lord Malkore, we are all grateful to you and for you." She raised her horn of mead to him. They all raised their horns to him.

Malkore was touched, "Well, thank you ladies. I had gotten to the point that I thought no one noticed, cared, or that any work I did really mattered to anyone here." Iyasiil leaned over and wrapped her arms around his arm and rested the side of her face on his shoulder.

Frigg looked at the two of them again. Then Frigg asked the question everyone had been pondering since first seeing Iyasiil and Malkore together. Pointing back and forth between them, "This isn't a normal Tending thing. Is this possibly something that will continue after the Tending is finished?"

Kalla exclaimed, "Yeah? Thank you!"

"Right?! Thank you!   I've been thinking the same thing." Dossa   added.

Iyasiil snuggled harder into Malkore's arm. He didn't say anything, but he was smiling.

Frigg pressed them, "Well?"

Iyasiil spoke, "We have been joking all day about how it would be foolish to trust feeling like you are falling in love after just two days, and much more foolish to trust those feelings if they happen during a ceremony, like a Tending. I have had some really intimate Tendings through the years, I am sure Lord Malkore has too. And we both have had very healing relationships in our travels. In all of that, I have never felt like I met someone, and it was the beginning of something that existed outside of the Tending."

Malkore added, "Same here. So, we have just kept it focused on right now. It feels better than any connection than I have ever felt with anyone, and I know that everything may fade fast as soon as the Tending is over. So, I am not getting attached to it."

Kalla asked, "How can you not?! I mean, look at you two, My Lord! I want you two to be together forever!"

Iyasiil laughed and told her, "So feel the love, right now. That is all any of us can do. This moment, right now, is the only moment that we can ever feel. This moment, right now, is all that exists in our lives. If this moment is full, we will be full – trying to make now something for the future is futile, because we don't want to create a future out of moments of not being present. Nothing lasts forever. Those feelings of wanting it to last forever, are just the feelings we are feeling right now. Essentially, "I will love you forever, for right now. And I will see how things go in the future. Let's see how I feel in three minutes."" Everyone laughed.

Malkore added, "Because relationships are only moments that happen one after the other."

Frigg asked, "So, Lord Malkore," she had a suggestive tone in her voice and a flirty look on her face, "You are in bed with four beautiful, loving women, who are here to support you in any way that you need to be supported. How may we serve you, My Lord?"

Malkore smiled, shaking his head. "I can't imagine anything better than the last two days. I feel so full and so grateful."

Iyasiil looked up at him and said, "Then, Lord Malkore, if you don't have any specific requests, you leave yourself at the mercy of us women."

All the women laughed, and Malkore, too. Iyasiil was looking at him with a smile and a look in her eyes that was a combination of flirtiness, immense respect, open-hearted desire, the deepest love, and raw lust.

Malkore smiled at her, then made eye contact with the three others and said, "I can't think of any better fate. I am just not sure if I should be scared or excited."

"Probably both." Kalla said, looking him in the eye, not holding back her love and excitement.

That was the first moment Malkore felt Kalla be so present with him that he wanted to hug her. He didn't say anything because he wanted her to feel her own way into it. If she was ready to hug him, she would be delighted if he initiated a hug. If she were not quite ready to hug him, she could fall back into her own resistance. So, he just felt the desire to hug her and felt how delicious the desire to hug someone is when they are present and loving.

Iyasiil spoke to the girls, "So girls, we are going to massage, Lord Malkore, all of us. This is a really important part of Tending, most of the time. It is vital to mind your own energy. It is a delicate balance to nurture someone's spirit and possibly their sexual energy and not have your own desire get greedy and want to be satisfied, because it may not match where they are, right then. And also, it is so important to keep your heart clear enough to feel and listen to their body, not just what your mind says they might want. Does that make sense?"

The girls nodded.

Frigg added, "Tending massage is amazing, and it can feel like a let-down to some people if your own desires are not aligned with what the other person needs right then. So, it is most important to build up their energy higher than you may think is possible."

Iyasiil told them, "This will be a teaching for the two of you. Frigg, maybe you, too, at some points. So, I may be really direct and have really strict instructions for you. Girls, this is not just about rubbing on someone's body. This is about nurturing their soul, *first*." She made eye contact with each of them, to make sure they understood. "It's about building up their lifeforce energy. There may be a lot of body work happening, too, we never know until we get started. Even when there is a lot of bodywork, it is always done in a stream of heart-nurturing and life-force building. It is really likely that you will feel more love flowing through you than you ever thought possible, it's not always easy to love that much without getting carried away in your own emotions, or your own fears, or your own desire. Sometimes, we get really turned on and it's not the time to satisfy our personal desire. We have to keep feeling all the love flowing through us, loving the person we are working on, without taking anything for ourselves."

Kalla nodded and looked like she understood.

Dossa nodded. She was a little unsure but felt like it would all make sense as the experience unfolded.

Frigg asked, "Lord Malkore, are you ready?"

"Yes, My Love. I am ready." He said to Frigg.

Frigg told him, "Very good. One thing, Lord Malkore, during your massage, there may be a little chatter at first, so we make sure Kalla and Dossa are on the same wave that we are, while working on you. Just ignore all the chatter, it will be short. Your job is to soak in all the love and nurturing, let your body relax, and let yourself be filled up."

Malkore nodded, "Of course. Not a problem."

Iyasiil then instructed him, "Lord Malkore, if you will stand up and take your clothes off, we will get you ready for your massage."

Malkore thought, *"I am ready now."* And he also knew that it had become the custom here over the last few centuries that a woman will bath him before a massage during the Tending. Sometimes it is really nice, sometimes it is really needed, and sometimes it is just really good insurance before having all your parts exposed to others.

He stood up and loosened the waist on his tan pants and Frigg pulled them down to the floor, then she pulled them away as he stepped out of them. Iyasiil loosened the lacing on the front of his shirt and pulled it off of him.

Iyasiil had a few fleeting thoughts wondering how this massage would go with four of them, and immediately dismissed the thoughts. She trusted that all would be in perfect order as things proceeded.

Dossa and Kalla had gotten the basin of warm water and several pieces of cloth to bath him with. When they returned to where Malkore was standing naked between these two beautiful women, Frigg was standing behind Malkore, Iyasiil in front of him. Iyasiil had both of her hands lying flat on his chest and her forehead resting on the top of his chest, right at the base of his neck. Frigg was doing the same behind him, she had her hands lying flat on the back of his heart with her forehead against the base of his neck.

Kalla wanted to get in on it. Part of her wanted to see if she could operate at the same level as her teacher, another part of her genuinely wanted to love and support Lord Malkore, and another part of her was excited by everything that was going on and she selfishly wanted to dance in that joy and love that was happening.

Kalla motioned for Dossa to wrap her hands around Malkore's thigh, just above the knee. Kalla knelt down on Malkore's left side and pressed her palms into the front and back of his thigh, then pressed her forehead slightly into the outside of his hip. As soon as she had her head against Malkore's hip, everything fell away. She felt her heart expand and fill up with love. She felt her body begin to tingle with a warm sensation she hadn't really known before, it felt bigger and still more relaxed than any type of erotic feeling she had ever had. The only way she could have described it was that she felt *so full.*

Kalla felt like she was filling up his leg with love and support, she had an image in her mind of her hands flowing red and blue love into his thigh and the love flowing upwards, mixing into a swirling shiny purple energy. She saw an image in her mind of that energy working its way to his heart, filling his whole body and head. She wondered if the color of the love she saw in her mind made a difference and made a mental note to ask her teacher about it later. Then she focused on letting that curiosity go, she took a breath, and refocused on flowing more love and support into Lord Malkore again.

Dossa did what Kalla was doing, kneeling down with her hands around Malkore's thigh. She peaked around Malkore's thighs to see if she was doing it the way Kalla was doing it before laying her forehead against Malkore's hip. She focused on how she wanted him to feel good. She started with the thoughts, *"I want your body to feel good. I want your heart and head to feel good. I am wrapping you in a blanket of love."* Then she had the thought, *"What if I were the blanket of love? I need to be that love, not just want it for someone . . ."*

Dossa then let go of any concern of "doing it wrong." In that moment, she gave herself permission to love Lord Malkore any way she could. She kept thinking, *"Just fall in love with him, again and again."* That was when she felt her heart really expand, she felt like her forehead melted onto his hip and she felt like her hands went inside his thigh and began filling up his thigh.

As if by magic, when all four women were in the same emotional and energetic place, they all took a deep breath at the same time, and Iyasiil began to speak a prayer, "Beloved Masters of All Nine Realms, let us be raised up to you. Look into the heart of this one. See the Grace and Wisdom that he is. Look upon him for all the days and let him always feel all the love flowing through him. Help us to support him so that he may be a light in the darkness for those who are lost and a shining sun for those who long to know their own light. Let him dance in battle and never know the taste of death. Let him know nothing but the greatest love through every drop of his blood."

Kalla had tears running down her face as she heard the prayer. She was feeling so much love for Lord Malkore, in that moment. She wanted to wrap her entire heart around him. She felt herself lean her forehead into him a little more. She took her left hand and wrapped it around to the inside of his thigh, as if she were hugging his leg. She took a deeper breath, just as her teacher would have instructed her to do. She imagined him being filled up with the greatest, most wonderful love and she felt like her heart was being pulled into him.

Malkore felt it. He felt all of it. He felt like he was being transported back into the heart of creation.

Each of the women took a piece of cloth from the warm water basin and began cleaning his body. His whole body was being cleansed; he didn't think he could have gotten any more clean if he had been bathing himself in the river.

"Lord Malkore, if you will lay down, we are going to have a talk with your body and spirit, now." Iyasiil said.

Frigg spoke to the girls, "Dossa, Kalla, the emotional place I usually go to right now is that I combine two things inside myself. One, I imagine all the love of the entire world flowing through me. Two, right now, I will feel how I am feeling about Lord Malkore and see if those feelings are helpful in giving him a nurturing experience."

Kalla responded, "Thank you, sis. I think I understand. I can do that easily, and the other thing is to make it all a giveaway, where I just think of it like it is all flowing to him, filling me up as it flows to him. Right?"

"Right." Iyasiil said. "In the process of flowing it through you, you will be filled up beyond belief."

Frigg was sitting on her feet between Malkore's shins. She had taken off her outer dress and was wearing only a light white dress that was mostly see through.

Iyasiil had only been wearing her lightest dressing gown the whole time. She was sitting next to Malkore's left shoulder and she wasn't getting a clear picture of what to do, yet. So, she laid her hands on the left side of his chest and left shoulder.

Kalla had gotten up on her knees and was sitting on her feet beside Malkore's right hip. She felt her attention going from the outside of his hip and up into his heart, so that's where she put her hands.

Dossa was by Malkore's left hip. She wasn't quite squirming, but she wasn't at ease. She looked like she kept changing her mind every half second for a few seconds. Iyasiil looked at her and put her hand on Dossa's shoulder. Dossa looked almost pained for a second, she motioned for her teacher to lean in.

Dossa whispered into her teacher's ear, "I kind of want to be up there," pointing to his head.

"Great! Do it. Go up there." Her teacher whispered back.

"But there's not room. He would have to scoot down." Dossa said, nervously. She was worried that it would be a disruption for Malkore to slide down. She was worried that she was not seeing things correctly, because she wanted to sit above his head.

"That's not a problem, sweet girl." Iyasiil whispered to her. Then in a soft and gentle voice, she said, "Lord Malkore, if you will scoot down, Sweet Dossa is going to hold your head and massage your neck." Malkore scooted down.

"Oh, it's that easy. Just ask for what you want." Dossa thought. Then she got up and moved up to the head of the bed. She pulled her long dress up, and lowered herself down above Malkore's head with her legs spread out wide. She immediately felt herself relax as she had followed through with what she felt pulled to do.

Malkore reached out with his hands and grabbed Dossa's feet and slid them into his ribs. He wiggled her feet into his sides to communicate that he was OK with her getting close and snuggly. She let out a slight giggle and wiggled her feet into him more. Then she laid her hands on his chest, closed her eyes, and took a couple of breaths to see what she wanted to do next.

Frigg used a lot of massage oil to saturate the tanned skin on Malkore's muscular legs. She covered the tops of his thighs and the sides of his thighs, not hesitating to work deep up into the crease between the tops of his thighs and his body. As she was feeling his muscles, she realized she may be doing a little more work than she originally thought.

Frigg tapped Kalla on the arm and motioned for her to come down onto Malkore's right shin as she moved to straddle Malkore's left shin. When Kalla was in place, Frigg leaned over and whispered to her, "Just do what I do." Kalla mirrored everything that Frigg did. They started off with their hands spread wide across Malkore's thighs, pressing their hands deep into his muscles from his knees up to the upper part of his inner thigh and angling out to the outside of his hip. After a few minutes, they were using their forearms, pressing deep, sliding up his powerful thighs. They weren't going so deep into the muscles that it would cause pain, they were just giving the muscles a good, deep flushing of blood. They kept this up for several minutes, then moved to the back of his knees, pulling upward, making strokes that went up the backs of his thighs.

Iyasiil was watching Frigg and Kalla working in unison, then looked at Dossa, who had moved her hands to the back of Malkore's neck and was digging her fingers deep into the muscles in the base of his neck then up to the base of his skull. All was going well with the massage part of it. All three of them seemed to be massaging him from a quiet and still, almost meditative, yet intense place inside. It looked fantastic; she wanted the same treatment for herself someday.

Iyasiil didn't see anything that needed to be done, at the moment. She took a couple of breaths and saw an image in her mind of being snuggled up on him – she didn't know or couldn't quite tell if snuggling up on him would be the best thing to do for him at the moment, or if that was her own desire. So, she just scooted her knees up to his ribs, her right knee snuggled into Dossa's toes. She put her hands on his torso, her left hand on his solar plexus, her right hand on his heart.

Iyasiil looked at Dossa. Dossa didn't even look like herself, she looked like she had been transformed into an older, wise healer – the woman Iyasiil always knew she could become. She was holding Malkore's head in her left hand, having turned his head to the left, making deep strokes with her right thumb down from the base of his skull behind his ear down to the point of his shoulder. *"Damn, I knew that girl was good."* She said to herself.

She looked at Frigg and Kalla, their movements were in sync and Kalla looked for the moment like she didn't need any direction at all. Seeing her girls being their biggest, best selves right in this moment filled her with such a gratitude and joy. She was so thankful for how this Tending was unfolding for everyone, and then there was Malkore. He looked totally at peace. She wondered for a second if this was a big turn on for him and looked to see if he had gotten an erection. He was just soaking in the nurturing.

Frigg guided Kalla's thumb right up under Malkore's balls and the two of them started making strokes from the inside of his thighs, to under his scrotum, across the front of his hips, and up into his lower abdomen. Frigg had motioned for Kalla to keep breathing, as a reminder. Kalla nodded that she understood and kept breathing.

Iyasiil kept breathing and kept checking in with her own heart. *"What am I going to do with this man?"* she asked herself. She knew that question was half asking what would serve him in the moment and half asking about her future with this man. She knew that the answer to both would only come as she kept breathing and feeling her feelings, so that's what she did. Her feelings started getting bigger and bigger inside. She laid her forehead on Malkore's solar plexus, but that didn't feel quite right, so she slid her left knee towards his hip and put her head right in the middle of his stomach. She felt like her forehead melted down into his stomach a little bit, *"That's the spot."*

Iyasiil felt tears welling up in her eyes, she still had her right hand on Malkore's heart. She could feel Frigg and Kalla's hands making strokes around his lower abdomen, right up against her hand. With each massage stroke, Frigg and Kalla would run their pinky on top of Iyasiil's pinky, loving on them both.

As Iyasiil was melting into Malkore's stomach she began to see images of his life. She saw thousands of battles, thousands of people, hundreds of lovers. She saw so much love flowing through him, and she felt so much pain that he had endured. She saw the time he went into the woods for what seemed like months to try and purify himself of the hurt and anger he felt from his youth. She saw the times he had been betrayed and blamed for things he hadn't done by small-minded, jealous people, trying to take what he had. She saw how he had grown. She saw how he had traveled from world to world, learning everything he could, teaching whatever he could. She saw the journeys he took to the heart of creation. And she saw how he had felt so alone at times, she saw how he filled up that aloneness with appreciation, and gratitude for all that is and created a sense of contentment.

Malkore reached down and touched Iyasiil on the shoulder to get her attention. She looked up and he motioned for her to come up to him. She moved up towards his head. He whispered something into her ear. It was a language she had only known as "The Prayer Language." She didn't understand any of the words, but she felt them -- she felt how the words landed with her heart. She felt her heart expand even more and she noticed that more tears started flowing. She felt like she could explode.

She only responded, "Yes, My Love."

Dossa had finished both sides of Malkore's neck and was getting up gently, so as not to disturb him. She went over to the table to get a drink. The intensity of this healing, loving energy felt so good to her. And it was a lot to let flow through her. She wasn't used to it.

Iyasiil's teacher brain was proud of Dossa for taking a break when she needed to. Her healer brain quickly checked in with what Lord Malkore might need if the energy shifted with Dossa getting up -- There was nothing that needed to be done. She slid her hands up his body to the fronts of his shoulders and laid the side of her head on his heart. The left side of her ribs were resting on his stomach, and her heart was on his ribs.

Dossa came back and laid across the head of the bed with her breasts right above Malkore's head and her legs down the left side of his body, her ankles were on top of Iyasiil's feet. Dossa had propped herself up on her right elbow and had her left hand on Malkore's chest right above Iyasiil's head. Dossa was feeling so grateful to be a part of what was going on. She was feeling a level of nurturing going on that, even though she was helping to facilitate, it was healing a deep hurt in her.

Most men that Dossa had ever been around could only get about five percent of this much nurturing before they went straight to sex. She had gotten to the point that she didn't even like being nice to men most of the time, because any kindness was often quickly followed up with them trying to have sex with her. Being there with Malkore was opening something up inside herself that felt like it had been hidden so deep inside her that she didn't even know it was there. She felt her heart open like she had never felt before, she felt so grateful and so honored as a person and as a woman that she wanted to fill Malkore and her teacher up with so much love and nurturing.

Dossa looked down at what Kalla and Frigg were doing, they were almost moving as one person. It was only when one of them needed to get their entire hand deep into Malkore's groin that their movements were not synchronous. They traded off, then fell back into rhythm as if it was practiced.

Dossa wanted to put her cheek on Malkore's forehead, she didn't know why, and she didn't do it. Then, she remembered

Kalla talking about feeling an impulse to do something. She scooted to where she could rest her cheek on Malkore's forehead and when she did, he took in a big breath. Dossa felt her heart so big; she felt kind of mothering in that moment. She felt like she was starting to understand how feeling her own love, in the proper situation, can be healing and can have a big impact on someone else. Without even realizing it, she rolled her head down and kissed Malkore on the forehead. He let out a sound that she couldn't describe. It was a part-moan, part-squeak, part-cry. She just rested her cheek and lips on his forehead. Then kissed his forehead again, then again, and again. For whatever reason, that really touched him. He had a couple of tears falling out of his eyes.

For centuries, he had kept his erotic energy mostly inside himself, never sharing it with anyone, because he never felt like anyone could see into the deepest parts of him. With Iyasiil, he felt met. He felt like every part of him was seen, understood, known, and welcomed. Because he felt met so deeply, he felt his erotic energy freely flowing and ready to come out.

Frigg and Kalla were doing a great job of nurturing him and when they sensed that his heart and spirit were full, they continued on to nurturing his erotic energy. As they had been massaging all around his genitals, his cock had started to get thicker.   Frigg had made several strokes with her hand, massaging his cock. She wasn't trying to excite him, she was simply sharing that nurturing energy with that part of him, too.

Kalla looked at Frigg with a question on her face. She wasn't even sure what the question was, but she felt something.

Frigg leaned over and put her lips against Kalla's ear and softly whispered. "Cradle it in your hands and say a nurturing pray, honoring the man that he is." Kalla nodded, that answered her question.

Frigg took Kalla's left hand and put it on Malkore's stomach right against the base of his cock. Frigg laid his cock on Kalla's hand and covered it with Kalla's right hand.

Kalla took a deep breath to empty her heart and mind and began whispering a prayer so softly that Frigg couldn't even hear her words. "I wish you the greatest joy. Thank you for all you do and will do for the people." She felt overwhelmed with love and awe. She had tears dropping from her eyes. "I love you. I love the man that you are. Thank you for today. Thank you for every day. Thank you for loving me. You are the greatest man. Thank you. May you know the greatest joy." She felt his cock grow as she kept repeating, "Lord Malkore, I wish you the greatest Joy. I wish you the greatest joy. I wish you the greatest joy." She wanted to lay down with her head on his hip, right next to his cock, but she didn't.

Then she looked at Frigg, smiling, with tears rolling down her cheeks. She wasn't sure if she should be embarrassed for feeling so much, but she was learning over these days that she probably shouldn't be embarrassed.

Frigg could feel what a powerful place Kalla was in. She could see that Kalla was radiating the energy of the Divine Goddess. Frigg was impressed with her ability to bring so much healing and loving energy through her. Frigg nodded to Kalla, approving of what she had done. Frigg then slid her right hand under Kalla's hand, Kalla pulled her hand away. Frigg cradled Malkore's cock and leaned down, resting her forehead on it and began a prayer, "Lord Malkore, Father of Asgard, the people are ready for you. We are your people. We are *your* people. Please, Father Malkore, teach us and mold us into what we can become. Thank you for being patient with us. We honor your strength and wisdom and thank you for becoming the man we need. And personally, Lord Malkore, feel my love – I love you so much. Feel my gratitude. Feel how happy I am that you are here. May you be blessed everyday of your life. May you know the greatest joy." She gently kissed his cock and rested her forehead back on the underside of it for another breath.

Frigg noticed Kalla had slid her hand up under his scrotum, supporting his balls in one hand, gently massaging his stomach with the other.

Iyasiil felt his breathing get a little heavier. She felt his erotic energy stirring, because she felt her own energy stirring as well. And as she was breathing him in, she felt a deep tenderness in him. He was totally relaxed, and she could feel his total presence. She didn't know if it was a good thing or a bad thing for Malkore's Tending but she was consumed by her own feelings at the moment, just as she had cautioned the girls against. She wondered if Malkore was being taken such good care of that she had the space to only feel her own feelings without needing to tend to him, or if she was lost in her selfish desires which may make him miss out on something important. There was also the possibility that his needs could be met through her desires, which only happens in the most heightened states, when people are very clear.

Right then, Malkore reached down and pulled on her shoulders to pull her up onto him. She wasn't sure if he wanted her straddling him or just to come up and hug him. She got her knees under her and leaned up to his face and whispered, "Yes, My Lord?"

"I am yours. Come into my heart." He whispered.

She whispered back, "It's the only place I want to be, My Love." She climbed on top of him with tears welling up in her eyes, straddling him and made sure she was far enough forward on him so that Frigg and Kalla still had plenty of room to work.

Dossa reached down from above Malkore's head and put her hand on her teacher's head. Iyasiil had her chin on

Malkore's collarbone and her arms under his shoulders. Malkore felt like his heart was reaching out of his chest and pulling her in. She wished she could burrow inside him. She kept reminding herself to breathe. When she did breathe, she felt like her heart was pounding and exploding with love, all at the same time. She felt like she couldn't pull herself into him hard enough. She wanted to be closer and closer.

She felt Frigg mend her dress, so it wasn't wadded up beneath her, and she felt Frigg's hands slide to the outside of her hips and slowly pull her hips down to Malkore's hips. Iyasiil moved her head to the center of his chest, right below his chin. She could feel his stiff cock against her wet yoni as she slid her hips down.

Frigg motioned to Kalla to move around to his right side. Frigg moved to Malkore's left side and sat next to them with her left hand on the back of Iyasiil's heart and her right hand on the outside of Malkore's chest. Kalla moved to Malkore's right side. Kalla put her right hand on her teacher's sacrum and her left hand on top of Frigg's hand, on the back of her teacher's heart. Dossa was still resting her cheek on Malkore's forehead, occasionally kissing him on the forehead whenever she felt like it.

Frigg began to speak in a tone of voice that the girls didn't recognize, she sounded like an old, wise woman – she sounded a lot like Iyasiil did when she was teaching the most important lessons. Frigg spoke as if she were making a pronouncement, "The Mother and Father of Asgard have come together to out of their love of the people, so the people may know the greatest love. May their love bless the people, and their wisdom guide us to the greatest heights. And more importantly, may their presence in each other's lives be the greatest comfort and the greatest inspiration, so they may live in more love and joy than anyone has ever known."

Dossa began sobbing. Frigg had tears pouring down her cheeks. Kalla, again, wanted to lay down and soak up all the love that was radiating from the two of them, so she did. She laid down with the front of her hips against Iyasiil's shin. She put her right hand on her teacher's back and put her forehead against the outside of Malkore's shoulder, and she pressed the tip of her nose and her lips into his shoulder. She took a deep breath and let herself melt into him – she imagined that she was pushing love through her mouth into his heart. Anything else would have felt like she was holding back and Malkore and Mama had been teaching her to not hold back, so she tried it and it felt good.

Frigg said, "We are creating something great here that will spread throughout the kingdom and teach love to all the nine realms. The Mother and Father of Asgard will teach the people how to find the deepest, greatest places so they can love like no people who have come before. It is an honor to be with the two of you." Frigg pulled up the back of Iyasiil's dress and took Malkore's cock in her hand, putting the tip of it right against the opening of Iyasiil's yoni. Iyasiil gasped as she slid down onto it.

Frigg began singing a sacred song. Kalla could feel the energy rise even more. She didn't know what was going on, but she wanted to make love with them both, and she felt like she was making love with them both, just not sexually.

Frigg had the sense that this was a type of marriage, maybe not the kind of romantic, living-together, kind of marriage, but definitely a bonding of spirits/bonding of visions kind of marriage.

Dossa didn't raise her head, even when Malkore's body kept rocking with Mama moving his whole body with her hips. Dossa still kept kissing him periodically, even though he was now having sex with her teacher.

Frigg noticed Iyasiil fidgeting with her dress, making half-hearted attempts to adjust it.

Frigg carefully reached across and tapped Kalla on the shoulder, she knew Kalla may not even acknowledge her. Kalla did. Kalla gently, but still quickly sat up. Frigg motioned that they were going to pull Mama's dress off of her. Kalla nodded.

They began gathering Iyasiil's dress up around her waist, then gently pulled her shoulders up to where she was vertical. Iyasiil gasped at the sensation, being penetrated deeper, both physically and emotionally. Frigg and Kalla began lifting the dress up beneath her shoulders. Iyasiil didn't really seem to notice what they were doing, because she was lost in her own experience. Frigg and Kalla lifted Iyasiil's arm with one hand and raised her dress above her head with the other hand.

Dossa felt like she was seeing the most beautiful thing she had ever seen. The two of them were glowing the most beautiful golden light. She felt like she was getting washed and blessed with the love of the Creation, itself. She kept breathing as slowly and as softly as possible, but she couldn't stop the tears from pouring. She couldn't believe how much love she felt for these two amazing people – for everyone here. Her whole body was tingling. She loved Mama so much and wanted to crawl inside Malkore's chest and curl up there for the rest of her life.

Iyasiil kept sitting up as she made love to Malkore.

Frigg felt the impulse to put her hands on Iyasiil's heart, she could tell that Iyasiil was at least halfway off in the spirit world. She put her right hand between Iyasiil's breasts and her left hand between Iyasiil's shoulder blades, on the back of her heart. Iyasiil let out a half-gasp/half-moan.

Kalla saw this and saw how beautiful it was and thought about how beautiful it would be to have the support of a sister when making love, especially if the love making had a connection as intense as this. She looked down at Malkore and felt so much gratitude for him, she felt so much love for him, and she loved what was happening when Malkore and her teacher were together. As she looked at him, Kalla started seeing her own hands on his heart in her imagination, so she tried it. Kalla put her hands on his heart.

He gasped, too. He brought his left hand up and put it on top of her hands, while continuing to hold Iyasiil's leg with his right hand. He pressed Kalla's hands into his heart and let out a deep, guttural growl while his whole body tightened up, reaching as deep as he could inside Iyasiil with his hips. He had tears in his eyes, and he could feel Dossa's tears dripping down the right side of his head.

Iyasiil made a few short, gasping screams in rhythm with her rocking motions, then her whole body started shaking. Malkore half-growled/half-screamed. A few more seconds of this and Iyasiil collapsed onto his chest. Screaming, sobbing, and still shaking through her whole body. Malkore was shaking, too. He wrapped his arms around her.

Frigg quickly pulled her dress off and pressed her body against Iyasiil, and Malkore's left arm. Frigg wrapped an arm around Iyasiil and held Malkore's shoulder, pulling him a little harder into Iyasiil.

Kalla felt like lightening was shooting through her body. She felt like her whole body and spirit was orgasming repeatedly. Kalla noticed that Frigg's body twitched several times, too. Kalla leaned on Iyasiil, wrapping one arm across her teacher's back, holding onto Frigg and reached up with the other hand, laying it on Dossa's head. Kalla could feel her breasts pressed onto Malkore's arm and she wished she had taken her dress off too.

They all kept breathing. Every one of them felt like they had their own blessing, healing, and full-filling experience. They all kept breathing and feeling what was happening.

It took about fifteen minutes for the energy to settle down a bit. Iyasiil and Malkore still had some of those waves of lightening shudder through them every couple of minutes. Everyone kept breathing and feeling the most intense connection, love, and gratitude that any of them had ever felt.

When Iyasiil's breathing had returned to normal, she started to sit up. Frigg leaned up and put her left hand on Iyasiil's hip and the other hand on Malkore's heart. Kalla laid down with her head on the front of Malkore's shoulder and he wrapped his right arm around her. He kept his eyes closed for a minute as he was breathing, still coming down from such an intense thing.

Iyasiil felt like collapsing on him again. She could still feel his cock still occasionally throbbing, deep inside her, and she didn't ever want to let it go.

Iyasiil barely cracked her eyes open to see where Frigg was. She reached out and put her hand out on Frigg's shoulder, then closed her eyes again.

A few moments later, as her eyes were opening again, she saw that Malkore was just opening his eyes. When they made eye contact, they smiled at each other and Iyasiil started giggling. She was beaming.

Iyasiil leaned over to Frigg and put her forehead against Frigg's forehead, and they both took a long, slow breath. Malkore pulled Kalla closer into him with one arm and tilted his head up towards Dossa, while reaching over to Dossa's leg with his left hand.

Dossa reached down with her left hand and wrapped it around his jaw, kissed him on the forehead again and said, "Me too." Everyone laughed, except Frigg who hadn't heard the running joke of the day.

Kalla scooted her hips harder into Iyasiil's leg and said, "I love you two so much. I love you all so much."

Frigg kissed Iyasiil in the lips, then looked her in the eyes and said, "Me too."

Kalla said, "Frigg, too." They all laughed more, except Frigg. Frigg had a curious, confused look on her face.

Dossa laughed and said, "I'll explain later, Frigg. It's been my theme all day." Frigg smiled and nodded.

Frigg leaned down, pressing her breasts into the left side of Malkore's chest, and kissed Malkore on the lips and asked, "So, Lord Malkore, have you ever made 4 women orgasm at the same time before?" The room erupted in laughter. Frigg was laughing, looking Malkore in the eyes. His whole body was shaking with laughter. She grabbed the right side of his head and kissed him again.

Kalla was laughing so hard she started crying, the crying turned to deep sobs. Malkore pulled her tight to him again.

Kalla cry-squealed, "I don't know why I am crying." A l the women felt it and teared up a bit themselves.

Iyasiil leaned down and kissed her on the forehead and said, "Just let yourself cry. Cry as long as you need to."

Frigg pointed one finger in the middle of Malkore's chest and said, "Lord Malkore, have you ever made four women cry at the same time, like this?" Everyone laughed again. "Lord

Malkore, seriously, I have never met a man like you. I don't know what you do or how you do it, but I think I speak for everyone here when I say, I am ready at any moment to do this again. I have never felt anyone except Mama who has a heart and love like yours."

Dossa, using her smallest, most meek voice said, "Me too."

Without lifting her head, Kalla said, "Dossa too."

"Thank you, ladies." Then looking at Iyasiil, "Thank you, My Love." She just smiled at him, and they kept making eye contact.

"Now there is good news and bad news." Frigg said, and they are both the same thing. "Lord Malkore, your Tending is soon over. And you will never lose the love of the women in this room. Even though I haven't been here the whole time, we will always carry the best part of each other with us."

Malkore nodded and smiled at Frigg, then kept looking at Iyasiil. They both felt a tinge of sadness and a little fear that the energy and connection between them would be lost soon.

Frigg continued, "The marriage of the Mother and Father of Asgard is complete. You both have so much work to do, and the people need you both so much. It seems like now is the time for the work to begin. No matter what happens with the two of you as the Tending fades, you both will feel a support with each other that will never end – it will help guide you and strengthen you as we make Asgard what it is meant to be. I love you both so much!"

Without picking her head up off of Malkore's shoulder, Kalla pointed up at Dossa. Dossa said, "Me too."

Kalla said, "Me too."

Malkore kept looking at Iyasiil and quietly said, "I love us, too." Iyasiil wiped tears from her eyes and whispered, "Me too."

Frigg said to them all, "Now, you wonderful, beautiful people, there is still a party going on in the great hall. I suggest we all have a drink as we let our energy come back down to as close to normal as we will ever get again after this, then let's go get some food in the great hall. I, personally, won't be up for much, but it is always good to go to the great hall after a Tending is finished to reintegrate with the people, even if just for a short time."

Iyasiil said, "That sounds good." Then she looked at Malkore, "Lord Malkore, would you like to walk into the great hall after making love with four women?"

He laughed. "That sounds great."

After several more minutes, they all slowly began to stir and move, and they resumed their original positions on the bed, Kalla and Dossa took turns refilling everyone's drinks. They all talked, shared stories, and laughed for a while.

As they started getting up and getting ready to go to the great hall, Malkore reminded everyone, "All our plans for Odin need to stay a secret, no matter what happens. So, everyone be careful." Everyone agreed.

- - - - - - - - - - - - - - - - -

They were all walking to the great hall, Iyasiil had her arms wrapped around Malkore's right arm and her head on his shoulder as they walked. Frigg had been doing the same briefly on his left arm, then said, "Thank you, Lord Malkore. For everything. I will take my leave, now. I should make sure everything is going well in the kitchen." Frigg reached out for Kalla to take her hand, when Kalla did, she pulled Kalla in to take her place walking with Malkore.

Dossa had been walking on the other side of Iyasiil and saw Kalla wrap her arms around Malkore's left arm. She slowed down to get two steps behind them and in a playful, joking tone, Dossa said, "Me too! Me too!" and ran and jumped on Malkore's back, draping her arms over his shoulders to hold herself up. And just for comedic effect, since she couldn't wrap her legs around Malkore with both women on either side, she spread her legs out wide squeezing Kalla's left hip with one foot and her teacher's right hip with her other foot. All three women were laughing, feeling playful. Malkore spread his elbows out wide from his body and Dossa wrapped her legs around his waist. They only had another thirty steps before they got into the great hall, and Iyasiil laughed at what people might think when they saw the four of them walk into the great hall like this.

It was a cooler night and the doors to the great hall had been closed. The two men guarding the door saw them coming and went to open both doors wide, "Lord Malkore, welcome. There is still so much food and drink. All of you enjoy!" After Malkore, Iyasiil, Kalla, and Dossa got into the great hall, the men closed the doors and looked at each other and one of them said, "Did you see that? He must be the greatest warrior if he can make three women smile so big!" They both laughed.

Everyone looked at them as they walked in. Everyone cheered at the new arrivals. Screams came out of the crowd, yelling Malkore's name. Several of the women yelled, "Mama!" and ran over to hug her. Dossa let herself fall down off of Malkore's back.

The four of them made their way into the crowd. A couple of people got up to give Malkore and Iyasiil their seats just beside the head of the long table. They had only been sitting there a few moments when Kalla and Dossa put plates of food ir front of them.

Chapter Nine
Iyasiil Says Goodbye

Late that night, everyone had enjoyed their time in the great hall. Malkore spent a bit of time talking with the men and many of them had lots of questions about the training they would begin in two days. Malkore didn't say much to them about it, he just told them to get a good night's rest the following night.

He had enjoyed being in the great hall with Iyasiil, and as much as he enjoyed the renewed energy among all the people for what they would be learning from him, he selfishly just wanted to spend time with alone with her. The girls sat across from them as they ate, normally the girls would have eaten their meal off in the wings of the great hall. Tonight, Iyasiil told them to sit at the main table, which they had been about to do without even thinking about it. After the experience they had all just had, they were more family, not just students.

At times, it was almost hard to eat and finish a conversation between them, because so many people were coming up to Malkore and Iyasiil. The men wanted to touch base with him and so many of the women had missed her being around her in the last several days. She was surprised to hear so many women express so much love for her and wanted so much of her attention.

At one point, Odin called out to Malkore. He wanted to tell a story to a few men about how Malkore had him chasing a wild boar in the woods when Odin was just in his adolescence. Odin had never told any of those stories to his men. Malkore had the sense he was trying to prepare the men for the training that awaits them.

Odin wanted Malkore to tell a few stories about great battles that Malkore had been in with Odin's father. Malkore told a few stories, always using his big, warrior's voice. Iyasiil could see how much he hid his real self, when he was playing that part of the loud warrior with the men. Then, as she watched him, he would change. He would stop. The men would stop yelling in response to the story. They would lean in closer, so they didn't miss anything. He turned every story into a teaching. When he was teaching, he wasn't hiding. He used that loud, raucous persona to blend with the men, so he could get their ear.

She saw how much work it was to gather up all their attention with an old battle story and craft it perfectly to lure the men into something they needed to learn, then once he was sure that they understood the lesson, he would finish the story with a point that would cause the men to yell in celebration again. Malkore is a master storyteller – He is a master teacher. And now he was getting a chance to teach again.

She loved watching him do his thing, it was wonderful to see. As much as she wanted this for him, there was a part of her that was feeling bad inside.

In her head, she knew it was just the end of the tending, and her heart was feeling all the massive energy of the last few days dissipate.

Her heart, while normally unflappable, was aching a bit. This was a big one. She had a terrible fear that everything she was feeling was going to go away -- that it was all just a part of his healing.

The woman warrior in her knew that this might happen, and she was willing to let it go – let him go, because as they had been saying the last two days, "It's what we do." If it is her place to be what he needed for a short time, to help build Asgard, and especially to help him fulfill his life's mission, then she will be that. She thought to herself, *"It really is kind of stupid to think you really can fall in love like that in just a couple of days."* She could feel the energy draining out of her body.

"Oh, wow! Girls, I can feel my body shutting down. I am going to go back home and get a good night's sleep." She told the two of them.

Dossa said, "OK, Mama. Do you want us to walk you back home?"

"No, sweetie. Thank you. But I do need something from the two of you tomorrow." She told them.

Kalla responded, "Of course, Mama. Or should I say," Ka la looked around to make sure no one could hear her, "Mama of Asgard. What do you need?"

Iyasiil could feel how full and excited Kalla was still feeling, and she could feel her own energy dropping. "Letting go of the energy of the Tending can be really hard sometimes, and this one may be really, really hard for me. So, I need to go spend some time in the forest tomorrow, and I need your support. I would like the two of you to take a walk with me. It will be a good time for teaching and a great way for you two to see how much support we all need after we have been in a place of service and support for several days."

Dossa asked, "That's it? Just go for a walk?" Dossa looked at Kalla, then back at their teacher. "I think we can handle that." Dossa was feeling playful, then she looked at Mama with a serious look on her face, "Mama, I love you so much. Thank you for this."

She smiled at Dossa, "Of course, My Love. So why don't the two of you come get me in the morning and we will go for our walk." She could feel a wave of sadness welling up inside.

Dossa looked at her, "Oh Mama, I can see how tired you are. Go home and get some sleep. Should we bring you breakfast in the morning?"

"No." Then she thought about it. "Yes, I think that would be great. Whatever we don't eat, we will take with us to eat on our walk. Thank you girls, for giving me your very best the last several days."

"Will Lord Malkore be joining us tomorrow?" Kalla asked.

Iyasiil looked like she was about to vomit and was keeping the feelings deep inside, "No, I'm afraid the Tending is over. It will just be us."

The girls looked a little sad and they both looked like they had questions, but they didn't ask.

Malkore had been looking back to where Iyasiil and the girls were sitting periodically while he was talking with the men and telling his stories. He knew it would be good if he planted a few seeds of teachings with the men tonight, and he did. But, he could feel a distance from her that didn't feel good to him. "*So, it begins.*" He thought. "*Oh shit. I am doing it, aren't I?*" He thought. "*I really am trying to make something of the energy of the Tending and it's just going to hurt.*"

He continued talking and telling his teaching stories with the men.

Odin was still in full celebration mode. He kept bringing up stories from his youth and battle stories he had heard from his father where he painted Malkore as a glorious warrior and a masterful teacher. Malkore could tell Odin was trying too hard to make everything seem amazing, but it was a good first step. *"We will see how he does when the training really begins."*

Malkore was in the middle of a story about how he and Borr had created an attack strategy, even practiced it a little with their men to defeat an army three times their size when Odin was just a boy. At the time, no one in Asgard had ever created battle plans ahead of time and certainly never practiced so that everyone knew what they would do. That kind of preparation had not been implemented in centuries, and certainly never under Odin's reign. Since that seed was planted, Malkore delivered the kicker to the story, "If you thought this was a celebration, we had mead and orgies for a month after that one!" The men all yelled.

Malkore looked over to Iyasiil, she was getting up to leave, he wanted to go with her, and he felt a little sense of panic, a sense of desperation inside – like he was losing something. He felt fear. *"Fuck! What the fuck is wrong with me?!"* He rarely ever got scared of anything anymore. *"There it is."* He thought. *"If it's meant to be. It will be."* He tried to be OK, but the pangs of fear and the resulting sadness were still there. *"Well, if I am going to be a fool, a fool I shall be. I will try and see if she is truly gone."*

"Men, I will leave you to it, tonight. Enjoy yourselves." Malkore said to the men he had been talking to.

As he was walking away from that group, one of the women who pretty much lived in the great hall during celebrations screamed out his name, "Malkore! You beautiful man! I am going to kiss you right now!" She walked up and gave Malkore a huge kiss on the lips. Malkore smiled and talked to her for a brief moment.

Iyasiil and the girls heard the woman scream Malkore's name just as Iyasiil was getting up to leave. Iyasiil put her best warm smile on her face and said to the girls, "See, He probably won't be in any kind of shape to walk with us in the morning."

The girls looked confused and a little sad, but they just couldn't believe that so much love could fade so fast. Dossa felt her heart sink, she had felt so much hope that her life could change and now she was feeling like she had been tricked somehow.

When he looked for Iyasiil, she was gone. He saw Kalla and Dossa sitting there at the table and made his way to them. On his way to them, several people tried to get him to stop and talk. He politely excused himself and said he would find them soon.

When he got to the girls, he asked, "Where did she go?" He still felt a little urgency inside and didn't like it, then resolved himself again, "*If I am going to be a fool, then a fool I will be.*"

Kalla told him that she had been tired, that letting go of the Tending had left her drained. Then she asked, "Is it really over?"

Malkore grabbed a chair and pulled it up close to both of them.

"It sucks, doesn't it?" He responded. "Normally when a Tending is over, it can feel like a relief to be back to normal. I was thinking about something. And I would like the two of you to help me, if you are willing. You do not have to help. I am not your teacher. And I think it could be really good."

Kalla looked like she was about to cry. Dossa asked, "What is it, My Lord?"

"I am feeling great. I do not need Tending anymore. But what I want to do is give her a time of nurturing and honoring, like a Tending – to honor her for the woman she is and to honor her for everything she is doing and will do for the people. I am still feeling totally in love and, like we talked about before, trying to not be attached to a relationship with her. While I feel a bit of fear of her going away, the love has not."

Kalla was building up to start crying, "So you don't want it to be over?"

Malkore saw how emotional she was and said, "Of course not! I am trying to only feel my love and gratitude for her at the moment, and disconnecting is really hard."

Dossa said, "So it really is over?"

Malkore took a breath and thought for a moment. Then he looked at each of them and said, "I have two answers to that. One, if it's over, it's over. That would suck, but that's how it is. *And*, she will never stop being important to me and the two of you will never stop being important to me."

Kalla wanted to crawl into his lap, wrap her arms around him, and cry.

"I feel like crying, too, Kalla." He said.

"What's the second answer?" Dossa asked.

His face changed. He had the quiet, confident look of a warrior's determination on his face and said, "It's not going to be over if I have anything to say about it."

Dossa smiled. She felt a little hopeful again. "Lord Malkore, I have a selfish question."

"Ask me anything, My Love." He responded with a warm compassionate tone.

Dossa looked meek and a little scared to ask, "Even if it doesn't work out, can we still talk? I don't want to stop learning from you too."

Malkore smiled, "Of course, Sweet Dossa. I will always be there for both of you, until the end of time. That will never change. It's like Frigg said, "We will always carry the best part of each other with us.""

Kalla was still fighting back tears.

Malkore said, "Kalla, if you are OK with it, come sit here." He sat up straight and patted his right thigh. She nodded and got up to sit on his lap. She wrapped her arms around him and laid her head on his shoulder. "I love you, sweet girl. I love you and I am so thankful for you." He had his arm wrapped around her. He started to wrap both his arms around her, but Dossa chimed in "Me too. Me too." Dossa got up and sat on his other leg. Kalla let out a little laugh. Dossa put one arm around Kalla's arm and her hand on Kalla's head. She looked Malkore in the eye, put her other hand on his heart, and softly said, "Thank you." Then she kissed him on the forehead, again.

Malkore asked, "How you doing, Kalla?"

Kalla didn't even pick up her head, but asked him, "Lord Malkore, have you ever had your ass kicked by a woman not even a hundredth your age?"

Malkore chuckled, not knowing what she was talking about, "No. I don't recall that ever happening before."

Kalla said, "Well, that's what's going to happen if you go away."

Malkore kissed her on top of the head and said, "I can live with that deal. I'm right here, sweet girl. I'm right here."

Dossa kissed him on the forehead again, and asked, "What do you need from us to support Mama?"

"I want to make it a full day, so it will have to be tomorrow, I am going to be busy at high sun every day for a couple of days after that."

Kalla told him that they were supposed to bring breakfast to their teacher, then go for a walk in the forest tomorrow. She said that Mama had been really sad before she left the great hall and was having a hard time with the Tending being over.

"OK. I would never tell anyone to defy their teacher, but how about you two go with me on this. I would like to make breakfast for her, so don't bother coming in until you bring lunch. She is such an amazing woman and if nothing else, I want to honor her for how amazing she is. So, I am going to make a day where it is all about her and what she needs and what she wants."

Kalla started crying harder. "I love you so much!"

Dossa kissed him on the forehead again and said, "Me too."

"Good? It's a plan?" Both girls nodded. "Then maybe at some point, you two can help give her the same kind of massage that you helped give me tonight. How does that sound?"

"That sounds great." Dossa said.

"Now, I am going to go snuggle in her bed, unless she has already disconnected and turns me away."

"We will walk you over there." Dossa said.

They got up to go to Iyasiil's chamber, Dossa filled a pitcher of mead, and the three of them left.

When they got to her door, Kalla knocked on the door softly, then opened it. Her teacher was not there.

Dossa asked, "Didn't she say she was coming back here?"

Malkore said, "Nothing to worry about. You two head on home and have a good night. I'll just wait outside for her."

Kalla walked outside to look around. She walked back in and whispered, "Lord Malkore. Come with me." She took his hand and walked out the door about ten or twelve paces, then turned around to look back at the door, then pointed at the roof.

He smiled.

- - - - - - - - - - - - - - - - - - - -

After Iyasiil had returned from the great hall, she had climbed up on the roof of her chamber and was looking at the stars.

She had tears in her eyes. The tending had been the most powerful time of growth she had ever witnessed. The transformation and unfolding of him into his true self had been amazing. Malkore didn't need to heal when he got home, he just needed to give himself permission to be the man he really is. She had been honored to be a part of that.

Iyasiil sat on the ridge of her roof, wrapped in Malkore's big bear skin robe. The Tending was over, but she wasn't quite ready to give him back his robe, yet. It would always take a day or so to fully disconnect after a powerful Tending, but this might be harder. Sometimes, the mothering urge to look after someone would linger for a couple of days. Sometimes, when someone came back from battle feeling totally broken, bloodsick, and angry, she felt like she needed to go off in the woods by herself for a couple of days and be alone.

This time, she expected she would just lean on Kalla and Dossa for a few days and get them to spend time with her. This one was going to hurt. She knew enough to know she would need the girls Tending to her a bit, just as she had been teaching them to Tend to others.

Even though Malkore's first day of training the men didn't start until the day after tomorrow, Iyasiil knew the Tending was over, just as Frigg had said. She was having a hard time with it at the moment.

She thought he would remain in Tending at least until after that first day of training the men. She thought it would be good, in case he needed any extra support in the transition. She knew he wouldn't need any support at all, and she wanted to make sure it went well. In her heart, she knew it would go well and he wouldn't really need her support. But she didn't want it to be over, she didn't want to pull away.

"Oh, look at me." She said to the stars, "I am a mess." She didn't want it to end.

She heard some people walking on the road behind her, she didn't care who it was. She felt alone and so sad.

Then she heard some clunking behind her. Then she heard his voice, "Thank you, girls."

"Shit! He found me." She thought. *"I am up here feeling sorry for myself and he's just going to go on as if it doesn't matter."* She felt herself being guarded.

"Has anyone seen the Mother of Asgard?" She heard him ask.

She laughed, his voice was comforting, but she didn't want to be comforted right then.

She turned her head, "Lord Malkore. How are you feeling?"

He sat down on her left side a couple of feet away. He wanted to sit right behind her and wrap his arms around her, but he was worried that she was pulling away and wouldn't want him to be that close. So out of respect for what she may be feeling he didn't get what might feel like "too close." He responded, "No. That's not what we are talking about, right now. How are *you*, My Love?" He handed her a horn of mead.

She took the horn of mead form him and poured half of it into her cup, then handed it back to him. "Thank you." She wiped tears from her face, then shook her head.

"Hey, it's still me. What's going on?" He asked.

"I'm a mess." She said.

"I see that. What has you so messy, Love?" He knew what it was, he just didn't know if she wanted to talk about it.

She looked away and up at the stars. She was trying not to cry, "Oh, Lord Malkore. I am sorry I took your robe; I just didn't want to give it up, yet." She burst into tears. She started crying harder and harder. He scooted over to be closer to her. When he raised his arm to put it around her, she collapsed on his lap.

"The robe is yours if you want it. I love seeing you wear t. What I don't like is feeling you so far away and I don't like being unsure whether or not you would be OK with me holding you."

She wrapped both of her arms around his thighs and almost screamed, burying her face in his knee. "It's the only place I want to be."

"Then, tell me. What is going on? Why are you so upset? No. wait. Let me guess. Better yet, let me say this: I am not finished with you, just because my Tending is over. Even if *we are over*, it's going to take me a little while to stop wanting to be with you and hold you every second. If you need me to go away, I will. Otherwise, I am not going to stop. I don't want to stop."

She turned her head towards him and rested her ear on his thigh, "OK."

He went on, "I may be a fool to think this will go on. If that's the case, then I am going to be a fool – and I am OK with that. I have been a fool a thousand times over. I'm not scared of being a fool for such an amazing woman. But I know who I am, and I know how peaceful my heart feels when I am with you."

"Yeah, there's that. That part is pretty hard to ignore." She said.

"So, I want to propose something to you. OK?"

"What is it?" She asked.

"Don't take care of me. Only take care of you, from now until the end of time, just as you normally do. If you want time away from me, say so and I will stay away. If you want to spend time with me, say so and I will get as close as we both want to get. And I will do the same. We will just see what happens. How does that sound?"

She squeezed his thighs in a hug, "That sounds good."

"Good." He said.

"Then you're OK if I have trouble letting go of the Tending and keep wanting to be with you for a while?" She asked.

"It's what we do." He responded.

She laughed. The way he said it meant almost the opposite of how they had used that phrase before. They had always used it to describe the actions they took when they were very emotionally clear. He had just used it to say that he, too wanted to spend time with her, even if it was just the feelings lingering from the Tending.

"Then you're a mess, too." She said.

"Yeah, but I will be *your* mess for at least a few more days. *If* you will have me." He said.

"Yes, My Lord. I will have you." She sat up and wrapped her arms around his arm, then scooted as close to him as she could. "Will you stay here tonight? Or do you want to go home and sleep in your own bed?"

"Well," he started speaking in a brighter tone that got more and more sarcastic as he went on, "a good warrior will always assess a situation and then take right, decisive action. Right?" She nodded. "So let me assess this situation. There is a woman, with whom I am completely enamored, who is the only woman I have met in the last Forty-Five or Forty-Six Hundred years, since I was just a wee child, that I feel like is my equal, who I also think is the most beautiful woman I have ever seen in my life — I mean, she really is *my kind* of beautiful. When I am with her, I feel a peace inside that I have only felt in connection with nature and with the deepest parts of myself. When I interact with her, there is a fluidity, like a tide that ebbs and flows between us . . . It's quite remarkable. But apparently, she does this thing that is really annoying. I don't know what I am going to do about it. You see, when she is feeling emotionally run down and she needs nurturing, she will get some crazy thought in her head that is really scary. She will tell herself the scary story in her mind and she just fucking runs with it . . ." She laughed. "Now I would prefer if she would come sit in my lap and say, "Lord Malkore, I need you to hold me. I just got scared. I am tired and worn down and I had a few stupid ideas run through my head that told me I should doubt how much you love me. I am sorry for not being perfect, but I need to feel you loving me until I let the stupid ideas go."

Iyasiil got up and sat on his lap, wrapping him up in a hug. "So, you really want to do this? Even if it's just going to face in a couple of days?"

Malkore in a sarcastic, reprimanding tone said, "Excuse me, young lady. I wasn't finished."

Equally sarcastic, she said, "Oh. Forgive me, My Lord. Please finish."

He went on with even more sarcasm in his voice, "I was assessing the situation, as any good warrior would do, right?"

"Yes, My Lord."

"Yeah, did I say the part about there being this woman with whom I am totally enthralled?"

"Yes, My Lord. I believe you said that part." She was starting to giggle.

"OK. Did I mention the part about her heart and presence and that whole thing about never finding an equal in the last Forty-Five centuries?" He asked with mock earnestness.

"Yes, I believe you did, My Lord."

"OK. Now I think I was responding to her question about whether or not I want to stay with her tonight or be at home. Is that right?" He was really having fun being playful with her.

"Yes, My Lord, Malkore. The question was about if you wanted to stay with her tonight, or if you would be more comfortable at home." She said.

"OK. Thank you." Then with a very rich genuine tone, "I think I want to be home tonight."

"OK, My Lord." She said, hiding her disappointment.

"Excuse me. I wasn't finished." Again, he looked at her with mock sternness. "I was saying that I want to be home tonight. And nothing," he began to speak with animation, "has *ever*, in *all* my life, in all of my *5000 years*, felt more like home to my heart, than you." He dropped the sarcasm and just let his words settle into her as he looked into her eyes, reflecting the bright moon light.

Her whole body relaxed. "Oh, Lord Malkore, I am going to kick your ass."

He laughed. "I love you so much, for as long as it lasts . . ." His voice trailed off, "For as long as it lasts."

"I am tired, will you come snuggle with me in my bed, now?" She asked him.

"It's the only place I want to be, My Love." He said, repeating her words from earlier.

They climbed down off the roof and went into her chamber. She actually felt a little nervous to take off her dress in front of him. Without the energy of the Tending, she felt like this was the first time she was getting naked with him. What a strange mix of feelings . . .

He came over and hugged her and looked at her with a warm, compassionate look on his face. He didn't say anything, but she could feel him looking deep within her soul. Just the fact that he looked so deep into her was enough to fall in love with him, but she saw such a kind and gentle heart in him, and so much wisdom. That's just more of why she was falling in love. She took a breath and let herself feel that. She didn't try to feel it really big or intense, she just let herself feel it however it was happening. As she looked at him, she felt like her dress had fallen off of her and she felt playful. "Take your clothes off, big guy. It's time for bed."

He smiled. He could feel her again. "Yes, My Love."

They laid down and snuggled into each other. She let out a long sigh, "This is where I want to be."

"Let yourself sleep, My Love. I am right here." And within minutes, they were both sound asleep.

Chapter Ten
Payback is Hell . . .

They had woken up and rolled towards each other. Their hands met somewhere in the middle, and they held each other's hand as they made eye contact, and both enjoyed the moment. "I have plans for you today, My Love." He said.

"You better make it quick. I am taking the girls for a walk, this morning."

"Oooohhh. No. Sorry." He said with a sarcastic tone. "Last night, I let them know that your teachings would have to wait until tomorrow. You'll only see them when they bring us our midday meal."

Acting offended, she playfully said, "You get to spend time with the greatest woman you have ever known and now you go sneaking around trying to control her and change her *sacred* teachings without asking her?!"

"No, No, No, No, No. No teaching today. No watching out for the people today, not the soon-to-be-queen, not the girls, not anyone." She recognized her own words from their first morning together being used against her. It was deliciously fun!

He was smiling so big, and he was wrapping her in loving sarcasm, "You will not teach or serve anyone today, not even me, My Love. Today is all about you - Only what you want, only what YOU need. You have done so much for this entire kingdom, already. And you have served and raised up kingdoms and empires before this one and you have served them more than they ever even knew. You will continue to serve again, but not today."

He continued in an animated way with his eyebrows raised as if he was enlightening her from a lofty place, reveling in his victory of using her own words to win their playful banter. "You have served the people more than they have even let themselves realize. Because you are the greatest kind of woman, you make the people great in every way. You carry yourself in such a way that the people learn to live their own heart's love in the greatest way."

Then he got on top of her, straddling her. He was holding her arms above her head, she was pinned down, not trying to break free. She was smiling and whispered so softly it couldn't be heard, "I love you."

Ignoring her, as if he was still "laying down the law" to her, he went on, "So, you are taking the entire day to only take care of you. You and I are going to stay right here, we are going to eat some delicious food, as soon as I prepare it, and we are going to do nothing today except what feeds your soul. And if you try to get up and go do anything for anyone else, I will KICK YOUR ASS so hard . . . Are we clear about this, My Love?!"

She had tears rolling down her face. She felt loved in a way she had not ever felt loved before. She had never had anyone offer to take care of her with the same depth and breadth of presence with which she Tended to others. No one knew how, because they hadn't touched their own hearts deeply enough, not until this man.

Just then, the door opened. It was Kalla and Dossa with their arms full of food. They hadn't been asked to bring breakfast, but they knew what a powerful day this was and wanted to support Malkore in supporting their teacher.

She made a sarcastic, scared pleading voice and said, "Thank the blessings you are here, girls. This man is trying to take me captive and hold me here, I need your help! Help!!! Please Help Me!"

The girls were laughing, Malkore was smiling.

Iyasiil said to Malkore, "My girls are here to rescue me. You don't even have your sword, old man. You are about to lose your fucking head."

The girls had put down the food. Dossa tended the fire and built it up strong. Kalla brought over two cups of morning tea. Malkore sat up, still straddling her, not pinning her arms down anymore. He had barely covered his nakedness with the edge of a blanket, but his bare chest, muscular back, and most of his ass were on full display. She was completely naked, only her hips and legs were covered by Malkore and the blanket.

Kalla leaned over put her hand over her teacher's heart, kissed her teacher on the forehead, then kissed her lovingly on the lips, and said, "That really sucks for you, Mama. I hate that you've been taken captive, but I am afraid we have already made other plans for today."

Malkore roared with laughter, reveling in another victory.

Kalla looked her teacher in the eye, she had such a big smile on her face.

Kalla turned her attention to Malkore, "My Lord, thank you for what you are doing today. Thank you for loving this great woman so well." She reached out and took his face in her hands and kissed him on the cheek, he thought she was going to kiss his lips. She wanted to kiss him on the lips, then she got scared and stopped herself. She did use a flirty tone to say, "Now, My Lord, if you're *not* still making love with her when we return with your midday meal, then you are truly not worthy, and I *will* be forced to take your head." She kissed him on the cheek again, bowed her head with a smile, and the two girls left.

He grabbed Iyasiil's hands and pinned her to the bed again. "You're creating monsters, My Love. It's amazing to see such a transformation in them, so quickly."

"I told you, it all shifted after they started seeing us together. That was one of the early clues." She said.

He got off of her and started to lay down next to her, instead he got up. He held his hand out to help her raise up, then grabbed the bolster to put behind her back. "I was about to lay down and ask you to tell me more, because I am curious to hear more. But you are *not* working today, so I will get you food and you can tell me tomorrow."

She watched him walk across the room naked, *"Fuck! Is he really here? This feels so easy."*

- - - - - - - - - - - - - - - - - -

As the girls were walking away from their teacher's chamber. Dossa said, "I can't believe you said that! What did his face look like when you said it?"

Kalla said, "He looked excited. He was smiling like he smiles at her."

"I thought you were about to kiss him right on the lips." Dossa said.

"I did too, but I got scared. I wanted to." Kalla said with a giggle.

"They are so sexy! If you had kissed him, I would have just gotten naked and fucked all three of you, right then!" Dossa said.

Kalla laughed, "I know! I want to fuck both of them so bad! Could you feel what they felt like? It seems like everything is OK, like they are back to normal . . . Well, normal for them. It's like they are made of sex and love and honor and wisdom! It's all those things and I want to fuck every one of those parts of both of them."

They kept talking until they got back to the kitchen. Once they were in the kitchen, not a word was said - they honored their teacher's privacy. No one needed to know what Malkore and their teacher were up to today.

- - - - - - - - - - - - - - - - - - - -

After they finished their morning meal, Malkore had gotten them both a second cup of tea. She stayed in bed, he got up, put on his robe, and took their plates to the table.

She watched him walk around her chamber. She had never felt such a masculine presence. This man wore a robe made from the hide of a bear he had killed with nothing but a knife - he could walk away from battling a hundred men without a scratch, and he has such a tenderness about him – the greatest warrior has the greatest compassion and an inner peace in him that she had never seen in anyone before. Her heart sang in the space this man made with his presence.

As he walked back to the bed, he asked, "Are you ready?"

He got the oil, and he removed his robe. She was smiling so big and was fighting back more tears. She felt like she couldn't speak for a moment. All of her fear from the night before was gone. She felt so happy to be right there in that moment, she only nodded to him.

Inside, she felt a kind of expansive freedom. It was freedom mixed in with the kind of gratitude she had only ever felt for the blessed path she walked in her own life, never having met an equal with whom she could fully share all of who she was.

She was starting to not feel so alone in the deepest part of herself. She whispered the words, "Thank you, My Lord."

After a few moments, he felt her go away a little. "I hope the girls aren't disappointed. They had been excited about what we had planned for today."

He rolled over on top of her straddling her and holding her hands to the bed, pinning her down again. "You didn't hear me." He said with a mock, stern voice. "I said, NO. NO. NO. NO. NO. You will NOT be taking care of anyone today, not even your students, not even me. Are we clear?!"

He meant to keep acting rough and playing dominant with her a little longer, but as he looked down on her face and saw her smiling at him, he was startled by the love he was starting to feel for her. He almost gasped with that feeling welling up inside. He looked into her eyes. Then he looked a little deeper into her eyes.

With a gentle, heartful tone he said, "To answer your question: Obviously not! Did you see them just now?! After you left the great hall last night, I told them I was planning a day where you would be tended to like they had seen you tend to me. I told them that it would be starting with me cooking you breakfast, then massaging you for as long as you want. They were so excited for you. They are happy for us, in whatever this thing is that is brewing here in this room. They love you so much."

"They love you, too, Lord Malkore." She said.

Then he started laughing uncontrollably and halfway collapsed on her but was still pinning her arms to the bed.

"What is it? Tell me."

He was laughing so hard that she began laughing too. He said, "It was adorable and cute and like watching a newborn horse figure out how to use its legs." Then he laughed again. "Except she did it! She did great! No wobbling."

"What are you talking about? What did she do? Who? Kalla?"

He was laughing and nodding, "Yes, it was Kalla. Oh, My Goddess! I love that girl! She looks up to you so much and loves you so much and she is in such a hurry to learn everything she can from you. So here is what she did: They were sad and scared for a minute that this thing between us was over, then after I talked them down from that, Kalla shifted her own energy. She started using *your* medicine woman voice and she said, "There is a deep-hearted love that is growing between the two of you. None of us here have ever seen a connection so deep, a connection that goes all the way to the depth of your souls. You are wrapped in golden light when you walk together." It was beautiful. It was fucking beautiful!"

She was laughing and feeling grateful that one of her star students was stepping up so much. She was enjoying his enjoyment of Kalla's attempt at impersonating her style of teaching. "I love those girls. And there are more coming."

"I see that, too. There are a lot more coming. You're going to be busy, My Love." He said to her.

"This thing between us feels big. Thank you. But you made a mistake, My Lord."

"What mistake did I make?" He asked.

"I'll tell you if you kiss me." She said smiling.

As he leaned down to kiss her, he loosened his grip on her hands just enough. She quickly pulled his hand down towards his knee, where she pushed his knee down with a force that he wasn't expecting. With his weight going forward to kiss her, she was able to lift and twist her hips, rolling his weight towards the other side of the bed. In an instant, she had moved so quickly, so forcefully, and so gracefully that before he knew it, she had gotten on top of him, pinning his shoulders down.

He didn't resist. *"She moves like panther!"* He thought.

"What mistake did I make?" He asked.

"You mean beside dropping your guard and being toppled by a frail, little woman?" She asked with a hint of gloating in her voice.

"Yes, besides that." He was smiling. He rarely felt caught off guard.

"You haven't kissed me yet, My Lord. I can't tell you until you kiss me." She said.

He pulled her close to him and kissed her. She let her weight go heavy on him as they both took a breath.

"Thank you, My Love." Referring to her as "My Love" was starting to take on a different meaning. He'd had a dream of something he had never seen. Sometimes he wondered if this dream could be real. This thing with her felt real so far.

While she was resting all her weight on top of him, he tried to muscle her back over to the other side of the bed. She reacted so quickly, deflecting his arm that tried to push her. As he was rolling, she slid sideways, seeming to hover over him until he was lying face down on the bed with her still on top of him. She got him again.

He thought, *"This woman has some serious secrets to teach. Where did she learn that?"*

She leaned down to whisper in his ear. In a mocking tone, she said, "Your mistakes keep piling up this morning, My Lord. What I've been trying to tell you is that you made a mistake in thinking you were going to cook me breakfast to start the day." She rolled him back over onto his back and got back on top of him. "You couldn't cook me breakfast because I've already taught my students too well."

He didn't want to move. She felt so good lying on top of him. "Yes, indeed, My Love. Now, will you lay down? I need to talk to your body. There is a conversation I want to have with your skin and your heart."

She smiled and slowly slid off of him and lay on her stomach. He grabbed the oil and began to massage her calf muscles. After spending ten minutes on each calf, he moved down to her feet for another ten minutes or so on each foot. Next, he was massaging the back of her knees, then began making strokes up the back of her thighs.

She wondered if he was about to go straight to her butt and start having sex, which she would have loved. But when other men had done that with her, years and years ago, it had been disappointing — it felt rushed, and something was lost in the experience. It wasn't that she didn't like sex, she loves it! The disappointment was because her energy hadn't been stoked up as high as it could have been in those moments. The men just didn't know what was possible. She wondered if he would be in a hurry. He wasn't.

Malkore understood the first and necessary part of deep intimacy was the unlocking of the body and the mind, to release any daily stresses or any resistance that hides in the tissues of the body and the far recesses of the mind. In his mind, there had been so much abuse and dishonor of the feminine on a collective level. Everyone, but especially women, need to be given the space to unfurl into trust, otherwise their experience cannot rise above thoughts and fears to the place where their spirit dances free.

After working the back of her thighs for a while, he moved up and straddled her upper thighs. He asked if she was comfortable. He did rub the oil into the skin on her butt, and as he moved, she could feel his cock dangling on her thighs, but he wasn't getting turned on. He started to make firm strokes into the muscles of her ass. She didn't even realize that she had some tightness and tension that needed massaging. Again, she thought, *"His cock isn't even getting hard."* She wasn't used to that.

He began massaging her lower back. He started at her sacrum and slowly worked his way up. Forty minutes later, he had worked his way up to her neck, including reaching deep into her sides in slow, loving strokes of his hands. She could feel the strength in his hands, and she could feel the gentle nurturing-ness of his heart.

He laid his chest down on her back and he imagined his heart was reaching in through her back to hold her heart. She felt it. He whole body shuddered as she gasped and then took in a long breath. She had never felt a man who could penetrate her with his heart. She'd only been with him a couple of days, but she had been amazed by him in so many ways, she shou dn't be surprised. She felt so seen and so loved and so honored by him when they were together. She always felt happy and content in her life, and these last three days she had felt a little extra happy, almost giddy at times.

He traced the back of her ear with the tip of his nose and it both melted her heart and sent tingles through her whole body. She could feel his cock laying on her ass, it felt good. She hac the thought, *"Is this where the massage ends?"*

"Roll over, My Love." He whispered.

She rolled over onto her back. He settled in straddling her thighs. He leaned down and brushed her chin with his nose and check, then put his forehead right over her heart and breathed a prayer of gratitude. He was giving thanks that this woman existed, honoring her for all that she is. He was saying a selfish prayer of gratitude that he was getting to be blessed by this woman's presence today.

"By the Love of All, I want this man." She thought. She wanted to say, "I am yours."

He sat up and looked into her eyes. Her eyes were dancing with excitement. He looked at her with a smile and almost with a laugh said, "I am so fucking *YOURS*."

She responded, "Please. Yes." Then she realized he had read her mind again.

Instead of getting between her legs and sliding inside of her, he put one hand on her heart. She felt like he was reaching all the way into her chest. She felt like the love of the universe was being pushed into her, filling her up. She couldn't tell if she was about to take off on a soul-journey through the stars or if she were just going to explode in ecstasy. With one hand still on her heart, he put his other hand on her lower stomach, right over her womb, *"pretty close to exploding in ecstasy,"* she thought.

"Breathe, Love." He said softly.

He reached for more oil. He began making long strokes with his hands from the bottom of her stomach and outsides of her hips, over her heart, and up to the base of her neck, then out to her shoulders. She was startled with how excited she got when he stroked up at the very top of her chest. He touched her collarbones, and her breasts got hungry to be touched.

He went up the sides of her ribs and squeezed her shoulders on the front and back. With every slow stroke of his hands, he kept breathing and feeling how her body felt to his hands.

"Where did you learn this, My Lord?" She asked.

Without pulling his focus from her skin, her body, and her energy, he said, "The same place I imagined you did, I dreamt it. It's been a series of lessons through the years, dreams and visions while asleep and awake."

"Yes, same here. We have to teach the people how to do all of this." She said.

Without missing a beat, he started a new massage stroke up her right side and cupped her right breast with his left hand. He was pushing the mass of her breast up into the air and slapped it with his right hand.

She giggled deliciously; she knew exactly why she had just gotten slapped in the tit.

Teasing her again, he said, "No. No. No. No. No. No teaching. No thinking about teaching. I applaud your dedication to serving the people, and right now, it's time you only focus on you." His voice softened, now speaking with no sarcasm, "It's time to discover what else is possible. You're safe here, I have you."

"Yes, My Lord. Discovery and dreaming only, understood." She said, recognizing her own limitation in that moment. She closed her eyes, took a deep breath, and rested back into her own senses, feeling her body from the inside.

He put his hands on the outside of her hips, sliding them to her lower abdomen, right on her pubic bone, then up her stomach, between her breasts and made wide circles around her breasts. She half gasped, half inhaled, and her whole body twitched. It felt like a soft bolt of lightning shuddered her entire body.

For her, this felt like a playful dance of seduction and surrender – a game where she was begging his fingers seek out the points within her that want to release at his touch; a game where her trust builds as he is trying to find the spark that keeps flying away from his touch with giggles of joy, until she is happily caught.

He put one hand on her heart and the other on her solar plexus, he leaned down and touched the back of his hand that was over her heart with his forehead. Then he slid his hand away and rested his forehead and nose on her heart. She wanted to reach up and pull his head down into her chest and hold him in her heart.

He couldn't even tell himself if he was saying a prayer, or honoring her, or feeling her spirit – it felt like all those things. He felt like there was no ripple between them energetically, emotionally.

He took in a deep breath to feel more and be even more present with her. He could feel her feeling it.

With his forehead over her heart, she slid his hands up her sides with his thumbs moving up the sides of her stomach. His fingers were firmly sliding up her ribs. His hands stopped at the base of her breasts, supporting her breasts. He was breathing her in.

He spent fifteen minutes massaging all around her breast, not touching her nipples, just slowly building up and teasing up her energy. He kept building up her energy until the slightest touch of her nipple made her entire body shudder. He spent about ten minutes doing the same with her other breast before returning his lips and nose to that energy center between her breasts.

Then he pulled his chin down and pressed his nose and forehead into that spot between her breasts, while pushing both breasts against the side of his face. Then he tilted his head up again and his lips and tongue were moving slowly against her skin. His lips and tongue were making love to that space between her breasts, loving her heart.

She felt intoxicated. Every cell in her body was softly, confidently screaming "*yes.*" She moaned and felt her yoni twitch as her chest was heaving with her breath and her hips were curling up, reaching for his cock. She felt like her heart and soul were being fed and feeding him at the same time. She could feel the energy of the Divine Mother flowing through her.

His left hand wrapped around her breast as he slid the side of his face over onto her left breast. She could feel his rough beard lightly grazing her soft breast followed by his soft tongue and lips all around her nipple. It felt like lightning through her body.

He gently loved on her breasts for a while, holding her ribs in his hands from the sides, squeezing her sides with the inside of his forearms. She was loving it, feeling both like she couldn't take it anymore and like she didn't want it to end, wanting more and more. She had already been more excited than she had ever been with anyone.

He scooted backwards to where he was sitting on her shins and began circling her knees with his thumbs. Then making deep and still gentle slow strokes up her thighs with his fingers spread out wide. When his fingertips reached the crease between her thighs and body, they swept out to the outside her hips and up her sides. Then the same thing again and again.

As he was about to touch her again, she pulled her legs up and put her feet on the outside of his hips. She pulled his weight down to her with her heels in his back and had her hands on his shoulders. "Please . . . Now."

He barely had to move his hips to slide his cock inside her. It felt like she was wetter and more open than anything he had ever felt, even though he knew they could have built up her energy even higher.

As he slowly slid his cock inside her, her yoni almost pulled him in. He kept looking into her eyes. They both stopped and felt each other, they just felt what that moment felt like. There was nothing to say. Tears rolled down her face.

As he lowered his face down to hers, he grazed her cheek with his cheek and nose, resting his nose on the back of her ear.

She could hear and feel his breath and he began to slowly and powerfully slide his cock in and out of her. She was speaking a language he had only heard in the deepest spiritual states, a prayer of thanks, a prayer of praise.

He felt like his heart was growing so big, it felt like it was growing bigger than his chest. He felt like his cock was growing bigger than ever. As he was breathing a low, guttural growl started coming out of him. He felt like his whole body was being drawn into her heart.

She felt like her whole body was being wrapped in his heart. Whenever she focused on her heart melding with his, she was distracted by how good every little bit of movement of his cock felt. She felt like every slow, powerful thrust of his cock was going to make her shatter into pieces and whenever she focused on how good he felt, she felt how delicious his heart was.

"Thank you, My Lord." She wasn't sure if she'd said it out loud, but he heard it. He slammed his cock inside her and held it deep inside her, growling.

"My Love, it's what we do." He said. She started giggling, then giggling harder. He started laughing, she started laughing harder. She pulled him down onto her even harder and pushed his hips deeper into her hips with her calves. She was holding on so tight. Her heart was exploding with joy, with gratitude for this moment, with such a full heart that she wasn't sure she could ever please him as much.

In a whisper into her ear, he said, "This is more than I have ever felt before, too. My Love."

"Shit! He really can hear my thoughts!" She jerked her head to look at him.

He smiled. "It's what we do, My Love." He said as he slid his cock deep inside her again and again.

She was squeal/screaming and pulling his body into her with every thrust, then she burst into tears as her yoni was throbbing. Her body was shaking, and she was crying, wrapping him tighter and tighter with her arms, wrapping him tightly with her legs, she held on like she didn't ever want to let him go.

He pushed his heart into her heart. She felt it. He kept holding her and kept feeling so much love. He pushed one hand underneath her to hold the back of her heart. The other hand reached up and cradled her head from behind, his massive hands seemed to hold her entire head as he gently pushed her head into the side of his face, just another way to hold her.

She kept crying. The crying turned to wailing. The wailing turned to a kind of tortured sounding cry. She managed to say "Yes" to let him know all was good and held him even tighter. She was crying and wailing to release the emptiness of every moment that she ever had where she felt alone or like no one was there who could feel *all* of her and touch her in the deepest ways. She let out a half whine, half scream and pulled him even closer. "Yes." He pulled her closer, too.

He kept plunging both his heart and his cock as deep inside her as he could. He kept wanting to tell her how amazing she is and found himself unable to make any sound but that growl he kept hearing coming from deep inside.

He felt like crying. He kept hearing the voice inside say, *"Thank you. Thank you. Thank you."*

Her whole body was shaking, and she was crying and screaming in both pleasure and pain. "Yes." She said again.

Her body seized. She stopped breathing, but the crying didn't stop. He kept holding her while feeling how good it felt to be here with her. He only made micro movements with his hips, just enough to keep energy flowing, not enough to distract her from what she was feeling in that moment.

He kept being amazed at how thrilling it is to feel a real woman. *"You are delicious in every way."* He thought.

Then she exploded in a gasping scream and pulled him into her harder. She kept shaking. He stayed there, cock deep inside her, supporting his own weight on his knees and forearms. He nuzzled his face into the side and base of her neck, and he kept hearing that growl come from deep inside.

He kept feeling her, as if they were still making love, because they were – this part is just as important and powerful as any other part of making love.

He kept breathing and feeling his love and gratitude. He just kept holding her.

It wasn't until her breathing had returned to normal that he rolled off her and sat up at the head of the bed while scooping her up and putting her sideways on his lap. She melted into him.

She was like a raging storm inside, raining the power and passion of the world on him. He was a mix of feelings – he wanted to hold her forever, he felt "awe" at how immense her heart is, and he didn't ever want to stop making love with her.

As she settled, she thanked him, "Thank you. I didn't know that was going to happen. It's not often that I get to feel *just* my own energy when I am around anyone else."

He said, with caring in his voice, "I know. That's why being with you feels so good." She nodded. "You give so much to the people, and you give so selflessly. We all need to get filled back up and supported. Being of service feeds us in so many ways, but it can't touch all the places that need to be touched. And none of that has anything to do with me loving you. Loving you feels like the most selfish thing I could do. Making love with you is the ultimate selfish act."

"I like you touching all those deep places inside. Please keep being selfish with me." She paused and took a breath. "You know for a tough guy, you sure are sweet and wise." She nuzzled her face into his shoulder.

"It's what we do." He said, unable to contain his laughter. It had become their saying.

She laughed, too. She melted a little more and her whole body started shaking as she was laughing. The laughing turned to sobbing a little more.

"If I could pull your entire body into my heart and hold you like that, I would." He said.

"That's what this feels like. It's like being held in your heart. If I didn't need to get up to get something to drink and go to the bathroom, I'd stay here all day." She said.

He reached over to the shelf beside the bed and grabbed a cup of tea, "The drink I can help with."

She sat on his lap nursing the cup of tea for at least Twenty minutes, "I don't know if there any one specific thing I was crying about, and I know it doesn't matter." She drained the cup of tea and handed it back to him. "Is there any more food sitting around."

She slid off him, he got up and walked over to the table across the room. Watching him walk across the room naked was magical. He came back with food, and they sat and ate in silence for quite a while then talked a while, too.

She felt fresh. She felt like how the air is clean after a big storm, like she had been wrung out and filled back up with pure light.

"Today is still my day, right?" She asked.

He nodded and asked, "What would you like? How can I support you now, My Love?"

"Let's go for a walk in the afternoon." She said.

"Whatever you want, My Love." He said smiling.

"Good. I'd like that." She closed her eyes with a smile. Sipping the last of her tea, she asked, "OK, you big burly man, what do you have in store for me now?"

He was leaning against the wall at the head of the bed, he pointed to a spot on the bed a foot in front of him, "Put your butt right here, facing me, and lay on your back."

"Yes, My Lord." She started to move towards him, "But first." She climbed up on him, straddling him, and wrapped her arms around him and laid her head in the side of his neck.

He put his hands on her hips and slid his hands up her back. *"I love this woman!"* He thought.

She pressed her heart and her breasts into him and said, "I love this. I am so thankful." She wiggled her whole body on him.

He pulled her a little farther into him and said, "It's what we do."

Several minutes later, he slid his right hand between his chest and hers, putting his hand on her heart, leaning his forehead into hers. He put his other hand around the side of her neck then around the back of her head. Holding her head firmly, he pulled her in and kissed her passionately. Then again. And again.

"Now, My Love." With his hand still over her heart, he pushed her back onto the bed he said, "I said to lay down." He reached for the oil and started massaging her from the knees to her hips.

"More? Oh, Shit." She said.

"My Love." He said with mock sternness, again, repeating her words back to her. "You would never do less for me, would you?" He responded.

"No, My Lord. I wouldn't. It's just that this is already better than anything I have ever known. I don't need more." She relented and took a breath, relaxing her body.

With more sarcastic forcefulness, he said, "My Love. During the time of your Tending, you will have to learn to accept that I am far, far wiser than you. Therefore, I have a much better sense of what your body needs." She was giggling hearing her own words used against her again. "You know, for such a wise and powerful woman, you sure are stubborn sometimes. Do you know that?" She just smiled and laughed.

In a subservient tone, she said, "Yes, My Lord. I will try to remember." Then, dropping the sarcasm, she said, "You know, if any other man even jokingly said he knows what my body needs, I would laugh at him. How could anyone know my body better than me . . . it's not possible. But you . . . I can actually feel that you are feeling me. I've never felt anyone so in tune with my whole body and heart."

"It's what we do, My Love." His voice was soft, with a generous tone, "Seriously, the way I think about is that I don't know what your body needs better than you. I think our bodies know what we need better than we do at times. We all lose focus and don't listen to our highest self like we could, at times. So, with you, my job is to listen to your body and let it guide me. Does that make sense?"

"Oh, yes. Well said, My Lord. That's beautiful." She said.

"Now, let yourself sink into the bed and feel nothing but your own energy. Forget that I am here." He said.

He kept massaging her thighs. After he felt her body relax more, his thumbs went from the inside of her knees up to the soft skin between her thigh and her vulva. At the end of each stroke like that, he held slight but firm pressure to the area besides her vulva. His focus was not on pleasuring her, although it was wonderfully pleasurable to her.

He only wanted to give her that chance to feel her own sensuousness as freely and as abundantly as was possible.

Malkore heard the girls come in through the back door, Kalla and Dossa were bringing in their next meal. He was surprised it was lunchtime already.

Iyasiil didn't even flinch being naked, laid out on the bed.

"Mama, is he taking good care of you?" Dossa asked as they were putting food on the table. She hadn't read the energy in the room before she spoke. Malkore held his finger over his lips to let her know to be quiet. Then he motioned for them to come on into the room.

Iyasiil called out to her students, "Girls, join us for a little while. I want you to learn this." Then quickly looked at Malkore and said, "I am not teaching them today. You are."

He was caught off guard a little but wasn't surprised. He had never taught this before, but quickly adjusted, "Yes, My Love. I guess *this* is what we do." They both let out a little laugh.

Kalla brought over a pitcher of water and filled their cups and put down a small plate of bread and cheese on the side table beside the bed. Dossa stoked up the fire and added a few pieces of wood to it.

Then both girls sat on the bed on either side of their teacher. Dossa was sitting on her feet, and she looked a little nervous, like she didn't know what she was supposed to do – she didn't want to screw anything up. Kalla wasn't sure if things were about to get weird, after last night, she kind of wanted them to – she was feeling really playful.

Malkore could sense Dossa's nervousness. "Girls, I just want you to feel your own flow of love. So just breathe." He went back to massaging Iyasiil's thighs. "While you are learning this energy, I want you to just imagine sitting in the water or the beach and feeling the waves gently flowing into you. Don't try to control it, you can't get hurt and you *can't* do it wrong, just feel the rhythm of the waves. Make sense?"

The girls nodded their heads.

Iyasiil stopped feeling his hands. She stopped feeling her own energy for a moment because she was thinking about him. "*Wow! This man is such a natural fucking teacher. He opens the heart first, then pours wisdom into the open heart.*"

Turning back to Iyasiil, "And you, my precious and wise woman, if you stop feeling your own energy and start focusing on me or the girls, I am going to send them home until we are done." He kept looking her in the eye.

"Yes, My Lord." She said with a giggle. Then she closed her eyes and returned her awareness to her own sensations, emptying her mind.

He laid his hand on her heart and said, "Iyasiil, My Love. When I speak to the girls, I want to you ignore me. I want you to see and feel nothing but your own energy."

"Yes, Love." She said.

Then he spoke softly, "Now, Dossa and Kalla, keep breathing and letting the energy of what you see and feel wash up into you like the gentle waves on a beach. If you need to lay down next to her while you are doing that, then do it. You both did so well last night, this isn't any different." They both nodded again.

Dossa whispered, "OK, this is *just like* last night. Right?!"

"Yes. Just breathe, there is nothing you have to do. And there is no way to do this wrong, as long as you are present in your own heart. So, make feeling your own feelings your top priority." He said.

"OK. Just feel it, whatever it is. Got it." Dossa said. She relaxed and her nervousness faded quickly.

He turned to Kalla, "You are joining us at the end of this part, I have been massaging her since you two left here this morning. So, whenever you do this on your own one day, just know that there is a lot of build up before you get to this part. Up until now, the sole focus has been relaxing and nurturing her body - relaxing and nurturing her spirit - honoring her as an amazing woman, and making the space that is not about me, not about my pleasure, not about my desire. My job is to make space for her to feel her own energy and then to meet her there in whatever she finds within herself."

Kalla shook her head in amazement for a moment as she took in all of what he had just said. Then she nodded, "Wow. Yes."

Iyasiil felt Dossa relax and reached out to her side to touch Dossa's leg. Feeling her teacher's touch, Dossa relaxed even more. She looked at her teacher and felt her heart get warm, she felt how much she loved her teacher and how thankful she was to have Iyasiil in her life now. That brought a smile to her face. She leaned down and kissed her teacher on the lips, then laid down and put her hand on her teacher's heart and her head on her teacher's shoulder.

Malkore looked to see if Iyasiil was using too much of her own energy to take care of Dossa, it didn't look like it. He gently touched Iyasiil's forearm and said, "Teacher, be mindful not to give anything away. Just feel your own energy. I am teaching the girls right now, My Love."

Iyasiil nodded, "Yeah. We're good."

Kalla was watching Malkore's hands, wanting to know what it felt like to him. *"How does he do this?"* She could feel the energy in the room, it felt magical. It was like Malkore and her teacher were in another world. *"I'll never be able to do this. They are amazing."* She didn't even realize right then that she had done the same thing with him last night. She looked up and made eye contact with Malkore with a look of wonder on her face.

He smiled a soft, easy smile and very deliberately let out a long exhale, telling her to breathe. Then when he took the next long, deliberate inhale, she caught on and started breathing. He started making his breath into a wave like sound. She remembered and nodded, *"Beach. Waves. Breathing. Got it."* She thought.

Kalla looked down at her teacher's beautiful, naked body. She didn't notice the nakedness as much as she felt a sense of wonder. She could feel the quietness inside.

Malkore said to Kalla, "We are always searching for that quiet place inside. That is where the magic comes from."

Kalla thought, *"Is this one of those times when he just read my mind?"*

Kalla wondered if she should lay down on the other side of her teacher, so she would be held on both sides, but her heart didn't feel warm when she thought about that, so she didn't do it. Then as soon as she let that thought go, she started feeling how much she wanted Malkore to be massaging her like this. She was a little startled by that and she tried to put that image aside for a moment. The thought of it almost took her breath away, her body responded inside saying, *"Yes! Yes! Yes!"* She tried her best to tell her body to shut up and be quiet.

Malkore quietly said to Kalla, "Just feel everything you are feeling. It is all welcome."

Kalla thought, *"I am not so sure about that."*

He looked her in the eye and said, "If it feels good, just let it flow through you. Use it. When you are feeling good, it's just you being totally present with you."

Kalla had a glimmer of shock flow across her face. *"Oh, shit! He knows."*

He smiled a gentle smile and said, "Just let it flow through your hands . . . Just let it all flow."

She lookec a little nervous but followed his instructions. When she touched her teacher, she felt like her hands were sinking deep into her teacher's skin and all her nervousness fell away.

Iyasiil had her knees up and spread out comfortably wide. Kalla was sitting next to her teacher's left knee and looked at her teacher again. She closed her eyes and took a big breath. She started feeling her heart get warm again. She felt the skin high on her left ribs get tingly, so she wrapped her left arm around her teacher's thigh, holding the back of her teacher's thigh in her left hand, cradling her teacher's knee under her arm. She could still see what Malkore was doing, and she relaxed her body as she squeezed her teacher's knee with her upper arm and ribs. She gently and still firmly held the outside of her teacher's left hip with her right hand. Then she looked at Malkore. He nodded his approval of what she was doing.

As he was massaging Iyasiil's thighs, he returned his full attention to Iyasiil and how she was feeling. He was still making long massaging strokes up the inside of her thighs starting right in front of Kalla's shoulder, going on either side of Iyasiil's vulva with his thumbs, then out to the front of her hips, back in to her lower stomach, and up to the bottom of her ribs.

As he pushed his hands up to her ribs, he touched Dossa's arm. She looked at him, wondering if she needed to move. He just wanted to make sure she was comfortable with the touch. "Dossa, if that's OK with you, just stay there." Dossa nodded.

He made several more of those long strokes up to Iyasiil's ribs. Then his next massage stroke went up the inside of her thighs with his thumbs on either side of her vulva and his fingers spread wide, fanning out across her lower abdomen, from hip to hip. He was pressing firmly but not hard into the sides of her vulva as his entire hands were slowly pulsing in rhythmical pulses.

Iyasiil could feel her body getting hungry for more touch. With each touch, he explored and found a new release; a release she felt in her mind, body, and spirit.

She wanted him to rub her inside and he was being so patient. He was building her energy and excitement up more and more and more. His patience was both frustrating and comforting. Her breathing was getting a little heavier, but still relaxed. Her body was making tiny, little moving with waves of pleasure.

Dossa was focusing on feeling and flowing love into her teacher's heart and spirit. She didn't know if she was doing it right, all she knew was that she loved her teacher so much and wanted her teacher to know how loved she is. Dossa remembered the thought she had last night about "being the blanket of love." Her whole body relaxed more. As she relaxed more, her hand started moving in small rocking motions, barely moving on her teacher's heart. Her skin was not sliding against her teacher's skin, she was just moving the skin between her teacher's breasts slightly as her hand gently moved. After a few moments, she realized the rocking motion she was making was synchronous with Malkore.

Malkore, moved to straddle Iyasiil's right knee. As he leaned forward, he put his left hand behind Dossa's back to support his weight. Dossa's legs were close to Malkore's legs, and she laid her top leg on Malkore's calf. Malkore was glad she was comfortable enough, within herself and with him, to do that.

Malkore started using his right hand to start rubbing from above Iyasiil's clitoris to the bottom of her yoni with two fingers on either side -- not touching her clitoris or her vulva, but exciting her and all the sensitive skin all around her yoni. Then having all four fingers together, he made a firm and gentle, flat stroke upwards with his hand. It was enough to bring a long gasp from her, but not enough to get her energy building towards orgasm.

Iyasiil felt the excitement and enticement from his fingers circling around the outer edges of her yoni. She felt her body begin to sing an invitation for him to know her deeper than anyone had ever known her before. She felt his fingers offering an invitation to which her body was a resounding, "Yes."

He leaned over to Kalla and whispered, "Building, building." Kalla nodded. Then he continued making those same long, gentle and still firm strokes with lots of oil on his hand.

Kalla was fascinated watching and feeling her teacher's energy respond to his touch. She noticed that her thoughts kept going back and forth between thinking it was the physical touch that was bringing her teacher's response and thinking it was the nurturing and presence that was creating the magic. She kept catching herself and remembering that it was the mixing of the two that created the magic.

Malkore put two fingers on the entrance to her yoni laying them flat against her skin so that the tops of those fingers were cradling her clitoris. He made slow, light circles with his fingertips, just barely moving the skin, massaging the sensitive tissue underneath.

She was loving it and wanting more, each invitation of his touch was met with a new eagerness to allow. She reached out and held onto Kalla's leg and squeezed it, holding on with the excitement.

Kalla felt her, she felt the deep resonance in her teacher's soul. She felt how free her teacher felt, no demands, no expectations – just free to feel.

Then, Malkore shifted his weight backwards and started using his hand at a different angle. Kalla was watching closely, wanting to learn. He slowly and gently put two fingers just barely inside her, only as deep as his fingernails. He was making light pulsing motions downwards towards the bed on the small spot of sensitive, wrinkled skin inside. Kalla looked up at him, curious what he was feeling. He just took a deliberate breath, reminding her to keep breathing.

That first moment when Malkore's fingers first entered her, Iyasiil felt a tightening through her whole body, but not out of fear or shock. It felt like the endless moment when a wave is at its peak, but holds on before it falls, collapsing, surrendering to what is next. She felt herself surrender beyond the boundaries of her own skin.

Kalla closed her eyes and took another long, slow breath. Then she noticed that she had begun moving her hands on her teacher's hip and thigh without even realizing it. She gently got up so as to not disturb all of what was happening, and she sat on her feet next to Iyasiil's stomach on the left side. She laid her left hand on her teacher's lower abdomen, right over her womb. With her right hand, fingers spread out wide, she started making slow strokes up the ribs on her left side. In a fluid movement, she cupped her thumb and fingers wide around the base of her teacher's breast. Without stopping, her fingers continued up to the front of her shoulder, to the top of her shoulder. Then she slid her thumb from the outside of her teacher's collarbone towards the center of Iyasiil's body as her fingers gently pressed into the base of her teacher's neck. She saw her teacher nod slightly. Kalla kept repeating that same massage stroke slowly.

She took a deep breath and looked at her teacher; she felt her love for her teacher again and smiled. Kalla felt so grateful to get to love on her teacher this way.

Malkore was impressed with Kalla getting quiet enough inside to feel the impulse to do something so natural and pure.

Malkore was still rubbing the back wall of Iyasiil's yoni in small, slow circles just a half-finger inside her. He slowly began making the slow circles go a little deeper, then his fingers strokes went even deeper and towards the inside of her right hip. Iyasiil was loving it, she couldn't think of a time when she had ever been touched there. She thought, "*Where did that spot come from?*" She felt like Malkore was introducing her to parts of herself she didn't know existed.

It wasn't creating the kind of pleasure that would build up to orgasm, it was gentle, a subtle pleasure that felt like it was freeing her spirit of any concerns she had ever had. She felt like her soul was being released into dancing and expanding bigger and bigger. Iyasiil could feel her desire growing, too.

Kalla kept making those strokes up her ribs and with each stroke cupped the outside base of her breast a tiny bit more, then Kalla gently moved Dossa's hand down to their teacher's stomach and started making wide circles around her teacher's left breast at the end of each massage stroke. She could feel Iyasiil's breathing get heavier, and her body start twitching.

Kalla began using her left hand to push across the bottom of her teacher's ribs and pulling with slight pressure against the area beside Iyasiil's right breast. Malkore saw what Kalla was doing and noticed the slow speed of Kalla's touch, and he could empathically feel the presence and love that Kalla was feeling at that moment.

Malkore spent several minutes gently and still firmly massaging the right side of Iyasiil's vaginal cavity, then moved back to the center and began ever so gently massaging the base of her cervix. He moved to the left, back area of her vaginal cavity and kept making slow elongated circles. Anytime he found a spot that felt tight, either physically or emotionally, he made smaller gentle circles on it with his fingertips until her breathing showed him a small release of some sort.

Iyasiil had thought the night before while watching Frigg, Kalla, and Dossa massage Malkore that she would love to receive the same herself someday. She didn't know it would be today. She expected that Malkore would be doing a lot more teaching, she thought, "*It seems the girls had picked up the energetic part of it easily and have found a place to fall into the massage, easily.*" Then she felt Malkore, lean down and bite her knee. She was giggling and gasping while still wiggling with pleasure.

Malkore softly and gently said, "Bring your awareness back to your body, Love."

Iyasiil didn't even smile, she just said, "You fucking witch, get out of my head." She was joking with him, but she loved being seen so deeply. She felt sexy and beautiful when he noticed what was going on inside. She had gotten to where she always felt love flowing through her in her life, but she never felt loved like this by other people. No one had ever been present enough within themselves to be able to love like this, she felt like he could make flowers bloom on dead branches and make springs appear on dusty ground.

"Breathe, My Love." He said back to her.

Kalla was worried for a second that she had done something wrong that had distracted her teacher. She looked at Malkore wondering if she had messed up.

He looked back at Kalla and whispered, "Keep going. You're doing great, Kalla. You both are."

Kalla laid her hands on her teacher's heart and took a big breath herself. When she felt herself settle again. She began moving her hands in unison, alternating between her left hand on the outside her teacher's right breast, pulling from the back of her ribs with all her fingers together, up to the base of her breast, pushing the mass of her breast up into the air and her right hand pressing into her teacher's heart. Then, the next stroke, Kalla would have her left hand massaging Iyasiil's heart while Kalla's right hand came up the outside of the left breast.

Dossa had her hand flat on her teacher's lower abdomen, right over her pubic bone. She got lots of massage oil on her hand and began making slow, gentle, loving strokes out to Iyasiil's left hip, wrapping her hand around her hip, then slowly pulling her hand back across to her right hip. Then making a circle around Iyasiil's stomach and back to her teacher's left hip again.

Malkore began making very small circles deep on the front wall of Iyasiil's yoni, the flats of his fingers were lightly grazing the wrinkled tissue just inside. Iyasiil's breathing began growing heavier and heavier. Every spot that was being touched felt like the best spot, until he moved to the next one.

He slowly increased the pressure he was putting on the front wall of her yoni. Iyasiil reached down and grabbed the shoulder on Dossa's dress, holding on. Her pleasure was building, but not just in her yoni or her breasts. She felt like every cell in her body was about to shoot lightning out in every direction, she could feel the charge building up inside of everywhere. Her light moans turned to soft groaning, gasping whines.

Malkore increased the pressure he was using on the wrinkled tissue on the front wall of her yoni. His rhythmical pulses sped up, but just ever so slightly. Iyasiil began moaning louder and her body was shuddering and twitching more and more. She was ready for more.

Iyasiil let out a screaming moan of pleasure and a river flowed out of her. She felt like she was getting pummeled by crashing waves of ecstasy. It was unstoppable. She felt exposed and seen. She felt honored and held. She didn't want it to ever stop.

Kalla looked up at Malkore and motioned to Iyasiil's breast, asking if it was time to touch her breasts directly. Malkore nodded.

Kalla put both hands wide on the sides of Iyasiil's ribs and pushed her hands up firmly into Iyasiil's breasts, pushing them up into the air, then pressing her fingers into them, grabbing Iyasiil's breasts and lightly pinching her nipples. Iyasiil let out a growling, moaning scream, "Yes!'

Malkore kept increasing the speed of his movements inside while increasing the pressure on the most sensitive part inside. He began curving his fingers slightly to put a little extra pressure on the wrinkled area on the front wall of her yoni.

Iyasiil grabbed Kalla's wrist, pressing Kalla's hand harder into her breast, then she grabbed Kalla's leg and squeezed it.

Kalla made eye contact with Dossa. They smiled at each other, both amazed at what was happening. They had both had a lot of sex in their lives, but they had never been taken to this level of intensity. This is what Dossa had always dreamed about, but this was even more than she dreamed was possible.

Malkore was now working Iyasiil's body quite hard, his strokes had gotten faster and faster with more and more upwards pressure until Iyasiil was orgasming repeatedly and her cervix was reaching down to Malkore's fingers in pulses.

Iyasiil began screaming, her whole body tensed up, then began shaking harder and harder, and when her screams passed their peak, Malkore stopped. Iyasiil's whole body was shaking and squirming, she was gasping and moaning.

Malkore wanted to tell the girls to stop and be still and keep flowing the nurturing and love and didn't want to distract Iyasiil from her experience. Dossa looked up at him, he whispered, "Hold her." Dossa reached over and tapped Kalla on the arm and motioned for Kalla to lay down. As Kalla laid down, Dossa took Kalla's hand and held it still on Iyasiil's heart. Dossa kept her hand on Kalla's hand and laced her fingers in between Kalla's fingers.

Malkore said, "Keep breathing and soaking in the love."

The girls both had their heads on Iyasiil's shoulders. Iyasiil was still shaking and shuddering, she wrapped her arms around both girls, pulling them in tightly. Dossa kept her hand on her teacher's heart. Kalla reached up and wrapped her hand around her teacher's head, holding the back of her neck, resting her forehead on her teacher's cheek.

Malkore laid down so he was halfway on his left side with his left shoulder right against Iyasiil's yoni, he laid his head on her stomach and began nuzzling his face into her stomach. He wrapped his right hand around her left leg and held her.

Iyasiil wrapped her legs around his body. Iyasiil's whole body was tingling, she felt like lightening was shooting through every part of her. Even the smallest movements from any one of them set off another lightning bolt inside.

Malkore kept feeling how much he loved her and how thankful he was to have her in his life, even if it is just for another couple of days. He had never met anyone who touched such a deep place inside, it had been millennia since he had felt really excited to be with someone. He felt beside himself in happiness and gratitude.

Over the next Fifteen minutes, Iyasiil's breathing returned to as normal as she would ever be again. Malkore got up on his hands and knees and put his knees on the outside of hers and leaned down to kiss her. With the girls still lying beside her, he had to put his hands on the outsides of both girls to lean down to kiss Iyasiil.

He looked her in the eye, smiling and said, "Hello, My Love. Welcome back. I hope you had a beautiful journey."

"The best." She said, smiling at him. "What do you think girls? Shall I keep him?"

Malkore and Dossa laughed. Kalla said, "If you don't keep him, Dossa and I will!" Kalla leaned up and kissed Malkore on the cheek.

Malkore began shifting his weight to get up and Dossa said, "Wait. Me too." She reached up and pulled his head down to kiss him on the cheek, too.

Malkore stepped his knees backwards, when his knees were beside Iyasiil's feet, he leaned down and put his forehead on her stomach, right above her yoni. He took a big breath and said a prayer, silently to himself honoring her for the amazing woman she is. Her body shuddered and she let out a little gasping yell.

Kalla looked at her, then looked at Malkore with her jaw hanging open. "How do you do that?!" She had never seen anyone be able to cause another person to have an orgasm cr nearly an orgasm, just with their intention or whatever it was he was doing, she wasn't sure.

He looked at Kalla and said, "I told you. I grew up."

Chapter Eleven
A "Walk" in the Woods

The four of them kept laying on the bed for a while. Then Kalla got up and got everyone a plate of food. Dossa tended the fire but kept it just low enough to where she would have coals left for the evening when she would build it up again.

They all sat on the bed and ate, and not much was said for a little while.

When they had finished eating, Dossa took everyone's plates to the table on the other side of the room. Kalla filled up everyone's horn of mead, then the girls got back on the bed.

The girls looked like they had so many questions. They could feel that this was not the time to ask and Kalla was feeling so eager to learn more. "Sometime in the next couple of days, could the two of you sit down with us and tell us everything that just happened and has been going on over the last several days? I have so many questions."

Dossa added, "Yes, please. I feel like there is so much that I don't know. And it is all amazing."

Iyasiil laughed, "Of course. I am so happy that you two have stepped in so much over these past days. I am so proud of both of you."

Malkore looked at the two of them, he was smiling a very happy and grateful smile.

"What?" Dossa said, looking at him.

"I am feeling so grateful that you two have been here. It has restored my hope for the people in so many ways. And it has been delightful getting to know you two a little bit." He told them.

Kalla smiled and dropped her head and took a breath. Then she looked back up and said, "I don't think this Tending was for you, Lord Malkore. I think your Tending and this Tending today for Mama is just a cover. I think this has been for Dossa and me. We are the ones who have gotten the most out of it."

"Yeah, I feel the same way. But I am scared I am going to lose it." Dossa said.

Iyasiil asked, "How so? What do you mean?"

"Well, I feel like I don't ever want to leave this room with you two, the four of us. I feel so good. I am scared the feeling will fade and I will lose it. I want to feel the magic all the time and this is the only place I have ever known it. I don't want to live without it." Dossa responded.

"Yeah, I get that. Well, now that you know what's possible, you can call it in whenever you want and the more practiced you get at it, the easier it will become to call it in. But I know that doesn't really help. How about this?" Iyasiil took a long breath, then said, "We are going to keep working together for as long as you both want. So, we will keep building, no matter what." She paused again as she collected her thoughts, "I agree, this is a special kind of magic that has been happening." She turned to Malkore, "Magical for me too, I am so thankful."

"It's the same for me." Malkore added.

Iyasiil went on, "So Lord Malkore, if you are willing to help, how about if for as long as this thing between us keeps going, the four of us get together to spend time together?"

Dossa said, "Yes, please."

Kalla was starting to cry softly and was trying to hide it.

"Girls, I told you last night that no matter what happened between your teacher and I, that I wasn't going away. We are family now." Malkore said. He wanted to emphasize his point, "Dossa, you and I are family now. Kalla, you and I are family now. That doesn't change, unless you want to change it."

Kalla couldn't keep it in anymore and she exploded in tears. She almost dove across the bed to lay on Malkore's lap. She had her shoulders on his thighs, with her arms wrapped around the outside of his hips, and her head sideways on his hip, facing Iyasiil. "I was scared you were going to say "No."" She grabbed the sheet wrapping around his hip and pressed her head into his hip.

He cradled her head in his hand and rubbed the middle of her back with the other hand. "Oh, sweet Kalla, I love you. I love you so much. I love you just as much as you love me. I am not going away."

"Me too?" Dossa asked.

"Yes, sweet Dossa. You too." He said.

"Me too?" Iyasiil asked playfully.

He looked at her and smiled. He leaned over and kissed her, "All day. For as many days as we have."

"Good." Iyasiil said in her cutest, happy little girl voice. He smiled at her and took in how adorable she is.

He looked at Kalla and brushed her hair back with his hand, "I love you sweet girl. Take a breath and see if you can feel it."

Kalla said, "Yeah." But everyone could feel that she didn't really mean it.

"Look, one of the most powerful things I have learned is to ignore the scary thoughts that pop in my head. Scary thoughts never stop coming, just like the hopeful and happy thoughts. The thing that makes the biggest difference in how well our lives go is how much we feel the excitement of the happy and hopeful thoughts and let the scary thoughts float right on by. So Kalla, how do you feel when you think I might go away?" Malkore asked.

Kalla nuzzled her head onto the outside of his hip more and said, "I hate it. I don't want you to go."

"Right. Now, get a picture in your mind of you and I staying connected for a long time. Feel what that feels like. Do you have it?" She nodded her head. "Now feel it again, feel it more. Watch it happen in your mind for a second or two and feel what it feels like. What does that feel like?"

She said, "Like I am in trouble . . ." Kalla meant it to be funny, and it was.

They all laughed, including Kalla. Iyasiil was laughing too hard to form words and she was trying to ask how Kalla felt like she was in trouble. Malkore pressed his hand a little harder into her back as he laughed.

Kalla said, "I just, I don't know, I . . . I don't know." Then she let her body fall even harder onto his lap. She took a breath, then she started to get up. She sat up on her feet and looked at both of them. "I don't know" then she looked at Dossa and asked, "do you feel the same way?" Then she waved her hand, brushing the idea away. "Of course, you do." Then she looked back at Malkore and her teacher. "I feel like I am falling in love with both of you. And it is totally different with each of you, and as if falling in love with two people at once isn't enough, I am soooooo crazy in love with you two together. I am so happy that you two found each other. I never would have guessed, but being with you two, I can't imagine the world without you two together. You two being together makes the world better. No, that's not it. You two being together makes the world a magical place." Then she felt relief at having said all that. Then she said, "So basically, I want to fuck the shit out of both of your feet with my feet. And if you two aren't fucking the shit out of each other's feet with your feet, then something is wrong with the world."

Iyasiil screamed with laughter and fell over on Malkore's shoulder. Malkore, let out his big warrior's laugh. Dossa fell over on the bed laughing, "Girl, you are too much! You're just too much. You're going to get us both in trouble . . ."

"Shut up, you bitch! I am not too much! I am just the right amount! So, hold on! I am becoming even more, so fuck you!" Kalla responded.

Dossa pushed herself up and said, "That's right! Yes! But be careful, it's dangerous. You're still going to get me in trouble."

Iyasiil asked, "How is she going to get you in trouble?"

Without hesitation, Dossa said, "Because if I keep hanging around her, she is such a bad influence, pretty soon, I am going to start telling you how much I want to fuck your husband's feet with my feet."

Iyasiil was taking a sip of her mead and almost spit it out, she was laughing so hard. Malkore didn't know what to do, he wasn't used to this kind of attention, and he just shook his head, laughing. Kalla screamed, laughing. Kalla fell over on Dossa's lap, then rolled so she was laying on her back, her head was on Dossa's lap, and she was looking up at Dossa.

Dossa looked down at Kalla and said, "I always want to fuck your feet with my feet."

Kalla reached up with her right hand and made the squawking sound of a goose as she squeezed Dossa's left breast.

Malkore was laughing, he had never seen these two so playful. It was obvious how close they were, and he could see how wonderfully dedicated they were to each other.

Iyasiil put her horn of mead down and wrapped her arms around Malkore's arm as she leaned on him, she started to speak with a very serious tone, "Here we are. We have been named the Mother" she paused for effect "and the Father" she paused again, "of Feet Fuckers. That's quite a title to hold. Can you handle it, Lord Malkore?"

It totally caught him off guard. He was laughing so hard, and he couldn't stop. He was laughing so hard that he started crying. It took a minute, then he said, "By the eyes of Ve, my eyes have been opened, I finally found my purpose in life!" They all kept laughing for a bit, then he said, "Ladies, thank you. You have touched my heart more than you know." He looked at each of them. Then his eyebrows shot up as a new idea popped in his head and he spoke with a very serious voice, "We talked about how the things that happen in Tending are not to be talked about outside of the Tending, right?" The girls nodded.

"It would probably be good if you ladies don't refer to me as Lord Feet Fucker outside of here." They all laughed.

Iyasiil said, "How does it feel to have three women falling in love with you? Can you handle that, My Lord?"

Malkore shook his head slightly and said, "I don't know. But I can tell you that my heart feels *so full*. I am curious how it is all going to unfold, I have no idea. But to answer your question, I can handle it. I love all of you so much and I am so thankful."

Iyasiil responded, "Yeah, none of us know how it will turn out, either. That's why we live, to see how things unfold."

"My Love today is your day. How are you doing? You have three people here that love you. How may we serve you to make your life awesome?" He asked.

"Well, I think this has probably been the greatest day any woman could have asked for. Girls, I am so proud of the two of you and all the opening up and stepping into your real, true selves that you both have done the past several days. That s probably been the greatest gift you could have given me – it's what I want for you both. And you, you big-hearted bear, I couldn't have asked for anything better. I would really like to go for that walk while we still have plenty of daylight, then we can all have dinner with the people in the great hall or we can just come back here and the four of us have dinner. I'll see how I feel when the time comes."

The girls looked at each other, they had both been hoping they would get to spend more time with Malkore and their teacher. They were both happy that they were going to get to spend more time with them today.

Malkore said, "That sounds great. So, girls, since today is all about your teacher, I am going to take her out for a long walk in the woods now. Is there anything else we need to finish up before we go?"

Kalla said, "No. I don't have anything. I am going to go walk down to the river, then probably take a nap. This has been a big day – a big couple of days." She looked at Dossa to see if Dossa had anything to say.

"Yeah, that sounds great. I'll join you if that's OK." Dossa said.

Kalla reached up and squeeze/squawked her breast again, twice.

- -

Malkore and Iyasiil started off on their walk. Iyasiil didn't say anything, but she definitely seemed to have a destination in mind. She walked at a pace that was a little faster than Malkore expected, she didn't walk like she was in a hurry, but it was faster than their walk the days before, that was at a leisurely pace.

As they approached the forest, he could feel her energy fall away. It wasn't exactly away from him as it was that she expanded into communion with the entire forest. As she got about twenty paces inside the tree line, she stopped. She stood there with her eyes closed and took in a long breath. He could feel her breathe the forest in and start to hum a tune. The tune felt familiar, even though he was sure he had never heard it before.

He stopped and took in a breath himself. He had always come to the forest alone to regain his peace, sometimes spending days getting quiet enough inside to hear the vibrations of all that was alive around him, but he was certain that he never made it look this good.

Watching her walk among the trees, he was caught without breath at what an amazing creature he'd found.

He stood back from her and didn't want to disturb her conversation with the forest. Then he spoke to the forest, himself, "Does getting lost in her beauty betray the power and depth of her soul? You'd think I'd never ask that question, for they are one. And they are the greatest beauty ever born. My Heart grows bigger than the world itself as I look at the most prosperous spirit ever to walk. Prosperous in Peace. Prosperous in Harmony. Prosperous in the Love that flows from every drop of her. I am thankful for who she is. I am ravenous with desire, and I am ravenous with gratitude. The feel of her skin, the depths of her heart, the smell of her, the love born of peace, and the wisdom born of an amazing life, that is what fills my heart today."

She turned back with a smile, "Join me. There's a place I want to take you."

He'd dreamed of grace and beauty like this, but never seen it in an actual person. He has seen beautiful women, his whole life, but none like this. He felt this grace inside most of the time and was content to only feel it inside. Years ago, whenever he'd lost track and felt like something/someone was missing, he learned to stop and meditate to fill himself and the world with that grace, and then move in it, everywhere he went. But he'd never seen it personified in another.

"I thought I was taking you out for a walk." He said playfully.

"Well, maybe I used my witchy ways to crawl inside your mind so you would think that walking in this direction was your idea." She said, although they both knew that wasn't true. She kept walking.

Then she realized something was different. It was a tiny sense that something was gone, a vulnerability – a danger not present.

He had just caught up to her. She stopped and turned around to face him. She took his hands, "My Lord, during your tending, I told you that you would not look out for anyone but yourself for the days when we were chambered. I told you that you would not protect anyone, not even me." He nodded. "My Lord, I am not in need of your protection. If I do need it, you will know – You will hear me tell you clearly in your heart. But do not extend one drop of your life trying to protect me from anything the world has coming to me."

He'd just had his ass handed to him in the most loving way. He was smiling. *"How did she know?"* He thought. *"Of course, she knows . . ."*

He is a warrior. He is always protecting everyone. She had just told him to *not* do that. He would always scan the area as he walked, as they entered the woods, he looked all around for any danger that may be hiding from them. He is a warrior; he would never let anyone get hurt when he was around.

"You are truly amazing, My Love. I am truly amazed. You could feel me protecting you, that's impressive. But I am never going to stop." He said.

"I know. And of course, if anyone ever tried to hurt me, you would tear them in half. That's not a problem, I would do the same for you. It's about you wrapping me in a bubble. I do not need protection. First off, there are probably only five or six warriors in Asgard who could best me in a fight. Second, if there is no danger, there is no life. That would be like taking away all of a person's sadness and fear, thinking they would only be happy all the time. It doesn't work that way, as you know. It is the danger, sadness, and pain that creates the desire to grow. If I never face the possibility of danger, I never get to face the possibility of raw beauty and raw love. Does that make sense?"

"Absolutely." He said.

In a flirty voice, she said, "So, you big, sexy bear," she pulled his arms behind her back, pulling him closer, until he was hugging her, the she wrapped her arms around him, "Don't fuck with my flow, or else you'll find out whether or not you are one of the few who could best me in a fight . . ." Then she leaned up to him and kissed him, then she turned and started walking deeper into the woods again.

He sensed that she was serious, although he had never met a woman who was anywhere as good as any man in his army.

"That might be fun, to find out." He said as she walked off.

Without turning around, she kept walking and said, "Lord Malkore, I doubt you have the will to fight me as hard as you would have to fight in order to best me. I think you would be afraid to hurt me, then you would find yourself without a sword, blood draining from your body, and a fear that everyone would laugh at you for getting your ass kicked by a woman."

"At least she believes what she is saying, but I wouldn't put it past her." He thought.

She kept walking and said, "You shouldn't test me on this, My Lord." She turned and showed him a witchy smirk that turned into the most alluring face he had ever seen. She said to him, "If you catch me, you can have me." Then she took off deeper into the woods, moving like a panther, within seconds she was almost out of sight in the thick forest.

He laughed. "The chase is on." Then he took off at a really fast pace, he expected to catch her within a minute, she only had thirty or forty paces of a head start, that shouldn't be hard to make up.

He was running around trees, jumping over logs, jump spinning through bushes so as not to catch a branch in the face – He loved this! This was *his* kind of date. She had turned to the right and went behind a thick cover of brush, when he came around the brush, he realized he had lost ground on her.

"Oh Shit! This woman is for real." He took off at full speed, leaving a trail of dust and leaves behind him. After another two minutes, she was in sight again, but still fifty strides ahead of him.

She didn't even look back, she just kept going. She turned left around a thicket and disappeared out of sight. He looked to see if he could take a short cut and cut her off. No such luck. He was going to have to catch her with pure pace. He sped up, moving even faster. He came upon a log that was laying across the floor of the forest that was easily as high as her waist, *"Surely that would have slowed her down."* He thought, but she was nowhere in sight. He pressed on with a smile on his face. He was really starting to enjoy this.

He caught a glimpse of her as he came to a part of the forest with a little less ground brush. He was gaining ground on her, but she was still thirty strides ahead of him.

They were going up a rise. She was about to disappeared over the top of it, as he got to the top, he looked to get a good idea of the terrain. It opened up more, they had 150 strides before they would get back into thicker foliage. "I got you, witch." He said as he ran. Then he started laughing, he thought, *"The father of the Feet Fuckers is about to nab you."* He was breathing too hard to laugh aloud, but he was certainly going to yell that at her when he was about to catch her.

He was making up ground on her now. In another thirty seconds, he was only four strides behind her. He yelled, "You are about to be nabbed by" then in as big of a booming voice as he could muster while he was running at full speed, "The Father of the Feet Fuckers!"

She didn't even respond, she just sped up and kept running. Right as they were at the thicker part of the forest, he caught her. He wanted to grab her around the waist and slow down and she bent over and escaped his arms. He flew right past her. It took him several strides to stop, when he turned around, she was gone. He assumed she was hiding behind one of the large trees they had just flown past. He walked a few steps back in the direction from which they had just come. He looked behind several trees and didn't see her and didn't even see footsteps to tell him which direction to look.

"I'm up here, My Lord." She was standing on a hill, forty paces away, up to his left. There is no way she could have gotten there so fast.

"You fucking witch!" He yelled with a big smile. He knew she had used some kind of witchcraft to get up there so fast. He would have to ask her to teach him that trick someday.

"Giving up so easily, Feet Fucker?!" She yelled down at him, then turned and disappeared behind the berm she had been standing on.

He took off up the side of that berm. He caught a glimpse of her when he got to the top, she had about twenty paces on him. He was moving quickly up a small rise and saw her disappear to the left around a large bunch of bushes. When he got around the bushes, he caught a glimpse of her off in the distance when she got to an area of the forest with little brush, only tall old growth trees.

As he entered the old growth trees, he saw a few footprints, as he ran. He knew that would find her quickly. He had run fifty or sixty paces into the old growth grove, following her footprints, when he heard her yell from behind him, "Why are you going that way? I am right here."

He stopped as quickly as he could. And was turning around, looking to see which way to start running again. She had stopped. She was breathing heavily, her skin was glowing, and even though her mouth was hanging open, as she was catching her breath, she was smiling. "Oh, wow! I can't remember the last time I had this much fun. You are indeed a fierce hunter!" She said, gasping for breath.

He was stunned. "You haven't stopped surprising me, yet. That was amazing!" He had the biggest smile on his face, too. He wanted to walk up and hug her, but thought that if he tried it, she would take off running again. "You are . . . You are . . . I don't know what you are, but I like it. In five thousand years, I have never seen the likes of you, Iyasiil."

"Nor I, you, My Love." She put her hands behind her head, to stretch out her lungs, and took a couple of small steps, not heading any particular direction. "Oh, wow! That was fun. I thought you had me so many times."

He approached her slowly, as he was an arm's length away, he started acting cautious, he took small, slow steps, like he was trying to not trigger a flight response, as you would an animal you were trying to catch.

"No worries, Lord Feet Fucker, you caught me." She took a half step towards him, still breathing hard. He took a half step towards her, still catching his breath. He still wasn't convinced that she wouldn't disappear into the distance again.

"You got me. I am yours." She said with a flirty tone and an adoring look on her face. She took the last step to him and wrapped her arms around his neck. She laid her head on his shoulder and against his neck. "I am so fucking yours. All day. For as many days as we have."

He could still feel the adrenaline pounding through his veins, his eyes and all his senses were still sharp. He could feel her heart pounding against his body. He leaned down and lightly bit her on the base of her neck, where it curves into her shoulder. She grabbed his head and pressed it into that bite, and she was surprised how much it turned her on. She could feel his fierce passion. She let out a breath that was just short of a moan. That light bite turned into a kiss on the base of her neck, below her ear. Her whole body responded.

"You know, My Love, I have seen the rise and fall of empires. And one thing that I have learned is that a people can only move forward when the truth is spoken." He said in a very serious tone, using her words from their first night together. " f we are to be the Mother and Father of Asgard, it is important that you don't lie to me. That will be the downfall of Asgard."

"What? What are you talking about." She couldn't imagine what lie she had told him.

"That was not a *walk* in the woods." He said.

She burst into laughter. He had caught her off guard.

"I love you, Feet Fucker!" She said laughing. "Well, I'd like to take that walk with you now."

"How fast?" He asked with a grin.

"You'll know when I know." She said. They walked at a leisurely pace, holding hands. At this pace, they could both take in the beauty of the forest. She took in a few long, deep breaths. "My Lord, I've long since waited for a man worthy of sharing the depths of me, as you have waited too. Now, I'm excited to bring you to my sanctuary. Are you ready?" She asked looking deeply into his eyes with a girlish excitement.

"With you, I would go anywhere, at any time." He thought, *"Wow! Each moment with her is better than the last."*

As they were walking there was an area ahead that was so dense with trees and leaves and vines there was no way through it, and she was walking straight for it. As they got close, she kept moving forward, holding his hand. *"Is her sanctuary just a spot next to this giant thicket?"* He wondered.

She turned slightly and let go of his hand to walk between two trees and as he followed, she turned again and walked through an opening in the thicket that he hadn't seen. It was hard to believe that such a clear opening could even be here, it wasn't cut – it had grown this way. It was nearly a perfect circle of a clearing inside, wide enough for 20 men to lie head to feet across.

She stopped just at the entrance to the clearing. Something shifted in her. He had never seen her looked rushed or nervous, but all of a sudden, she had a touch of frantic energy inside. She turned to him and stepped towards him, about to quickly untie the lacing on the front of his shirt. He reached up and held her hands to stop her. He was almost giddy with excitement for whatever this place is.

"My Love." He paused to get her to slow down. "What is this place? Did you build this? How long has this been here?

I've walked all in these woods for millennia and I've never seen it before."

"I don't know. This is why I left to come be with the people now. I started dreaming of this place and had no idea where it was or how far away I had to go to find it. I grabbed a few things, said goodbye, and started walking this way. It took me years to find it, and when I did, I knew this would be my new home."

"Wow! That's amazing. That's about like how I came to live with the people. But I didn't see a place in my dreams. I saw a boy." He said.

She looked confused for a moment, then smiled when she realized it was Odin he had seen and that it was being Odin's teacher that had called him here. Then her mouth opened n "awe." It wasn't that he had been asked to be Odin's teacher once he got to Asgard, he was *called* here to be Odin's teacher. Then she looked deeper into his eyes and realized the full weight of this mission he'd been given of being Odin's teacher. She knew Frigg's potential, but she had not felt into who Odin really was or of what Odin was really capable.

"Wow, I didn't realize Odin was that important, but he will have to be every bit of that to be worthy of Frigg as she keeps stepping into who she is. This is the place we will bring Odin to help him make his transition." She said.

"Oh." His eyes lit up. She had mentioned that she had a place to do the ceremony to transform Odin into a woman.

"Yes, this is the place. When we step fully inside, you will see why. She responded.

She had indeed slowed down inside when he took her hands, now she seemed content to stand here with him, getting lost in each other again.

Without breaking eye contact, he quietly said, growing a smile, "So, tell me about your sanctuary."

"Yes. Sorry, I got a little distracted looking at this man . . ." She turned to look to the center of the circle. "I wish I could tell you more, but I am just learning about it myself. The little that I know is that it is a portal through which we can journey almost anywhere in the universe. You'll see more as we step inside."

She reached up to begin un-lacing his shirt, slowly this time. She pulled his shirt off and laid in across a branch on the side of the thicket. Then she loosened his pants and dropped them to the ground for him to step out of before laying them on the branch. She removed everything but his necklace with his medicine herbs in it and his bracelet on his left wrist.

As she was stepping out of her dress and laying it aside, she got a bit of that frantic energy back. Her tone of voice changed, and she started talking a little faster. "My Lord, I am going to go on as if this thing between us is everything I dream that it is, even though we only just met and we met in Tending."

"Agreed. And we have a safeguard." He said. He was wondering if this was what was behind her frantic-ness.

She slightly shook her head quickly, trying to shake off something that didn't make sense. "What do you mean? What's the safeguard?"

He took a breath, "Whatever this is, it is huge and real and amazing. The only question is time. The dream is about living in this magic for a long time. Now we both know that nothing lasts forever, not even us. And we both know that if we stop doing all the things that have made us who we are; if we stop walking our individual paths that we have walked that got us here, the relationship will turn to shit."

"Agreed." She said, still listening.

"As long as you keep doing what makes you so wonderfully you, it won't matter how long we get to dance together, because your life is going to continue to be wonderful – that's the life you have created. And if you stop being you, I'll be bored with you and move on down my path quickly."

She nodded, understanding what he was saying. "And I won't stop being me." She said matter of factly.

"And I'd rather die than abandon who I am, because if I abandon who I am and stop doing what makes me the man I am, we would both be better served if you just kill me right there. It is *only* in us both walking our individual path –" She was nodding to all of this. "- the path that made us each who we are, that will be satisfying, whether we are in each other's lives or not."

Still nodding she finished, "And being together is only a consequence of feeling good within ourselves and having fun together."

"Yes." He said.

"There's just one problem." She said.

He cocked his head, "What's the problem." He wondered what problem she could have with what he had been saying.

She took a deep breath, looking from his eyes, down his naked body then back up to his eyes. "I can't stop thinking about you! All day! Every day!" She said with almost a squeal.

"Well, yeah. That part is different." He said.

"I always feel this much love flowing through me. It's like standing under a waterfall and having all of it go through me and go out to the world sweetened in my flavor, just as you have your own flavor." She said.

"Yes." He nodded in agreement, grinning so big, feeling happy inside.

"This is different. So, this is a learning place for me. I haven't had sex in millennia, except a few times when Tending, and that was only to soothe them enough to begin healing."

He interrupted with a joyous smile, "I bet he was blown apart and you put him back together and everyone thought it was a miracle."

"Yes, of course. Now, My Lord, shut up and let me finish!" She said, slapping him playfully on the chest. Then she took on a different tone, talking faster, thinking faster, she was untying a knot in her brain. "the last people I came from, are a people who will never grow into the place we have both grown to – They just aren't a people who will grow. These people can, their hearts are fantastic, they just don't know what's possible, yet. I'm sure that's why I was called here. That's why we both are here. Here's my problem. It's taken you how long to get Odin just to the place where he is now?"

"A long time." He was about to cut her off and ask what brought up the distress she was feeling and wasn't sure if she would get there on her own.

"Right. And as he progresses, the people will follow, but the mass of them need to be taught. If I'm right, the men have been deaf to you, just a complete waste of your time?" She asked.

"Pretty much." He responded, nodding in a non-cholent way.

She went on, "Some of these women were a little hungry, and they are starting to become really hungry to learn and grow."

"That's the effect you have." He said admiring her.

"It's not all me, the people have to have the potential, and Frigg is ready to really start her journey. And you and she will teach Odin from both sides."

"Still not hearing a problem." He said jokingly, stealing a glimpse of her spectacular body and almost losing his train of thought in the looking.

"Well, My Lord, Malkore - Lord of Sarcasm," She said looking up at him with an endearing look. "That's exactly it! *This*!" She motioned back and forth between them.

He thought, *"Oh hell, she saw me getting lost in her body."* He just smiled. He knew that what was between them would only help, although he didn't fully see how, just yet.

She went on, "Frigg could still get lost and get stuck for way too long if she doesn't dive deep, dive hard into her own work. So, there is a bit of urgency. And Odin will still need you more and more as Frigg begins to grow. In fact, your most powerful work with him will begin in the coming years."

"Sooooooo . . ." He was still waiting to hear her concern.

Her eyes darted around looking through all her thoughts, then she landed on the thought she was searching for. Her face looked back up to him, her tone totally changed again. She came back to her sexy, playful, alluring self. She wrapped her arms around him. "The problem, My Lord," she kissed him, "is there is no way for us to teach our people during this crucial time" she kisses him again, "while I am keeping you in bed every day, all day, being selfish with you, never letting you out of my bed to do your work in the world." She kissed him again, "And all my students will have to come to get in bed with us to learn anything."

He laughed. He knew just how she felt. He was feeling totally enthralled with her. "Yeah." Then mocking what will the people say, "Has anyone seen Malkore and Iyasiil? They disappeared into her bed chamber three years ago and no one has seen them since . . ." She laughed.

"Exactly." Then she looked deeply into him and said, "This is going to take some getting used to. I have felt so distracted the last three days – longer than that, since I first saw you in my dream."

"What brought all this on just now? What happened that you got scared?" He asked.

"Oh. I don't know. We were walking here after our run, and –" her eyes shot wide-open. "That was it." She started to tell him, "Oh, Lord Malkore. Do you know what it was?" He shook his head. "It was when I was feeling so excited getting to have that run with you – feeling like every part of me was alive with you – feeling like it would take every part of me to keep up with you, and every part of you to keep up with me."

"Yeah, what is the problem with that?" He asked.

"I was feeling so excited to be with you and had an image in my head of us being together for a long time and how exciting that would be."

"Sounds awesome to me!" He said.

"Yeah. It sounds good to me, too." Then she put on a cute, girlish charm, and said, "And I got scared for a second." She said.

He laughed and grabbed her, hugging her, swinging her back and forth. "Before we met, after you saw me in your dream, when the women were preparing for the feast, did you do what needed to be done to support the people and guide the women well?" He asked.

"Yes."

"Did you make contact with everyone in a way that offered them the chance to meet you deeper?"

"Yes."

"My Love, did you Tend to me masterfully? Tending to my needs while keeping your heart open to honor your own feelings?"

"Yes."

"Did you accurately assess the situation during my tending and see clearly how the normal rules of tending would not serve me, because the situation was different?" He asked.

"Yes." She was smiling and wondering how long he would keep pointing out how ridiculous it was for her to be scared, and she was loving feeling his ironic, sarcastic love.

"Did you quickly and easily adapt to an unorthodox situation in the Tending to maximize the teaching benefit for Dossa and Kalla?"

"Yes, My Lord." She said.

"Did you do it is such a way that also maximized the benefit that I would get out of the Tending? Did you do it in such a way that I would feel restored and be in a better position to serve Asgard with all the changes that need to come?"

"Yes, My Lord. I think you have made your point." She said, wanting him to shut up so that she could kiss him and do what she had come here to do, show him her Sanctuary.

"No. I haven't, My Love." Then with a sarcastic tone, using an animated voice, he said, "My point is: I think Asgard will crumble if you ever stop loving me!" Then in a soft, meek voice, he added, "for as many days as we have together."

She started laughing. "Ahh, so for Asgard, I should love you? I see."

Still sarcastically, with his face lit up, and his eyes sparkling, he said, "Yes. It doesn't really matter to me, you understand . . . I don't feel at all like I have been preparing and waiting for this for Five Thousand years. It's not that I can barely catch my breath because I am so fucking enthralled with you. It's not that every thought is of you. I am just here to do whatever is best for Asgard." He paused for comedic effect, "You know . . . because I am a warrior."

She stepped forward and pressed her entire naked body against him, wrapping her arms around his waist and sliding her hands up to the back of his heart. She felt her fear melt away. "I guess I have been putting a bit of pressure on myself."

"I know a good way to let all that pressure go. It works every time." He said with a slightly flirty tone, looking at her with admiration.

It was her turn to pour on the sarcasm, "My Lord? Have you been keeping a secret from me? You know a way that would help me to not hold on to pressure I put on myself, and you have been hiding it from me? Oh, Lord Malkore, Father of Asgard, *King* of the Feet Fuckers, a people can only move forward and grow when the truth is spoken. And a lie of omission is one of the worst kind of lies. You should tell me now."

Dropping the sarcasm, he said, "My love, I will. But it is not something I can tell you now. It is something that can happen only under proper conditions. If those conditions ever happen again, I will show you. I promise."

"Fair enough, Lord Malkore. May I introduce you to my Sanctuary now?" He nodded, still smiling at her. They were still standing at the opening to the cleared circle, "As we enter, just breathe and try not to be shocked. OK?"

He looked at her confused and cautiously, he couldn't imagine what she could be talking about. *"What could be shocking about a clearing in the woods with a wall of brush surrounding it that is twice as tall as my head?"* He thought. *"Well, when I put it like that, I guess I better be prepared for anything."*

She reached under a bush at the entrance and grabbed a rattle made from a turtle shell. "Take a deep breath, My Lord." She started, shaking the rattle all around his head as she walked in a circle around him. "This rattle came from Midgard. Going there was the first gift this place gave me. Rattles fracture awareness and help any crystallized structures in our energy to fall away or get re-oriented. You're really clean after all you have just been through, and it never hurts to have a little help."

He nodded. "Indeed. We are always grateful for all the help we can have."

"Now come with me, My Lord, Father of Asgard." She took his hand and turned him towards the center of the clearing. She began singing a song in a voice so big he was surprised in was coming from her.   The song was in a language he didn't recognize.   The resonance in her voice sounded like she was singing her own harmonies. As she sang, he began feeling his heart flutter. After the first part of the song, she took a step forward and he stepped with her.

His vision went dark.   He felt like he was floating.   He couldn't see anything but black. He felt her hand and turned to look at her. She looked like she was floating in pure blackness. *"I guess this is what she was talking about.   Oh Shit!"* He thought.

As she finished the second section of the song, she took another step forward and he stepped with her. He felt like he saw a flash of a blinding white light that was so quick that he didn't even flinch. He couldn't believe what he was seeing. It was the same clearing, with the same wall of brush around it, but there was nothing but black sky directly above, and the entire Sanctuary was filled with colored lights, like clouds of glowing color, hanging in the air, drifting around. The clouds of colored light as wide as his arms stretched out. And there was a large tree in the center of the circle. She continued singing and walked slowly to the center of the Sanctuary. She still had her eyes closed as she walked and sang. He could see that there were things piled up in the center of the sanctuary that had not been there before they entered. She stopped about two paces away from the pile of things there. He kept looking around in wonder. She sang until she got to the end of the song. Then she slowly opened her eyes.

"Oh!" She sounded surprised. "We are still here. I never know what will be here or where I will be when I come in here." Then she turned to him, "Are you OK?"

"Yes. What is this place? This is magnificent!"

"I don't know. I am just learning from it." She said.

He looked down at the stuff in front of them, "Did you leave this stuff here and it stayed hidden until we came in?"

"No. The Sanctuary provides whatever we need. Sometimes, I have opened my eyes and I have been on other worlds. Sometimes, different things will just be here waiting for me when I arrive."

"Wow! So, whatever you need is just here. So did you ask for this stuff?" He asked.

"No, it seems that the Sanctuary puts the things here for me to have the experience or do the work that I need; at least that's how I think it works." She said.

"Well, what do they have in store for us today? We have drinks, snacks, and blankets. Imagine that!" He smiled at her.

She chuckled, "Yeah. Imagine that. What do you think they want us to do?" She meant that question to sound flirty, but it came out of her mouth sounding like she was puzzled, which she was.

"Let's just sit and eat and drink and see what happens. Eh?"

"Yeah, I guess so." She picked up one of the blankets that looked the thickest. She had never felt a blanket this thick or heavy before, it was as thick as many blankets together, but not too heavy. She began to unfold the blanket and spread it out with one edge right against the tree in the center of the Sanctuary. Then she moved a couple of other blankets right against the edge of the tree. She reached for the bag of food and the skin of water, but she looked uncomfortable. She was sitting on her feet by the base of the tree in the center of the Sanctuary, looking around as if she had lost something.

"What is it?" He asked.

"I am not sure. I thought we were just going to lay down or something, but –" She kept looking around, then looked at him with a slightly disturbed look on her face. "I am not sure." She looked up at the tree and asked, "What do you guys want?" She reached out and put her hand on the tree in the center of the Sanctuary. She took a deep breath and felt herself get light-headed for a second, then the sensation faded. Then she gasped. She had her eyes closed and she dropped her head. Malkore stepped over and got on his knees right next to her. He wasn't sure what was happening, but suspected this was why they were here.

Iyasiil collapsed right into his arms and seemed to be unconscious, except her eyes were darting around beneath her eyelids. He held her for a moment, then picked her up in his arms. He maneuvered around to lay her body on the blanket that was laid out, her head on the folded-up blankets against the tree, and he carefully positioned her so that the top of her head was touching the tree. He wasn't sure if that was the right thing to do, or if it was even necessary, because she already seemed like whatever was happening had already begun, but as she had said, "It never hurts to have a little help."

She was in vision. He could see her lips twitching and her jaw barely moving as if she were talking in a dream, but the words were not coming all the way out. He laid down next to her and propped himself up on one elbow, looking at her.

- - - - - - - - - - - - - - - - - - -

She felt herself gasp. Then she stood up and looked on the ground and there was a seed that had fallen from the huge tree that had grown in her sanctuary. She picked up the seed and held it in her hand and looked up. She began lifting up towards the black, starry sky above her sanctuary. When she left the Sanctuary, she went through a tunnel of light and saw just ahead of her and opening in the tunnel of green grass. As she went through the opening of the tunnel, she landed softly on the hillside of green grass and looked down at the large seed she had in her hand. She heard the word "Yggdrasil" in her mind.

She knelt down on one knee and said her prayer, "Yggdrasil, take care of these people. Grow strong. You will be the source from Asgard. Teach them to find their own greatness. Nurture their spirit. Grow their hearts." Then she plunged her hand deep into the soil and left the seed. Then she spit on the ground above the seed and saw her spit turn into a trickle of water that soaked into the soil.

She looked up and saw a circle of clouds in the Midgard sky. She wondered if it was time to go back home or if there was more for her to do here. She saw the center of the circle of clouds above her turned black and she could see the stars. She began lifting up into the air again.

- - - - - - - - - - - - - - - - - - - -

She slowly opened her eyes a little bit and could see Malkore's head against the dancing clouds of lights. She was back in her Sanctuary.

Malkore saw her start to open her eyes, but they were pointed in different directions and still darting around. Her eyes didn't even get half open and immediately closed again.

"Yggdrasil." She said in a whisper, not quite fully back in her body.

He couldn't understand what she said, but knew she was not fully conscious, yet. "Breathe. Just take a breath."

"Yggdrasil!" She said again, more forcefully, but still with her eyes closed.

"Yggdrasil." He said, repeating it to her.

"Yes." She whispered, as if she was only barely able to speak. "Remember." Then her body relaxed. She wanted him to remember what she had said. Then she seemed to fall completely asleep.

He put his hand on her heart. Her heart was still beating. Her breath was soft and easy. To help him remember, he said softly to himself, "eeg -- drah – seel. eeg – drah – seel." He had no idea what that meant, but knew it was important, and she needed him to remember.

After several minutes of lying there, looking at her and hoping she could tell him what she had seen when she woke up, he scooted his body right up against her body and laid his head down and started to drift off to sleep himself.

When they began to wake up. They were still in the Sanctuary, but there was blue sky above them and no dancing clouds of colored lights around, just normal daylight from the sun. The tree was still there, along with the blankets and the food. She took a couple of big breaths and slowly sat up, then scooted back to lean against the tree. She put her hand on Malkore's head and then patted her thigh, wanting him to put his head on her leg. He shuffled his weight around and laid on his back with his body moving off to her right side with his head on her thigh.

"Welcome back." He said.

"Yeah, that was quite a trip. It looks like the tree might be here to stay."

"Can you tell me what you saw?" He asked.

"Yes, My Lord. I went to Midgard, again. I planted a tree from one of these seeds here." She looked at the ground around them but didn't see any seeds. She laughed, "Well, there were seeds here. I planted a tree on a hill on Midgard to guide the people there. But the tree had a name. I can't remember the name."

"Yggdrasil?"

"Yes! Oh yes. Thank you. Wait. How did you know that?" She asked.

"When you came back, you told me to remember it." He said.

"I did? I don't remember that." She said.

"I'm not surprised. You were just barely here, only enough to barely say two words." He said.

"Then I saw what I am going to do after you are gone." She said, not really realizing what she had said.

"What?! After I am gone? What does that mean?"

She laughed. "No. Not like that." She looked down at him. "We both are going to have so much work to do here for a long time, My Love. By the time you go, you are going to be glad to go on your next mission, just to get away from me." She said with a giggle. "I don't want to think about it. We have Five Hundred lifetimes before we have to worry about that." Then she realized what she just said.

"What?" He sat up and looked at her.

She started grinning as if she had just given him really good news, which she had. Tears started welling up in her eyes. She nodded.

He smiled back at her, "So I get to keep you for a while?"

She nodded again, looking like she was going to burst with happiness. They showed me how Asgard would grow and when the work was done, they showed my what my next task would be. It won't be until after you are gone. They said you would be gone for Five Hundred lifetimes, but I don't know what that means, you know? We're already Five Thousand years old, how long will you be gone to live out five Hundred lifetimes? It doesn't make sense, but I'm sure it will all be clear when the time comes."

"What am I going to do?" He asked. "I am going to leave?"

"Don't think about it, we have millennia to prepare. And we have so much work to do, My Love. You wouldn't believe what Asgard will become!" She said with a look of wonderous excitement on her face.

"The great hall, made of gold?" He asked?

"Yes! She exclaimed. "You've seen it? It is so amazing. I can't wait!" She was bubbling with energy, and her body was wiggling with excitement as she talked about it. "Oh. I finally feel like I have the full picture of what I am doing here – of why this place called me here."

"Ooooooo, that sounds good. Tell me." He said, excited to hear.

"Not yet, I will tell you very soon, but there is something I must show you first, or it won't make sense. OK?"

"OK. I can't wait to see it. Show me." He asked.

"Soon. Very soon. In just a few days, it won't be long. Oh, it's going to be so fun." She said. He reached for the skin of water and handed it to her. "By Ve, yes! Oh, I am so thirsty. Do we still have food?"

He reached for the bag of food and opened it up between them and laid all the food out. There was spicy cheese, dark bread, light bread, spread wrapped in a thin hide, and some meat wrapped in hide, too.

"Wow, the sanctuary really wants us to eat well, today." He said.

She was still glowing with energy. "Yggdrasil. I am pretty sure I was on Midgard." She was eating like she hadn't eaten in weeks. She was moaning with pleasure at the taste of the food. "Oh, listen to me. I sound like you when you eat." Then she giggled.

"You must be happy, then." He said.

She stopped chewing and looked at him with a mouthful of food. "I am so happy." She said. It wasn't that her face was smiling at him, her whole body was radiating the warmth and fun of her smile.

"You are so adorable. I am a very blessed man." He said, preparing her another piece of bread with the buttery spread in it and two pieces of bread with meat and spicy cheese in them.

She took another bite and looked up at the sky above them, wiggling her whole body. "Oh, wow! This is the best food I have ever eaten. Oh, what a wonderful day." She looked at him, still glowing. "What a wonderful day, with such a wonderful man."

"I am so happy. I wanted to make a day for you that was wonderful." He said, smiling.

"You know, we don't need a portal for this, but it's always good to have a sacred place to sit and do what we do." She said with a smile.

It always struck him that she never smiled to communicate anything, she only smiled because her inner beauty and peace were leaking out of her body from her face.

"What do you mean?" He asked.

"I haven't learned to do it, yet, but I've seen in vision where it's possible to get quiet enough and clear enough inside to travel to other worlds without a portal, like this one." She said.

"I've suspected that. But you weren't shown how to do it?" He asked.

"No, I guess I will have to keep coming here until I figure it out." She said.

"How about when Frigg pulled that horn out of her robe the other night? Is that one of your tricks, too, you witch?" He asked.

"No, that's not one of mine. We all have different gifts. I think I have done it a couple of times in a panic situation, but I am not sure. Each time, it was one of those scary situations where my memory was jumbled. And it was a long time ago."

"Well, *there's* a story to be told." He said, wanting to hear the story.

"No, not really. I just found myself in some scary situations a long time ago and needed to fight my way out. Now, if I found myself in such a scary place, it's easier to disappear." She said with a giggle.

"Yeah, I have been meaning to ask you about that . . ."

"Oh, Lord Malkore. I can't give up all my secrets, yet." She smiled a coy smile at him.

"Uh huh." He said, not buying whatever she was trying to sell.

They continued talking and relaxing for a little while longer. Then they got up to go back to the entrance of the Sanctuary. She really liked the thick blanket and wondered if the Sanctuary would let her take it back to her house. They stopped at the inner boundary of the Sanctuary. She stopped and held out her hand for him to hold it. When he took her hand, she squeezed it in hers.

She began singing again, and they slowly walked through the barrier between the inner Sanctuary and the rest of the world. When they got out to the branches where their clothes were hanging, she still had the thick blanket across her shoulder. She smiled and turned back to the center of the Sanctuary and said, "Thank you, dear ones." Then she blew a kiss towards the center of the Sanctuary.

He noticed the huge tree in the center of the Sanctuary was gone. "It's gone."

"What?" She asked.

"The tree." He spent all of one second running through ideas in his head, trying to make sense of what he was seeing.

Then he realized that the best way to appreciate magic is to enjoy it. "Wow."

She looked back in, "Yeah, it looks so plain now, doesn't it?"

"Yeah, not a single dancing cloud of light, anywhere." He smiled at what an amazing place she had found.

"Yeah, funny how that works, huh?" She laughed, enjoying his wonder.

They got dressed and started walking out. When they got about 20 paces away from the Sanctuary, he looked back, wondering if he would be able to find this place on his own. "Mother Fucker! It's gone too." He was looking at a wide, clear sloping hillside with trees and a thick canopy cover, high above the ground.

She started laughing and kept walking, "First time being married to a witch, My Lord?"

He was still looking back, stopped in his tracks, trying to see if he could see any indication of where he had just been. His jaw was hanging open . . .

She turned to see if he was still walking with her and laughed out loud. She walked back to him and wrapped her arms around his arm. "You'll never find it, unless it chooses you."

"Oh shit! I mean . . . I mean . . . Oh shit!" He had the biggest look of wonder on his face.

"I figured this would be the place to bring Odin, when the time comes." She said.

"Yeah! Oh, wow! Yes, that will be perfect. I may not even have to do the part I was thinking about. Your Sanctuary may do it all." He said as they turned and started walking towards home.

"I don't know how it all will go, so we better be ready for anything. What's the part you were thinking? Can you share?" She asked.

"Well, when Frigg mentioned that Odin would be in a state of physical flux, I pictured giving him a massage, much like you got today."

"Oh, yes! OK, I see it now." She interjected.

"I just saw you and Frigg there talking to him, as he was lying there. You two were creating a new awareness in Odin as she begins coming out of her transition. I have no idea what you would say to him/her, but I trust you two amazing women to know what to do when the time comes." He said. "Now that I say it, it doesn't sound like much, but it felt pretty big at the time. I hope we can do this."

"My Lord, I don't know if you realize the power you carry in your heart and in your hands." She said.

"What do you mean?" He looked at her with a puzzled look on his face. He took the heavy blanket off her shoulder and was going to carry it home for her.

"My Lord, when you were massaging me this morning. I had to stop you at one point because I didn't know whether or not I would take off and journey through the cosmos and never come back. It wasn't like massaging you. I left and went and touched the heart of Creation, these people call it the fires of Muspell, it's known by lots of names in lots of places. But the point is: You sent me there – No teas, no herbs, no little dream mushrooms, no fasting in the forest for days and weeks at a time. You did it with your presence and how you managed my energy, and how you filled me up as you made space for me. No one does that!"

"Wow! Thank you, My Love. But I am not doing anything anyone else can't do. It's just a matter of getting clear enough inside to listen and letting enough love flow . . ." He said.

"I know. Just like pulling a drinking horn out of an empty robe, or making a man think you have disappeared when he's chasing you through the forest. Anyone can learn, but not many have. And that doesn't take away from how amazing of a gift it is to offer to someone -- it doesn't take away from how amazing you are *to me*. You got that, Lord Feet Fucker?!"

He laughed his big, boisterous warrior's laugh and grabbed her around the waist, picking her up in the air. He swung her around, hugging her, then set her down and kissed her. "I really hope that name doesn't catch on. Please, please don't let that catch on. You and the girls are the only ones allowed to call me that."

"My Lord, it would be impossible for anyone else to call you that, because no one else will ever hear it. Unless Asgard gets boring, and we need to create salacious rumors about you and your three wives and all the crazy kinds of sex you all like to have." She couldn't keep herself from laughing at the thought.

He looked at her like she was crazy. Then he smiled and said, "If it comes to that, I am going to challenge Odin for the throne myself and change the name from Asgard to FeetFuckia." She laughed again, then he went on, his words dripping with sarcasm, "Then you will be forced to call me King Feet Fucker! And there will be severe punishments if you don't." He looked in her eyes, adoring her. "You don't want me to have to punish you, do you?!"

"My Lord . . . excuse me . . . King Feet Fucker, being punished by you sounds like the kind of thing that would be awesome in the land of FeetFuckia!"

That caught him off guard. He turned to the side, bent over, stumbling forward, about to fall, laughing so hard. "You funny fucking witch!" He was laughing so hard, he was almost gasping to catch his breath.

She walked up to him and took his hand and said, "My Lord, take me home. I want to show you what my feet can do." She smiled at him and started walking towards home again.

He started laughing harder, again. "I love you, woman! You are so much fun in so many ways! I think I have laughed more in the last three days than I did in the last three years."

"Hold on, Lord Feet Fucker, It's only going to get better from here." She said with a confident smile on her face.

Chapter Twelve
Listen to the Forest

They got back to her chambers, and he asked her what she would like to do the rest of the day. She was taking her dress off to clean her body up with the cloth in the warm water by the fire. She got a really pensive look on her face. "Remember when we were in the Sanctuary, I told you that I would have to show you something before I could tell you about my long-term plans?"

"Yes, of course." He walked over to her and took the cloth from her hand and started wiping down her skin, as she had done to him their first night together.

She smiled. It was such a nice gesture, "You are so thoughtful. I am not used to that."

Without really responding to what she said, he stayed focused on washing her body. "Yeah, I'm not used to it, either. Keep telling me about what is so heavy on your heart, My Love."

"It is something I am wrapping up and putting in the ground for a few days until I can show you and we can talk about it. I am sorry to be so secretive, but that just can't be helped. Just know that it's really big for me. It will be the culmination of all that I have done, my entire life. Well, that's pretty dramatic –

But it feels that way, right now." She turned and looked at him. "It scares me, and I will need lots of support in making peace with it."

"Anything! Just tell me what you want, when it's time. Tell me what you need. I'll be there." He said.

"Thank you. And thank you for understanding that I can't tell you, right now. It's too scary to talk about it without you seeing what I have to show you, first. I know that's stupid, and I know you would probably take it all in and see the vision right along with me."

"I understand." He said, washing her ass with the warm water.

"Mmmm. That feels good." She said, closing her eyes and taking a deep breath.

"As it should, My Love." He finished washing her legs and her feet. "Did I miss any spots?"

"My lips." She said, looking into his eyes.

He rinsed the cloth out in the warm water several times, then started to reach up to her lips with the cloth. "No, not that way. Use your lips. Please." She used her alluring look to try and hook him and reel him in.

He dropped the cloth in the water basin and slowly looked at her, starting at her feet, and worked his eyes slowly up her body. When he got to her face, he looked into her eyes and stepped the half step closer, so his body was touching hers, then pointed at his own lips with his finger, "These lips?" He asked.

"MmmmHmmm." She said, nodding her head.

"You want me to use these lips, to clean your lips?" He asked, flirting more.

"Yes, please." She said, looking up and down from his eyes then to his lips, then back to his eyes again.

"But what if I get your lips really clean that way and you get spoiled? Then you are going to want me to do this all the time." He said with sarcastic concern.

She responded in such a soft, sensuous tone that was the opposite of her sarcastic response, "Such a wise man! You figured that out all on your own, did you? Now quit fucking around, Lord Feet Fucker, I can't stand my lips being this dirty."

He was laughing too hard to kiss her. He hugged her, then picked her up and carried her over to the bed and got on top of her, straddling her hips, laying his chest against her, and kissed her several times. "Is that better, My Love?"

"Not yet. My lips got *really* dirty while we were on our walk today." She said.

"Well now, we can't have that can we?" He kissed her lips. He kissed the corner of her mouth, her cheek, the back of her jaw in front of the bottom of her ear, then he moved to her neck below her ear and down to the tip of her shoulder. He grabbed the massage oil and began rubbing her collarbones and the base of her neck, occasionally leaning down to kiss up the front of her neck, under her chin, and up to her lips again.

He could feel her excitement growing. He could feel how turned on she was getting, "Would you like to stay here for a little while? Or would you like to go get food in the great hall now, My Love?"

"My Lord, if you stop kissing me, I'm going to hurt you." She said.

He got up and took off his clothes, then knelt between her knees and began massaging her with long strokes, hands spread wide, from her hips up to the bottom of her breasts. After every three or four strokes, he would finish the massage stroke going wide around her breasts and across the top of her chest, onto her collarbones towards her neck. He let his weight fall onto his left fist on the bed and slid his right hand up her neck. Cradling the side of her head, with his fingertips behind her ear and his thumb on her jaw, he leaned down and kissed her again. "Iyasiil, My Love. I am probably the most disciplined man in Asgard. I almost never fail at my mission."

"OK." She said, with a curious tone, not sure where he was going with this.

"I had thought to give you a short massage. I think I am going to fail." He kissed her again. "It's horrible to put one's selfish desires ahead of the needs of someone during a Tending." He said.

She was in no mood for sarcasm at that moment. "I don't need to be taken care of. I don't need a massage right now. I want *you*. Now." She said.

He kissed her again. "So, I can be selfish with you?" He asked in a flirty way, pretending to sound surprised.

"If you don't be selfish with me, I am going to totally fuck you up!" She said with a come-get-me look in her eye.

As he moved backwards and leaned down to kiss her yoni. "Your day – your rules." He said softly. He moved her legs and put her thighs on his shoulders and slid his hands under her hips.

She was caught off guard. "Oh, fuck yeah! You keep surprising me." She said with a gasp.

He began lightly running his face and lips all around the inside of her thighs, gently stroking the sides of her yoni with the tip of his nose, and softly grazing the skin over her clitoris with his lips. "It's what we do, My Love."

He felt her body tighten, then he felt her body relax. He licked the sides of her vulva, slightly sucking the soft skin into his lips, then licking firmly up each side of her yoni. He spread the lips of her yoni with his tongue and spread his tongue wide and made circles from the very back until his tongue was resting softly on her clitoris. He shaped his tongue like a spoon and scooped it inside her yoni, finishing with the broad tip of his tongue reaching inside on the front wall of her yoni. Then making his tongue wide and flat again, he slowly licked up to her clitoris and wrapped his lips around it, lightly sucking it into his mouth and massaging it with his tongue.

He moved his body up above hers and snuggled his forearms under her shoulders. He pulled his knees up and scooted his hips as close to hers as he could. She pulled his hips towards her with her heels on his ass. She could feel his cock between her legs and wanted him to make love with her right at that moment, she was ready. Instead, he kissed her several more times, then raised his body up to bring his cock onto her stomach, then slowly slide it down. He slid his cock down so that the tip of his cock was touching her clitoris.

She reached with her hips, hoping to take him inside. He slid the entire length of his cock up her clitoris.

Her body was screaming, "Now! *More! I want you.*" She felt so excited and so open, like the only thing that mattered was having him inside her.

He slid his cock up and down her clitoris several more times before his cock slipped down to the entrance to her yoni. She reached for him with her hips, again. He pulled his cock back, so he wouldn't slide inside her. He held his body still and looked into her eyes. She looked back into his eyes.

He thought, "*I am yours, but you don't get to decide how or when.*"

She felt his words through his presence. She had never met a man with such a strong masculine presence, much less one who had his heart so present. She felt so met and like he could handle all of her. She didn't feel like she had to handle anything, she felt so easy and soft in his presence. She got to rest in her feminine with him. She had never felt that – not while feeling her own power. She shouldn't have been surprised at how erotic that was. She was aching to feel him inside, she could feel her insides reaching, trying to find him and pull him in, "Please, My Lord."

"I am yours." He replied and slid his cock inside her.

She felt like he went to the heart of her. She looked deep into his eyes, and he didn't shy away. "Yes." She wanted to say more, but there were no words.

He couldn't tell what was more powerful, right then. He felt like his heart was exploding. He felt so much love flowing through him, and he could feel her receiving it. It made him want to love her more. He had never felt his cock so engorged, and he shook his head and thought, "*It's the heart that pumps blood to the cock, not the other way around.*"

She saw him shake his head. "What?" She said, seeing his amusement.

With a half chuckle, he said, "Never. I have never . . . *this* is why I haven't had sex in forever . . . I know I bring a lot, and I quit having sex, because I couldn't feel anyone show up like you." He said.

She stopped and looked at him. "Yes. That's why you feel so good. I feel my heart so full. Thank you."

"No, Love. Thank *you*!" He said. He didn't know what else he could say. He leaned down and put his head on her forehead and gently rubbed his nose on the tip of her nose. "Thank you . . . Thank you for the path you walked to get you here." He emphasized his gratitude with a thrust of his cock. "Thank you for finding your heart." Another trust of his cock.

She looked at him and had never felt her own heart as big while with another person. "Yes."

"Thank you for not giving up when your path was hard." He said with another thrust of his cock deep inside of her. "Thank you for finding your way here." He heard that deep, gravelly growl come out. He wanted to say more; to tell her even more how blown away he was with her. And he was getting lost in feeling her heart and her body. Part of him only wanted to melt into her heart and part of him didn't want to stop thrusting his cock deep inside her.

He did both. At times, he felt himself melt his heart into her heart. Other times, he felt how much it shook his nerves to feel so amazing inside her. He wanted to feel them both at the same time.

She arched her back and tilted her head back and to the right. She was moaning and gasping and squealing and cursing and yelling. He leaned down, opened his mouth wide and kissed her throat, sucking on her throat, massaging it with his tongue, and wanting to hear everything that she would ever say.

She let out a loud half-scream, half-growl that she had never made before. She reached up and grabbed the back of his head and pressed his head into her throat, wanting to let every part of her out into him.

He growled into her throat, thinking, "*I want all of you.*" He felt himself falling into her like falling into an abyss. He felt like he was floating into the deepest darkness, a blowing blackness, the deepest part.

He could tell that his body was still moving, he could still feel amazing pleasure magnified by the depth of her presence and his spirit was falling into that deepest place. Her screams and moans faded. The feel of her skin against his skin faded. His vision faded.

He could only see a spot off in the distance of his awareness, he could feel himself going through that portal into another world. He looked around and he could see a vast jungle full of plants. Plants of all sizes, with flowers of all different colors. As he walked towards one plant that was as tall as he was, it spoke to him. "Thank you for answering."

"What? I didn't – Where?" He looked around and he could hear the voices of all the plants. Some of them were singing. Some of them were talking to him, thanking him for coming to visit. Some of them were honoring him, almost as if they were bowing to him, waiting for their chance to talk with him. "You look like a plant on Asgard."

"I am. We seeded all the planets. We gave them all the green life you see." It said.

"The plants there don't talk. Not like you do." He said, baffled by what he was seeing and hearing.

"Sure, they do. Just listen."

"No, I know. There are only a few of us who have learned to listen." Malkore said.

"We know. We are always talking to you. Take a walk around. So many of us want to talk to you while you are here."

He was drawn to some small flowers nearby. He looked at them as he was walking towards them. He started feeling happy and feisty inside as he looked at them. "Hey guys . . ."

"Malkore!" They yelled. "What took you so long? You o d bear!" They said.

He thought, *"Am I hearing that right? Are they fucking with me?!"* "Sorry guys, I couldn't see you. All the real plants were n the way." If they were offended, he was ready to apologize, but he went with his gut feeling.

They all screamed with laughter! "Malkore, you old statsa root, I'm going to tell the next jorta pod you eat to go rotten n your stomach!"

"These guys are hilarious!" He thought. He was laughing. "You guys are awesome. I never knew plants could be funny." He said.

One of the flowers seemed to stand a little taller and say, "Hey man, we aren't like those fuckers from the reptile planet . . ." Malkore laughed, but also wondered if all the reptiles on Asgard were seeded there too from the reptile planet. "Of course they were, how else could something so ugly grow on a beautiful planet covered in all of us, man!"

"Oh shit. He just read my mind." He thought.

"Of course I read your mind, old man. Hey, you probably think I'm a fucking witch, eh?!" Then all the plants laughed.

Malkore screamed with laughter. "So, you know my witch? Huh?"

"Hey man, who do you think led her to you?! Who do you think built that Sanctuary that called her to you?!"

Malkore looked stunned. *They see everything. Wow!*" He thought.

"Of course, we see everything, old man! Unless you are in a cave somewhere . . . then we have to go ask the rock people to give us a report on what you guys were doing in there."

"Wow! Why am I here?" He asked.

A soft voice spoke from behind him. It sounded like a patient, loving, feminine voice. "Tell Frigg that Seven will do and as soon as Odin wakes up, give him the red grass tea. For everything else, you will have what you need. Goodbye, Lord Malkore." He tried to turn around to see who had spoken to him, but it was fading too quickly.

He felt himself slowly start to wake up, as if he had been sleeping. He was back with Iyasiil. He heard a long growl that turned into a scream and as he was landing back in his body. His whole body went numb. He heard a scream. It took a second to get back into his body. It took a second to catch up with what his body was doing. He was orgasming. It felt like an orgasm without end. His brain was fractured and fracturing, his voice was screaming and growling.

He heard another scream. It was her. He looked at her. She was OK. Then he felt like he had been struck in the back by a falling tree, hit by lightning. He collapsed on her. All he could do was make that growling scream. Then his body shook inside her.

She grabbed him with her arms around his shoulders and dug her heels into his low back. All she could do was scream. She buried her face in his shoulder and screamed, pulling him into her with all her strength. She kept trying to say something but only gasps and moans came out.

He said, "Grass tea." As he was saying it, he realized he was in no condition to try and talk.

"What the fuck did he just say?" Her brain wasn't quite working, either. She tried to catch her breath and regain her senses quickly. He was quieter inside than she ever felt him. They had been making love so hard, she hadn't even checked in with how he was doing. "Malkore. What?"

He rolled off of her and pulled her up onto him so hard she thought that she may fly off the bed onto the floor, then she felt his strong arms pull her right into his chest. "Grass tea. Grass tea for Odin."

She started to realized how far gone he was at that moment. *"Grass tea for Odin? What the fuck does that mean? What is grass tea?"* She thought. Then she slowly realized that he was trying to tell her something and he wasn't able to. *"Wow. He's gone. I need to come back to make sure he is OK."* She thought.

Under any other circumstances, she would have felt him slip off into vision or begin to soul travel, but she had been lost and was only feeling her own energy and everything that was flowing through him. She didn't notice him leave, she only felt like her heart and body had gotten shattered in the most amazing way. "Take a breath. I am right here. Just keep breathing." She looked at him, and he had a far-off stare in his eyes. He was still halfway into a journey or vision.

He was breathing. He was slowly coming back into his body more. He started laughing a little. "They were so funny." He said. "They were so funny." Then a tear rolled down the side of his face.

She knew she was going to be in for a hell of a story when he got fully back in his body. "Keep breathing. I'll remember, "grass tea" and "they were so funny."

"They put it all here. Everything." He said. Then he turned his head and looked at her and smiled, then he started laughing again. He started to try and say something, but only started laughing harder.

She couldn't imagine what was going on with him, but she started feeling lighter.

"They . . . they agreed with me. They said you really are a fucking witch!" Then he started laughing even harder. After another 20 seconds or so, he was able to take a full beath, and then another. "Oh, Love. I love you so much. I met the ones who built your Sanctuary. It was the little spicy flower people that were so funny. Oh wow!" Then he started chuckling again.

She was laughing, too, his laughter was infectious, but she still had no idea what he was talking about. "Wow. Sounds like an awesome ride. Welcome back."

"Yeah, Shit! I didn't see that coming. Wow." He said. Then he took a big breath and looked at her, "I hope I didn't kill the mood."

"You didn't kill my mood. I was cumming so hard, a didn't even know you were gone." She said.

"Good."

"I did feel like my heart got blown open right there at the end, so maybe I was feeling something." She said.

"Yeah. I hope so." He was still trying to fully catch his breath and looked at her. "I'll tell you the whole thing in a minute, but Love, it was so beautiful! It was the planet of plants – like it was the home planet of all the plants." He started talking a little bit faster, "They said they seeded all the planets, so all the planets would have green plants. And they talked; they thought and talked. And they said that we all need to listen to them, that the plants here are not any different, that we all should listen to them," he looked at her, "like you do."

She looked at him smiling, wanting to hear more. "And?"

"And the first one who spoke to me told me there were lots who wanted to speak to me. I went over to these little guys who were hilarious. They started fucking with me before I even got there. Iyasiil, it was incredible!" Then he started laughing again, "they said that they weren't like." He was trying to tell her the story but kept laughing too hard. She was getting tickled by his happiness and how fun it sounded. "Oh man, I told them that I never knew that plants could be so funny. And they said, "Of course we are. We aren't like the reptile planet." He roared with laughter, remembering what he had seen.

She looked at him, amused by his laughter, hoping she was going to understand. "What?"

"OK. Apparently, all the life here was seeded here by other planets. They showed me a picture of the reptile planet – a planet of smart, talking reptiles, who seeded all the other planets with their kind of life, along with the plant planet. All the plants and trees here, come from there." He paused and stared off into his vision. "I don't know what any of that means, but it was beautiful."

She slid off of him and laid next to him, propped up on her elbow. "What about my Sanctuary?" She asked.

"Oh yeah! That was so cool! They said that they built if for you. They built it for you because you listened to them -- all the plants and trees, that way they could tell you how to find Asgard." He looked at her stunned.

"What is it?" She asked.

He was feeling good enough to get back to his usual flirty sarcasm, he looked at her with a very-satisfied-with-himself look on his face, "Well, I am not saying that I am a great catch, or anything. But they said, they built your Sanctuary so you could find your way to me." Then he shifted to a small, pathetic demeanor, "Or maybe they just were taking pity on me and figured I needed an amazing woman to keep me from living a miserable, pathetic life." He smiled at her.

She smiled, "Lord Malkore, I think you're the best catch anywhere besides the fish planet."

He screamed laughing. "What the fuck, woman! No one's humor ever catches me off guard. Ever! And you keep smacking me in the back of the head with the funniest shit! Oh, Goddess. You are amazing."

She was laughing. Then asked. "What about the tea?"

"What tea?" He asked with a confused look on his face.

You said, "Tea for Odin."

He shook his head as if he were just snapped back to awareness, "Oh shit. That was the point of the whole journey. That's why they sent me there. They said to give him tea."

"What? They called you there to tell you to give Odin tea?" She asked, not understanding what that could mean.

"No. No. I don't remember. It was something about Odin." He said, still feeling lost to remember the rest. He got up on one elbow facing her.

"But no idea why we need to give Odin tea?" She asked.

"It was something about Frigg." He looked at her shaking his head. "I am sorry. I don't remember. Maybe it will come to me." He said.

"Frigg and grass tea . . ."

"Grass tea! That was it! They said it would be enough and to give him grass tea." He looked at her. "Do you . . . it was red grass tea. Does that make any sense?" He asked.

"Oh. Yeah. Of course, the tea from the red tinged grass. Yeah. That's what I gave you the other night. But what about Frigg?" She asked.

With a clear voice, he said, "They said it would be enough."

"What would be enough?"

"Shit. I don't know. They just said to tell Frigg it would be enough." He shook his head. "All seven. That's it. Tell Frigg that Seven would be enough. And then give him the red grass tea."

"OK. That all makes sense now. Frigg was talking about giving Odin seven of her herbs. We just need to give him some tea when she does." She said.

"No, after he wakes up, they said."

"Ok, after he wakes up, we give him tea that will knock him back out, again. That should be interesting. We may be there a while." She said.

"Yeah, sounds like it." He said.

"Wow! Sounds like a hell of a trip that you had, Lord Malkore." She said.

"Yeah." Then he looked at her and asked, "Did I ruin your day of Tending by going off and talking to smart-ass little plants without inviting you?" He asked.

"Oh. No. Absolutely not, My Lord. I had quite a journey myself. I went straight to the orgasm planet and got my soul blown open. No ruining happened here while you were gone." She said.

Still feeling a little worried, he asked, "Really? Are you being serious?"

"Oh. Lord Malkore, I will never be the same . . ." She said with a smile and a look of wonder on her face.

Then with a flirty tone that had just a hint of gloating in it, he said, "Yeah, The Father of Asgard put it on you good?"

She laughed and replied, "No, but Lord Feet Fucker knocked me the fuck out!"

He roared with laughter.

Just after the sun began to set, Malkore and Iyasiil got dressed. They met Kalla and Dossa in the great hall. Malkore looked around and for some reason thought about the boy. He almost wanted the boy to come join them, but he hadn't seen the boy all day.

Several people stopped by where they were sitting and asked Malkore if he was ready for the warrior training that would be happening the following day. Malkore always responded, "Absolutely. Make sure that you are ready." Some of the men took it in stride, some of them took it as a warning not to drink too much that night.

All four of them were really hungry. All the emotional activity over the last days burned a lot of energy. They all enjoyed eating and the food was delicious.

After they ate, the crowd thinned out and the four of them stayed in the great hall to continue their conversation.

One young lady came by and got their plates and refilled their horns. It was usually Kalla and Dossa doing that, they weren't used to anyone doing anything like that for them.

Kalla and Dossa wanted to hear all about how the day had gone for their teacher and Lord Malkore since they had left their teacher's chambers at lunch time, but they could sense that the stories would have to wait for another day.

Kalla was sitting next to Iyasiil, she looked at her teacher and asked, "If you are free, could I have some time with you tomorrow, just the two of us?"

"Yes, of course, Love. Is everything OK?"

Kalla said, "Yes. Everything is amazing and if tomorrow is not too soon to talk about it all, I just want to ask you a couple of hundred questions. That's all."

Iyasiil smiled, and laughed, adoringly at Kalla, "Oh My Goddess, you are so beautiful. I love you so much. Of course. I think we should go out to the East woods and go for a walk."

"OK, thank you, Mama." Kalla said.

Iyasiil said, "Why don't you pack up some food and come get me at high sun." Kalla nodded.

Malkore asked, "Dossa, are you not going to join them tomorrow?"

"No, My Lord. Not tomorrow." Then with a funny, self-deprecating tone, she said, "Whenever we have not been with the two of you, the last several days, Kalla has been working overtime, Tending to me. I have needed lots of holding this week. I have never felt better, but you and Mama sure know how to fuck a girl up." The all laughed.

Malkore put his hand on her shoulder, "Just the fact that you can joke about it that way, is a good sign. It means that you aren't beating yourself up about it and you aren't shaming yourself, too hard."

"No, not really. I just wish I'd started sooner." Dossa said.

Malkore said, "Ah, yes. I wish I had started sooner, too." Iyasiil snickered at his response.

Dossa looked at him, not sure if he was serious or not. "Seriously? Look at everything you have done!"

"Dossa, as long as you work with your teacher, and really commit to walking the path that she will help you find, you will do so much more than me by the time you are my age. I didn't have a teacher who already knew what mistakes to avoid. I had to learn the hard way how to learn to do things the easy way. Some things you'll have to learn on your own, but even in that, you'll be able to learn everything faster than your teacher did or I did." He said.

"Lord Malkore, you haven't really had anyone to guide you either, have you?" Iyasiil asked.

Malkore smiled and felt a hint of how hard his life had been, "No, I learned by trying all the different ways that *don't* work, first. Only after trying all the wrong ways to do something, did I ever find the right way. I am kind of stubborn and not very bright when it comes to that." They all laughed. He looked at Iyasiil, "I expect that you floated beautifully and gracefully into every lesson. You learned and were carried off on the wings of butterflies and rainbows, right?"

She laughed. "Yeah, No. That's not the path that I signed up for, initially, either. I, too, chose the stubborn, figure-it-all-out-the-hard-way path." Iyasiil said. "I wouldn't trade it for anything, I am thankful for every step I've taken." Then she looked at Dossa, then Kalla and said, "By the way girls, when you learn the lesson, you never have any regrets, remember that." Then turning back to Malkore, "Ya know, looking back, there really wasn't any other way. It wasn't like I was trying to do everything the hard way, there just weren't any teachers like us." motioning between herself and Malkore, "I looked. But there were no teachers around. But that's not anything new to you, either. Is it, My Lord?"

He shook his head, "No. The way I think about it now, the way I want it to be for everyone, is that: It was our job to be there for you when you were young. We failed you, by not preparing our elders to be ready to teach you. You should have never had to walk that path, learning the hard way."

"You were just a boy, and you had to find your own path. There was nothing you could have done, then, My Lord." Iyasiil said to him.

"I know. But, that doesn't mean that it isn't my responsibility, and Kalla's responsibility, and Dossa's responsibility to make sure we are ready to make the world a better place for the ones to come. Kalla and Dossa are the teachers of the next generations. If the children born a millennia after them, don't have teachers, it is because none of us sitting here have done our part."

"That feels like a lot of responsibility." Dossa said.

Iyasiil said, "It *is* a lot of responsibility. And right now, you doing your part is letting yourself soak in the love available to you and learning to accept yourself. Today, can you handle the responsibility of letting yourself soak in the love from the three of us?"

Dossa smiled. "Yes, I can handle that. I just wish I could give all of you more, like you are giving me."

Kalla interjected, "So you are not good enough because you are letting yourself be loved? Is that it?! Dossa, shut up! You always putting yourself down like that?! I hate it when you do that!"

Malkore said, "The first lesson is to learn to accept yourself more than you judge yourself – the more you do that, then you can start to laugh at those fears that lead to judging yourself. When those fears pop into your head, they show you the places that you haven't learned to love you, yet. Put it this way, Kalla, how has it been for you loving on Dossa a little extra the last several days?"

Kalla's face lit up, "It's been wonderful! She is finally lett ng me love her like I want to."

Malkore asked, "Does loving her feel good?"

"Yes." Kalla said, looking at Dossa.

"How good?" Malkore asked.

"So good!" Kalla looked at Dossa, "I feel like I could cry and melt because I love you so much." Kalla said to her.

Malkore went on, "So Dossa, you could beat yourself up for needing love, or you could get love from someone who loves you. If you beat yourself up or hide your heart in any other way, you take all that away from Kalla," he paused for effect, "and you take it away from your teacher," he said pointing at Iyasiil. "And if you beat yourself up, I don't get to love you either."

Dossa leaned over on Malkore's arm. She was still unsure and looked at her teacher to see if her teacher had a problem with her leaning on Malkore's arm. Iyasiil just smiled at her and nodded her head slightly. Iyasiil said, "Feel how his arm feels, even sitting here at dinner. He loves you that much. And loving you feels just as good to him as it does to you."

Dossa wrapped her arms around his arm and hugged his arm, then looked up at him.

He leaned down and kissed her on the top of her head. Then caught himself, "Was that OK? I didn't ask if you were OK with me giving you a kiss."

She nodded, "Of course. It's OK. I want you to kiss me, it's just . . . I . . . uhhhh." Then Dossa let out a frustrated groan, "Uuuuuggghhh. This is going to take some getting used to. I am not used to *not* feeling like a fuck up."

"Yeah, that's the first lesson. I am glad you are paying attention." Malkore said to her.

Dossa asked, "So, how do you do things if you aren't a fuck-up? I can't even imagine how that works."

Malkore looked at her, "Well, how do you feel right now, hugging my arm?" He could tell she was thinking about it. He laid his other hand on her arm, "Really, how do you feel doing that, right this second?" She was struggling to feel like she had a right to feel loved. "Check in with your body and your heart. Take a big breath. What does your body feel like on my arm?" He asked her.

"It feels good." She said.

"Of course, it does. So, that's how you do it. When you are with someone safe and someone who loves you and cares about you, of course it will feel good. It feels just as good to me. So, if you want, and it is entirely up to you, stay there as long as you want, I'll keep loving you and I will keep feeling your love. How does that sound?" He asked her.

She nodded. "Me too." She said, wanting to be funny, acknowledging that she wanted to stay where she was.

They all stayed and talked for a little while. The conversation meandered all over the place. The intensity of the last several days was falling off. Others came to join them for short periods of time, then went on their way. They had all had a very intense few days. At one point, Iyasiil yawned. Malkore took that as a sign that they all should break for the night.

The day had been very full and Malkore knew the next day could be very intense depending on how Odin approached training. He hoped the day would go well and he was prepared to easily challenge every man in Asgard if that's what it took to begin training the men how he wanted to.

They got up to leave and Iyasiil hugged Kalla. Kalla hugged her then pulled her head back to look at her teacher, then said, "I love you so much, Mama – all day." Then she kissed her teacher on the cheek.

"I love you, too, sweet Kalla."

Dossa got up and stood on the bench to hug Malkore. Standing on the bench, she was barely taller than him and she kissed him on the forehead. Dossa said, "Good night, sweet forehead. I love you."

He laughed. "Good night, sweet Dossa. Carry our love with you."

Kalla saw Dossa kiss Malkore on the forehead and said, "Me too. Me too." She jumped up on the bench and was several inches taller than him. "Wow! I like it up here. I'm taller than you, are you scared of me now, big guy?"

He laughed, again. "Should I be?" He asked.

"Probably." She said, playfully.

"OK. I am not scared, yet. Right now, I just want to hug you, and I want you to have a great night, tonight. Sleep well and have awesome dreams."

"I am going to dream of fucking your feet with my feet." Kalla said. Malkore laughed.

Dossa heard that and started laughing as she was hugging her teacher, and quietly said, "I would say there is something wrong with that girl, but I kind of feel the same way."

Iyasiil laughed. "I love you so much. And, in addition to that, you crack me up! Have a good night and sleep well, sweet Dossa."

They all walked out of the great hall. Kalla and Dossa walked towards the house where several young ladies lived.

- - - - - - - - - - - - - - - - - - - -

Iyasiil and Malkore returned to her chambers and got ready for bed. They talked for a little while, once they got into bed. They talked about everything that had been going on the last several days.

"Can you believe we only met four days ago?" He asked.

"It's hard to believe. I know this is going to sound weird, but after last night, when Frigg was here, I feel like we have been married for a month already. I just can't wrap my brain around the fact that we just met and that we only just came out of ceremony. It seems like so much has happened. It doesn't seem like it could have all possibly happened in just four days." She said, then she realized how she had said the part about marriage. "I hope that didn't sound weird. I am not assuming that we really are married, now."

He laughed and smiled, "No, I get it. It really has started to feel like we have been married for a while. Whether we are married or not, I want to be here with you right now. I want to hold you tonight and wake up next to you in the morning."

"Yes. Me too, My Lord Malkore. Being held by you, right here, right now, is what I want, too." She said.

He started chuckling, to himself.

"What is it?" She lifted her head off of his shoulder and looked at him. "What are you laughing at?" She asked.

"Well, we have had sex four or five times now, and" he started laughing harder and was having trouble getting the words out, "each time there has been some kind of big emotional release or journey, right?"

"Yes. Is that a problem, My Lord?" she asked sarcastically, knowing it was an amazing blessing.

"No. No. I just had the thought, and it made me laugh, that maybe, in the morning, we should try having sex like normal people. You know, sex where so one spirit travels; no one feels like they get broken in half and rebuilt, emotionally; sex where no one is incapacitated for a while afterwards." He was still laughing.

She was laughing too. "Yeah, that sounds great. I am sure we both can happily stay disconnected from our own hearts and from each other enough to stop it. All we have to do is betray what feels like the unstoppable force of our spirits dancing half-way into the other worlds together. That sounds awesome."

"See! I knew you would understand." He laughed more. "Seriously, feeling disconnected is why I quit having sex, forever ago. I am all in for transformational love making, as well as silly, playful, deeply connected sex, --"

"Fuck, yeah! Playfulness is the best!" She interjected and laid her head back down onto his shoulder.

"Right?! And sometimes, it was strange missing sex so much, and never having it because I was never satisfied when there wasn't the kind of deep-connection I have enjoyed with you. I guess I was holding out for something that I wasn't even sure was possible."

"Yes. I feel the same." She said.

"Having gotten to experience it, with you, now I feel different. I feel free, like a part of me is free to come out and play." He said.

"Oh, Malkore, *yes*, please. That feels so good."

"So, selfishly, I want to ask, if we could keep this up for at least another day or two." He said.

She laughed. "OK, but only for another day or two." She said sarcastically, "Otherwise, it might get too distracting to get to make love with you every day. I am not sure I want to feel that much love flowing through me every single day." She lifted her head to look at him, "Besides, if it keeps feeling so good all the time, we will get bored. Neither one of us wants that. You don't want to get yourself into a relationship that is boring with the same old Joy and deep-connection and support and unpredictable fun, all the time, do you?"

"No. Of course not. Just for another day or so, then we can stop. OK?" He said.

"You know, there is another thing that we both need to be aware of." She said with a serious tone.

"What's that, My Love?"

"We don't really know what each other is like when we are in our daily life. There is a chance it could be really different. I don't know what you are going to be like when you wake up on a daily basis, and you don't know what I am like when I come home from teaching and need to decompress. We just don't know, yet." She said.

"Yeah, I was thinking about that. So, let's just see how tonight goes and see whether or not we want to see each other tomorrow night. How does that sound?" He asked.

She climbed up on him, straddling him. She spoke with a measured tone that hinted at her excitement and her confidence that she would still like him after all their teaching tomorrow, "Yes, My Lord, that sounds good. If you still like me tomorrow, after training and after I get back from my walk with Kalla, then maybe we will have dinner together and see if we want to spend time together again, tomorrow night."

They both knew they would want to spend time together the following day.

They both knew there was a possibility that things between them could change when their regular, day-to-day lives resumed.

While they knew it was a possibility, they both knew that trying to prepare for that possibility was pointless.

They both knew it would be a bitter disappointment if they didn't get to keep exploring this magic between them. They had both been feeling so deeply met and deeply connected, they had gotten their hopes up that it would continue for a while.

He looked at her trying to contain his smile and said, "Right. Tomorrow, I might not like you at all. So, If I bump into you somewhere in the village tomorrow, I'll just say, What? What would I say?" He said.

"You could just say how you are feeling." She said.

"I can tell you how I am feeling right now." He said. She nodded. "I want to spend all night with you tonight and spend all evening and tomorrow night with you, too."

"Yes. Me too." she said, sliding back down to snuggle him and resting her head back into his shoulder. "So how about this . . . Tomorrow, we either meet here or in the great hall, whenever both of us are finished?"

"Sounds good." He said.

"Is there anything special you need to do in the morning to prepare for training?" She asked.

"No, I already have a pretty good idea what I might do with them. I am going to base the lesson on how the fight went with Odin yesterday." He said.

"Oh, how so?" She was curious what kind of a teacher he was with the men.

She had seen how he was with the girls, and she had felt his presence with her, but she had been around enough men to know that things can be drastically different when there are no women around. So many men will behave differently when they are just with men. It is usually out of insecurity, trying to be accepted. She had seen thousands of times when a man would behave one way, trying to seem genuine around women, then turn into an adolescent in a man's body when he didn't know there was a woman around. It was not attractive. She didn't expect that of him, but it was still a possibility in her mind. She had dreamed of a man, of a whole world of men, who knew who they were, had integrity within themselves, regardless of what company they kept. She would love to hide and watch the men's training tomorrow, maybe someday she would.

Malkore said, "When I put him against the wall, he was off balance. He was off balance because he hadn't trained enough to keep good form when he is scared or angry. And he was scared that he wasn't good enough. As I am sure you know, when we are scared that we aren't good enough, we either shy away from our weaknesses or we sabotage ourselves to make it look like our fear is true."

She was nodding her head with it still laying on his shoulder. "So true. You're pretty wise for a big, dumb, warrior type, you know?"

"Yeah, thanks." He said with a chuckle. "I am looking forward to it. It should be good, tomorrow."

Chapter Thirteen
Today is the Day

They had both woken up early. He woke up feeling playful. He rolled over to her and kissed her.

"Mmmmm. That is the kind of good morning I like to have." She said, but she seemed like something heavy was on her mind.

"What is going on? You haven't gotten tired of me already, have you?" He laughed.

"Oh, goodness, No!" She closed her eyes and took a big breath. "I am just feeling so full, I woke up feeling sort of blown away that you are still here, and that you are real. Feeling so much has opened up a part of me that I didn't know was there. I have been waiting for centuries to be shown what to do next. Now it's here, it is big. It's just a lot to do. The good thing is that we only have to do the work of today, and today is going to be fun. I probably shouldn't even think about all there is to do in the future."

"I get that. It is a lot to carry. It is even harder to carry it alone. And it is impossible to carry, if you feel like you have to do it all at once." He said.

"Yes. That's it. I forgot for a second that I don't have to do it all right this moment." She said.

Jokingly, he said, "Yeah, the only thing you need to do right now is, give the Father of Asgard a big kiss. And you have to act like you like it, too."

"I like it!" She climbed on top of him straddling him and kissed him repeatedly. "I really like it."

"Me too. Me too." He said, imitating Dossa.

"Any plans before training today, My Lord?" She asked.

"No. I am all yours, if you will have me. Would you like to go get some food in the great hall this morning?"

"I don't know. Let's wait a few minutes and see if the girls show up with any food. What about after the morning meal?" She got up to tend to the fire. "Keep talking, I'm still listening. I am going to stoke up the fire." She said.

He sat up and sat on the side of the bed. "I was thinking about that. I woke up with a question in my mind and a question on my heart. It was a question for you. I was wondering: Is today the day?" He asked with curiosity and a very slight hint of arrogant amusement.

"And which day would that be, My Lord?" She asked. She was kneeling by the fire stoking it up to knock the early morning chill out of the air.

"When we first met, while I was still being tended to, you said that someday you would show me how to use my sword. Then yesterday you said there were only Five or Six men in Asgard who could best you in a fight. I was just curious if today was the day." He said it as if he didn't care and was only being playful, but was curious - there was something in her voice when she said it. She didn't say it like she was better than him, she didn't say it like she was just playing. She said it with quiet confidence.

She looked up at him with a wry smile. Then feigning innocence, her voice dripped with sarcasm, "Surely there's nothing that a little, weak, frail woman like me could teach the great Lord Malkore -- the greatest warrior in the kingdom, the greatest warrior who has ever lived. No, there's nothing that little bitty me could teach such a man."

He was smiling so big. "Yes, of course. Just like if you tried to run away from me in the woods, you couldn't get more than a few strides down the trail before I caught you."

"I don't know what you are talking about. Maybe that was just a dream you had while you were taking a lazy nap in the Sanctuary, while I was planning Asgard's future." She said with a grin while walking towards him.

He let out a big laugh. "Oh, yes. I dreamt it. That must have been what happened. An old, frail woman like you probably can't run anymore anyway, right?!" She leaned down and kissed him.

Then with a serious tone, "Do you want my serious answer?"

He looked surprised by her serious tone. "Please."

"I don't remember saying that to you, when we began your Tending. I am sure I did, but I didn't know I said it, and I wouldn't have known *why* I would have said it until we were in the sanctuary yesterday. I want to tell you what I saw in my vision, and it is really scary to share it. I want . . . I need . . . I need your support. This vision scares the shit out of me in the best way possible. It's amazing! And it scares me. I'll share it with you. But we won't tell Kalla or Dossa or Frigg, or anyone else in Asgard, especially not any of the men." She had a powerful look on her face. "This one scares me. And I can't hold it myself — I can't carry it by myself. I need you. I need the Father of Asgard."

"Of course, My Love. What can I do?" He asked.

She smiled at him then got that mischievous grin of hers and said, "Eat a good breakfast, My Love. You're going to need it."

He grabbed her by the waist and pulled her down onto his lap. She wrapped her arms around his neck and shoulders and was trying to keep from crying. She was a mix of emotions.

"Is there anything I can do for you, right this moment?" He asked.

She said, "All I want to do is make love with you all morning, and I am too excited and too scared. You asking me about the sword work is at the very heart of it. So, My Lord Malkore, Yes, today is the day."

He pulled her in tighter, "I am excited. Let's go get some food, then we will figure out what we need to do before training today. How does that sound?"

She nodded.

They got up and got dressed and started walking towards the great hall. Just as they were getting there, Kalla and Dossa were just arriving, too.

Iyasiil asked, "Join us for morning meal, My Loves?"

- - - - - - - - - - - - - - - - - - -

After breakfast, Malkore and Iyasiil headed back to her chambers. He asked, "What do we need to do, this morning?"

"Let's go back home. I need to get something, then we will go find a place that is private." She said. They got to her chamber. She walked in, picked up a long bag that had a shoulder strap on it. She threw it over her shoulder and grabbed an empty skin to carry water. They started walking towards the oak grove and stopped by the spring to fill the skin with water. They got past the oak grove and halfway to the river.

Iyasiil could feel her excitement and her nervousness grow even stronger. She stopped. She dropped her head. Her shoulders slumped.

He stopped and looked at her, "What is it, My Love?"

"I have not felt like this in millennia. I hate it when I forget that everything is OK. I hate it when I forget that everything is magical." Iyasiil started to reach for her bag, then stopped herself. She took a big breath, then screamed a scream that gave Malkore chills. Then she took a couple of gasping breaths. Then a few more longer breaths to slow her breathing down, then she looked at him. *"That* is how big this is for me."

"OK, well let's get at it, then. I am right here with you and whatever comes and wherever it takes us, I'll be right there with you, and we will do it together." He stepped towards her.

She reached out for his hand, and they continued their walk towards the river. After another couple of minutes, she pointed off to the left where there was a section of trees that cut into the grassy meadow. "Let's head over that way."

When they got there, she took a big sip of water, then handed him the skin. He took a drink, too. She sat on her feet and set her bag down in the grass and said a prayer with her hands on the bag. She opened it up and pulled out a roll of cloth. She laid the cloth on the ground in front of her and began to unroll it. There was a sword rolled up in the cloth, as he had suspected. She picked up the sword and pointed to a spot about five feet in front of her and said, "Join me." She laid the bag flat across the ground in front of her and laid the sword on top of it. She folded up the long piece of cloth and laid it in front of where she had asked him to sit. He knelt down and sat on his feet, following her lead. "Now, Lord Malkore, I don't know if I could ever express how thankful I am to have you here. I'll tell you everything and answer all your questions after we are finished. For now, will you join me in a few moments of quiet meditation?"

"Of course." He said.

She closed her eyes. Then he closed his, too. The sat quietly for ten or twelve minutes. Then she let out a long deep breath that was loud enough for him to hear it. She opened her eyes. Moments later, he opened his.

She took another breath, looking deep into him. "It's pretty amazing how much I love you already. Thank you so much for being here."

He nodded at her, "Of course, I feel the same."

"Lord Malkore, I may be out of practice, I don't know. If I am out of practice, do not go easy on me, not even for a second. If I remember my training, then you have about one minute to prepare yourself before you get your ass handed to you." She looked at him and smiled.

"OK. I am ready when you are." He said, his eyes dancing with excitement.

"You better hope so." She said with a confident smile. Then her body relaxed, completely. She picked up her sword, stood up, and began walking away from him off to his right.

He had not laid his sword down on the cloth in front of him, as she had done. He got up and slowly began walking towards her, giving her the space that she needed. He felt excited and curious about what was happening and what he was about to see.

After another twenty seconds, she turned around and walked towards him slowly. When she got about five strides away, she stopped and held the handle of her sword between her hands, palms facing each other with the tip of the sword pointing at the ground. He looked at her and how she was holding her sword. This was not a fighting grip. She made eye contact with him and waited for him to acknowledge her. She bowed to him. He nodded to her.

She took a breath, then her face changed. She was no longer a beautiful and graceful woman. She looked at him like she was about to destroy him and not care either way if he lived or died.

"Yeeeesssssss!" He yelled. He saw a focus and clarity in her right in that moment that he only ever saw in the greatest warriors. There was no anger, there was no fear – there was only clarity and confident determination.

She came at him using a fighting style he had never seen. Her sword was pointed directly at him with the butt of the sword over her left shoulder. Her left hand was flat against the butt of the sword so that her palm was facing him.

He was expecting her to try and strike his body, he was prepared for any strike she could make. That was his first mistake.

He was watching her eyes, to see where she would attack. That was his second mistake. Watching the eyes to see where an attack is going only works with people who have been trained only up to a certain point. Only advanced training will teach people to use their eyes for misdirection. He was about to learn that he had underestimated her, again.

She was not trying to make an attacking kill stroke on him, she was intentionally trying to disarm him. His sword was on his left hip. By not trying to attack him, she caught him off guard.

She was looking at his right shoulder, in an attempt to misdirect his attention. The tip of her sword caught the hilt of his sword and began lifting it out of its scabbard. Her intention was to flip his sword out of his reach, either catching it herself or staying between him and his sword. It almost worked. When he realized what was happening, his sword was halfway out of its scabbard. He started to grab the handle of his sword, but knew if he missed the handle, then his hand would have been around two blades, neither of which he had full control. He twisted his body to his right, giving him a chance to disconnect her sword from his, and lunged his left shoulder into her, closing the distance between them, hoping to knock her down, giving himself a chance to regroup and prepare for another attack.

She had almost flipped his sword up into the air. It was a risky first attack, but worth the try. She felt his shoulder slam into her chest, it knocked her back a step. She used that step to turn and aim for his back as he went past her. It happened so fast; she was sure she could at least slap him in the ass with her sword as he was moving away. She heard him make a growling sound as he landed his shoulder into her and she knew he wasn't holding back, so she went for a full crippling stroke into his ass.

He expected the attack as he was moving past her. He was able to get his hand around the handle of his sword and pull it the rest of the way out of its scabbard and turn back to his left and defend an attack that surely would have cracked his pelvis and severed every muscle he needed to stand upright. He deflected that blow and felt his mind shift from lightly sparring with someone to assess how good they were to a state of alertness that surprised him.

She could feel her mouth get dry. She knew that making him pull his sword already meant that she had surprised him and gotten him on the defensive. Without hesitating, she attacked again, faking right, just enough to get him to defend, then attacking left. Before her sword was even close to attacking his left hip, she had already started her real attack towards his waist on his right side.

He responded to both the dummy attack to his left and the kill stroke to his right. When the attack stroke came to his right side, he took a step back with his right foot to create distance to disarm her. He let the force of her sword begin his disarming stroke, which would take his sword from the inside of her sword to the outside and push it in a large circle low to his left, up high to his left, across to his right above shoulder height, and down to his lower right. If executed properly, this disarming move is nearly impossible to defend against. She defended the move.

As he was trying to disarm her, she almost moved too late, which would have left her swordless and out of position to move quickly to a safe distance. *"I am terribly out of practice; he almost got me."* She thought.

Because she was shorter than him, she was able to defend the disarming move, by spinning her body around keeping enough pressure on his sword to make him continue to think he could disarm her. She timed her spin, so she was turning with her arms above her head, facing away from him as he was pushing her sword at the top part of the disarming circle. She wasn't vulnerable to having the sword twisted out of her grip in doing this. It was a risky move against someone of his skill level, but there was a chance she could go directly onto a straight thrust at him from here. She did. He was ready for it.

As she went for her straight thrust, he brushed her sword to his left enough to step forward to her left and reached for her ribs as grabbed her at the base of her ribs, where he thought she might be ticklish, and made a honking sound as he went past her.

He expected her to take another step forward which would give him distance, but she quickly changed to a reverse grip with her right hand and thrust her sword backwards towards his upper body. He was at the very edge of her reach and the tip of her sword just touched his ribs on the left side a hands width below his shoulder. She was already turning and brought her left hand up to the bottom of the sword's grip to steady it in case he countered immediately.

"Too close." He thought. *"It's time to back her up."* He looked at her and saw a different woman than he had known the last four days. There was no grace in her. She was a total block of focus. Normally this is where he would make some kind of comment that would either inspire a student or frustrate an opponent. After millennia of fighting, those comments came pretty naturally, he didn't have to think about them. Before he could open his mouth, she attacked again. He decided to see how she would fare if he didn't evade her attacks, so he blocked each attack she made and made no offensive moves himself. He wanted to see if she would either get frustrated, get tired, or lose focus in the monotony of only attacking. He lost count at thirty-two quick, consecutive offensive attacks; she was relentless.

"Shit, she's good." He had to keep his effort up at eighty or eighty-five percent of his maximum to keep from walking away bloody. He was having to work as hard sparring with her as he did with the best of the men in the Asgardian army.

She didn't stop. "Are you going to cut that shit out now, My Lord?" She said through labored breath.

He was breathing hard, too; she is a formidable warrior. "What shit would that be, Mother of Asgard?"

She swung her sword even harder at him two more times before she answered, "I told you not to hold back, Feet Fucker." She said.

After three more attacking strikes from her, he saw his opening. She made a straight shoulder strike he moved it to the side, pushing her sword hand higher than the level of her shoulder. He stepped in moving the tip of his sword to her throat, immobilizing her sword out to his left.

He wrapped his left arm over her sword, putting his left hand on the inside of her right wrist. He looked to her left hand to see if she had been hiding a knife that she could pull on him if she needed to. He didn't see anything in her left hand, so he stepped hard to his left into a deep lung, giving her the option to hold onto her sword and break her wrist or let go. She let go.

He started taking a few steps away from her with her sword still cradled under his arm and he swung his own sword in a circle with his right hand.

In a relieved tone, as if she had finished her effort, she said, "By the fires of Muspell, you are good. Shit! What a turn on! I want to fuck you so bad, right here, right now." She took three quick steps and jumped on his back, hugging him around the neck. She leaned her head around and started kissing him on the right side of his face. Malkore dropped his own sword from his right hand. After three quick kisses, her hand reached the grip of her sword, in front of his left shoulder.

His right hand quickly went up to the butt of her sword and squatted down and bent over with such force that even with her heels hooking into his hips at the last second couldn't keep her from flying over his shoulder and landed on the ground. She rolled a half roll and did a half twist, so she was facing him, laying on her back.

"You won't get me with that move either, witch." He said with a tone that was half guttural warrior, half heartless killer.

She didn't try to get up. She lay there in the grass and let her body relax as she caught her breath. "OK. OK. I am done. I made my point, when I catch my breath, I can tell what I want to tell you."

He looked at her, not sure if she would try to play another trick on her to gain an advantage.

Her voice changed, "Malkore, My Love, Father of Asgard, King of Feetfuckia, no more today. You can hold onto my sword if you don't believe me. I am done."

He went over and picked up his own sword and held it strong in his right hand while slowly walking to her. He didn't walk towards her feet; in case she might still try to kick him and keep fighting. He took a second to look a more closely at her sword as he walked towards her. Once he had gotten far enough out to her right side, he took the two more steps towards her.

Then his demeanor changed. He was smiling his flirty smile at her, then he stepped on her chest with his right boot. With his flirty, sarcastic, mock-dominance tone, he said, "Now, My

Love, if you think you can behave yourself, you may have this back." With that, he offered her the handle of her sword. For a little emphasis, he put a little more weight on her chest with his boot. "Are you going to behave yourself, young lady?"

She took her sword in her left hand and laid it on the ground to her left and moved her hand away from it. He knelt down beside her.

Still catching her breath, speaking with a thrilled and happy tone, she said, "Oh Malkore, thank you. Oh shit, you are good. I believe what they say about you. You probably are the greatest warrior who has ever lived. That was everything I had, everything. I am out of practice, but not by that much. Oh Shit, My love. You are the best. That was so fun."

He had just about caught his breath. He started laughing. "A woman, who is as highly trained with a sword as any man in Asgard, tries with all her might to land a kill stroke on her new husband and says, "That was so fun." So, tell me again why they ran you off from the last village where you lived, My Love?"

She laughed and looked at him with happiness beaming from every cell in her body, "I'll tell you, if you kiss me."

He didn't return his sword to its scabbard, he laid it on the grass to his right, where she couldn't reach it, if she tried. He leaned down and held both of her wrists in his hands as he leaned down to kiss her. He still wasn't sure she wasn't setting him up to attack again.

He kissed her several times. The kisses felt really good to him, but not as good as when he didn't feel guarded. He laid down on his side, next to her, capturing her right arm under his shoulder as he scooted closer to her.

"Maybe we need a safeword." She said. He looked at her confused, not knowing what she meant. "So that we know the training is over. No tricks, no ploys, just kissing."

"I'm surprised you didn't try to fake an injury to get me to drop my guard." He said.

She laughed, "That would never work on you. You didn't believe it when I jumped on your back and kissed you."

"No. I didn't believe it, because *you* didn't believe it. That was the only time you ever sounded like you were trying to convince me of something. I couldn't feel your heart and your desire when you said it." He said.

"I do desire you, Lord Malkore, a lot!" She said.

"Not in that moment. If you had really wanted to fuck me right then, you'd be naked right now. In that moment, you wanted your sword back." He said.

"True. So, what should be our safeword?"

"I'm afraid I am not going to believe anything you say while we are sparring or running." He said with a chuckle.

"That's the problem with being a master of misdirection in combat . . . How about this: With swords, I will put my sword in the ground and say, "I am done." Will that work?"

"We can try that, Love." He leaned down and kissed her.

"So how did I do?" She asked.

He laughed, "You start training the army at High Sun in a couple of hours. You better get ready. I am going to take a day at the hot springs."

She smiled at him, then got a serious look on her face, "No, seriously. I want you to tell me the truth."

"I am serious, My Love. You were right there are probably only 5 or 6 men in Asgard who could best you in a fight. I couldn't believe what I was seeing, but from everything you have shown me so far, I wasn't really surprised – not surprised, just amazed." He said.

"Really?" she asked.

"Yes, really. Now tell me what this is all about. You didn't bring me out here just to show me how good you are with a sword. Something is brewing in you." He said.

"No. I wanted you to know what I *can* do before I began telling you what I *want* to do. I know what I want, I see it clearly, but I am not sure I have all the words to describe the change that has to happen before I can make my dream happen." She said.

"OK. I am listening." He said.

"Let's go get some water and find a place to sit in the shade to talk." She said as she started to get up. He flinched dramatically as if he might need to defend against a surprise attack. She laughed. "No, My Lord. Now you know that if you slip up a tiny bit or lose focus for a second, I could make a pair of boots out of your skin. See, we need a safeword."

They got up, she grabbed her sword, and they walked to where her bag was lying in the grass. She picked up the skin of water and took a sip, then handed it to him.

"Smitten." He said.

"What?" She looked at him funny.

"I am feeling pretty smitten with you. That's the safeword." He said.

She smiled and laughed a little, "OK. "Smitten" it is. I need to put this away before anyone sees it. Come sit with me for a second." She knelt down in front of her bag. She took out a rag and wiped down her sword and inspected the blade for any knicks or any places where the edge was rolled from impact. Then she closed her eyes and took a long breath. She took the cloth that her sword stayed wrapped in and wrapped up her sword, put it in the bag, fastened the bag closed, then closed her eyes and took a big breath again. When she was finished, she looked at him, and her face had fully transformed to look again like a woman in love. "Smitten. Yup."

He looked up at the sky, they still had several hours until High Sun, when he would start training the men. "We still have a couple of hours until training begins. Where would you like to sit and talk?"

She said, "Let's go back up to the oak grove and find a spot in the shade. We can refill the water if we need to."

He had lots of questions about where she learned to fight so well, and she had a story to tell. He didn't ask, he would just wait to hear the story. She had been so wound up before and wanted to show him that she is a serious threat to anyone in a fight, he was more impressed that he could ever express in words. He couldn't imagine what was bigger than sharing what she could do with a sword, so he stayed quiet while being attentive to her as they walked back.

As they were walking back, she stopped a couple of times. He stopped when she stopped, each time she would playfully say, "Time for a hug." She hugged him and grabbed the sides of his head and kissed him. He could feel her heart flowing its love through her skin. She was glowing and smiling, and he could still feel that she had something big to share. Her love felt genuine, and he could feel her relief that she had impressed him with her fighting skills. *"This is going to be a hell of a story."* He thought.

When they got to the oak grove. They sat down in the shade, and she looked relaxed. He leaned against a tree; she sat leaning against a rock just a few feet away. All her nervousness was gone. "I am so excited to share this. I am still scared, but I think you'll hear me."

"Oh, My Goddess, you are amazing. You could tell me anything right now and I would just smile at you." He said.

"OK, here it is. I have had an idea of something I wanted to do for years. Then when we were in the Sanctuary yesterday, I saw the whole thing. I am going to build an entire army of women."

He got it! His eyes darted back and forth as he saw all the parts of it growing and playing out in his mind. "Yes." He saw the power the women would hold within themselves, and how they would be respected among all the people. Then he looked her in the eyes, "Yes!"

She saw that he was lit up with what he saw. "Yes."

Malkore was excited for her, "Do it! Do it now! How can I help?! I would love to help!?"

She looked at him, "The men aren't ready. You told me that I am "creating monsters." Not monsters, warriors – Women Warriors. Some of them carry the Goddess energy as healers, some carry it as both healers and warriors. It's time for the women to begin learning their true power as women. You have seen the change in just days in Kalla and Dossa, but that is just the beginning of their journey. Dossa will make a great warrior; she has everything she needs – except the training. Kalla will be able to best more than half your men, when she's ready. And Dossa may someday challenge St'laad."

"Oh, I totally see that." He said.

"Do you want me to help train them?" He asked.

"No. Trian your men. Part of their training needs to be training their hearts to truly honor the goddess in every woman."

"Yes, absolutely." He responded.

"We will do our own training for quite a while. When we are ready, we will come challenge your men. We will earn their respect on our own. It won't happen soon, but we begin now." She said.

"Yes." He said with wonder and excitement on his face.

"You know how you taught Kalla and Dossa?" She asked.

He looked at her like he had no idea what she was talking about. "Uhhhh. No, what do you mean."

"I was watching. It was amazing to watch how masterful you taught them from the first moment . . . You spoke to their heart; opened their hearts. Then, when their hearts were open, you poured wisdom into it. That's how you teach." She said.

"Wow! Thank you. I never thought about it like that. Hmmmm." He said feeling kind of honored and kind of surprised.

"Yeah, you teach better than anyone. You are amazing. I want you to do that with the men! I want you to introduce them to their hearts – Sorry, this is how I really want to say it to you, You need to introduce them to their hearts. Show them what it's like to be a strong, powerful man who has his heart intact. Show them how amazing it is to walk with your heart, not just your balls. It will help after Odin spends his time as a woman and comes back as a man."

He laid down, propping himself up on his elbow and looked at her, smiling, "I could sit and listen to you all day, please don't stop talking. You have about forty-five minutes before Iyasiil's Warrior Training begins. Have your first lesson ready."

"Only if you go and teach the women how to stand in their power . . ." she responded smiling.

He leaned forward and crawled forward to her and kissed her. She kissed him and looked at him with an intensity and caught his attention. She said, "Together, we can make this happen. I couldn't do it by myself. You have been killing yourself trying to teach all you have to teach. Now, we can do t. I need you to teach the men, which is what you want to do anyway. You are the most amazing man, no one else can do this. The women need to know what we know, and it's time the men start learning."

He was nodding. "How do we do this?"

She stopped. She looked at him and took a breath. "Well, for the next two days, I suggest you let yourself fall madly in love with me."

"I can do that." He said smiling.

"We can make a new plan again in two days, in case you don't like me anymore." She said, smiling.

"OK." He said laughing. "Good plan."

She looked at him, and he felt like she was looking so deeply into him. "Malkore?"

"Yes, My Love?"

"I love this." She said.

He looked at her and was smiling. In a playful, high-pitched voice, he said, "Me too. Me too."

She pushed him back onto his butt crawled up onto him, sat on his lap, straddling him, and kissed him. "Thank you for today. I have an army to build."

He couldn't stop smiling at her, "Me too. Me too."

She kissed him again, then rested her cheek on his cheek. "Malkore. All day. For as many days as we have."

He grabbed her by the hair on the back of her head and kissed her, passionately. He wanted to get lost in her, but knew his time was getting short before he needed to get ready to start training.

"All day. For as many days as we have." He said.

She sat back against the rock she had been sitting against. They kept talking for a while and she felt like a huge weight had been lifted off of her, while at the same time, she felt a huge responsibility. The responsibility didn't feel like a burden, she felt excited, she just had to build it slowly.

St'laad was the first one to show up for training. He was really early for training, but wanted to practice moves with his sword and he would spar with anyone else who showed up early.

He saw Malkore and Iyasiil sitting at the edge of the oak grove and called out to them from thirty paces away. In his big, booming, Asgardian warrior's voice, he yelled, "You're only on time if you are early. If you're on time, you're late."

Malkore smiled at him and yelled back, "St'laad! The only man in Asgard that could best me in a fight!"

As he got close, St'laad nodded his head to Iyasiil in greeting. "Old man, you know that's not true. We both know it, so don't lie to me. We only get better when the truth is spoken." Malkore and Iyasiil looked at each other, smiling. "Am I interrupting? I just wanted to say "Hello.""

Iyasiil got up and hugged him and kissed him on the cheek. "Hello, brave Asgardian Warrior. Are you excited for training to begin today?"

She began to sit back down. He looked at Malkore and said, "I am. And the men are excited, too. I think we need this, Lord Malkore." St'laad looked at Iyasiil, and pointed to her as he looked back at Malkore. "Is Sanshii your secret weapon in preparing your lessons for the men?"

Malkore said, "More than you know. St'laad, please sit down, join us for a minute." St'laad sat down to join them. Malkore offered him a sip of water from their skin. Malkore looked at Iyasiil, "Are you ready for the people to know, My Love?"

She nodded, looking like she was falling in love with him more, every moment. Letting the people know who she really was felt like it added a lot of power to their relationship, and it felt like the first step in putting her plan into motion with the people. Her name, the legend of her, carried weight with the people. Everyone had heard the stories about the great healer, a goddess-like woman named Iyasiil.

Malkore spoke with a heartfelt tone, he had a lot of respect for St'laad. "St'laad, you are a man of great honor, and you have earned the respect of the people."

"Thank you, My Lord."

"Besides her two students and Frigg, you will be the first person in Asgard to know. This woman was called here to Asgard because she is a great teacher and carries a wisdom as old as the hills. It is time the people to know who she really is. Her real name is not Sanshii. She is Iyasiil."

St'laad looked at him as if to say, *"No big deal, so what."* Then it dawned on him, St'laad's jaw dropped, "Iyasiil? *The* Iyasiil? I thought those were just legends." He leaned down on the ground, so his elbows were touching the ground. "I had no idea. I am so sorry."

"No apologies, great warrior. I didn't want anyone to know, until it was time. I just didn't know it would be this soon." She said.

"Right. I understand, I think." Then he looked at Malkore, then back to her. "Wow! I mean . . . I mean . . . And the two of you. Is this a thing? If you don't mind me asking."

Malkore looked at her to see if she had any reaction. She looked at him in a flirty way, as if to say, *"I don't know. Is it?"*

Malkore smiled and said, "Well, we decided that we are going to be madly in love with each other until sundown, tomorrow." Iyasiil laughed. Malkore was trying to not laugh to keep up his serious demeanor.

St'laad looked confused for a second, then said, "Ahhh. I see, you have finally gone senile, old man. You lost your mind, and she is to be your nurse in your final days. I understand now."

Malkore roared with laughter. "Oh son, that was funny! No, we don't know what this is, so we are just going to ride it out and see what happens."

St'laad was one of the few men in Asgard who could joke like that with Malkore, he had earned enough of Malkore's respect to do that. "My Lord, Sansh – I am sorry. Iyasiil, the people are talking about you two, quite a bit."

Iyasiil smiled, "What are they saying? This ought to be good."

"No, My Love. They are saying you two glow and are carried in a golden light when you are together, that you are more Gods than people. People have already started talking about how you two are different than any couple in Asgard."

She looked at Malkore, Malkore looked at her. She responded to St'laad, but kept looking at Malkore with her flirty look, "Well, it certainly feels that way." Malkore smiled at her. Then she shifted gears. "Great warriors, I have a date to take a walk with a beautiful young woman this afternoon -- you two should be so lucky." she said with a flirty tone. "So, I will take my leave of you." She stood up and put her bag over her shoulder. "Lord Malkore, thank you for this morning. I can't imagine doing this without you." She looked at St'laad, "Hand me that skin and I will fill it up before training begins."

Malkore said, "Thank you, Love." Both men watched her walk away a few steps. When she was about thirty steps away, St'laad lunged at Malkore, from his sitting position and tackled him, and said quietly, "You old dog! Leave it to you to grab the sexiest woman in Asgard! Who else could hold a goddess's heart, but a god, like you!"

Malkore was surprised that he felt so happy and giddy – he felt smitten. Normally, he would not really roughhouse with them men, unless he was making a point. But today, he just smiled. "Thank you, son. I am a very lucky man."

St'laad responded, almost reprimanding Malkore, "No, My Lord. There is no luck to it. No other man in Asgard is worthy of such a woman."

"Thank you, son. Thank you." Malkore said. "Now is there anything I can do for you?"

"My Lord, I don't know what you have planned for training today, but could we practice for a few minutes before anyone else arrives?"

"That's what I wanted to hear! Of course!" Malkore said in his big, warrior's voice.

They walked to a spot at the edge of the oak grove, where they could see men begin to show up as it approached High Sun, they began sparring. St'laad began at about seventy-five percent effort and Malkore matched his intensity. After a few minutes, St'laad slowly began increasing the intensity at which he attacked. Malkore matched his intensity stroke for stroke, never giving St'laad more than he could handle, but forcing him to constantly improve to handle what he was being given. They kept going for about ten minutes and it was quickly getting as intense as any training any man in Asgard did besides Malkore himself.

Iyasiil was bringing the skin of water back before she went to meet Kalla for their walk. She left it where they had been sitting.

She could see Malkore and St'laad sparring and every part of her wanted to go join them. She was wondering how she would fair against St'laad in a straight up fight. He was good. She could see that he was *really* good. She took a deep breath and trusted that she would get her time to go play, but it startled her how hard it was to walk away and not join in. She tried to rationalize joining them in her mind but couldn't sacrifice her plan.

She took a second to look at Malkore and watch how he moved. *"He really is an incredible force of nature."* He was beautiful to watch and beautiful to touch. She couldn't wait to touch him again. She put her hand on her heart, *"Malkore, My Love, My King. Heart of My Heart. Soul of My Soul. May your day be beautiful."*

Chapter Fourteen
High Sun - Malkore's
Warrior Academy

The men gathered for training, most all of them were there, including the boy. Odin and Malkore had already begun the first lesson. Two men walked up a little late. Odin yelled to ask the group, "What time do we start training?"

"High sun." The men responded.

Odin turned to the men who were late and said, "When any of us doesn't take our challenge seriously, we all suffer! Take a run to the river and back!"

The two men dropped their heads. One of them looked at Odin and said, "Really?"

Odin yelled, "Get out of my face! Either go home or come back with wet boots, just move!"

The men started off on their run. Malkore looked at the group of men, "If they run hard, they can be back in 12 minutes. I bet they won't be back for 15. When any one of us doesn't take our challenge seriously, we all suffer. Who is going to make sure those two are not late tomorrow?"

About ten men spoke up, "I will."

Malkore said, "Those are your brothers, do you want those two to die in battle because they weren't properly trained? Who is going to make sure they get here on time tomorrow?" This time all the men answered. Malkore went on, "They have almost a two-minute lead on you. Who is going to beat them back here, men?!" No one moved.

Odin yelled at them, "Get off your asses and run! Everybody! Go!" Everyone, including the boy, started running to catch the first two men.

Malkore turned and looked at Odin with a pleased look on his face. Malkore looked relaxed. He felt relaxed, like he had all the time in the world. He took a step towards Odin with his hand resting on the hilt of his sword and said, "Maybe you actually were listening all those years ago."

Odin nodded, "Lord Malkore, I heard every word. You were right, I just got lost for a bit. Now I realize how much I need you. Now more than ever."

Malkore was rarely surprised, but that surprised him. Still not rushed, Malkore said, "Son, they have almost three minutes on us now. You and I need to be the first ones back here."

Odin's eyes got big. "Oh shit! Yeah, of course. Oh shit!" Odin started running.

Malkore didn't move. As Odin passed him, Malkore said with a big grin, "Yeah. Oh shit!"

Malkore wasn't worried about catching and passing everyone in the group. He didn't know if Odin could keep up, though. He turned and started running. He caught up to Odin within ten seconds. Running alongside Odin, he said, "Consider this little run and all of today's training to be your first real test as king, My Lord."

Odin started laughing, "Yes, My Lord. But Malkore, it would serve you to not train me very well."

Malkore asked, "Why is that, son?"

"Because one day, I am going to kick your ass!" Odin sped up his pace slightly. Malkore was smiling and sped up, too. He kept Odin in the corner of his eye and made sure to stay two steps ahead of Odin, no matter how fast Odin ran. After a couple of minutes, Odin was breathing heavily, but still running strong. After about Five minutes, they had almost caught the back of the group. Odin yelled, "Malkore, you bastard! Your mother was never married!" He meant this as an insult, but Malkore just laughed.

Malkore ran with a smile on his face. It actually felt good to feel his student back, instead of the pompous ass who had been wearing Odin's skin for so long.

Malkore didn't even seem like he was breathing heavily, and yelled back, "Odin, I was born of the wind and the rain. There is proof my parents are still together every time a storm comes!" And Malkore took off into the back of the group so quickly Odin could hardly believe it.

Odin sped up again and started making his way slowly through the back of the group. The front of the group had almost caught the first two men when they reached the river. Only one person had passed the first two men already, the boy. Malkore saw the boy headed back the other way and looked to make sure his ratty boots were wet, they were. Malkore thought, *"He's a quick little fucker. If he can climb, he would make the perfect scout."*

The boy and Malkore almost ran into each other going different directions about fifty yards from the river. The boy didn't know Malkore would be running, too. Malkore yelled out to him, "Don't let me catch you, boy!"

The boy almost tripped trying to run sideways to yell back, "Yes, My Lord, Malkore."

Malkore got to the river and jumped in, filled his hands with water and took a big drink. He let out a big, "Aaahhhhhh!" with his arms held up to the sky. Then he started running back to the oak grove again. He was leaving the river just as Odin got there to get his boots wet.

Odin saw this as his chance to keep up with Malkore. They quickly joined the front third of the group, headed back to the oak grove and Malkore yelled, "Odin and I gave you lazy bastards a three-minute lead and you let us catch you already?! Run like the fate of Asgard depends on it!"

Odin was tired. He was feeling the effort in his legs. His breathing was heavy. He was keeping up with Malkore, he was keeping up with the group.

Malkore yelled again, "What time do we start training tomorrow, men?!"

The men yelled, "High sun!"

Odin was right next to Malkore. Odin was hurting, this pace was tough. His lungs were starting to burn. "Oh shit." He said to himself, out loud. No one but Malkore could hear him.

"Odin, don't worry. You don't have to run fast; we can just find a man much more worthy to lead Asgard. Maybe I will give the throne to that quick little fucker up ahead." Then Malkore let out a laugh and started speeding up.

Odin just started thinking about making each stride two inches longer, same leg speed, just longer strides. He picked up speed a little. At this pace, only Malkore and the boy would beat him back. He could live with that. His legs were burning to the point that every few seconds he wanted to quit. He thought, *"Just two inches longer with the stride. Just two inches longer."* His stride started to smooth out, he still hurt, but it was a little more OK if he just focused on his stride. Then he thought to himself, *"I am king, and I am only thinking of myself."* He blew out all his breath and took in the deepest breath he could and yelled, "Do you want to quit? Is Asgard not worth your full effort?!" The men hardly responded; they were hurting too badly.

The oak grove was in sight and Odin was almost at the front of the group. Malkore had almost caught the boy.

Malkore pulled his sword and was running towards the boy. "My sword is out. It's pointed at your back. Don't let me catch you, boy!" The boy turned his head and looked terrified. It was just about everything Malkore could do to catch the boy. They were almost a hundred yards ahead of Odin and the men.

Malkore caught him right as they reached the oak grove where they started. Odin slapped the boy on the ass with his sword right as they stopped running. They were both out of breath, the boy had done well.

Malkore grabbed his skin of water that Iyasiil refilled for him and called to the boy to come over and get a drink. The boy thanked him and only took a small sip. Malkore told him to drink a lot, that he was going to need it. The boy took another big sip.

Odin was five yards ahead of the next man in the group. Malkore was impressed with his determination. Odin was breathing so hard; he wasn't sure he would ever catch his breath.

Over the next three minutes, men came in breathing hard, moaning, and griping about how hard that was. Odin grabbed his skin of water and yelled to the men to get some water and catch their breath.

The last 20 men were straggling in, Odin was still out of breath but yelled, "I don't care if you die today, just don't slow down. Don't stop running."

The last stragglers came into the shady area under the oak grove. Malkore was proud of them. No one slowed down. No one quit running, even though it hurt. "Good job, men! Everyone get some water and catch your breath." Then even louder, "Training will begin in five minutes!"

A lot of the men groaned that after a hard run, they hadn't even begun the day's training.

The boy came over, "My Lord, could I have another sip of water?"

"No, son. Take five big sips then hold on to it. Drink all you want." Malkore said.

The boy smiled with a funny look on his face, "Thank you, Lord Malkore." The boy wasn't used to anyone being nice to him.

Odin came over, to the boy. "What's your name, boy?"

The boy couldn't believe the king was talking to him. "Me? My name is Toofid, My King."

"Toofid? We have to get you a new name, son." Odin said with a laugh. The boy felt insulted, but it also felt good to get attention from the king.

Malkore came over to Odin and the boy, "Can you climb mountains, boy?"

"I climb like a goat, My Lord." The boy said with a smile.

Malkore turned towards Odin, "If he can really climb like he says, that's your new scout, My Lord."

"Scout." Odin turned to the boy. "Can you really climb like a goat? Tell me the truth, son."

"Yes, King Odin. I can." The boy said. Malkore noticed he didn't answer like he normally talked. He said it without any doubt. Malkore believed him.

Odin yelled to all the men, "Asgard. Come closer. Bring your water." All the men slowly moved over and gathered in front of Odin. "This is the newest member of our army." The boy snapped his head to look at Odin. He couldn't believe what he was hearing. "This little fucker just made you all look like fat, lazy bastards!" The men laughed. "His name is Scout!"

The men yelled "Scout!"

The boy looked at Malkore. Malkore just smiled and nodded to him, "Yes, Scout."

Odin asked the group, "Who is going to look out for Scout?"

Every man in the group said, "I will."

Odin turned to Scout, "Who will you look out for, young man?"

The boy wasn't sure, but he made a guess. "If I am Scout, I will be looking out for everyone, My Lord."

All the men yelled, "Scout! Scout!"

"Good job, son. Now, join your men." Odin told him.

The boy had never felt a part of anything before. He didn't quite know what to do. He looked at the men, then back to Malkore. St'laad was sitting in the front of the group and said, "Scout, come join us here." As Scout sat with him, St'laad rubbed his head, welcoming him.

Another man lightly punched Scout on the arm and said, "Good to have you with us, Scout."

Malkore would still keep an eye on him, but it was good to see the warriors accepting him, at least for now.

Odin put on his boisterous warrior's voice and said, "Now, are you ready to begin training today?!" The men had caught their breath, and their eyes were sharp.

Odin turned to Malkore, then turned back to the men. "Before Lord Malkore begins, I want to tell you a little bit about how my teacher teaches. You all began running, and it felt good to be synchronous with my teacher again. He slowly walked over to me. We talked for a minute or two, then he mentioned that he and I should be the first ones back from the run to the river." The men erupted in laughter. "He waited until all of you were down on the flats before reminding me that he and I would be running, too. I told you in the great hall that I wouldn't ask you to do anything I wasn't going to do myself. We are going to build something great here and every one of you are a part of it. Today is important, but it is only preparation for tomorrow. Tomorrow is when the real training begins."

Malkore knew exactly what he meant. He had spoken those same words to Odin a thousand times. He was still a little shocked that Odin remembered.

Malkore said, "Well said, My King."

Odin spoke again, "Now, if I catch any of you lazy, fat bastards not paying attention, I'll cut off your balls and feed them to the pigs for dinner. So, listen and learn what Lord Malkore is teaching." He turned to his teacher and said, "Lord Malkore, please train my men."

"Asgardian warriors, this will be the worst day of training you have ever had. It will be the worst because we are going to show you the worst thing about you." He paused for effect, but he wasn't asking the real question he wanted to ask. "Men, are you ready for that next-level shit you haven't been ready for until now?"

"I am." Odin said loudly. He was not only setting an example for his men. He really felt ready.

All the men began to chime in, "I am."

Malkore took a deep breath. *"Let's see how this goes . . ."* He thought. "If you really think you are ready, I will ask you my *real* question." A few men nodded to him. "How many of you have ever felt worthless or been scared that you are not good enough?" No one really responded with anything but looking around to see if anyone else was going to speak up. "No? No one. Because warriors have to be tough and they would never admit to being scared or feeling anything other than brave, right?"

Odin's lead warrior, St'laad, dropped his head and raised his hand. Then a few others, then Scout.

Then Odin spoke, "You're not just fat, lazy bastards, you're a bunch of fucking liars, too! Men, I've known since I can remember that I would be king. And I have been scared ever since that I wouldn't be good enough. Malkore taught me when I was young to surround myself with the smartest men, the most loyal men, and to *listen* to them. He taught me that no one could lead a kingdom by himself, that I needed all of you. When I became king, I forgot that. I was terrified that if I didn't seem perfect all the time, you would all kick me out of Asgard. That's the truth. So, you fat, lazy liars expect me to believe that Me, Scout, St'laad, and two or three others are the only ones who have ever felt like they aren't good enough. Men, show some fucking honor. Do not dirty our brotherhood with lies."

One by one, the men started raising their hands. All of them raised their hands.

"It just might work." Malkore thought. "Thank you, men. Now this is why I bring it up. Two reasons, actually." Malkore motioned for St'laad to come up and join him. "I know most of you will want to give him shit when I ask this, but for a moment, only tell the truth." He put his hand on St'laad's shoulder and asked, "How many of you know what a great warrior this man is?"

"I do." The men yelled out like a chorus across the group.

"And how many of you look up to him?" Everyone, including the king yelled out. "And how many of you have ever thought that he is a worthless piece of pig shit?"

St'laad's brother yelled out, "Do brothers count, Lord Malkore?" All the men laughed.

Malkore put on his serious teacher's voice and asked the man, "Are you trying to get your balls fed to the pigs today?"

Properly scolded, the man answered, "No. I am sorry, Lord Malkore."

"Seriously, do you respect your brother?" Malkore asked.

"Yes." The man said.

"*More* than you would ever let him know, right?" Asked Malkore.

The man looked his brother in the eye, then back to Malkore, "Yes, My Lord."

"And when he has needed help, you have been the first one there? And he has always done the same for you. Right?"

"Yes, My Lord." He said.

"Would you ever let yourself depend on someone who wasn't worthy?" Malkore asked.

"No, My Lord." He said.

"You trust him?"

"Yes."

"Probably more than anyone else, right?"

"Yes, My Lord." The man said with a tear starting to come up in his eye. He opened his mouth, then closed it again.

Malkore noticed, "What were you about to say, son?"

He wiped a tear from his eye, then turned to everyone, "You all know how hard I work at everything, right?" Then, he looked at his brother, "I always work hard because I never feel worthy of having you as a brother."

St'laad had a tear roll down his face.

Malkore thanked St'laad and told him he was finished with him. St'laad walked over and hugged his brother.

Seeing these brothers hug, who always fought and argued, bitterly, Malkore yelled out at the men, "That is Asgard!" Pointing to the brothers. "No one can defeat an army with a bond like that. No one can defeat a people with a bond like that." A silence fell across the group. "Now, before any one of you fat, lazy, lying fuckers starts giving them shit about talking about their feelings, first ask yourself if you want a brother like that. Men, I not only *want* brothers like that, I *need* brothers like that in my life! Agreed?"

All the men nodded and spoke their agreement.

"These two brothers have been fighting each other for a century because both of them were scared in some way that they weren't good enough and had something to prove. Understand?"

"Yes, My Lord." The men answered.

In a booming voice, Malkore yelled, "No one here has anything to prove! You are Asgardian warriors! Would it be good to honor that in each other?"

"Yes, my Lord." The men answered again.

"Would it be good to feel the power of every man here behind you, without any doubt of their belief in you?!" Malkore asked, still in his big, booming voice.

The men yelled their agreement.

Malkore went on, "There is only one way to make that happen – there is only one way to truly honor each other in the best way. Would you like to know what it is?"

The men all yelled, again.

"You have to honor it in yourself, men. When you feel weak, you have to ask for help without fear, trusting that you will only be stronger after getting the help you need. When you are scared, you have to have something stronger than fear to carry you. You have to know that you are worthy of Asgard's love and respect, without question. You have nothing to prove."

Odin continued the teaching, "Honor yourself and you will easily honor each other! You have nothing to prove."

Malkore hadn't expected that, "*Maybe they are more ready than I thought.*" "Yes." Malkore said to Odin.

Odin spoke up, "Asgard, when it is just us, here, together. I will continue to tell you fat, lazy, lying fuckers what fat, lazy, lying fuckers, you are. But never to tear you down, never because you are not worthy. Only to ask you to believe in yourself, like you never have. When you doubt yourself, I will call you out and we will crush your doubt together! That is my vision of what Asgard can be! Will you join me in that? I want an army who is strong and motivated and works so well that nothing will ever be able to stop it. Will you join me in that?"

The men yelled and cheered out of habit, but they were a little stunned by what had been happening, it was like they had been led into another world and didn't know how or why. They didn't know what was happening, but almost all of them liked it.

"The second reason I bring up that fear and doubt of not being good enough," Malkore asked Odin to pull out his sword and hold it over his head as if he were about to strike. "Come at me until I say stop." Odin started to strike down with his sword, but first he raised his sword up and behind his head a little. "Stop! Hold that position." Trying to hold that position, Odin took a small step back. Malkore turned to the men, "Did you see that? What just happened?"

Only two or three people noticed that Odin had taken a step back. St'laad said, "He stepped backwards." Odin hadn't even realized it himself.

"That's right. Now we all know how strong Odin is. We have all seen him kill hundreds of men with this very strike. But when we were practicing with swords two days ago, I noticed that his weight was moving backwards, that he was relying on his strength to make a kill."

Odin jokingly said, "Don't remind me." The men laughed; everyone had heard the story already.

Malkore said, "Tell me what happens if you take a man with this much strength who keeps his weight balanced and moving forward with this strike? Easy kill, right? When you are better than most men, you can get by ignoring your weaknesses for a long time. Hopefully." The men laughed.

Odin interjected, "There is always someone better than you, even if you have never met him. *That* is the man you train to fight – Not the men around you. You train to fight the man who is better than you. Understood?" The men all nodded.

Malkore continued, "Here is the thing: If you are scared that you aren't good enough. Somewhere inside you will sabotage yourself or shy away from the scary thing inside that you need to be whole – you will make it will look like you are not good enough. Look at these two brothers, one has spent a hundred years arguing with the man he respects more than anyone else just to try and prove he is good enough. They fight like brothers!" The men laughed. "They get a pass for that, when they are boys. But now it's time to outgrow those boyish fears and never doubt themselves or each other. Now it's time to realize that they are each other's greatest ally!"

Odin spoke again, "A man at war with himself, with his own heart, can go far, but not nearly as far as a man at peace with himself."

Malkore finished that sentiment, "When you are calm and at peace with yourself, you fight like a god!"

The men cheered at that one.

Odon interjected, "When you are at peace with yourself, you make love like a god with a cock of thunder, too!"

The men cheered even bigger at that . . .

Odin went on, "We are in this together. I want you to find the greatest part of yourself to add to what Asgard will become. I don't want your fear; I want you to learn to grow bigger than your fear. I want your inspiration. I want your dreams. I want you to fight like you are fueled by the sun itself, not just fueled by trying to beat your own fears and doubts."

Odin turned back to his teacher. Malkore was looking pleased with his student. Odin realized, right then, how much of his teacher's respect he had lost. It wasn't until he had a bit of it back that he saw how far he had slipped. "I told you I was listening, Lord Malkore. Please continue, My Lord."

To the group, Malkore said, "It is vital that you know what scares you inside. It is vital that you learn to *not* be scared of it.

We all have weaknesses. By the end of training today, you will be thankful to know how to build up your weaknesses. The worst warriors only focus on their strengths because they are scared that their weaknesses means that they aren't worth a shit."

Malkore called another man up and told the man to draw his sword and come at him. Within a few strikes and defensive moves, Malkore yelled, "Stop! Hold that position." Malkore notice the way the man was stepping into a strike left him a little off balance. He only wanted the man to move his step half a foot to the left when he made the strike, but it made all the difference in his ability to respond to changes.

Malkore demonstrated how off balance the man was by pushing onto the ground. Then, with the proper step, Malkore tried to push him over again. The man didn't budge. Malkore asked, "Did you feel that? I couldn't move you." The man nodded. "OK. Now you and Lord Odin go find a spot and practice with each other, until the proper movement of each of your weakest skills becomes automatic and your weakness doesn't come back."

Another man asked, "Will you show me, Lord Malkore?"

"Of course, son. Come on up." Addressing the group, "Keep paying attention and learn from what your brothers are going through up here. If you see one of your brothers making the same mistake that you make, then come up and grab him and the two of you go practice until you get it right." Then Malkore called out to St'laad, "St'laad, do you know what you need to work on?"

"Yes, My Lord. It is what you just showed me today." He said with an embarrassed smile.

"Good. I want you to take Scout. Show him how to help you work on your weakness, while teaching him one good move with the best form. Make sure you teach him one good piece of technique to use in helping you work on your weakness. That will teach him and help you." St'laad and Scout started walking off to practice together and more and more men started coming closer. The men were looking for their chance to learn. "OK. Who is next?"

In just 30 minutes, all the men had paired off to work on something. Clamoring swords could be heard all through the oak grove and into the valley. Malkore went to get a bit of water, then he walked around to all the men, giving them pointers, teaching a little when the men needed coaching. He would jump in to take the place of one of the men and have the other attack him to check the men's progress and point out what to keep practicing and praising what was working well.

After an hour or so, Malkore ended with Scout, looked at the one movement he was working on to help St'laad. It was good. "Now son, I want you to run a lap around and tell everyone to meet me back where we started. "Yes, My Lord." The boy sheathed his sword and began running to every pair of men in the meadow.

As Malkore and St'laad walked back to talk with the men, Malkore said, "St'laad, I want to ask you something. It's about Scout."

St'laad interrupted, "Lord Malkore, I would love to. I will work with him every day."

Malkore looked surprised, "Good. Thank you. Then, you and I will practice early, like today, so you don't get sloppy. OK?"

"We are Asgard. It's what we do. Right?!" St'laad asked. Malkore laughed. "Did I say something wrong, My Lord?"

Malkore laughed his big, warrior's laugh, grabbed the man around the shoulder as they walked and said, "You don't know how right you are, St'laad. It's what we do." It had become the theme. "It's what we do." He repeated.

When the men reassembled, after sword practice, Odin and his practice partner didn't come right away. Odin wanted to make a statement to all the men. He and his practice partner kept practicing for another two minutes just to show that they were working hard. Malkore didn't mind that, if they were practicing well.

Odin and his partner re-joined the group quickly and Malkore asked, "Do you guys want one more short lesson? Or is that enough for the first day?"

Odin added on, using his big, warrior's voice, "Choose well, because tomorrow you won't get a choice."

One man in the back yelled out, "Today is just preparation for tomorrow's training, so give us another lesson!"

Malkore's face lit up, he pointed at the man and said, "That man gets the first horn of mead tonight!"

The men yelled at the man, "First drink for you!"

"OK men. I have lived with a lot of different people in a lot of different places before I came to live in Asgard. I can tell you that there are a lot of miserable bastards alive in this universe. They really are miserable fucks." All the men laughed. "And the part that sucks the worst for them is that they will never outgrow it. They are miserable for one reason: They refuse to open their hearts; they are scared to face the pain inside and grow. That's it. So right now, I am going to guide you through something to help you to be a better citizen of Asgard, this will help you with your family, and it will help you in case some of you fat, lazy, lying bastards ever gets lucky enough to get close to a woman again." All the men laughed. "And it will make you stronger in spirit, because a man at peace with himself, cannot be broken. A people at peace within themselves, can never be conquered."

One man in the back of the group, had been making comments while Malkore was talking. Then he made a joke, not taking it seriously. Odin looked at the man, "Hey! Pigfucker! Get your shit together or leave and never come back." The man looked down; scared Odin might kick him off the raids. "You will come see me when we are done." The man was still looking down. "Look at me, Pigfucker! You will come see me after we are done."

The man looked at Odin and nodded, "Yes, My Lord."

Malkore joked quietly to the guys right in front of him, "You see how respectfully he called that man a Pigfucker. He meant no judgment there." The men close enough to hear Malkore laughed. "Seriously, Pigfucker back there is great with a sword, but not such a good guy to be around. He thinks too much of himself only to try and cover that he is scared of being worthless. He doesn't respect himself -- because of that, he really doesn't have any respect for anyone else. Does that make sense? Men like that, hold everyone back. When *that* man is at peace with himself, he will be the best man in the kingdom. Now, who's responsibility it to support that man?"

All the men who could hear Malkore talking said, "It's my responsibility, My Lord." But their tone was not convincing. None of them wanted to take responsibility to help the guy.

Malkore was still only talking loud enough for the men right in front of him to hear, "If your brother is an asshole, he's still your brother, right? Maybe he just needs someone to listen long enough to hear why he's such an asshole."

Another man in the back said loudly, "Lord Malkore, we can't hear you."

Malkore spoke up so everyone could hear him, "I was just talking to these men, saying that if your brother is an asshole, he is still your brother. And sometimes assholes just need a chance to tell their story of why they are such assholes. People usually act that way because they don't feel good enough. They are scared they aren't good enough! And it doesn't matter how accomplished they are, their heart is hurting really badly inside -- they believe they are worthless, and they believe that no one really cares about them. Most of the time they learned to believe that when they were little and never learned any better." Pig fucker was fuming inside. Everyone got nervous about what might happen.

Odin gave Malkore a look that said he shouldn't push this guy. Malkore wasn't scared, this is what he was here to do.

Malkore went on, looking right at Pigfucker, "I was saying that a man like that, when he finds peace within himself will be the best man in the kingdom."

Pigfucker mumbled to himself, "Peace is a joke. I'd rather kill a peacemaker." The man next to him hit him on the arm and told him to shut up and to calm down. Pigfucker responded, "Fuck you."

Malkore continued, "Men of Asgard, do you run away from a fight?"

"No!" the men yelled.

"When your mouth gets dry and your hands shake before battle, do you run away scared?"

"No!" the men yelled.

"After today, if you find a weakness in your fighting style, will you hide it and hope it goes away?"

"No!" the men yelled.

"Watch this! Odin, raise your sword up high and strike at me." Odin came at him strong, pushing off his back foot, supporting his weight on his lunging leg.

St'laad was in the front of the group and saw the improvement and yelled, "Yes. That's it!"

Malkore turned to the men, "Better?"

The men cheered for their king, "Yes, King Odin!" "You got it!" "Way to go, King!"

Malkore continued, "Better, right? All he had to do was put himself in that place of being *willing to learn*. Did that make him weak or worthless? Or did it make him stronger?"

"Stronger!" The men yelled.

"He got help and then only had to spend 30 minutes practicing it correctly. Right?"

The men cheered for Odin a bit more. They were sucking up to the king, but that's what you do with a king.

Malkore asked, "Are all of you better at one skill than you were when you got up this morning?"

The men all cheered.

"Doesn't that feel good?!" Malkore asked them.

They all cheered again.

Malkore went on, "Asgard, we all have battles to fight. Our training will make us better prepared than ever before."

Odin interjected, "We have even greater battles to fight within ourselves. We all have battles to fight in our own heart. If you want Asgard to grow, those are the most important battles to fight and to *not* run away from. You wouldn't run away from a fight with an enemy's sword. So, don't run away from the fight when that asshole in your head tells you that you're a piece of shit. Understand?"

Odin turned to Malkore and said, "Excuse me, Lord Malkore. Please go on."

"Well said, My King. That is all for today, men. You bunch of lazy, fat, lying bastards, remember that today is only preparation for tomorrow. Get the fuck out of here." The men all laughed. A couple of them came up and shook his hand and thanked him.

He walked over to Odin. Odin asked, "Good today, huh?"

"Yeah, good. After training tomorrow, if you don't die on our run, you and I will go sit down and have a horn of mead."

"Indeed. I look forward to it, My Lord. Go see that beautiful woman of yours, I will take care of Pigfucker. He will be a different man tomorrow."

"Why? How will he be different?" Malkore asked.

"Do I seem different than I did two days ago, My Lord?" Odin asked with a grin.

"Yeah, what changed?" That was one thing Malkore wanted to ask about when they talked tomorrow.

Odin looked at him with a glimmer in his eye, "I'll tell you tomorrow night after training. Have a good day, Lord Malkore."

Now, he had Malkore feeling curious what secret he was keeping.

Chapter Fifteen
Too Scared to Kiss Well

After that first day's training with the men, the energy in the village was buzzing. Many of the women had prepared a meal for all the people in the great hall and everyone was curious how the first day of training had gone. As the men began to filter in it turned into a party. Everyone was high on excitement for what they might be building together.

Malkore had gone back to Iyasiil's place to check in with her and to rest for a bit. She was not there, she and Kalla would be gone for several more hours.

Since he had begun his Tending, he was learning of these things called "naps." They had always been foreign to him, but he was beginning to appreciate them. He got a small plate of fruit and cheese that one of the girls had left in their teacher's chamber. He took off his boots, took off his armor, and put his sword by the bed. He sat at the head of the bed and started running all the day's events through his head.

He thought about how he had been curious to ask Iyasiil about the joke she had made about showing him how to use his sword. He thought about how that question was at the core of what had been troubling her. He thought about her vision of building an army of Women Warriors, and how powerful it would be to have a whole army of women standing in their power. He was trying to imagine how the entire culture of

Asgard would change when all the women learn to stand in their power. He didn't know what it would look like, but he wanted to. He had always suspected, and was just now getting to see firsthand, that being with a woman standing in her power is more thrilling and sexier and supportive and comforting and empowering and enlightening than anything. And he understood how a woman standing in her power could be incredibly intimidating to an insecure man.

One lesson he was always teaching is that "There is no strength outside of balance." It shows in fighting. When you are off balance in a fight, you won't last long. It shows in every aspect of life. If your spirit is out of balance, you suffer. If you don't feel worthy, your relationships get out of balance because you either try to put yourself above others or put yourself below others. Either way, you suffer because there is no real connection and people will not trust you, unless they are soul-sick, too, and need you to be bigger or smaller than them. When there is an imbalance like that, you can't connect with anything except the story you are trying to tell of your worthiness or unworthiness. He thought of how he would teach it to the men, *"If you are putting yourself below me, I don't get the real you, all I get is the story that you are small. And if you are trying to make yourself bigger than me, all I get to get close to is your ego, I don't get the real you. Maybe that is where we will start tomorrow, after we get Scout to run up the hill for thirty minutes or so and get the men to go find him."* He thought.

This is how Malkore, as a teacher has always come up with lessons for his students; he goes over what has happened, and thinks about what the next step is, then plans out how to teach that next step of learning and growth.

He was really proud of St'laad -- not just for showing up early, but for committing to showing up early every day to get his own training in, so he could work with Scout every day and teach Scout how to handle a sword. Scout was in good hands with St'laad as his teacher.

Malkore sat on the bed alone and took a couple of breaths. He thought about that nap, put the empty plate aside, and laid down. He hadn't laid down by himself in five days. After more than a millennia of sleeping alone, it surprised him how quickly the bed felt empty without Iyasiil there. He smiled at that thought and imagined her there with him. He imagined the feel of her skin and let his heart feel how it lit up with happiness he is when he could feel her presence.

He slept for about thirty minutes and woke up with a deep breath. He sat up and scooted to the head of the bed and started breathing for a few minutes of meditation. Within a few minutes, Dossa walked in with a pitcher of mead and a plate of bread, cheese, and berries. She didn't see him at first. She put the plate down and went to stoke up the fire just enough to have coals to build up in the evening. After she tended the fire, she turned to look and see if the bed needed to be made. She saw Malkore sitting there with his eyes closed. She gasped.

He thought, "*I guess I haven't mastered that invisibility thing, yet.*" He opened his eyes with a slight smile on his face.

"My Lord. I am sorry. I didn't know you were here." She said.

"That's not a problem, sweet Dossa. I was just sitting and breathing – just meditating." He said.

"I won't disturb you, My Lord." She turned and started to walk to the back door. She was acting like a slave girl, who's master was annoyed with her.

"Dossa." He said.

She turned back towards him, "Yes, My Lord?"

"Stop right now and take a breath. Tell me, if you want to, what are you so scared of right now." He said.

"I don't know, My Lord." She said without taking a breath.

"No, really. Take a breath. Settle into your body." He said. He wasn't sure she was ready to have a conversation like this without Kalla and Iyasiil here. "First of all, are you OK talking to me without your teacher and Kalla here?" Her eyes shot up at him. *"That was it."* He thought. "It's OK if you don't want to talk without them here. I totally understand. And if you would like to stay and talk, I'd love to have you stay." He said.

"You would be OK with that?" She asked.

He smiled, "Of course! But only if you are OK with it. We will make plenty of time to talk later if you don't want to talk alone." He could feel how scared she was, but he wasn't quite sure of what was scaring her so badly. "Take a breath."

She did. She took a breath. "Oh shit. This is one of those feet things, isn't it?"

Malkore laughed a big laugh. "Yes, sweet Dossa. This is one of those feet things. Bless you, sweet girl. The only thing for you to pay attention to is where do you want to put your feet, right this minute." He paused. "If you were free to do whatever you wanted and put your feet anywhere in Asgard, where would you put them right this moment."

She looked at the bed briefly and was wondering if it was OK to say what she wanted. She looked like she was shrinking with the battle in her own mind.

"I don't know." She said.

"Yes, you do. You just looked at the spot, didn't you?" He asked.

She laughed a little bit, then nodded her head. "Lord Malkore, why is this so hard?" Then she started crying softly. "Oh shit. I'm sorry."

"Dossa don't apologize. It *is* hard. It is hard to listen to your heart when you have had good reason to shut it down in the past." He said.

"I'm so sorry, Lord Malkore."

"You just did it again." She laughed a little. "Are you going to keep doing that?"

"Doing what?" She asked.

"Are you going to keep apologizing when you haven't done anything wrong? Are you going to keep apologizing or are you going to start telling the truth about what you are feeling, what you want, and what you think?" He asked. *"Oh, shit, Malkore. Don't push her too hard. She may not be ready."* He thought.

"Fuck! That's it! don't want to be scared to talk anymore." She said with more energy.

"Good. Good. Then take a breath, check in with your body and your heart. Ask your body and your heart where they want your feet, right now." He said. Then he thought, *"Wow! Maybe I wasn't pushing too hard."*

In a meek, small voice, she said, "On the bed."

He smiled at her, "Good job. Now it is time to proclaim to the bed and the entire universe that you want to sit on the bed.

And do it so the entire universe hears you." She looked at him like he was crazy. "Trust me on this Dossa. You are going to love how it feels to use your voice."

In a slightly less meek voice, she said it like a question, "I want to put my feet on the bed?"

"Good. But the universe didn't hear you declare it. Say it louder, like you mean it." He said, not sure she was ready to really say it.

"Like I mean it." She was telling herself to not hold back.

"Yes, like you mean it." He repeated. "Look me in the eye and say it like you mean it."

She took a big breath and looked him in the eyes and said, "Lord Malkore, I am declaring to you and the universe that I want to sit on the bed." Then she looked away, uneasy with having said it.

"Good job, Dossa. Now, say it again, even louder."

"Even Louder?" She said.

"You don't have to say it louder, but what you have to do is feel what you want even bigger and then give yourself what you want. Does that make sense?" He asked.

"Yes, My Lord. I think so." She said.

"Now feel it bigger than your fear of saying it. Then let the feeling come out of your mouth how you are feeling it." He said.

"Oh. Just like –" she let out a big breath. "It's just like when Frigg was here. I just have to see what I want and say it."

"What happened with Frigg was here?" He asked.

"It doesn't matter. I just need to see what I want and say it." She said, looking confident.

"OK. Do it." He said.

"Lord Malkore, I hope I am not disturbing you. I didn't know you were going to be here. But now that I see that you are here, I would love to sit down with you." She said.

He could feel her more, now. He smiled and felt his love and care for her. "Dossa, I would love that."

She sat at the foot of the bed on the opposite corner from him and tried to get comfortable. "Well, that was easy." She said making fun of herself for making it so hard to say what she wanted.

"Dossa, you know, if you had seen me and run and jumped on me and hugged me, that would have been OK too, *if* it was really how you felt. The only way to mess things up is to not be true to what you really want and who you really are."

"Well, then I mess shit up all the time!" She said jokingly.

"So now that you are here. What were you so scared of, specifically?" He asked.

"I was scared that you didn't want me here and that if I just came and laid my head on your lap that you would think I was a stupid little girl who was stupid – really stupid." She said.

"Now, what do you think of that fear? If you had come and laid down and put your head on my lap, would I have thought you were stupid?"

"It doesn't sound like it." She answered.

"What would I have thought about you if you had done that?" He asked.

"That I am pathetic." She said.

"Nope." He said.

"That I need too much." She said.

"Nope." He said.

"That I am crazy for wanting to put my head in your lap when I have only known you for four days." She said.

"Nope. He said.

"What would you have thought?" She asked.

"I would have thought, "Thank you for letting me love you." And then I would have pulled you closer." He said.

She started crying. "But what if I need too much love?" She asked.

"If that were the case, then I would tell you my secret. I would tell you my secret that no one else knows." He said.

She looked at him with a confused look on her face, "What's that? What's your secret?"

"Do you really want to know?" She nodded and her crying let up a little. "Dossa, I need *too much* love, too." He said smiling.

"You?" She couldn't believe it.

He nodded at her with his eyebrows raised, "MmmHmm. Me too."

"You don't act like it." She said.

"Well, I keep myself pretty full of love, these days, but that only makes connecting with someone even sweeter. I love it! And can't *ever* get enough of it. I need a lot!" He let his words sink in with her for a second. "Let's do one of two things. Either lay down here and put your head on my lap or let's try something else."

"What?" she asked.

"Trust your heart to make the right decision. Then if you choose it and don't want to do it, you can change your mind." He said.

"OK. I choose the something else, then." She said.

"OK. Great. Scoot over and sit directly across from me. I was meditating when you came in. When I heard you come in, I thought about having you join me in meditation."

"Why didn't you just say it, then?" She asked.

He smiled, "Do you want to know the truth? I was scared."

"Of what? Scared of me?" She asked, already beating herself up.

"No, not scared of you. Of course not. You have never had many men that you feel safe with. I was scared that if you felt me wanting to be closer to you, it would be scary to you." He said.

"Oh. No. No. You? I know I am safe with you. You are so safe. You may be the only one in the world that's safe. That's why I usually only date women, because not many men are safe. But you, *that's* why you are so scary, because you are safe!"

He chuckled. "How am I scary?"

"I don't know. I feel so big. I feel like I'm going to explode." She said.

"Explode how?" He asked.

"It's like, if I let myself be big, this big" she motioned between them, "then what if I can't do it?!" She said. Then she looked at him, looked him in the eye and said. "Oh shit. That's just me being scared that I am not good enough, isn't it?"

"Good catch. Yes, that's exactly it. Good job." He said, smiling.

"OK. And I need to learn to feel like I am good enough."

Malkore said, "That's one way. There is another way that might be easier, though. Do you want to hear what that is?" She nodded. "You can ignore those scary thoughts and the feelings that come from those thoughts and only feel what your heart wants."

"What do you mean?" She asked.

"For example, when you noticed that I was here, I get that you were surprised, but after that, go back to that moment in your mind. What did your body feel like right in that moment?" He asked.

"I don't know. I got scared so fast." She said.

"OK, so right now, go back to that moment and freeze that moment in your imagination. Imagine yourself standing there and you see me sitting on the bed. Take a deep breath and check in with what you want, right in that moment." He said.

"Is it OK for me to be here? That's what I felt." She said.

"OK, good. Do you mean you were scared that it wasn't OK for you to be here alone with me?" He asked.

She nodded. "Yeah."

"So, that was the fear that is blocking you from feeling what you really want. Does that make sense?" He asked.

Dossa looked confused, "No. What do you mean?"

"I mean that you are scared that it's not OK to be here alone with me, but that fear only came up because inside you wanted to be here with me once you saw me. If you didn't want to be here with me, the fear would not have come up." Malkore said.

"OK. Right." She said.

He continued, "Try saying this, "I want to be here with you right now and I am scared it's not OK to want to be here alone with you."" He said.

Her face lit up with recognition, "Yeah, that's it!"

"OK, good. So just feel that feeling of wanting to be here and trust that it's OK." She was struggling with that. "Take a breath."

"Are you really OK with spending time with me?" she asked.

"Of course, I am. When I heard you come in, I was excited to see you. I was wondering why I came here to take a nap, instead of going to the great hall. When you came in, it made sense. I am glad you are here." He said.

"Really?" she asked.

"How do you feel hearing me say that I am happy to get to spend time with you." He asked.

"It makes me want to cry." She said.

"Why?" He asked.

"Because I was scared you only wanted to be around Mama and Kalla and not me." She said.

"Another fear that you aren't enough, right?" He asked.

She nodded. She felt better getting that off her chest. "OK. I am tired of being scared. So, I am here now. What do we do?"

"How about you scoot over and sit directly across from me and let's sit and breath for a bit. Close your eyes if you want. After you feel like you get settled in, just say "OK" and then we will shift into something else." He said.

She scooted over to sit across from him, "I can do that."

She looked at him, then slowly closed her eyes.

He said, "Gently blow all your air out, then take in a big, fresh breath. Then breathe easy and listen to the sound of your breath."

She nodded her head slowly as she slowed down her thoughts, listening to her breath. Malkore could feel her presence a bit more as her thoughts slowed down and she began to make deeper contact with her own heart.

After several minutes, she kept her eyes closed and softly said, "OK. I'm ready."

He took another breath with a big exhale, encouraging her to continue breathing, then said, "When you are ready, slowly open your eyes and make eye contact with me."

She took another couple of breaths, then slowly opened her eyes and made eye contact with him. She felt her heart get warm as she looked into his eyes. A smile began forming on her face. She started feeling happy, she felt like her skin was glowing a little. She giggled.

"Hey, sweet lady." Malkore said, smiling back at her.

With the smile on her face, and with a relaxed tone, she said, "Hey, Malkore." Then she caught herself, "I mean, My Lord. Oh, I'm so sorry."

"You just did it again. You apologized when you didn't do anything wrong. You spoke from your heart and then stopped yourself." He winked at her.

"Oh fuck. I did, didn't I?" She said, but without breaking eye contact with him and without beating herself up. "I have so much respect for you. You deserve to addressed appropriately."

"I don't care how you address me, as long as you bring your heart like this." He said.

"Yes, My Lord." She said.

"Keep breathing and tell me how this feels now, Dossa."

"It feels good. I feel good. I don't feel like I'm behind that wall that is always there." She said.

"Yeah, that's the way it feels to me too. I feel like you are really letting yourself, be here with me." He said.

"Yes. Yes. That's exactly what it feels like. I just feel like I am here, just here with you. I don't feel scared, anymore." She said.

"Good. Now, as you continue to look me in the eye, I *invite* you to look more deeply into me. Look as deeply into me as you want to, I'm wide open and I won't hide any part of myself." He said.

She took a breath, and he could feel her presence even more, then he couldn't feel her anymore. "What happened? That felt like you stepped in, then went away."

"I'm sorry." She said. Then she realized she had apologized again, "Shit. I did it again. I'm sorry." Then she burst into laughter, "And I did it again! I just apologized for apologizing, twice!" She kept making eye contact while she laughed.

He started laughing, too. She was adorable when she wasn't hiding. "Dossa, what scared you, right then?"

"It's that thing that Kalla said." She was hoping he would know what she was talking about. She was scared she would be really embarrassed to say it.

"What did Kalla say?" He asked.

"You're going to make me say it, aren't you?" she asked.

"No, I can't make you do anything, but if you are going to talk about it, I would like to know what we are talking about." He said jokingly

"Kalla said that th ng about not knowing how to love you. She said all those different ways and she said she was feeling all of them . . . *that* thing." Dossa said.

"OK. *That* thing. Yeah, I remember. So, take a breath, look as deep into me as you want to, and feel all the different ways you love me right this moment. Let yourself feel them. Just keep feeling your feelings. It's OK to feel them, no matter what they are." He said.

She did. She felt her heart get warm again, her skin tone changed, her smile came back. He could feel her presence again Malkore felt his heart get warm, too.

"There she is! So, what do you notice inside? What does it feel like in there?" He asked.

"It feels good. I fee good." She said.

"Did those feelings about me come up again? Or was it something else?" He asked.

"Mostly the same . . . and I am feeling them. I'm not running away or getting scared." She said.

"I can feel that. I can feel you a lot more. What I notice is my heart gets warm when I can feel you really be here with me. And, it feels good to me, too." He told her.

Her smile turned into a different kind of smile. She looked grateful and looked like she might cry again. She nodded her head, receiving what he was saying. "I like this." She said.

He smiled and nodded. "Now, Keep breathing and keep making eye contact with me, and see if it feels any different if you focus on letting me look more deeply into you. See what it is feels like to let me see more deeply into you."

"OK." She said. Then she took a deep breath and refocused on looking him in the eyes. She stayed present with him for a while, after a couple of long breaths, her eyes got a little bigger and her breathing got more intense. She looked like she was breathing hard to stay focused through something painful. "Wow." She said.

"Yeah, wow. What were you feeling?" He asked.

"I felt like I was going to explode. I started feeling scared. I felt excited. And I felt like my whole body was jumbled." She said.

He smiled. "Yeah, that sounds about right. Good job staying with those feelings! What was scary? Can you say what was exciting? And how did your body feel jumbled?"

"First, I felt excited, then scared. Excited to be closer to you, and it felt good. It felt *really* good. Then I got scared that I was going to screw it up. Scared, again, that I would be too much. Then, as I stayed with it, and I didn't go away, that's when my body felt jumbled." She said.

He still didn't understand what she meant by "jumbled" but she kept saying it. "Did the jumbled feeling feel good? Or was it a bad kind of jumbled?" He asked.

She looked at him with a funny look on her face. She looked like she almost said something that she wasn't sure would be OK to say. "Do you really want to know?" She asked. He nodded at her, curiously. "I felt jumbled in that I-want-to-fuck-your-feet-with-my-feet kind of way." They both started laughing. "You asked . . ." She said.

"I still find it hard to believe that you are attracted to me but thank you for sharing that with me. Do you feel OK now that you told me that?" he asked.

"Lord Malkore, I am so attracted to you. I think you are the most awesome man I have ever met." She said.

"Well, thank you Dossa." He said almost blushing.

"It's the truth." She said.

"I hear you. Now take a deep breath and feel what it feels like to tell me that." He said.

She took a deep breath, while keeping eye contact with him, and said, "It's scary and I'm OK with it." She paused for a moment, "for now. I'll probably freak out later." They both laughed.

"Let me know if you get scared, again. I'd rather have you talk about it, than get scared and run away, and beat yourself up." He said.

"OK. I promise." She told him.

"Would you like to keep going? Or do you feel like that's enough opening up for today?" He asked.

"Oh, no. Let's keep going, this is fun, and I have to deal with this shit sooner or later. I just don't want to freak you out." She said.

"How do you think you could freak me out?" He asked.

"I don't want you to think I am weird or stupid for being so attracted to you, that's all." She said.

"Oh, no. Dossa, don't give that another moment of your attention. I'm flattered and I am OK with it. Besides, it's all about showing up and being who we really are. And I don't feel like I have gotten to see much of who you are, you're just now starting to let me see you, without hiding." He said.

She nodded at him, "Yeah, I am sorry about that. I'm learning. This is all new to me."

He playfully pointed a finger at her and gave her a look that said, "*I caught you.*" He said, "Try again."

Dossa smiled and didn't beat herself up for apologizing, "How about this: I want to love you so big, and I wish I had met Mama years ago, maybe then, I wouldn't be so scared now. How is that?"

"Better. And don't worry about where you are now. Just love where you are going – feel the excitement of what you are growing into. Does that make sense?"

"Yeah, so how do I do that?" She asked.

"Well, what do you think it will be like when you walk around every day without being scared to let people see who you really are?"

Her face lit up, "That will be awesome!"

"So, feel awesome now, don't wait." He said. She giggled at the simplicity of his suggestion. "So, try breathing and making eye contact with me and be the future version of you that isn't scared." He said.

Dossa cocked her head sideways, "But –"

He cut her off, "Try it. Feel that feeling of who you want to be. Then breath and bring that into connection with me."

She took a breath and made eye contact with him. "OK. Yeah. I can do this."

He nodded. "Good. Now, look as deep into me as you can."

She smiled and nodded, "Yeah, I can do this."

He took another breath. "Now, let me look as deeply into you as you can." She took a breath and looked like she was about to cry. "Keep breathing. Stay with it. Keep feeling it." Tears started falling down her face as her face slowly scrunched up into crying. She leaned forward and crawled across the bed and sat on his lap. She put her head on his shoulder. He wrapped his arms around her and held her as she cried. "I'm right here, Dossa. Keep breathing. I'm right here. I'm not going away."

As she was crying, she said, "Nobody has ever cared enough to really see me before."

"Yeah, sometimes it is too much for people because they don't want to feel their own feelings. That's why us "too much" type of people have to stick together. That's why we feel at home with each other." He said.

She started crying harder when he said that. She nodded her head while soaking the shoulder of his shirt with tears and mucus as she cried. She said, "So, that's why you and Mama and Kalla feel so good to me, then."

"Yeah. It's good to find your soul family. Those people always feel like home to us." He said.

She started crying harder. She cried really hard for several more minutes and he held her the whole time.

"Do you think you and Mama will stay together?" She asked.

"I don't know. Ask me again in a hundred years, OK? I'll have a better answer for you then." He said.

She laughed, "I hope so. I don't want to lose you."

"I am not going anywhere. I told you and Kalla that we can still talk even if things don't keep going with Iyasiil and me. We are all grownups. If there is a problem, we will deal with it." He said.

"Yeah. I know. I just love you and Mama being together so much, it makes my world better." She said.

"I know. So, feel that better world and carry it with you, always. And being with her makes my world better, too. It's hard to believe I only met her 5 days ago. I don't even think we talked before she started my Tending."

"I know. She is so in love with you." Dossa said.

"Really?" He asked, then he couldn't help but be distracted by all the happy feelings boiling up inside.

"Oh, yeah! She glows when she is with you. She didn't glow like that before. She glowed, but not like she does with you." She said.

"Wow! I think she's amazing." He said.

"You're different, too, Lord Malkore." Dossa said, pulling her head up to look him in the eyes.

"How am I different?" he asked. He was curious how he was seen by others.

"You have always been really good looking, but now it's like you flow sexiness out of every part of you. I didn't want you before, even though I thought you were handsome. Now, I feel like I can really see you and feel you and you are amazing." Then she realized how easy it was to say all that. "Oh shit!" Her eyes got big. "I'm not scared!"

He smiled at her, "Wow! That's so awesome. Feel what it feels like to not be scared."

She nodded her head and put her head back on his shoulder. "I feel like I —" then she stopped herself from saying the rest of that sentence.

He waited several seconds to see if she would finish. "You feel like you, what?"

She started laughing. Then in a really cute way, she said, "I got scared again." She kept laughing. "Give me a minute." She buried her head deeper in his shoulder and let out a mixture of laughter and a frustrated growl. "What the fuck?!"

You did great for a little while, "Next time you won't get scared for a little while longer, then even longer after that. So good job!"

"I was about to tell you that I wanted to kiss you." Then she hugged him harder, mashing her face into his shoulder, and this time she made a sound that was a mixture of frustration and fear.

"Oh, bless you, sweet Dossa." He paused and hugged her harder.

"Yeah, bless me, I can't even kiss a man without crying." She said.

"No, No, No. You could go kiss anyone here, but this feels different, doesn't it?"

She nodded. "This feels big. I feel big."

"Yeah, I don't think your fear is as much about kissing me as it is your fear of being big, your fear of being yourself with people and not hiding." Malkore said.

"But, I do really want to kiss you." She said, still feeling a little puny.

"I know, and when you aren't scared of it, and you can kiss me with your whole heart without being afraid and without holding back, you absolutely should kiss me. I would love that." He said, pulling her even closer. "Oh, sweet, Dossa, you are so adorable and beautiful and funny. Your teacher tells me that you carry some deep wisdom, too. I like it when you don't hold back."

"She said that? Really?" Dossa looked at him with a curious look on her face. He nodded at her. "Wow, I thought she just felt sorry for me."

"Now, Dossa, that's another of those fucked up, I'm-not-good-enough stories, isn't it?" He said.

"Yeah, I guess it is. I do that a lot, don't I?" She asked.

"Yeah, and when you do, you can't bring your best kisses — your best kisses stay locked inside and you stay frustrated." He said with a smile.

In an animated voice, she said, "Well, shit! I don't want to do that anymore!" they both laughed. "So, when I stop beating myself up, I can kiss you?" She asked in a flirty way.

"It's more like, when you let yourself feel how delicious you really are, I won't be able to stop myself from kissing you." He said.

"Oh, fuck yes! That's what I want!" She said.

He went on, "And when you walk around feeling delicious, everyone will want a taste of your deliciousness. That's when you learn to set boundaries . . . Or run like hell." She laughed. Look at your teacher, everyone can see how beautiful and how amazing she is. Does she hide who she is because she is afraid of the attention it might bring?"

"No, but no one would dare be disrespectful of her." Dossa answered.

"That's right. Why is that?" He asked. "She isn't any different than you, except in how she carries herself. How does she carry herself differently?"

"Well, she just does. I don't know. It's like she would never shrink, no matter what happened." Dossa said.

"That's right. Well said. She would never shrink and make herself small no matter what anyone else said or did to her. Do think she would shrink if she were the one saying mean things to herself?" He asked.

"No, of course not. She would just stop thinking about it and go on with something that was real, and she would go on with who she really is." Then Dossa's face lit up, she looked excited. "That's it! That's exactly what I do. I say scary shit to myself, and I shrink away. I just need to ignore the scary shit I say, then go make the fun stuff happen." Then she exhaled deeply, feeling like for the first time she understood why her life had been so hard. "You already knew all that, didn't you?

Malkore smiled at her and nodded. "I knew it the moment I met you. What I didn't know is just how much fun you would be, when you stopped doing it. You have let me see a couple of glimpses of who you are in there and it is pretty great to see."

She looked at him for a long moment and didn't shy away, she looked relaxed and calm. "Lord Malkore, I –" She paused. "No. No. No. I am just going to do it."

"Do wha –" Dossa kissed him.

It was a passionate kiss. She let her body melt into him, she felt her lips like she had never felt them before, and she slid her left hand around the back of his neck and up to the base of his skull. *"This is how I want to kiss him."* She thought. Even though she had been sitting on his lap, leaning against him and had her shoulders turned towards him a bit, she hadn't felt her breasts touching him before now. She felt like her breasts started glowing and singing. As she took a breath, she rolled her spine to feel her breasts moving against him. Every second of the kiss felt more delicious than the last. When she stopped kissing him, she said, "That is how I wanted to kiss you. That felt better than being scared."

"Wow. Yeah, that is *so* much better than being scared. I didn't feel any fear in that at all." He said.

"Lord Malkore, I may need lots of practice in not being scared." She meant it to be flirty, saying she wanted to kiss him a lot.

He grinned at her, enjoying being able to feel her. Right then, they heard someone coming in the back door. He felt Dossa tense up. He rubbed his hand on the back of her heart and said, "Don't be scared about this either. Everything is OK."

Iyasiil walked in. Her face was flushed, she looked like the warm afternoon sun had taken a little bit of a toll on her. She looked at the table where Dossa had put the food down when she first came in. Without seeing Dossa in the room, only commenting on the food that Dossa had left for her, she said, "Dossa, you are amazing." She was praising Dossa for being so thoughtful to stock her chambers with food and drink.

Malkore quietly said, "See, nothing to be scared of." He wasn't trying to be quiet, Iyasiil just didn't hear him.

Iyasiil grabbed a pitcher of water and filled a large drinking horn. She drank almost the whole thing, then exhaled. She took a couple of big breaths, then looked across the room and saw the two of them sitting on the bed. She made eye contact with Dossa and smiled a big, happy smile. Then she looked at Malkore and felt her heart melt a little bit for him. "It has been a day filled with beautiful things, and seeing the two of you, right there, may be the most beautiful of them all. Oh goodness, look at you two!" She was beaming, looking at them.

"Mama, come here. I want you to meet someone, I think you'll like him." She said, being playful.

Iyasiil looked at him and said, "I think I will more than like him." She looked back and forth between them for a second, then said, "Let me rinse my face off." She turned around and grabbed the bowl of water and a piece of cloth and wiped her face several times, then wiped off her neck and arms. She grabbed another piece of cloth to dry off her face, then refilled her horn with water and walked toward the bed. She set the pitcher and horn on the small table beside the bed, then she took a big breath and looked at Malkore as she crawled onto the bed, "What a day, huh?!"

Iyasiil straddled Malkore's left leg, standing on her knees and hugged Dossa, then kissed her. "Oh, you beautiful woman, I love you so much." Then she looked at Malkore and her face changed, she melted inside a bit, "Oh, you beautiful man, I love you so much. I don't know if I will ever be able to thank you enough for our talk this morning in the meadow. I am truly thankful." Then she reached her right hand around the back of his neck and kissed him.

After the kiss, he looked at her and kept smiling. He felt so happy and grateful that she was in his life.

Iyasiil went on, "It's going to take two days to catch up on everything that has happened since I saw you last. I have had the best afternoon, and I want to tell you both all about it but tell me all about how you two got here. Dossa, you look great, inside and out. How did this happen? And Yay!"

Dossa had a moment of fear flash across her face, then caught herself and took a breath and relaxed. "Well," she started off in an animated, sarcastic tone, "it happened like this. I got to spend the afternoon alone and really think about how much the last four or five days have changed me. I decided that I am not going to hide anymore, so I lured Lord Malkore in here so I could fuck his feet with my feet." Then she looked at Malkore, and said, "Did I leave anything out?"

They were all laughing. Iyasiil was smiling so big at Dossa. "Well, you couldn't have picked a better man."

Dossa took a breath and with a thoughtful tone said, "Mama, I feel like you picked me to go on a magical journey. A magical journey to . . . to myself, really. I still feel like I am going to fail and disappoint you, but this feels so good. I just want to love you forever." Then Dossa pushed her teacher back and crawled off of Malkore's lap and crawled on top of Iyasiil, pushing her all the way down onto the bed. Dossa laid on top of her, hugging her for a few moments, then raised up with her hands on the bed, smiling at her teacher, and said, "Thank you. Thank you. Thank you. Now, you may have your husband back." Dossa paused before getting off of her teacher and smiled at her, celebrating the moment of not feeling afraid to share the love she felt and feeling grateful for her teacher and Malkore.

"Dossa, you seem like a different woman. *This!*" Iyasiil put her hand on Dossa's heart, "This is the woman that I saw trying to claw her way out of that shell you always kept you locked in, except I didn't know how amazing you would feel when you came out of that shell. Keep it up, girl."

"Thank you, mama. Now, tell us about your day." Dossa got off of her teacher and felt like she had grown up.

Iyasiil spoke with an excited tone. "No. Tell me how you got here. I want to hear all about it." She looked at Malkore, hoping one of them would speak.

"Well, you see, she lured me in here . . ." they all laughed, again. "After training, I wanted to take a few moments to reflect on the day. I went straight into teaching, when you left the oak grove this morning. I came in here to sit, and I just rolled things over in my head. Then I sat in meditation a few minutes and Dossa came in and was terrified when she saw me."

"What?" Iyasiil said, reaching for her drink and then moving to sit next to Malkore.

Dossa took over the story. "I did that thing I do where I hide, I was scared I was wrong for being alone with him, even though I didn't know he was going to be here, then I was scared because I liked the idea of having time alone with him, then I was scared of telling him, then I was scared of passing up the chance to just sit and talk. And then, as if all that weren't enough to deal with, this big dummy," motioning to Malkore, "goes and tells me to take a breath and feel my feelings. The next thing I knew, I was crying so hard I couldn't breathe. Then he told me how stupid I was, so I kissed him."

Iyasiil and Malkore were both laughing so hard at Dossa's account of the day. Then going along with the humor, Iyasiil turned to Malkore and said, "You told her she was stupid? That's so mean, you big dummy."

Dossa went on, "Well maybe he didn't quite say it, but he showed me how stupid it was to be afraid of being stupid. Instead, he suggested I let myself do what I really want to do and let it all come out, and not be scared. So that's when I kissed him." She had a flash of fear across her face again as she looked at her teacher. She tried to take a breath instead of crumbling and hiding. "Oh no. I just got scared. Shit! I am doing it again."

Iyasiil reached out with her foot and touched Dossa's knee, "Instead of being scared, tell me this: He's a really good kisser, isn't he?"

Dossa was trying to hold on and not descend into her world of fear. She reached down and held her teacher's foot, like she was holding on to her own life. Then she reached for Malkore's foot, and he reached out with his foot and put it on her other knee. She took a breath and closed her eyes as she was breathing in, then at the end of her exhale, she opened her eyes.

Iyasiil said, "We are right here, we aren't going anywhere, we both adore you. You're OK. Keep breathing."

Dossa said, "I'm still here."   Every cell in her body was screaming to run away, hide. She knew that was just her fear of being her real self. "I am scared I am never going to get it. I'm scared I'm always going to have to fight my fear."

Malkore said, "Each battle against your fear gets easier and easier until you feel like you are swatting away a bug. Keep fighting, keep winning, just like you are doing now."

Dossa growled a fierce growl, as she was squeezing Malkore's and Iyasiil's feet. "When I get past this I'm going to fuck you both senseless."

They both laughed. Dossa was trying to laugh, but she was fighting too hard to not fall into her internal cave of fear.

Malkore turned to Iyasiil and sarcastically said, "I didn't believe her. Did you?"

Iyasiil picked up on where he was going immediately, it wasn't her style of teaching, but she was game to play along with where Malkore was going to lead the conversation. "No. I didn't believe her when she said that either. I wonder why not."

Having his head still turned to Iyasiil, Malkore, used his sarcastic voice and said, "It would have been more believable if she had said something like this, "As soon as I quit being scared, I am going to crawl over there and kiss you like this."" Then he leaned forward and exaggerated propping himself up on his arms right in front of Dossa's face. Then he dropped the sarcasm and looked deep into her eyes, genuinely. Then he leaned his head into her face and stopped his nose just a whisper away from the side of her mouth. He lightly grazed the side of her mouth with the side of his nose and the side of his mouth, then he reached up with his hand and held her head with his thumb on her jaw and his fingers spread from the base of her neck to the base of her skull. Then he kissed her gently on the lips and finished with the side of his nose slowly and lightly grazing up and down the side of her cheek. Then he pressed her head into the side of his head and took a breath. Dossa let out a big, easy sigh.

Then back in his loud, sarcastic voice, that was the total opposite of the gentle, tender, heart-full moment that had just happened, he turned back to Iyasiil and said, "Now if she had done *that* I might believe her. But I don't. How would she have to of said it in order for you to believe her?"

In an equally sarcastic, almost theatrical tone, Iyasiil said, "Well, I can think of two things that would have been *so* much more believable. First, if she had come over to me and done this," Iyasiil leaned forward so she was close to Dossa, then dipped her head so that her long hair fell down in front of her face. She started slowly moving her head back and forth with her head barely touching Dossa's shoulder, with her hair slowly swishing against Dossa's chest, face, and shoulder. Then she slowly dragged her left temple across Dossa's collarbones from one shoulder to the other, then popped her head up, sending her hair flying back, revealing her face again.

"Oh shit! Fuck yeah." Dossa said, her face looking mesmerized with wonder.

Malkore could only imaging how awesome that was to see, he wished he could have felt it, too.

Iyasiil continued, "And if she had held me," wrapping her arms around Dossa, turning her head back like she was still talking to Malkore, "you know that kind of holding where you feel like the person wraps their entire heart around you?" Then she pulled Dossa close and imagined that her heart was wrapped all around Dossa's body. Then she gently and passionately rubbed her eyebrow on the outside of Dossa's jaw until her nose was nestled under Dossa's ear. "And then she had kissed me in such a way that I felt like my whole heart was being loved on." She gently kissed Dossa on the lips and tenderly sucked on Dossa's bottom lip and licked it, then in the same rhythm, Iyasiil licked Dossa's tongue while caressing Dossa's bottom lip with her bottom lip. Then she slowly leaned back and made eye contact with Dossa, dropping the sarcastic tone of voice, she whispered to Dossa, "Don't give up no matter how hard it gets. If you give up, neither one of us will want to kiss you again." Then she smiled her infectious smile. Then with full sarcasm again, "Now that would be a real tragedy." Dossa was smiling and starting to have little glimmers of her glow again and tears were falling out of her face.

Iyasiil sat back next to Malkore, "If she had done something like that, then maybe I would have believed her. Lord Malkore, Father of Asgard, King of Feet Fuckers, do you think we should give her another chance to make a statement to us now?"

Malkore was fighting to keep a straight face. He loved how effortlessly she had gone along with his silliness and kept it going long enough to put it back on him to continue. "Do you think she has enough of a sense of how lovable she is to be able to say anything worth hearing? I mean, I know she did five minutes ago, but that was so long ago. Maybe she has forgotten how lovable she is." Then he looked at Dossa.

Dossa looked like all the fear had just been wrung out of her. "I don't know if you two are the most amazing things that have ever been created or if you are both completely fucking crazy, but I know I want more of it. Please, Mother and Father of Asgard, Lord and Goddess of Feet Fuckers, this is the only way for me. Thank you."

"I prefer King Feet Fucker." Malkore said with a serious tone. Dossa laughed, shaking her head.

Iyasiil said, "Lord Malkore, I think that was pretty good. If you will turn your whole body and face me." Malkore had no idea what Iyasiil was up to, but he was going to go with it. He turned to face her, as he was turning, she turned to him and lifted her legs to put his feet outside of her hips. She put her legs over his legs and her feet outside of his hips. "We should put her in the place of honor. She should sit upon the throne of Feetfuckia."

Malkore couldn't take it. He almost spit all over Iyasiil's face as his laughter burst from within. He was at a loss for words. All he could do was nod at her. He could see exactly what she was doing. She was giving Dossa the opportunity to be held by both of them in a way that would be easy and comfortable for all three of them physically.

Iyasiil turned to Dossa, "Sweet Dossa, please come sit here." She patted her hand in the space between her and Malkore. Dossa had a look of amusement and the look of really being touched by what the two of them were doing for her. She moved around and sat between them. There was just enough space for her hips, where her hips were cradled on each side by one of them and her sacrum was supported by their knees against the head of the bed, and her thighs were supported by their thighs.

Malkore and Iyasiil both put one arm behind Dossa's back and wrapped their hands around her ribs. Then Iyasiil wrapped her left arm in front of Dossa, across her body, and tucked her hand under Dossa's shoulder.

Malkore first reached around to the other side of Dossa's face and wrapped his hand around her head from her jaw to the base of her neck and leaned forward to press his head against

Dossa's head. Iyasiil leaned her head into the side of Dossa's head and her lips naturally rested on Malkore's middle knuckle on his middle finger.

Malkore had just been about to move his hand to the top of Dossa's chest, just below the center of her collarbones, but feeling Iyasiil's lips on his finger he didn't want to move at all. He gently whispered, "Breathe."

Dossa took a deep breath.

Malkore softly said, "Now take a breath and breathe in all the love we both have for you. Breath in our belief in you. Breath in how much we both adore you. And breath in and feel your worthiness to accept all that love and honor." Malkore couldn't tell if Dossa would start crying or if she would grow into that big place he was describing. Tears were pouring down her face. Her breathing was a little heavier, but still deep and long.

Iyasiil could feel Dossa's presence so strongly and she knew Dossa's presence was still fragile, she had just begun learning to be present in a big way. So, while Malkore was drawing Dossa's attention to her heart, Iyasiil felt like she was going to die if she didn't make a silly, playful comment. Iyasiil took a deep breath, and in a very serious tone of voice, the tone she uses in prayer, she said, "Wise grandmothers and grandfathers, we ask you to look upon this one and love and adore her as we do, and we want to offer up the greatest prayer we could ever pray." Then using a really high-pitched tone of voice, she said, "Me too. Me too."

Malkore joined in, "Me too. Me too."

Dossa was laughing with her heart wide-open. Fear averted.

Iyasiil then spoke seriously. "Dossa, I am going to need you more than you can imagine. I love that big, fiercely loving heart you have. I need all your too much-ness. Know this: You are important to me. I want you in my life. I can't wait to see the amazing woman that blossoms out of this sweet bud you have kept yourself in."

Dossa was crying and nodding.

Malkore added in, "And Dossa, if you ever decide you don't want to be scared anymore, I would like another one of those kisses someday."

Dossa turned her head towards him and rested her forehead on his forehead. Dossa nodded. "Me too. Me too."

Iyasiil smiled, *"He always knows just what to say to engage the heart, whether it's serious or playful."* She thought.

She didn't know that Malkore felt totally drunk from Iyasiil doing the same thing.

Chapter Sixteen
You Know That's Going to Stick.

Malkore, Iyasiil, and Dossa went to dinner in the great hall. Kalla was already there, talking with a few friends that she hadn't seen much in the last few days. When Kalla saw them, she waved and blew kisses to them. Kalla went back to her conversation, then glanced at Dossa again and noticed that something about her was different.

So many people either called out to Malkore or came over to greet him and thank him for the day's training. Several women came over to give Iyasiil a hug and say how much they had missed seeing her as much in the last few days, and either subtly asked if she and Malkore were in a relationship or made probing comments to see if there was a reaction. There was a lot of curiosity floating around about the two of them.

They found a seat at the main table. Malkore sat next to Iyasiil, Dossa sat across from them. Food and plates were already laid out on the table, they all started filling their plates.

Malkore heard some loud laughter across the great hall that was coming from a smaller table, far away. Laughter and yelling were common in the great hall, even during mealtimes, but it caught Malkore's attention, and he saw St'laad and his brother eating together. He hadn't seen the two of them eat a meal together in decades. They were eating with two women they were dating, St'laad's two sons, and the boy, Scout. It looked like St'laad had invited Scout to come to dinner with his family. It was a good feeling to see St'laad stepping up to work with the boy and welcoming him into his family.

Malkore tapped Iyasiil on the hand and said, "Look. The boy. He's eating with St'laad's family." As they ate, Malkore told the story of what had happened with the boy during training that day. He didn't go into detail about how he kept Odin back for a couple of minutes before they started running, but he did tell the part of the story where he was chasing the boy down by the end of the run. He shared how Odin had laughed at the boy's name and given him a new name, and how St'laad had committed to working with Scout without even being asked.

When he mentioned that he and St'laad would be training together early each day, because St'laad would be working with Scout, Iyasiil started thinking about watching Malkore and St'laad training together and what a mixture of feelings she had. As she replayed the scene in her head, she watched him with a sense of immense respect for the man that he is, mixed with an overwhelming erotic desire. She felt her body start to get turned on again, just remembering watching him train.

Iyasiil interrupted him. "My Lord, I am not so sure I can let you train early with St'laad every day." Iyasiil said with a reserved, rigid tone in her voice.

"Why is that?" Malkore looked at her confused. She didn't seem the type to be controlling, and he was certain he hadn't made any commitments that would get in the way. He didn't know why she would have a problem with this.

"My Lord, When I left you in the oak grove this morning, I filled the water skin, and came back to leave it for you —"

Malkore cut her off, "Thank you for that, by the way. That was really thoughtful of you and much appreciated."

"Of course, My Lord. It's an honor to serve if I can. But I saw you and St'laad training together, and I don't think you should be doing that." She said with a quite somber tone.

"My Love, what is wrong? Why?" He said, still confused, but wanting to understand what she seemed so disturbed about.

"My Lord, if you could only see what I saw, you would know why it's a bad idea . . ." She said. She glanced at Dossa. Dossa knew where she was going with this and was trying not to laugh.

"What? What did you see?" He asked.

"Seeing you in your element, seeing the mix of grace and wisdom with which you move combined with the absolute lethality which you wield, I almost had to come stop you and take you back to my bed and fuck your brains out for the rest of the day." She started grinning at him. Dossa erupted in laughter.

"*Fuck! She got me again!*" He was fighting back a smile. He turned to Dossa, "I hope you are *not* going to try to learn from her. She may be a bad influence on you."

Without missing a beat, Dossa said, "Oh no, My Lord. It's worse than that. I'm letting my true brilliance come out now, thanks to you, so I am starting Mama's next-level training tomorrow at high sun. We are calling it, "How to fuck with a big, sexy warrior man."" Dossa kept making eye contact with him to back up her sarcasm even more.

Iyasiil and Malkore both laughed out loud.

Kalla looked over when she heard Malkore and her teacher laugh and realized that as much as she had missed her friends in the last days and as much as she was enjoying talking with her friends, this new family that had been forming was so much fun and she wouldn't be able to stay away much longer.

Malkore said to Iyasiil, sarcastically, "Monsters. You are creating monsters, I say."

Iyasiil leaned over to him and pressed her breasts into his shoulder and with a really flirty voice, said, "I think you can handle a few monsters in your life, don't you, My Lord?" He smiled at her and nodded, feeling her warmth and feeling how thankful and happy he felt right in that moment. "Besides, I'm not creating monsters." She looked around to see if anyone would be able to hear her. "I am creating an army of empowered women warriors." She looked at Dossa. She hadn't told Dossa about her vision, yet. It was all still so new to her; she wasn't sure how she would begin to talk to the women about what they would all create together.

Dossa looked at her, not sure if she meant that literally or if she just meant that she would be teaching all the women to believe in themselves. Iyasiil winked at her.

Malkore said, "Yes. Dossa, I take back the joke that you giving me crap is making you a monster. You are not. You are beautiful. And you should be encouraged in every way possible to always share *all* of your delicious humor."

"But I wasn't joking, Lord Malkore. We start training tomorrow at high sun east of the village while you and the men are at the oak grove on the west side. You better get ready." She meant this to be funny, but Malkore and Iyasiil both got one of those feelings like something powerful was happening in that moment, their faces changed. Even Dossa noticed that her intended sarcasm wasn't sarcastic. It came out like a matter-of-fact statement. "What just happened?"

Malkore and Iyasiil looked at each other. At the same time, they said, "Clues."

Dossa could feel her fear starting to slowly creep up, "What just happened? Did I say something wrong?" She was scared that she was about to get really scared.

Iyasiil said, "No, sweet woman. It was so right! You just answered my question that I have been asking myself all day. Thank you." She turned to Malkore, "We start at high sun tomorrow on the east side of the village."

Without hesitation, Malkore said, "Do it!"

Dossa interjected, "Do what? What the fuck just happened? I felt like my brain spun around in my head. What the fuck is happening?" Dossa's voice had an edge to it. She didn't sound angry, but she definitely had an edge in her tone. Normally, she would have shut down in a moment like this, and now she wasn't shutting down. Essentially, she was demanding that her teacher and Malkore to teach her what had just happened, so she could understand it and *not* start beating herself up.

Iyasiil looked at her and said, "You just gave me a huge gift, thank you. We both felt like a huge truth was just being dropped on us as you were talking. I know it feels strange until you get used to it. Did you feel like the whole world around you got fuzzy and blurry and started slowly spinning around you?"

"Yes!" Dossa said.

"Did you feel like the top of your head expanded until it was as big as a boulder, but light enough that it was pulling you up into the air? She asked.

Dossa's eyes got big, and she slapped her hands on the table. "Yes." She kept looking at her teacher with an amazed look on her face.

"Did you feel like what you said took on a whole new meaning that was totally different than what you intended?"

Dossa couldn't believe her teacher was describing it so well. "Fuck, Mama! Yes!"

"Could you feel your heart really big?" She asked Dossa. Dossa looked at her like she wasn't sure. "Even though they weren't the same feelings as wanting to kiss one of us, did you feel like you were totally in your body?"

"I think so." Dossa said, but not sure. "That one is still kind of new to me. Everything got blurry but your faces."

Iyasiil was excited for Dossa, "Yes, that's it. What you felt is kind of a Cosmic Confirmation. It is a feeling that the universe is confirming that something is true or important to follow. That whole head swimming feeling is telling you that what was happening in that moment needs to be listened to or honored or followed through on."

"So, I said something really good without meaning to?" Dossa asked.

Malkore said, "Yes. We both felt it and we both are so used to it that it wasn't disturbing. We both just knew it was important. You will get used to it, too. The really cool thing, well, one of two cool things, is that *you* felt it. You feeling it is proof that you were really present, and your heart was open, just like what we were doing while we sat on the bed today."

"Oh, wow. It works both ways." Dossa said.

Iyasiil asked, "What was the second really cool part?"

Malkore looked deeper into Dossa's eyes and said, "When I was sitting in meditation and heard you come into her chambers today, I felt that same feeling telling me that the possibility of spending time with you was important, today."

She was looking deeply into his eyes too. She had never felt so seen and honored before; no one had ever treated her like she was important before, except Kalla. She felt herself swallow her next comment down three times before she decided to say it out loud. She thought, *"Oh, Fuck! I am actually going to say this."* Dossa leaned in towards Malkore a bit and motioned for him to lean to her. He leaned in as far as she did. Their faces were about two hands apart. "Lord Malkore, I am going to fuck your brains out. And when I am done, I am going to fuck your wife." She kept eye contact with him to make her point.

Malkore and Iyasiil both laughed out loud. Malkore said, "Please!" He smiled at her, and he felt really proud of her. "You know, when you don't hide, we get to see what a beautiful person you really are. It is wonderful to feel you so close. I like this so much more than feeling you hiding in your shell. Please keep it up."

Dossa smiled, "If you think you can handle it, old man." Iyasiil laughed out loud. She wasn't laughing so much at the insinuation that Malkore was old, but at the brazenness of Dossa's humor. "And don't be offended, thinking that I am being disrespectful, I married your old ass, under a waterfall in a dream, so it's OK." Dossa made herself laugh with that one.

Iyasiil almost had tears coming out of her eyes, she was laughing so hard. She had her arms wrapped around Malkore's arm and laid her head on his shoulder. Malkore's shoulder was bouncing as he laughed, too.

"Wo- Wom-" Malkore kept trying to talk but couldn't get the words out past his laughing. He finally was able to say, "Woman Warrior, not Monster . . . Woman Warrior, not Monster. I must remember." He, of course, loved this kind of banter, and his complaining was sarcastic and playful. He kept feeling like a part of him had been opened up and was free to come out into the world these last several days. He felt his heart being touched and welcomed and fully met, which he wasn't sure had ever happened before.

Just then, a man came up to their table, he was the best blacksmith in Asgard. He made the best swords anyone in Asgard had ever seen. "Lord Malkore, I see that you and Odin have found a way to make more work for me. With everyone training every day, there is going to be a lot more swords that need repaired and replaced." The man's presence felt horrible to Malkore and Iyasiil, his complaining felt like an energy drain on what had been a fun, playful, light, and enlightening conversation.

With a bright tone in her voice, Iyasiil said, "I hear you are the greatest swordsmith in all of Asgard. I am Iyasiil. It is wonderful to meet you. I haven't been with the people long and haven't gotten to meet you, yet. Do you have a minute? I have a question I wanted to ask you."

The man transformed in front of Malkore's eyes. He went from looking like he had dark, grey, dull skin to having color in his face and a spark of light in his eyes. "Of course. My name is Dessel. What can I do for you?"

Iyasiil looked at him with a thoughtful look on her face, "Well, the swordsmith is the most important man in the army, and usually doesn't get much gratitude and appreciation for all he does. So, first, I want to thank you for all you do to make Asgard what it is. Men like this," she patted Malkore on the shoulder, "couldn't do what they do in battle if every fifteen seconds they had to stop fighting and run into the woods to get a new stick to fight with."

The man's face was lit up. He smiled like he had been waiting for a hundred years for someone to notice how hard he worked. "Thank you. No one has ever talked about that."

Iyasiil went on, "Oh, you're welcome, My Lord, Thank you. The second thing, if I were to bring you . . ." she looked around as if she had a secret to keep and didn't want anyone to hear. "Maybe we should step over here." She did have a secret to keep, but she wasn't about to tell him the real secret. She would tell him a different story, then let everyone in on the truth later on.

They stepped away from the table to a place where no one could hear their conversation. "There are some of us who want to honor the greatest warriors and one of the women had a dream about a special metal and where to find it. She actually found it." Iyasiil paused. *"Why am I lying to him? Why am I not telling him the truth?"* She shrugged it off and continued with her story to the swordsmith. "If I bring you a billet of that metal and a drawing of a sword that came from that dream, will you make a special sword for me? These are special honorary swords that will only be carried by the greatest warriors. This metal makes greater swords than any other, but only a master can work the metal well, that's why I wanted to ask you."

"I am honored. Thank you. The billets we forge are the best you will find anywhere. But, I will be happy to try, for you. Of course, but without knowing the metal or the design, I can't promise anything." He said.

"Thank you so much, My Lord. I will come by in a couple of days to bring you the design and the billet." She kissed him on the cheek, which was customary in Asgard. "Thank you again, My Lord."

- - - - - - - - - - - - - - - - - - - -

Malkore was smiling when Iyasiil got up from the table to go talk with the swordsmith. He said to Dossa, "She is masterful at that, did you see how he changed as soon as she started talking to him?"

Dossa got a sour look on her face, "I don't like him. I mean, I don't know him. He just feels gross to me."

"Look at him now. How does he feel to you while he is over there talking with your teacher?" He asked. Dossa looked at him. A slight smile came across her face. "Not as bad, right?"

"Yeah, was I wrong about him?" Dossa asked.

"No, you were right. When he walked up, he was whining and complaining, that is a drain on everyone. She just blasted him with something he desperately needed, respect and honoring." He said.

"Why" Dossa asked.

"Like she said, a good swordsmith is vital to an army, and your teacher knows that he needs to know that and honor it within himself. And she also knows if he is going to help Asgard grow strong, he needs to feel that respect from others. So, in that respect, it is good for all the people. Plus, I suspect she is going to need a favor from him." Malkore said.

"What kind of favor?" Dossa asked.

"I am not sure." Malkore said. He was sure. He just didn't want to tell Dossa; he would leave that up to her teacher.

"Yes, you are. You know what it is. What is it?" Dossa said.

"Why do you say that?" He asked her, impressed that she felt that he was lying.

"I just know you aren't telling the truth. What is going on." She said.

"Wow, Dossa. Good job! A week ago, even a day ago, I could have lied to you, and you wouldn't have known the difference. Now, your heart is so much more open; you are so much more present, you could tell. You are right, I do know. I'm sorry I tried to lie to you. Good job seeing through it. And the truth is: It isn't my story to tell, but at the very latest, you will find out at high sun tomorrow."

Iyasiil returned to the table to sit with Malkore and Dossa. "Looks like I am going back to the Sanctuary in the next couple of days. I need to find the ore to match what I showed you this morning."

Dossa was ready to smack the both of them, "What the fuck is going on?! You two are cooking something up. What is it?"

Malkore was smiling at Dossa, admiring her for stepping in and sharing without hiding.

Iyasiil looked at Dossa with a sense of wonder and pride, "Dossa, that felt so good. Did you feel how you are staying with us here, even though you're frustrated?! That's awesome! I can really feel you, now!"

Dossa hadn't noticed until her teacher pointed it out. "Wow. Yeah. I did, didn't I?"

Iyasiil said, "Yes, six or seven days ago, you would have felt left out and started shrinking because you felt like you weren't good enough." Then with a suggestive tone, she turned to Malkore and said, "What did you do to her in my bed that magically transformed her, My Love?"

Dossa laughed loudly, "Not enough."

Malkore laughed, too. "I didn't do anything. She is a flower who has been afraid to bloom. All I did was ask her if she wanted to put her roots in water." Malkore said.

Iyasiil mocked Malkore by mumbling, "fucking witch." She knew that on one level that what he said was true. She also knew that only *his* presence and skill could have led her to opening up like this in only a couple of hours. If it had only been her and Dossa doing that same work, it may have taken years. She knew that Dossa would still have to work hard over time to integrate the change into every aspect of her life, but the immediate transformation is profound and should not be understated.

He laughed and looked at Iyasiil, "I am not a witch. I just marry them under waterfalls."

Something about his presence touched her deeply in that moment, she felt tears welling up in her eyes. She leaned over and kissed him then said, "Thank you for marrying me under a waterfall."

"Wait. Are you two really married now?" Dossa asked.

Iyasiil smiled and answered her with a very matter-of-fact tone of voice, "Yes, we are really married . . . until sundown tomorrow." Then she turned to Malkore, "Right, My Lord Husband?"

"Right, My Witchy Wife." He said, looking at her, then turning to Dossa.

Dossa looked confused. "Wait. Go back. Until sundown tomorrow? And you didn't answer me about what you two are talking about happening tomorrow. And what Sanctuary are you going to, your chambers?" She had so many questions.

"Dossa, I will answer all your questions. Every one of them. Maybe tomorrow morning, maybe later tonight. Oh, that reminds me, will you go ask Frigg and Kalla to both come see me before we leave tonight?"

Dossa was already getting up, "Of course, Mama, right away." She immediately went over to Kalla. Dossa sat down with their friends and spent a few minutes with them before going into Odin's chamber, in the back of the great hall to look for Frigg.

Iyasiil looked at Malkore and said, "I wish I could have watched you work with Dossa to see how you did it. You are truly, magical."

"No, My Love, I told you, I just marry magic under waterfalls." He looked into her eyes and felt like the world stopped, everything got blurry except her face, he felt like the world was spinning around him, and he didn't care. All he cared about that moment was kissing her. "Right, My Witchy Wife?"

"Right, My Lord Husband." The whole world seemed to slow down; she leaned over to kiss him. Neither of them could hear anything going on around them, nothing existed but each other's lips. She pulled her head back just far enough to be able to focus her eyes on his eyes, with a soft and sultry voice she said, "My Lord Husband, there is something really troubling me." She was looking at him with her most beautiful, alluringness and speaking with a tone that suggested he should take her back to her chambers immediately.

"You don't look troubled at all, My Witchy Wife, you look delicious." He said, flirting back with her.

In a coy voice she responded, "Well, you see, My Lord Husband, that's just it." She leaned even closer, put her lips right up to his ear, and whispered, "I am delicious. And I am deeply troubled that no one has tasted me all day. And we have both had such a busy day, we haven't had the chance to make love since yesterday. It's deeply troubling . . ."

"Yes, My Love. I don't want you to be troubled." He said.

Before they could get up to leave, Kalla came over to check in with her teacher. Kalla said, "Look at you two, I think the two of you are the most beautiful couple I have ever seen." She focused on Malkore and said, "Lord Malkore, I haven't seen you all day, I have missed you. Mama and I had the best time today, although she worked my ass off on our hike, it was everything I could do to keep up with her. We went up to the top of Solutot Mountain, then we sat and had the best talk. It was amazing."

Malkore was happy to see her, "That's quite a hike. You must have done it quickly. You weren't gone but 4 hours."

Kalla said, "It was fast. We were almost running up the mountain." Then turning to her teacher, "What did you want to talk with me about, Mama?"

"Can you keep a secret, Kalla?" Iyasiil asked her.

"From everyone but Dossa." Kalla replied with a smile. "Why?"

Iyasiil saic, "I'm serious. This is big. Dossa is part of it, you don't have to keep it from her, but no one else can know about it, OK?"

Kalla sat down on the bench across from them. She looked at Malkore to see if he would give her a clue about what was going on. Malkore only nodded to her. "Of course, Mama. What is it?"

Malkore was distracted by someone about five paces behind Kalla. "Hold on ladies, it's Pigfucker." Kalla locked at him confused. "I forgot to tell you that Odin gave two men new names today."

Iyasiil saw Pigfucker lurking behind Kalla. "Pigfucker? Really? Oh, you know that name is going to stick." He looked like he was either about to cause problems, or he wanted to talk with Malkore. Iyasiil knew she could put Pigfucker down hard. He wasn't as great of a warrior as his ego thinks he is, but she didn't want to show the people what she could do, yet. Iyasiil made eye contact with Pigfucker to let him know he was being watched, he had always had a darkness about him, she knew to *not* trust him.

Pigfucker was looking for a chance to talk to Malkore. When he saw Iyasiil looking at him so sternly, he realized that she didn't trust him. He felt apologetic for that. He bowed his head to her and put his hand over his heart. When he raised his eyes back to her, he mouthed the words, "I am sorry."

Iyasiil looked at him and saw a vulnerability and a sadness in him. Her mind and memory told her to be on high alert around him, but her heart suddenly felt compassion for him. She kept looking at him and pointed to Malkore, asking if he was looking to talk with Malkore. He nodded.

"Kalla, let's go find Dossa. Someone needs to talk with Lord Malkore." After, they had gotten away from Malkore and given him space to talk with Pigfucker. Iyasiil leaned against one of the support beams of the great hall and watched to see what was about to happen.

Kalla was so confused and wanted to understand everything going on. Kalla felt like something had been put in motion without her knowing it, she felt like she wasn't keeping up and she was supposed to be in the middle of it. She wasn't wrong. "Mama?"

Iyasiil saw that Pigfucker was behaving himself. She turned to look at Kalla and saw that she was looking confused and a little frustrated. Iyasiil stopped everything going on inside and only focused her attention on Kalla, "Take a breath, Love." Kalla took a breath. "I will explain everything tomorrow, when no one is around, but tomorrow at high sun, we will meet again to go for a walk. It will be you, Dossa, maybe Frigg, and me. I'm sorry for being secretive, and I don't want anyone to know, yet. When I tell you tomorrow, you will understand."

"Yes, Mama, absolutely. Does Dossa already know??

Iyasiil said, "Yes, Dossa knows. She is supposed to be getting Frigg for me."

"Mama, Frigg was looking for you. She asked me over an hour ago why you wanted to talk with her." Kalla said.

"Damn, that girl is good. I didn't even know until thirty minutes ago that I wanted to talk with her." Iyasiil said.

Kalla had a slightly concerned look on her face, "Mama, what is going on? And I have another question. Is it OK if I ask?"

Iyasiil stopped thinking about training women, she stopped thinking about Pigfucker, she stopped thinking about Malkore. She only focused on Kalla and looked into her eyes and took a breath, "What is it, My sweet cutie? I forget how beautiful you are, sometimes. You're just so beautiful." She was smiling at Kalla, touching her face. "I told you I would tell you tomorrow. What is the second question?" She asked.

Kalla took a half-step closer to her teacher and looked deep into her eyes, "What the fuck happed to Dossa? She's like a different woman."

Iyasiil smiled. She thought about how Malkore had facilitated the change in Dossa. Thinking about what an amazing man Malkore is, she looked over at him and got that woman-in-love look on her face. "Malkore happened to her . . ."

"That bitch!" Kalla said, pretending to be jealous. Iyasiil laughed. "If she got to kiss him before I did, I am going to kick her ass! I knew I should have kissed him yesterday!" Kalla was joking, of course, and it was funny.

"Oh, you should have seen her fight through her fear and not shut down, it was beautiful! I wasn't there for the whole discussion. I just saw what Dossa was like after their talk. It was delightful to see."

Iyasiil saw Frigg and Dossa across the great hall. Frigg and Dossa were coming out from the back of the great hall where Odin's chambers were.

Kalla had so many questions. "What did they do?" She asked.

Iyasiil waved at Dossa. "Come on, sweet Kalla, let's go talk with Frigg." They made their way over to where Frigg and Dossa were standing.

Dossa looked at her teacher like she had just seen a miracle and was struggling to make sense of it. Frigg got a look of relief on her face when she saw Iyasiil.

Dossa looked at Kalla as if to say, *"You wouldn't believe what I saw."* She grabbed Kalla and hugged her and almost started sobbing. Dossa took a couple of breaths as she settled her body and heart, then she and Kalla just watched and listened to Frigg and their teacher. Dossa was standing with Kalla on her left side, and she still kept her arm around Kalla's waist and held on to her, feeling Kalla's support. Then she laid her head on Kalla's shoulder and put her hand over Kalla's heart and whispered, "Thank you."

Kalla had her right arm around the back of Dossa's shoulders, with her hand wrapped around the right side of Dossa's ribs. Kalla would wait to give Dossa crap about kissing Malkore. Right now, she could feel that Dossa needed her support.

Frigg grabbed Iyasiil in a big hug and said, "Oh Mama, thank you for being here." Frigg hugged her like she wasn't ever going to let her go. "Don't stop hugging me for about three days, OK?"

Iyasiil could feel Frigg reaching out with her heart. It was good to feel Frigg finally reaching out for support. Her relationship with Frigg would be different than with Kalla and Dossa, but Frigg wasn't trying to grow her medicine alone, anymore. Right now, Frigg needed to know that everything was OK, she needed to know that she was OK. "Blow out all your air, Love. Now, take a big breath and let it go too. You're doing so well. Breathe."

"Yeah, I'm OK. I have just never done anything like this before." Frigg said.

Iyasiil kept hugging her and spoke with such a warm and accepting and nurturing tone, "It's always hard breaking through new barriers, and growing into bigger things. You're doing great. Can you tell me what's happening?"

Frigg took a big breath, then let her body relax into Iyasiil's hug even more. She slowly leaned back and looked Iyasiil in the eyes, then smiled. Frigg patted the herb pouch she wore around her neck, "I think these little mushrooms really are magic." Then Frigg started crying again and hugged her more.

Iyasiil kept holding her as they stood there in the back of the great hall. When Frigg was finished crying again, she said, "Mama, why the fuck am I crying?"

Iyasiil swayed her body back and forth as she held Frigg, "Sweet lady, we carry *so much* for the people, *especially* us natural born healers. We hold such a big space for people, so they can grow into the best versions of themselves. It's *a lot* to hold. When we get full, then we need to flush it out. Sometimes we cry, sometimes we have to go kick someone n the face." She meant to make Frigg laugh with that comment. It worked. Frigg started laughing.

Frigg got a look of overwhelm on her face and said, "Oh, Mama, speaking of kicking someone in the face, I am going to kick Odin's ass."

"What? What happened." Iyasiil said laughing.

Frigg looked around, "OK, do you see the guy talking to Malkore right now?" Iyasiil nodded. "After training today, Odin brings him into his chambers and the guy is pissed off and complaining about Malkore, saying that Malkore is such an asshole and that he doesn't know what he is talking about." She paused. "He always complains about everybody. I don't like him. *He's* the asshole, not Malkore."

"I've never liked him, either." Said Iyasiil.

Frigg started telling the story about what had happened. "Odin spent a couple of hours talking to him and he kept wanting me to stay with them, but I didn't want to. I stepped out a few times, but kept feeling like I should be in there, for some reason. Then Odin told me that he wanted me to give the guy one of my mushrooms. He didn't even ask me if it would be OK, he just decided that I needed to do it. I'm going to fucking kill him!"

"I heard that Odin will be really different in a month or so. I heard he is going to learn to respect women in a really big way, so don't worry." Iyasiil smiled.

Frigg and Dossa laughed as they remembered their plan to change Odin into a woman.

Iyasiil said, "That reminds me, Malkore had a vision. He traveled to the plant planet, and they said that seven of your medicine pods will be enough for Odin when we help him make his transformation. His vision just confirmed it, and we will also give Odin some of my red grass tea after he wakes up."

Frigg pulled her head back to look at Iyasiil's face, "What?! Did he know I wasn't sure?"

"No, but apparently the plant people must have known you needed confirmation." She said laughing. Frigg nodded.

Kalla was just trying to keep up with everything that was going on. It seemed to her like that the whole world had changed in the last couple of hours. Her teacher was lit up about something, but wasn't sharing what it was, Dossa was a whole different person, Frigg was freaked out. Kalla thought,

"and Dossa got to kiss Malkore first – everything is just wrong!"
She made herself laugh with that thought.

Frigg looked at Iyasiil with a sparkle in her eyes, "Oh, Yes! Oh, Yes! That will be great! There is so much going on, I forgot Odin's dick-ish-ness will be over in a month."

Iyasiil said, "OK, so finish telling me about Pigfucker."

Frigg laughed out loud. "That's what Odin kept calling him, too. Don't you just know that name is going to stick with him forever?! Odin told me about it. Odin called him Pigfucker, like it was his name." All four of the women laughed. "Anyway, I gave him one of my mushrooms."

Dossa said, "That's when I came in."

Frigg got an excited look on her face, "Mama, you would have been so proud of Dossa! She handled it like a pure Goddess," she turned to Dossa and winked at her, "which she is!" Then Frigg turned back to Iyasiil, "He was out for about 20min, just like Odin was the other day. Then when he woke up, Dossa and I brought him back, slowly, talking to him. I knew he was going to be really fragile, and Dossa was a master."

Iyasiil looked at Dossa. Dossa said, "All I did was breathe and listen to him. That's what I thought you would have done, Mama."

Frigg added, "You did more than that. You told him what an ass he had always been, and you did it in a way where he didn't get defensive and angry. You reached his heart while it was open. It was amazing. You even made him cry."

Dossa looked at Iyasiil, "Well, yeah. I told him if he ever tries to touch me again, like he did several months ago, that I was going to rip his balls off."

Iyasiil laughed, enjoying how open Dossa was and how she was sharing so openly. She was also impressed that Dossa had the stuff to threaten an Asgardian Warrior that was twice her size and make him be glad that he had been threatened.

Frigg added, "She said it in a way that he believed she would do it . . ." Frigg took a big breath. "And you know what happened?! The fucker apologized! Pigfucker *actually* apologized! I couldn't believe it! Anyway, the mushrooms worked their magic. He is a different man." She looked over at Pigfucker again, "Look at him. Look at the way he is talking to Malkore. There is no way he would have been able to do that this morning. I guess these little mushrooms really are magic." Then Frigg looked at Dossa, "Speaking of big changes . . . what the fuck happened to the scared, quiet little girl I used to know and love?"

Dossa got a look on her face like she didn't know what to say.

Kalla chimed in pretending to still be mad at Dossa again, "The little bitch kissed Malkore! That's what happened to her! She kissed him before I did and I'm never going to forgive her for that." Then Kalla looked at Dossa and murmured, "Slut."

Frigg looked at Dossa in disbelief.

Dossa nodded as if to say, *"Yeah, that's what happened."* Then, with a matter-of-fact tone, Dossa said, "His kisses make women glow. Just look at Mama . . ."

Frigg looked at Iyasiil in disbelief. Iyasiil nodded and said, "It's true."

Frigg looked to see if anyone would show that they were joking. When she looked at Kalla, Kalla was still pretending to be mad and was still fake-glaring at Dossa and added, "Bitch!"

Dossa looked down and stepped very slowly around to face Kalla as if she were confidently accepting a challenge, then Dossa slowly looked up to look Kalla in the eyes. Dossa said, "You know what?" Then Dossa grabbed Kalla by the back of the head, pulled Kalla's head down to her lips, kissed her really hard, then release Kalla's head and said, "I'm *your* little bitch. That will never change." Then Dossa reached up with her other hand and made the sound of a goose as she squeezed Kalla's boob. All four of the women laughed.

Frigg still wanted some clarification. "So, are all three of you dating Malkore, now? Is that it?"

Iyasiil said, "Well, you performed a marriage ceremony for Malkore and me, two nights ago. So, we are married now. He and I agreed to stay married until sundown tomorrow."

Kalla said, "Just until –"

Dossa cut her off and said, "All three of us married him under a waterfall in a vision. But we don't know how long it's going to last." Iyasiil started snickering at Frigg's confusion.

Then Frigg gave up on trying to understand and decided to join in on the fun and said, "Well, I prayed over his cock, so can I be married to him, too?" They all laughed. "Now back to business. Mama, could I talk to you in the back for a minute? I have a question about something."

"Sure." Iyasiil said.

In her new normal, sarcasm, Dossa said, "Yeah, don't worry about us, Frigg. Kalla and I are just going to go fuck our new husband. After all, we may not still be married to him after sundown tomorrow." Then Dossa turned to start walking back towards Malkore's table. Iyasiil looked back, leaning over as if she were about to stumble because she was laughing so hard. Frigg just shook her head and kept walking into Odin's chamber.

Kalla followed her with a look on her face that said, "*I can't believe what you just said.*" Kalla loved seeing Dossa let her real self out. Dossa was this funny all the time when it was just the two of them, but she wasn't used to seeing Dossa be like this with other people. Kalla said, "Girl, he must have put it on you *good*! I have never seen you like this."

Dossa waited a step for Kalla to catch up to her and held out her hand for Kalla to hold her hand. She turned to face Kalla again, "No, My Love. I put it on *him* that good." They both laughed.

Kalla was so proud of her, but really was feeling a little jealous that she hadn't kissed Malkore already, too. After a few more steps, they saw Malkore still talking with Pigfucker. They stopped and waited for Malkore to finish his conversation.

Then Dossa took a long breath. She looked at Kalla and took in another long breath, breathing Kalla in. "Kalla, I don't know if I have ever thanked you for being such a good friend to me over the years. I know I can be a lot to handle. And please just know, that your love has kept me from dying inside."

Kalla was stunned. "Wow. Dossa, I love you so much. I've loved you since the day we met. It's your world, baby. I'm just living in it. I was thinking it was you who has kept me from dying inside. You always have my heart."

In response, Dossa squeeze-squawked her boob again and winked at her. "Malkore is finished, now. It's your turn to kiss him. Let's go sit down."

As they got to the table, Dossa led Kalla by the hand to sit next to Malkore. Dossa sat back down across the table from Malkore and said with a smile, "Hello my waterfall husband."

Malkore laughed, "Hello, My Love." Then he turned to Kalla to say hello.

Before Malkore could say anything to Kalla, she poured on the sarcasm in her voice and said, "Did Dossa tell you what a bitch she is?"

Malkore laughed as he made a look that said, *"What in the world are you talking about?"* Then he just started laughing, "I love you two so much. I just smile when you two are around. I never knew you were both so funny."

"Well, you wouldn't want to have waterfall wives who were boring, would you?" Dossa said, smiling a happy smile at him.

He started to answer her and Kalla cut him off, "Bitch! No one asked you to speak." Then laying on the sarcasm, "I am sitting over here having never kissed my waterfall husband and you are just sitting there still glowing like a radiant Goddess. Go fuck yourself, you little bitch!"

Malkore chuckled at her, "So that's what this is about."

Kalla got a serious tone, "Lord Malkore, do you remember when we came in and brought you and Mama breakfast yesterday? You had her pinned down and she was screaming for help."

Malkore laughed as he remembered it, "Hard to believe it was just yesterday, but yes."

"I started to kiss you, then I got scared and I kissed you on the cheek. Well, I don't want to kiss you just because it would be fun. Lord Malkore, you really are amazing in so many ways. And I still remember what I said about loving you like a brother, like a father, like a lover, like a man I respect. I want to kiss you all those ways." Kalla said.

"I don't want you to kiss me *any* of those ways." He responded.

"What?" she asked, looking confused.

"If you are going to kiss me, I want you to kiss me because you love the taste of you and me being together." He said looking into her eyes.

Dossa exclaimed, "Oh, fuck yeah!"

Kalla and Malkore kept looking into each other's eyes. Kalla looked like she just had a shock to her heart and her breath had been taken away, "Yes, My Lord. You are right." She got up and moved over to his chair, pulled up the front of her dress, sat on his lap, straddling him, looked deep into his eyes for a moment, then kissed him.

Malkore put his hands on the outside of her hips when she straddled him. When she kissed him, his hands slowly slid up her ribs until his fingers were spread across her shoulder blades, touching the back of her heart, with his thumbs lightly holding her sides and her upper back.

Dossa said, "Yeeeeeeesssss! There she is! That's the woman I love!"

Several people noticed the kiss happening and cheered. There was usually a lot of cheering whenever kissing happened in the great hall after mealtimes or anytime during a celebration.

Kalla kept kissing him, feeling like her heart was about to explode. She wanted to suck every bit of his sensuousness, his presence, and every bit of his awesomeness out through his lips and tongue. When she stopped kissing him, she kept her eyes closed and let her lips hover over his for a few moments, savoring the feel of him, feeling out of breath, resting her forehead on his.

He was just as stunned by how good that kiss felt and how much he could feel her heart and her presence. He slowly opened his eyes. She was just opening her eyes. She pulled her head back slightly and said, "Lord Malkore." She felt like she couldn't breathe. "Thank you."

"Kalla, thank *you*." He said.

She leaned her forehead against his forehead again and said, "No, not for the kiss. Thank you for helping me to wake up to the kind of woman I can be. I love who I am when I am with you."

"Kalla, you are so easy to love. It's a selfish honor. Really, it's what any man should do. I am just lucky to be loved so well." He responded.

Dossa, breaking the mood to give Kalla grief, said, "Kalla, can you finally calm down, now?"

Kalla kept her forehead against Malkore's forehead for a moment and said, "No, Dossa. That kiss just made me hungry for more." Malkore laughed and pulled her close to hug her.

She wrapped him up in her arms. When she stopped hugging him, she pulled her head back, then popped her lips on his lips again, quickly. She moved back to her seat.

Dossa, still poking fun at Kalla, asked, "Now that Kalla isn't panicking about kissing you anymore, what happened with Pigfucker just now? I was there when he woke up in Odin's chambers."

"What was he doing asleep in Odin's bed?" Malkore asked confused.

"Odin made Frigg gave him one of her magic herbs. She said it knocked him out for about 20 minutes, just like it had with Odin." Dossa said. "He seemed totally different when he woke up. He actually apologized for being such an asshole to me in the past."

"OK, that makes sense, now. I was wondering what had changed so much." Then his jaw dropped when it registered that Odin had gotten the same herb. "That's what happened to Odin after he challenged me the other day, because right after that, he came out and made the announcement about starting the training with everyone." Malkore let that realization settle in. "OK, it's making sense, now. Odin was totally different with me in training today and Odin told me that, what's his name, Pigfucker would be different tomorrow."

Kalla asked, "So, he was different with you, too?"

Malkore acted surprised when he thought about it, "Yeah. He was like a different man. He apologized for being disrespectful during training. He apologized for a lot of things he had done. And asked what he needed to do to be a better man and a better warrior."

Dossa asked, "What does "best man in town mean?""

Malkore smiled, "Where did you hear that?"

Dossa told him, "Pigfucker said it when he was first waking up. I didn't understand."

Malkore said, "Ahh, I see. In training today, I was trying to piss him off and I had said that he didn't respect himself and that's why he was an ass to everyone. I said that a man like that, when he makes peace with himself, will be the best man in town."

Kalla said, "He's scary. Why were you trying to piss him off?"

Malkore said, "I'm sorry he's been scary to you, and I wanted to piss him off to get his attention. I was hoping he would come challenge me, but it seems that Odin took care of it. His anger needed to be addressed if he is going to be trusted by the men I am training. So, I was going to bring all his anger to a head, so that we could get to the bottom of it and give him the chance to heal it."

"So, you were trying to piss him off so he would come fight you?" Dossa asked.

"Yeah." Malkore said with an understated confidence. "What could he do to me? And if he gets pissed off enough, it could be a great opening to get him to look inside himself, instead of being an ass to everyone."

"Whoa!" Dossa said.

"That's so badass, Lord Malkore." Kalla added.

"Warriors don't run from a fight that is worth fighting. If fighting him is the way to get through to him, I'll be happy to do it." Malkore said.

- - - - - - - - - - - - - - - - - - - -

Iyasiil and Frigg went into Odin's private chambers in the back of the great hall. Iyasiil asked, "What can I do for you, Love?"

Frigg took her hand and walked her over to the bed. She led Iyasiil to sit on the side of the bed, near the foot of the bed. Frigg sat towards the head of the bed and reached down and pulled something out from underneath the bed. "Can you tell me what this is and why I was supposed to go find it early this morning."

Iyasiil's eyes got wide, then she started laughing. Frigg looked at her confused. "Frigg, you are amazing! I just lied to Dessel and told him that one of the women had a dream about where to find this ore. I didn't know why I had lied to him when I said it, but obviously, you had actually found it."

Frigg responded, "Well, I guess you didn't lie, then, did you?"

"Apparently not." Looking at the chunk of metal, Iyasiil said, "I didn't know if I could find it here, on Asgard. Where did you find it?" Iyasiil looked over this jagged piece of metal ore with wonder.

"Find what? What is this?" Frigg asked.

"Hand me that knife off the table, I will show you." Iyasiil took the knife and scraped a thin shard of the metal sticking out. "Look at the color. I just promised the swordsmith I would bring him a billet of this, but, had no idea where I would find it."

"What is it for? Why was I woken up from a dream that told me to go find this? Does it have to do with these?" Frigg walked over to the corner of the chambers and pulled a blanket off of four wooden practice swords. "This afternoon I had a waking dream where I stole these and gave them to you. What the fuck is going on? Are we starting training, too."

Iyasiil smiled and told her, "Don't tell anyone. We will keep it a secret until the people are ready for it. The people, not the men nor most of the women, are ready to honor women and women warriors, yet. I wanted to ask you tonight if you would join Kalla, Dossa and Me."

"Of course." Frigg answered.

"Great, thank you. Kalla and Dossa don't fully know what we are doing, yet. I will tell all three of you as soon as we get to the top of Solutot Mountain. Get four pieces of scrap cloth as long as your arms outstretched and wrap these up in a blanket and we will meet on the east side of the village tomorrow, just before high- sun. Get ready, the training won't be easy."

"So, the metal is for a sword?" Frigg asked.

Iyasiil nodded. "Where did you find this? Is there more?"

Frigg said, "I bet we can find more. It was next to a rocky outcropping on the west side of the mountain, out from your chambers. Instead of going up to the springs at the big turn, you have to climb down off the side of the mountain."

Iyasiil nodded again, thinking about how much more of the ore she would need to eventually make enough to arm an army of women. "OK, good. Thank you for paying attention and thank you for following your vision. You're growing into quite a witch, Frigg." She said with a smile and a wink.

"Mama, I am just trying to learn what I can." Frigg said.

"OK, wrap this chunk of ore up and don't let anyone see it. I will come and get it from you in a day or so." Iyasiil said.

- - - - - - - - - - - - - - - - - -

Iyasiil went back out to join Malkore and the girls. As she walked behind Malkore to sit on the other side of him, she dragged her hand across the back of his shoulders as she passed. "My Lord, if we are going to stay this busy, we may never get to enjoy being married before our marriage is over tomorrow night."

"Is everything going well?" He asked.

"Yes, amazing. It is so wonderful when things go better than you could have imagined. I'm so excited. Frigg found what I needed. I thought that I lied to Lord Dessel that one of the women had a dream where she was guided to a special metal ore, like the metal I showed you this morning. Then, Frigg just let me know that she had a dream and went to where the dream pointed her, and she found the metal ore but didn't know what it was or what it was for."

"Wow. That is so cool! So, it's the same as what you showed me this morning?" He felt a little uncomfortable keeping the secret from the girls and talking about it in front of them, but it was her secret to keep.

Iyasiil was feeling the same way, she looked at Kalla and Dossa, "I am sorry girls. So much has happened today, I am trying to keep up with it all in my head. I promise, I will tell you everything and let you in on all the secrets tomorrow when we go for our walk."

Dossa said, "OK, but it better be good. You have built it up so much . . . you better not gather us together and say, "I've gathered you here to discuss a new spice I want to try in Teeda Root Stew.""